Three women.

To ...
to lose one's innocence and...
to conceive a child.

Each will take the privileged
Crighton world by storm in

Women & Love

Three compelling stories in Penny Jordan's
acclaimed family saga.

Penny Jordan's favourite books are sagas and when she became a writer her dream was to create her own series of connected novels, following the dramatic lives and loves of one particular family, across the generations. Now, with the Crightons, she has succeeded in her life-long dream! Each story will draw you deeper into their fascinating world.

The saga launched with *A Perfect Family* and continues in this special three-story collection.

All of the novels featuring the Crighton family can be read in isolation, as each tells its own compelling story, but if you wish to read the whole collection, then these are the novels to look for:

Women & Love

PENNY JORDAN

MIRA® BOOKS

*MIRA is a registered trademark of Harlequin Enterprises Limited,
used under licence.*

*This edition published in Great Britain 2002
MIRA Books, Eton House, 18-24 Paradise Road,
Richmond, Surrey, TW9 1SR*

Women & Love © Harlequin Books S.A. 2002

The publisher acknowledges the copyright holder
of the original works as follows:

The Perfect Lover © Penny Jordan 1998
The Perfect Father © Penny Jordan 2000
A Perfect Night © Penny Jordan 2000

ISBN 0 7783 0014 5

134-0902

*Printed and bound in Spain
by Litografía Rosés S.A., Barcelona*

CONTENTS

The Crighton Family

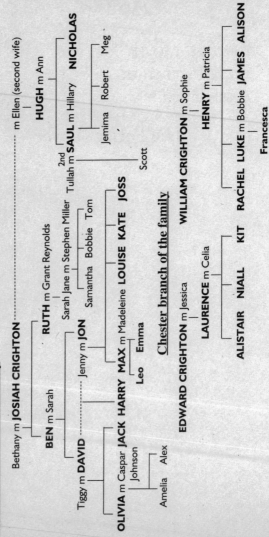

Haslewich branch of the family

m Ellen (second wife)

Bethany m **JOSIAH CRIGHTON**

HUGH m Ann

SAUL m Hillary   **NICHOLAS**

Jemima   Robert   Meg

Tullah m **SAUL** (2nd)

Scott

RUTH m Grant Reynolds

Sarah Jane m Stephen Miller

Samantha   Bobbie   Tom

LOUISE   **KATE**   **JOSS**

Jenny m **JON**

BEN m Sarah

Leo   Emma

HARRY   **MAX** m Madeleine

Tiggy m **DAVID**

JACK

OLIVIA m Caspar

Johnson

Amelia   Alex

Chester branch of the family

EDWARD CRIGHTON m Jessica

WILLIAM CRIGHTON m Sophie

HENRY m Patricia

LAURENCE m Celia

ALISTAIR   **NIALL**   **KIT**

RACHEL   **LUKE** m Bobbie   **JAMES**   **ALISON**

Francesca

The Perfect Lover

CHAPTER ONE

'MY GOODNESS, we *are* honoured, aren't we? It isn't very often these days that you manage to tear yourself away from the bureaucratic delights of Brussels.'

Louise tensed as she heard the sarcastic voice of her elder brother, Max. They had never got on particularly well, even as children, and in her view maturity had done nothing to improve either their relationship or her brother.

'It was commented at Christmas that you weren't around,' Max continued jibingly. 'But, of course, we all know Saul was really the reason for that, don't we?'

Louise gave him an angry look before retorting, 'Perhaps if you spent more time thinking about your own relationships and less talking about other people's you might learn something genuinely worthwhile, but then you never were much good at appreciating what's really of value in this life, were you, Max?'

Without giving him any opportunity to retaliate, Louise turned on her heel and walked quickly away from him.

She had promised herself that on this, her first visit home since she had started working in Brussels over twelve months ago, she would prove to her family just how much she had changed…matured…and just how different, distant almost, she was from the girl who…

Out of the corner of her eye she caught sight of

Saul, her father's cousin, who was standing with his wife, Tullah, and the three children from his first marriage. Tullah had her arm around Megan, Saul's daughter, while Saul held the little boy they had had together.

The large drawing room of her grandfather's house seemed to be filled by the presence of her peers, proudly showing off their growing families.

Clustered around the fireplace were her cousin Olivia, with her husband and their two children, talking animatedly with Luke, from the Chester branch of the family, and his American wife Bobbie and their little girl, while Maddy, her brother Max's wife, kept a discreet eye on Gramps, who was becoming increasingly irascible.

According to her mother, Maddy was close to a saint for humouring him the way she did. When Jenny Crighton had made this comment this morning, over breakfast, Louise had immediately pointed out that if Maddy could put up with being married to Max, then her grandfather must come as a form of light relief.

'Louise,' her mother had protested, but Louise had remained unrepentant.

It was no secret in the family that Max was not a good or kind husband to Maddy, and privately Louise couldn't understand why on earth Maddy stayed with him.

'You're looking very cross.'

Louise grimaced as she saw her twin sister. Twins were a feature of the Crighton family, in the same way that poppies were a feature of a field of corn—they sprang up all over the place, although as yet there were no sets in the current new generation.

'They'll come,' her father's aunt Ruth had predicted.

'I've just been receiving the benefit of Max's brotherly conversation,' Louise informed her grimly. 'He doesn't change…'

'No…' Katie looked at her twin. 'You know, in a lot of ways I feel quite sorry for him. He—'

'*Sorry* for *Max*?' Louise exploded. 'What on earth for? He's got everything he's ever wanted—a cushy place in one of the country's leading sets of chambers, with his pick of all the best briefs—and all he's had to do to get it is to persuade poor Maddy to marry him.'

'Yes, I know what he's got in the material sense, Lou, but is he happy?' Katie persisted. 'I think he feels what happened with Uncle David far, far more than he's ever shown. After all, they—'

'They were both made in the same mould. Yes, I know,' Louise cut in. 'If you want my opinion, it would be a good thing for this family if Uncle David *never* surfaced again. Olivia as good as told me that her father had been guilty of serious malpractice when he and Dad were partners, and that if he hadn't disappeared when he did…'

Both of them were silent for a moment as they remembered David Crighton, their father's twin brother and Olivia's father, and the near disaster he had plunged the family into prior to his disappearance some years earlier.

'That's all in the past now,' Katie reminded her gently. 'Dad and Olivia have managed to sort out all the problems they had been having with the practice—and in fact they've built up the business so much that they've decided they need to think about taking on an extra qualified solicitor to cope with the increased workload. But Gramps still misses David, you know. He was always—'

'The favourite. Yes, I know. Poor Gramps. He never has had very good judgement, has he? First he makes David the favourite, ahead of Dad, and now it's Max.'

'Mum's really glad that you were able to make it home for Gramps's birthday,' Katie told her sister quietly. 'She was…upset at Christmas when you didn't come home…'

'When I *couldn't* come home,' Louise corrected her sharply. 'I told you at the time. My boss put me under pressure to put together a report on the legal aspects of a new community law she thought might be passed, and I had no option but to agree. It wouldn't have been worth coming home for what would have amounted to just about forty-eight hours, even if I could have got the flights.'

Three months after leaving university, and not wanting to take the next stage in her training to become a barrister immediately, Louise had taken a temporary post working for a newly appointed Euro MP who'd wanted someone to work for her as a legal researcher.

Six months ago the temporary post had become a permanent one, and while the hours were long and the work extraordinarily demanding, Louise had thrown herself into it with determination, knowing that the contacts she was making in Brussels would ultimately equip her to make a change of career should she want to do so.

Their choice of careers couldn't have been more different, Katie acknowledged as she silently and sympathetically studied her twin. While Louise, true to her nature, had chosen to fling herself head-first into the maelstrom of politics and intrigues in the hot-house melting-pot atmosphere of Europe's bureaucratic capital, she had opted to join a still very youthful and emergent new charity which had been set up to help young children across the world who had been made orphans and refugees by war.

'Have you spoken to Saul and Tullah yet?' Kate asked her sister softly.

Louise reacted sharply to her question, tensing and almost physically backing off from her as she replied angrily, 'No, I haven't…Why should I? For God's sake, *when* is everyone in this wretched family going to stop behaving as though…?' She stopped, and took a deep breath.

'Look, for the last time, Saul means nothing to me now. I had a silly, stupid crush on him, yes. I made a total and complete fool of myself over him, yes. But…' She stopped again, and shook her head.

'It's over, Katie. Over.'

'Mum thought when you didn't come home at Christmas—' Katie began.

Louise wouldn't let her finish, breaking in bitterly, 'That what? That I couldn't bear the thought of seeing Saul? Or, worse, that I might—'

'She thought that perhaps you'd met someone in Brussels.' Katie overrode her with quiet insistence. 'And that you weren't coming home because you wanted to be with him…'

Interestingly, a soft tide of warm colour started to tinge her sister's skin, and, even more interestingly, for once in her life she seemed almost lost for words as she turned her head and looked down at the carpet before saying quickly, 'No. No, there isn't anyone…at least not like that. I…'

It wasn't totally true—there was someone, of sorts—but she knew perfectly well that the relationship Jean Claude wanted with her was one based on sex only.

Jean Claude was twelve years older than her, and moved in the higher echelons of Brussels' diplomatic circles. He was, as he himself had told Louise, a career diplomat, who currently held a post connected with the French fishing industry.

Louise wasn't quite sure as yet how she felt about him. He had a suave, dry sense of humour, and the kind of Gallic good looks that fell just short enough of outrageously handsome to ensure that he was very attractive to the female sex. Politics and the law, as Jean Claude had already teasingly commented to her, could make very exciting bedfellows.

'Brazen, I think you mean,' Louise had corrected him firmly.

'Be careful if you're looking for commitment,' a colleague had already warned Louise. 'He's got a reputation for liking variety.'

Louise had shrugged away the other woman's comments. Commitment was the last thing on her mind at the moment, and would be for a very long time to come. She might be over Saul in the sense that she was no longer suffering from the massive crush which had caused her to make such an idiotic fool of herself, but she was certainly far from over the feelings of humiliation and searing self-disgust—self-dislike—which had resulted from the sharp realisation of just how dangerously and potentially destructively out of control her feelings for Saul had threatened to become.

She would certainly never make that mistake again. *Never* allow herself to become such a victim, such a slave to her emotions ever again—she didn't really understand how it had happened in the first place. Right from her early teens she had set her sights firmly on aiming for a career. Marriage, babies, emotions, although she'd once have openly welcomed them with Saul, were more Katie's forte than her own. The terrifying force of her feelings for Saul had been an abberation, and the behaviour they had resulted in so totally abhorrent and repugnant to her that even now, nearly three years later, she could scarcely bear to think about it.

Yes, it was possible now for her to look at Saul with Tullah and the children without suffering even the smallest flicker of the emotion which had torn her apart and threatened every aspect of her normal life during those months when it had held its strangulating, choking grip on her life. But what *wasn't* possible, what she suspected might *never* be possible, was for her to forget just how traumatic that time, those *feelings* had been.

Louise frowned, her thoughts switching from the past to the present as she recognised the suspiciously furtive way her younger brother Joss and their cousin Jack were edging their way towards the French windows.

Discreetly following them, she waited until Joss was on the point of unlatching the door before demanding sternly, 'And just where do the pair of you think you are going?'

'Lou...'

Considerably startled, her brother released his hold on the door handle and spun round to face her.

'We were just going down to the greenhouse,' Jack told her with virtuous innocence. 'Aunt Ruth is growing some special seeds there and...'

'The greenhouse?' Louise questioned loftily. 'This compelling expedition to view Aunt Ruth's seedlings wouldn't have been taken via the TV room, would it?'

The look of contrived injured innocence her brother gave her made Louise's lips twitch slightly, but Jack wasn't quite such a good actor, and his fair skin was already starting to flush with guilt. Both boys were ardent rugby fans, and Louise had overheard them pleading with her mother, without success, earlier in the day to be allowed to sneak away from the family party in order to watch their favourite game.

'The All Blacks are playing,' Joss told her pleadingly.

'You'll be all black, or rather your good behaviour record will be, if Mum catches on to what you're up to,' Louise warned him.

'If we go now, we can just about catch the last half,' Joss told her winningly. 'And Mum won't even notice. We'll be back before she knows we're gone.'

'I don't think...' Louise began, but Joss was already reaching up to give her a fervent hug.

'Thanks Lou, you're the best,' he announced. 'And if Mum should ask...'

Louise shook her head firmly.

'Oh, no...don't drag me in. If you get found out, you're on your own, the pair of you.' But she was smiling affectionately as she returned her brother's warm hug. After all, it wasn't such a very long time ago that she herself had found such family gatherings rather dull, and had, like Joss and Jack, made her escape from them just as quickly as she could.

'Bet you wish you could come with us,' Joss whispered to her with an engaging grin before quickly sliding through the French window.

'To watch the All Blacks? No, thanks,' Louise retorted with a small female shudder, but she was smiling as she discreetly closed the French windows behind the two boys.

On the other side of the room Tullah, who had been watching the scene, touched Saul on the arm.

As he turned to look at her she took their son out of his arms and told him, 'I'm just going to have a word with Louise.'

Frowning slightly, Saul watched her. She had totally transformed his life, and the lives of his three children from his first marriage.

Louise stiffened as she saw Tullah making her way towards her. She looked quickly over her shoulder, but the door from the drawing room was blocked by her father and Aunt Ruth, who were deep in conversation. Katie, whom she might have expected to be her ally, had somehow or other managed to melt away, and now there was no escape for her. Tullah was already at her side.

'Hello, Louise…'

'Tullah.'

'You've had your hair cut. I like it. It suits you…'

'Thank you.'

Automatically Louise touched one of the short feathery curls of her newly shorn hair. She had had her hair cut on impulse the day before she had flown home, and the feminine cut showed off the delicacy of her bone structure and emphasised the shape and colour of her dark eyes. The weight she had lost while away at university had never totally been replaced. She looked, Tullah acknowledged inwardly, almost a little too fine-boned and fragile, and she could well understand, as a mother herself, why Jenny should be a little bit anxious over her well-being.

As the silence between them stretched Louise was acutely conscious of the fact that virtually everyone else in the room was probably watching them and remembering...

As she turned to move away from Tullah, baby Scott reached out and, grinning winsomely at Louise, patted her cheek with one fat baby hand, pronouncing solemnly, 'Pretty.'

Over his downy head Tullah's sympathetic eyes met Louise's wary, startled ones.

'Oh, dear. I think I'm going to sneeze.' Tullah told Louise. 'Could you take him for me?'

Before Louise could protest she found herself holding a solid armful of gurgling, beaming baby, whilst Tullah dived into her jacket pocket for a tissue.

'No. No, it's gone...' Tullah announced when the threatened sneeze was not forthcoming, but she made no attempt to take her son back from Louise as she commented, 'It's so nice to see virtually all the family here. I know your grandfather isn't always the easiest person to get along with...'

'You can say that again,' Louise agreed wryly, gently detaching the baby's clutching fingers from the gold chain she was wearing around her neck. 'He's got your colouring but Saul's eyes,' she told Tullah. 'How have the other three...?'

'So far, so good,' Tullah told her, showing her her

crossed fingers. 'It's probably been easier for them, and for us in one way, because they live with us full time. So there's no question of them feeling that Scott, here, gets to see more of their father than they do.'

Scott, for some reason, had quite obviously taken an immediate liking to Louise, and much to her own astonishment, and Tullah's patent amusement, he started to press loud juicy kisses against her face.

Louise, despite her determination to focus on her career, had always liked children and enjoyed their company. As a teenager she had often babysat for Saul, and had formed quite a close bond with his three, and now, to her chagrin, she suddenly felt her eyes filling with emotional feminine tears as Scott's baby kisses touched her skin.

Quickly she handed him back to Tullah, telling her chokingly, 'Tullah, I'm sorry…'

And both of them knew that it wasn't what was happening now that she was apologising for.

Very gently Tullah touched her arm.

'It's over, Lou,' she told her softly. 'Forget it. We have. You were missed at Christmas—by all of us…' As she turned to return to Saul and the children, she paused and dropped a light kiss on Louise's cheek.

'Forget it', Tullah had said. Louise closed her eyes as Tullah walked away. If only she could. Tullah and Saul might have forgiven her, but she doubted that she would ever be able to forgive herself…

'Is everything all right, darling?'

Louise forced a determined smile as she read the concern in her mother's eyes.

'Fine,' she assured her. A quick look around her grandfather's drawing room reassured her that she was no longer the object of everyone's discreet attention.

Taking a deep breath, Louise commented as steadily as she could, 'I was just saying to Tullah that Scott has Saul's eyes but her colouring...'

'Yes, he has, hasn't he?' Jenny Crighton agreed gratefully, relief leaking through the anxiety that had gripped her.

In one sense it had been a relief when Louise had finally agreed to come home for her grandfather's birthday, but in another...

Louise was her daughter, and she loved her, worried over her—how could she not do so?—but she had to admit that she had been anxious.

Louise had a quick temper coupled with a very easily bruised sense of pride. Watching Max talking with his sister earlier had made Jenny pray that Max wouldn't do or say something to upset his sister and put her on the defensive.

Tullah and Olivia—Jenny's niece and Louise's cousin—had both tried to reassure Jenny that everything would be all right, that teenage crushes were something that happened to everyone, and that it was just Louise's misfortune that hers had happened to be conducted under such a public glare of family attention, and that the object of her untrammelled teenage passion had been a member of her own family.

'She behaved so very badly,' Jenny had reminded them sorrowfully.

'Things did get a little out of hand,' Tullah had agreed. 'But since Louise's behaviour resulted in Saul and I getting together, and recognising how we really felt about one another far more quickly than we might otherwise have done, I have to admit that I feel more inclined to be grateful to her than anything else.'

'Louise made a mistake,' Olivia had added. 'Making mistakes is something we all do, and personally I think she'll end up a better, more well-rounded person for having had it brought home to her that she is fallible and human. She *was* rather inclined to think herself above everyone else,' she had reminded Jenny ruefully. 'A combination, perhaps, of a certain Crighton gene plus a very, very shrewd brain. What happened has softened her, made her realise that she's a human being and that there are some things she can't programme herself to achieve…'

'Have you had anything to eat yet?' Jenny pressed now. Jon, her husband, kept reminding her that Louise was now an adult woman, living her own life and holding down a very high-pressured job, but to Jenny she was still very much one of her babies, and to a mother's concerned eye Louise looked just that little bit too slender.

'I was just going to get myself something,' Louise fibbed. She was well aware of just how generous Tullah had been in coming over to her like that, but despite that generosity there was still a small knot of anxiety in Louise's stomach which made her feel that it would be unwise trying to eat.

'I was just on my way to wish Gramps a happy birthday,' she told her mother, and hopefully, once she had done so, she would be able to leave without the others thinking that…that what? That she was running away?

Running away. No, she wasn't doing that, had *never* done that, despite what some people chose to think!

'European Parliament…bunch of committee-making bureaucrats who are far too removed from what's going on in the real world…'

Louise gritted her teeth as she listened to Ben Crighton, her grandfather and family patriarch, a few minutes later. As she was perfectly well aware, so far as *he* was concerned the only real way, the only worthwhile way, to practise the law was from a barrister's chambers.

Excusing herself before she allowed him to provoke her into an argument, Louise couldn't help feeling sorry for Maddy, who had moved into the old man's large country house following an operation on his hip the year before.

The move, at first merely a temporary one to ensure that he had someone to care for him in the short term, had turned into a more permanent arrangement, with Maddy and the children living full time in Haslewich with Max's grandfather while Max spent most of his time living and working in London.

Louise couldn't understand how or why Maddy put up with Max's blatant selfishness—and his equally blatant infidelities. She certainly would never have done so, but then she would never have married a man like her brother in a thousand lifetimes. She knew how much it distressed her parents that he had turned out the way he had. Max was as unprincipled and selfish in other areas of his life as he was in his role as a husband.

Unlike their uncle David, Olivia's father and her own father's twin brother, Max might never have actually broken the law, but Louise suspected that he was perfectly capable if not of doing so, then certainly of bending it to suit his own purposes.

'He doesn't change, does he?' The rueful, familiar tones of Saul's voice coming from behind her caused

Louise to whirl round, her face a stiff mask of wariness as she watched him.

The last time she and Saul had spoken to each other had been when he had consigned her to Olivia's charge, having just made it clear to her that, far from returning her feelings for him, he would really prefer never to have to set eyes on her again.

Words spoken in the heat of the moment, perhaps, but they had left their mark, their scar upon her, not least because she knew how richly deserved his fury and rejection of her had been.

'I suppose at his age...' Louise began, and then shook her head and agreed huskily, 'No. No, he doesn't.'

Ridiculous for her, at twenty-two, to feel as uncomfortable and ill at ease as a guilty child, but nevertheless she did.

Whatever malign fate had decided to make Saul the object of her teenage fantasies and longings had long since upped sticks and decamped from her emotions. The man she saw standing in front of her might not have changed but she certainly had. The Saul she saw standing before her now was once again, thankfully, nothing more to her than another member of her family.

'Your mother says you're only paying a flying visit home this time.'

'Yes. Yes, that's right,' Louise agreed. 'Pam Carlisle, my boss, has been asked to sit on a new committee being set up to look into the problems caused by potential over-fishing in the seas off the Arctic. Obviously from the legal angle there's going to be a lot of research work involved, which I'll be involved in.'

'Mmm…sounds like a good breeding ground for potential future Euro politicians in the Crighton family,' Saul teased, but Louise shook her head.

'No. Definitely not,' she denied firmly. 'Politics isn't for me. I'm afraid I'm far too outspoken for a start,' she told him ruefully. 'And politics requires a great deal more finesse than I'll ever possess.'

'You're too hard on yourself,' Saul told her. 'In more ways than one,' he added meaningfully, forcing her to hold his gaze as he added quietly, 'It's time for us to make a fresh start, Lou. What happened happened, but it's in the past now…'

Before she could say anything he added, 'Tullah and I will be coming over to Brussels some time in the next few months on company business. It would be nice if we could meet up…go out for dinner together…'

Saul worked for Aarlston-Becker, a large multinational company whose European head office was based just outside Haslewich. He and Tullah had met when she had gone to work in the company's legal department under Saul.

Unable to do anything other than simply nod her head, Louise was stunned when Saul suddenly reached out and took her in his arms, holding her tightly in a cousinly hug as he told her gruffly, 'Friends again, Lou.'

'Friends,' she managed to agree chokily, fiercely blinking back her tears.

'And don't forget…write to me…'

Louise grimaced as she listened to Katie's firm command. 'Why on earth did you have to go and get yourself involved with some wretched charity outfit that can't even run to the expense of a fax machine?' she groaned.

'*You* tell *me*…but I do enjoy my job,' Katie pointed out.

They were saying goodbye at the airport, their mother having dropped them off on her way to a meeting of the charity she and their great-aunt Ruth had set up in their home town some years earlier.

'Sorry I can't see you off properly,' she had apologised as they climbed out of her small car.

'Don't worry about it, Mum; we understand,' Louise had consoled her.

'You could always come over to Brussels to see me, you know,' Louise told her twin abruptly now. 'I'll pay for the ticket, if that would help.'

Katie gave her a brief hug. She knew how difficult it was for her sister to admit that there were any chinks in her emotional armour, even to her twin. To the world at large, Louise always came across as the more independent one of the two of them, the leader. But in reality Katie believed that *she* was the one with the less sensitively acute emotions, even though she knew that Louise would have sharply denied such an allegation. Louise had always taken upon herself the role of the bigger, braver sister, but Katie knew that inside Louise was nowhere near as confident or as determinedly independent as others seemed to think.

Even their parents seemed to have been deceived by Louise's outward assumption of sturdy bravado, and consequently *she* was the one who was always treated that little bit more gently, the one for whom extra allowances were always made, Katie acknowledged. A fact which made her oddly protective of her sister.

'Oh, by the way, did you know that Professor Simmonds has been seconded to Brussels? Apparently he's been asked to head some committee on fishing rights in the North Sea,' Katie told her vaguely.

'What? No, I *didn't* know,' Louise responded, her face paling.

'No? I thought that perhaps you may have bumped into him,' Katie told her innocently.

'No, I haven't!' But if what Katie had just told her was true, Louise suspected that she was certainly going to do so. The committee Katie was talking about had to be the same one that Louise's boss had just been co-opted onto. Of all the unwanted coincidences!

Louise's thoughts rioted frantically, her stomach churning, but she dared not let Katie see how shocked and disturbed she was.

'I know you don't *like* him,' Katie was saying quietly.

'No. I don't,' Louise agreed curtly. 'After all, he cost me my first, and—'

'Louise, that's not fair,' Katie objected gently.

Louise looked away from her. There was so much that Katie didn't know, that she *couldn't* tell her.

Gareth Simmonds had been her tutor at Oxford at a particularly traumatic time in her life, and he had been a witness not just to that trauma, and the way she had made a complete and utter fool of herself, but he had also...

Louise bit her lip. The feeling of panic churning her stomach was increasing instead of easing.

'That's the final call for my flight,' she told Katie thankfully, giving her twin a swift hug before grabbing hold of her flight bag and heading for her gateway.

Gareth Simmonds in Brussels!

That was all she needed!

CHAPTER TWO

GARETH SIMMONDS in Brussels! Louise gave a small groan and closed her eyes, shaking her head in refusal of the stewardess's offer of a drink.

Trust Katie to wait to drop *that* bombshell on her until the last minute. Still, at least she *had* warned her, and forewarned was, as they say, forearmed.

Gareth Simmonds. She ground her teeth in impotent fury. She had been halfway through her first year when he had stepped into the shoes of her previous tutor, who'd had to retire unexpectedly on the grounds of ill health, and he and Louise had clashed right from the start.

She had resented the far more pro-active role he had made it plain he intended to play as her tutor. She had been used to his elderly and ailing predecessor, who had, in the main, been content to leave her to her own devices—something which had suited Louise down to the ground, giving her, as it had, ample opportunity to give the minimum amount of attention to her studies whilst she concentrated on what had become the far more important matter of making Saul fall in love with her.

The situation would have been bad enough if Gareth Simmonds had merely concerned himself with his official role as her tutor, but, no, that hadn't been enough for him. He had had the gall…the cheek… the…the effrontery to take it upon himself to interfere in her personal life as well.

26

Louise's tense shoulders twitched angrily. The last thing she needed right now—just when she was beginning to feel she was getting her life back on an even keel again, just when the events of the weekend had made her feel that at last, *finally*, she had begun to reclaim her sense of self-respect—was to have the whole ugly mess of her past dragged up again in the person of Gareth Simmonds.

He was going to Brussels to head a committee, Katie had said, when repeating to her the information she had garnered at an informal reunion of her old university classmates, and not just any committee either. Louise could feel her body starting to tense defensively. The thought that she might have to have any kind of contact with Gareth Simmonds was unacceptable, untenable. Anger, pride and panic started to well up inside her, causing her throat to tighten as though her own despairing emotions were threatening to choke her.

Gareth Simmonds. They had clashed straight away, something about him sending sharp, prickling, atavistic feelings of dislike and apprehension quivering through her body, and that had been *before* that disastrous confrontation between them at the end of her first year at Oxford, when he had sent for her and warned her of the potentially dire consequences of her not giving more time and attention to her work.

She had been far more headstrong and self-willed in those days, and the fact that he had had the gall to challenge her over anything, never mind the torment of her love for Saul, had driven her to retaliate. But he had been too quick for her, too subtle…too…

She had hated him with much the same intensity with which she had loved Saul, and with just as little effect, and the last thing she wanted or needed at this stage in her life was to be confronted with the physical evidence of her own youthful stupidity.

She could still remember…

There had been a good deal of giggling and gossip when he had first arrived at Oxford—the youngest Chair they had ever had, and the sexiest, according to his female students. Louise had shrugged her shoulders in disdain. *However* sexy *others* might find him, *she* was not interested. In her eyes he could never match up to Saul. No man could.

True, he might be over six feet with the kind of Celtic colouring that produced a lethal combination of thick dark hair and incredibly brilliant dark blue eyes, but for all Louise cared he could have modelled for the hunchback of Notre Dame.

'Have you *heard* his voice,' one besotted student had breathed, wild-eyed. 'I could orgasm just listening to him.'

Louise had looked witheringly at her. *Saul's* voice made her go weak at the knees, and Gareth Simmonds sounded nothing like him. In fact, the only things they did have in common were that they were both in their thirties—although Gareth Simmonds was a good seven years younger than Saul—and they could both display a decidedly brutal verbal toughness when they so chose. From Saul, the merest hint of a sharp word could reduce her to choking black misery. From Gareth Simmonds it tended to provoke a fierce desire to retaliate in kind.

He *might* have been her tutor, but that hadn't given him the right to interfere in her life in the way he had done—and besides… But, no, she must not think about that—not now.

Abruptly Louise realised that the plane had landed.

Automatically she stood up and reached to retrieve her bag from the overhead locker, and then froze as the man occupying the seat behind her also stood up to do the same thing.

'You!' she whispered as she came face to face with the very man who had just been occupying her thoughts and exercising her temper.

'Hello, Louise.' Gareth Simmonds acknowledged her calmly. Shakily Louise grabbed her bag and turned her back on him. What an appalling coincidence that *he* should be on the same flight as her!

Determinedly keeping her back towards him, Louise edged her way into the aisle and headed for the exit.

A sharp wind whipped across the tarmac as they left the plane, and as she hurried towards the arrivals lounge Louise reassured herself that her quickened pace was caused by the chilly evening air, and certainly not by any fear of coming face to face with Gareth Simmonds a second time.

Once through Customs Louise headed for the taxi rank, giving the cab driver her address at the large block of apartments where she lived. The apartment she rented was small, and fearsomely expensive, but at least she lived on her own, she comforted herself as she paid off the taxi driver and walked into the apartment block foyer.

While she filled the kettle, Louise ran her answering machine tape. A small rueful smile curled her mouth as she heard Jean Claude's familiar, sexy, smoky French accent. She had dated the Frenchman casually a few times, but was well aware of his reputation as an incorrigible flirt.

He was telephoning to ask if she was free for dinner during the week. Louise went to pick up and open her diary. She was due to accompany her boss to an inaugural meeting of the new committee in the morning. She suspected it might possibly run on until after lunch, and then at night there was an official dinner.

'The French contingent especially are going to be asking some tricky questions,' Pam Carlisle had warned Louise. 'They're none too happy about the fact that the Chair appointed is British. It's only the fact that he's known to be pro-European that's persuaded them to give their grudging acceptance of his appointment. The disputed waters are, after all, still officially British.'

'But they want to change that...' Louise had guessed.

'Well, they certainly want to get their own legal right to fish the waters.'

They had gone on to discuss the legal ramifications of the situation, and Louise had never thought to ask her boss the identity of the committee's Chair. Why should she have done? It had never even crossed her mind that the new appointee could possibly be her ex-tutor and protagonist Gareth Simmonds. Hadn't his prestigious lectureship coupled with the doting adoration of half the female student population been enough for him? Louise wondered bitterly.

'I'll bet he's absolutely heaven in bed,' she could remember one of her co-students breathing excitedly. 'And he's not married.'

'Heaven in bed'. Louise tensed abruptly. He had certainly been hell out of it! To her at least.

'He's rumbled us,' Katie had warned her. 'He's

guessed that I've been sitting in at lectures to cover for you. He actually *called* me Katherine yesterday…'

'So…?' Louise had said grittily. 'That *is* your name, isn't it?'

'It's *my* name,' Katie had agreed. 'But at the time I was attending one of his lectures pretending to be *you*.'

'He probably made a genuine mistake,' Louise had told her irritably. She had gone home to Haslewich, on the pretext of having left some of her books behind on her last visit home, but in reality so that she could see Saul. To her chagrin, though, Saul had been away on business, and the whole exercise had proved to be a complete waste of time.

In those days she had not always treated her twin as considerately as she might have, Louise acknowledged now, as the boiling kettle disturbed her reverie, and in fact it was probably very true to say she had often been guilty of bullying and browbeating Katie into doing as *she* wanted.

Things were different now, of course. She had done what she could to make amends, and, as she was the first to acknowledge, there were areas in which her twin had shown considerably more strength of purpose and determination than she could ever have exhibited herself.

She had been in her late teens then, though, and so totally obsessed with Saul that nothing else, *no one* else, had been important.

Briefly she closed her eyes. This afternoon, when Saul had put his arms round her to give her that firm fraternal hug, initially her body had totally recoiled from his touch—not out of rejection but out of fear, a deep-rooted, instinctive, self-protective fear that there might be some hidden part of her that was still susceptible to her old romantic dreams. But to her relief what she had actually felt, *all* she had actually felt, had been a warm and very reassuring sense of peace and release, coupled with the knowledge that there was nothing, after all, for her to fear. Being hugged by Saul, being held in his arms, had meant no more to her than if he had been Olivia's husband Caspar, or one of the Chester cousins, or indeed any other man of whom she had reason to be fond in a totally non-sexual and uncomplicated way.

She had *known* then that she was truly and totally free of the past, at least where *Saul* was concerned.

Frowningly she stirred her coffee.

She had behaved foolishly when she had been at university, there was no getting away from that fact, but she wasn't alone in having done that—many other students had done the same.

She picked up her coffee mug too quickly and some of the hot liquid spilled onto her hand. She cursed angrily under her breath.

Damn Gareth Simmonds. *Why* on earth couldn't he have stayed safely where he was in Oxford—and in her past?

The *last* thing she needed right now was having him around studying her…watching her with those too perceptive, too knowing evening-sky-blue eyes of his…judging her…just *waiting* for her to make a mistake…

Louise started to grind her teeth.

Well, she'd got news for him. She wasn't the Louise she had been at Oxford any longer. She was a *woman* now, an adult, holding down a highly responsible and demanding job, proving that she could control and run her *own* life, that she didn't need the constant back-up and support of her twin sister to be there at her side all the time, to do her bidding, to make her feel whole and complete. God, but she had hated him for throwing that accusation at her—just one of the scathing criticisms he had made of her!

It should have been *Saul's* denouncement of her, after she had so dangerously tricked Tullah into following her into the maze and left her there at the masked ball, that should have remained like a scar on her consciousness, a dialogue that ran for ever through her head as she tried to argue her way out of it, but oddly it wasn't. It was her arguments, her confrontations with her tutor about which she *still* had bad dreams, and still, in times of stress, played over and over again through her memory.

Oxford, the time after she had finally been forced to realise that Saul would never love her, that in fact he loved someone else. Oxford and Gareth Simmonds. Oxford, Italy—and Gareth Simmonds. *Italy* and Gareth Simmonds.

Picking up her coffee, Louise walked into her small sitting room and curled up on the sofa, closing her eyes. She didn't *want* to relive those memories, but she could feel the weight of them pressing down on her, pushing their way into her consciousness just as Gareth Simmonds seemed to be pushing his way into the new life she had made for herself.

As though the debacle of the masquerade ball had not been punishment enough for her to contend with, that following week she had received a letter from Gareth Simmonds. A curt letter informing her that he wished to see her as there were certain matters concerning her work which he wished to discuss with her.

Her parents knew she had received the letter, and there had been no way she had been able to keep its contents a secret from them—although Katie had been sworn to secrecy over the worst of her excesses in skipping tutorials. If her mother and father had not actually stood over her while she went through the humiliation of telephoning Gareth Simmonds and making an appointment to see him, they had certainly left her in no doubt about their feelings of shock and disappointment at the way she had been abusing both her intelligence and the opportunity that going to Oxford had given her.

Furiously she had blamed Gareth Simmonds for adding to her problems, while having to give way to her parents' firm insistence that they would drive her to Oxford for the interview, where she planned to stay for a few days in order to try to catch up with her work.

They had set out after breakfast, her mother patently unhappy and trying to control her tears and her father unexpectedly grim-faced and distant, and Louise had known what was going through both their minds. Was *she*, like her elder brother Max, going to turn out to be one of those Crightons who had inherited the same genes as her uncle David—the 'S' gene, as she and Katie had nicknamed it as teenagers. The 'S' standing for selfish, stupid and self-destructive.

She had *wanted* to reassure them, to tell them that there was nothing for them to worry about, but she had still been deep in shock herself, still traumatised not just by *what* she had done but by the frightening emotions which had given rise to her dangerous behaviour.

'I can't believe you could behave so appallingly,'

her father had told her grimly, his voice shaking slightly with emotion as he'd confronted her with the full enormity of what she had done after the ball.

'What were you going to *do*? Leave Tullah in the maze until—'

'No… No… I just…' Tears streaming down her face, Louise had turned her head away from him, not able to bring herself to admit that she had been so obsessed by her need to make Saul see her as a woman, to make him *love* her as a woman, that she had simply seen Tullah as a hindrance who was standing in her way. Someone who was preventing Saul from seeing her, Louise, properly, and recognising that they were meant to be together.

Katie had travelled to Oxford with them to give her some moral support. She was also going to use the time to see friends who'd stayed up in Oxford to earn some money waiting at the local bars and restaurant. While her mother had fussed around her rooms, tidying up Louise's discarded clothes and books, Katie had simply taken hold of her hand and gripped it tightly in a gesture of sisterly solidarity and love.

It was only when her mother had gone to shake her duvet and straighten up her untidy bed that Louise had finally moved, pushing her away and telling her fiercely, 'I can do that…'

What had already happened was shameful enough. To have her mother move her pillow and discover that she slept with Saul's purloined shirt beneath it would have been the ultimate humiliation.

When they were on their own Katie asked her awkwardly, 'Do you…do you want to talk about it…?'

Angrily Louise shook her head.

'Oh, Lou,' Katie whispered sombrely, her voice full

of pain and despair at what her twin had done, and love and pity for Louise herself.

'Stop fussing,' Louise commanded her.

'I'm sure Professor Simmonds knows what we've been doing,' Katie warned. 'I didn't want to say anything in front of the parents, but, as I told you, he's definitely rumbled the fact that I've been standing in at his lectures for you,' she went on. 'Have you got the notes I did for you?'

'Yes,' Louise acknowledged shortly. 'But how could he know of our switch? We've played tricks on our friends before now, and they've never realized.'

Katie waited several seconds before responding quietly, 'It's different with Professor Simmonds. He just seems to know. It's almost as though he's got some kind of sixth sense which allows him to tell the difference between us.'

'Some sixth sense?' Louise derided, scoffing. 'He's a professor of law, not a magician.' But even so she was left feeling uneasy and on edge. Something about Gareth Simmonds challenged her to defy him and to get the better of him, and it infuriated her that so far all her attempts to do so had ended up in her ignominious defeat.

'He called me Katherine,' Katie reminded her. 'Even though I was wearing your clothes and the others all believed I was you.'

'Arrogant, self-assured pig,' Louise muttered aggressively. 'I *loathe* him.'

But nowhere near so much as she loathed herself.

After Katie had left to let her sister draw her thoughts together—they had made the decision that, although they both wanted to go up to Oxford, they did not want to live together, nor to be thought of as an inseparable pair, and so were taking different courses and rented separate accommodation—Louise picked up the course notes her twin had left for her. But although her eyes skimmed over their contents her brain was simply not capable of taking in their meaning. How *could* it, when it, like her emotions, was still struggling to come to terms with the death blow that events had dealt her?

She had been in love with Saul and had dreamed of him returning her feelings for as long as she had been capable of knowing what being in love meant, and it had simply never occurred to her that she would not ultimately win him. Why should it? Every other goal she had ever set herself she had reached, and it had never entered her head that securing Saul's love would be any different.

Katie's writing started to blur in front of her eyes. Shakily she flung the papers down, wrapping her arms around her body. She felt so cold inside, so empty, and yet at the same time filled with such an enormous weight of fear and pain.

Automatically she went over to her bed and felt beneath the pillow for Saul's shirt, hugging it to her, closing her eyes and breathing in the warm Saul smell of him which still clung to it. But for once his faint but oh, so evocative scent failed to comfort her.

It wasn't his shirt she wanted to hold, she acknowledged as she threw it away from her with a wrenching shudder. It was the man himself. *Saul* himself. But he had made it cruelly plain to her that *that* was never going to happen.

'Saul, Saul, Saul...' Helplessly she cried out his name, whispering it over and over again inside her head as the tears started to flow.

Worn out by the intensity of her emotions, she finally fell asleep, only to wake up in the early hours, cold and shivering, her eyes sore and hot.

She was still fully dressed. She hadn't eaten, but she knew that the very thought of food was totally repugnant to her. As she got up she caught sight of the discarded notes that Katie had given her, and her heart gave a small, anxious thud.

Gareth Simmonds wasn't like old Professor Lewis. There was no way she would be able to sweet-talk him into overlooking the falling standard of her work—and Louise knew that it *had* been falling—but how could she be expected to concentrate on her studies when her thoughts, her heart, her whole self had been focused so totally on Saul?

'Ah, Louise. Good. Thank you for returning to Oxford at short notice. Did *your sister* come with you?'

Despite the calm and apparently friendly tone of his voice as he invited her into his study, Louise was not deceived by her tutor's apparent affability, nor by the way he'd emphasised the words 'your sister'.

Her plan of action, before her arrival here in Gareth Simmonds' study, had been to attempt to bluff things out, and to stick determinedly to the fiction that she had attended all his lectures and that *he* was at fault in mistaking her for Katie. But one look at his face, one brief clash between her own still sore and aching dark beautiful eyes and his far too clear and penetrative navy blue gaze, had been enough to alert her to the disastrous potential of such an unwise course of action.

'Sit down,' he instructed her when she failed to make any response—a first for Louise. She was not normally short of quick, sassy answers to even the most awkward questions.

It was a new experience for her to feel unnerved enough to hold her tongue and apprehensively await events. She could see a mixture of pity and irritation on his face that hurt her pride. How dared he pity her?

To her chagrin, she could feel her eyes starting to burn with the betraying sting of her emotions. Quickly she ducked her head. The last thing she wanted was for the urbane, controlled and hatefully superior man seated in front of her to guess that she wasn't feeling anywhere near as sure of herself as she was trying to pretend, and that in fact, far from not giving a damn about what he was saying to her—as she was desperately trying to show—she was feeling thoroughly and frighteningly vulnerable, and shocked by the situation she had got herself into.

Blinking furiously to banish her tears, she was unaware of the fact that Gareth Simmonds had got up from behind his desk until she suddenly realised that he was standing beside her, the muscled bulk of his body casting not just a heavy shadow but inexplicably causing the air around her suddenly to feel much warmer.

'Louise. The last thing I want to do is to make things hard for you. I know things haven't been…easy for you and that emotionally…If there's a problem that I…'

Immediately Louise stiffened. It had been bad enough having to cope with the mingled anger and pity of her family, but to have Gareth Simmonds offering her his lofty, condescending 'understanding' was more than she could bear.

'The only problem I have right now is you,' she

told him aggressively, relieved to be able to stir up her own anger and use it to keep the humiliating threat of her tears at bay.

She thought she heard him catch a swiftly indrawn breath, and waited for his retaliation, but instead he simply said humorously, 'I know that legally you're an adult, Louise, but right now you remind me more of my six-year-old niece. I'm not your enemy, you know. I'm simply trying to help you.'

'Don't you dare patronise me. I am not your niece,' Louise retaliated, standing up, her cheeks flushed with temper, fully intending to storm out of his office.

But before she could do so he stopped her, taking hold of her wrist and gently but determinedly pushing her back down into her chair. And then, before she could voice her anger, to her consternation he knelt down beside her chair, so that their eyes were level as he told her, 'Stop making things so hard for yourself. You've got a first-class brain but it won't do you any good whatsoever unless you stop letting it be overruled by that stiff-necked pride of yours. We all go through times in our lives when we need other people's help, you know, Louise—'

'Well, I don't,' Louise interrupted him rudely, adding fiercely, 'And even if I did, the last person I would turn to for it would be you.'

There was a long pause before he finally said softly, 'That's a very interesting statement, Louise, and if I may say so, a rather dangerously challenging one.'

He was, Louise recognised with a sharp thrill of awareness, looking not into her eyes any more but at her mouth.

'He is just so sexy,' she remembered her fellow female students saying when they talked about him, and now, like someone hurtling recklessly into un-expected danger, she knew exactly what they meant.

As immediate as that recognition, and twice as powerful, was her panicky, virginal rejection of it. She didn't want to see Gareth Simmonds as a sexually compelling and desirable man. She was only allowed to have that kind of reaction to Saul.

'I want to go,' she told him unsteadily. 'I…'

'Not yet. I haven't finished talking to you,' he had countered calmly. But he stepped back from her, as though somehow he had guessed just what she was feeling and wanted to make things just that little bit easier for her—which was totally impossible, of course. Louise knew that he disliked her every bit as much as she did him, and that he enjoyed making life difficult and unpleasant for her.

Holding her gaze, he said, 'Very well, Louise, if you want to do this the hard way then that's your choice. I do know what's been going on, Louise, so don't bother to waste my time or your own apparently failing brain power in trying to lie to me. In your shoes it would be pointless wasting the energy and intelligence you very obviously need for your studies on dreaming up unrealistic scenarios.

'In *my* experience there are generally two reasons why a student suddenly fails to live up to his or her forecast academic expectations. One of those is that quite simply, and unfortunately for them, they can't. By some fluke of fate and the examination board they've managed to get themselves onto a degree course they are in no way intellectually equipped to handle. The other…'

He paused and looked calmly at her. 'The other is that for reasons of their own they have decided that they don't want to, that there are other and no doubt more important matters to claim their attention. The solution in both cases is, however, the same. For those who don't have the ability to continue with their course, to bring it to a swift end is, I think, the kindest way to end their misery. To those who have the ability, but who don't wish to use it… It isn't so much *their* misery one wants to bring to an end, but one's own, and that of their fellow students…'

Louise stared at him in furious disbelief.

'You're threatening to have me sent down. You *can't* do that,' she told him flatly.

Gareth Simmond's dark eyebrows had risen.

'No? I rather think you'll find that I can. But forgive me, Louise, I assumed that this must be what you wanted. After all…' he picked up her course work and threw it disdainfully across his desk towards her '…to judge from this, continuing with your course is the last thing you really want to do.

'Look,' he went on, when Louise continued to glare at him. 'If I've got it wrong, and the problem is that the work is too taxing for you, please tell me and I'll try my best to get you transferred onto a less… demanding course. There *are* university standards,' he reminded her, with deceptive gentleness, 'and I'm afraid that we do still strive for excellence rather than the mere pedestrian. If you feel that you're not up to the work—'

'Of course I'm up to it,' Louise snapped angrily at him, her eyes flashing. How dared he stand there and suggest that she wasn't up to the work? His predecessor had told her on more than one occasion, albeit perhaps in a roundabout way, that he considered her

to be one of his most promising students. His predecessor... Louise clenched her fists.

'When a student's grades suddenly start to fall,
some people believe that it's more the teaching that's
at fault, rather than the pupil,' she challenged him
feistily.

Gareth eyed her thoughtfully.

'Some people might,' he agreed coolly. 'But others
might more intelligently suspect that the pupil's non-
appearance at nearly half her lectures and tutorials
might have something to do with the situation.
Wouldn't you agree? I'm not a fool, Louise,' he said,
at her look of surprise. 'I know very well that your
sister has been standing in for you at my lectures.

'Look,' he continued, when Louise made no reply,
'we could argue about this all day. The fact is, Louise,
that you've been skipping lectures and missing out on
vital course work. And you've lost weight,' he told
her abruptly, causing Louise to stare at him in astonishment. How on earth could he tell? Not even her
twin or her mother had commented or appeared to
notice—and with good reason, since she had taken to
wearing loose baggy tops over her regulation jeans,
knowing how much her mother would start to fuss if
she thought for one moment that she wasn't eating
properly.

Olivia's mother, although only a Crighton by marriage, had suffered from bulimia for many years, and
her behaviour during the years of her marriage to
David, her father's brother, had left its scars on the
family. Her own mother was fervently keen on
healthy, sensible eating—mealtimes, until Louise had
left home, had been old-fashioned family affairs, with
everyone seated around the same table. Not that

Louise had any problem with that—at least, not usually. She liked her food, and had a good healthy appetite, but just recently she had found herself unable to eat, too sick with longing and need, too hungry for Saul's love to satisfy her appetite with anything else.

'I appreciate that you're having personal problems...' Gareth said now.

But before he could finish, and suggest that she might benefit from talking them over with someone, she jumped in, demanding aggressively, 'Who told you that? They—'

'You did,' Gareth interrupted her levelly as he studied her mutinous face. 'You've lost weight. You're obviously not sleeping and you're certainly not working,' he reminded her quietly. 'The facts speak for themselves. I don't need a degree in psychology to interpret them.

'Professor Lewis told me that he confidently expected you to get a double first. On the basis of your current course work I'd say you'd be lucky to make a third. It's up to you, Louise. Either start giving your work some serious attention or...'

'You'll have me thrown out,' Louise guessed bitterly.

Without giving him the opportunity to say any more, she snatched up her papers and stormed angrily out of his room.

God, but she hated him. *Hated* him!

'Well, how did it go?' Katie demanded. She had been waiting anxiously for Louise to return from her interview and now, as she came hurtling out into the quadrangle, almost running, Katie had trouble keeping up with her.

'Slow down,' she begged her, catching hold of her arm, 'and tell me what he said.'

'He *said*… He *threatened* to have me sent down,' Louise told her flatly.

'What? Oh, Lou, no! Did you tell him, explain…? Did you…?'

'Tell him what?' Louise asked bitterly.

'About…about Saul… Did you explain? Did you—?'

Abruptly Louise stopped moving and turned round to face her twin.

'Are you *mad*?' she asked her grimly. 'Tell *Gareth Simmonds* about Saul?' She closed her eyes as she remembered the revolting pity she had seen in his eyes. How *dared* he pity her? How *dared* anyone?

'He's given me until Christmas to catch up…'

'Well, that shouldn't be too difficult.' Katie tried to comfort her. 'We've got the rest of the summer vac. And I can help you.'

'I don't *want* your help. I just want—' Louise began angrily, and then stopped.

The force, the futility of her own feelings frightened her. She felt oddly sick and light-headed.

'Why don't we spend the evening together?' she suggested to Katie, trying to make amends for her earlier bad temper. 'We could have supper and share a bottle of wine. I've still got that case in my room that Aunt Ruth gave us at the beginning of term. She said it would come in useful for student parties…'

'I'd love to but I'm afraid I can't,' Katie told her regretfully, shaking her head before explaining blushingly, 'I…I've got a date and…'

'A date? Who with?' Louise questioned her sister. But Katie shook her head and told her awkwardly,

'Oh, it's no one you know… Oh, Lou,' she pleaded as she turned to give her twin a fierce hug, 'I do understand how you must feel, but please, please try to forget about Saul.'

'I wish to God I could,' Louise told her chokily. 'But I'm not to get the chance, am I? Not if I get sent down and I have to go back to Haslewich. Oh, Katie…' It was on the tip of her tongue to plead with her twin to cancel her date and spend the evening with her, but then she remembered the look she had seen in Gareth Simmonds' eyes when he had told her that he knew she had been using Katie to stand in at his lectures for her, and she resisted the impulse.

She was not, she assured herself fiercely, the selfish, thoughtless, self-absorbed person his look had implied. She would have done the same thing for Katie…if Katie had asked…

But Katie would not have asked, a small inner voice told her.

The summer afternoon had given way to evening. Louise stared tiredly around her room. Papers and textbooks covered every surface, and her head was swimming with facts she couldn't assimilate; they floated in her brain like congealing fat on top of her mother's home-made stock, coagulating and clogging.

Saul. Where was he now…? What was he doing…? She got up and walked into her small kitchenette. She couldn't remember the last time she had eaten, but the mere thought of food made her feel sick.

Out of the corner of her eye she caught sight of Aunt Ruth's wine stacked in a dusty corner. Dizzily she went and removed a bottle.

Aunt Ruth had quaintly old-fashioned ideas about

how Oxford's modern-day undergraduates lived. The wine she had chosen for her great-nieces had been carefully selected for its full-bodied richness. Ruth had imagined it would be drunk at the kind of undergrad gathering that featured in expensive TV dramas—adaptations of books set in a glittering gilded era.

Louise opened one of the bottles and poured herself a glass. She was not normally a drinker. Oh, she enjoyed a decent glass of wine with good food, and she had gone through the normal student ritual of drinking at the bar in the students' union during the first few weeks at university, but that had simply been a rite of passage, something to be endured rather than enjoyed.

The red wine was rich and fruity, warming her throat and heating her cold, empty stomach.

Louise sank down onto the floor, owlishly studying the mass of paper she had spread all around her. Katie's handwriting danced dizzily before her eyes. Frowningly she blinked as she tried to focus and concentrate, quickly finishing off her glass of wine.

It was making her feel distinctly better—lighter, number. It was even making it possible for her to think about Saul without that wrenching, tearing pain deep inside her, threatening to destroy her.

Saul…

As she walked erratically back from the kitchenette, having refilled her glass, Louise tried to summon up Saul's beloved mental image and found, to her consternation, that she couldn't—that for some reason his beloved, adored features had become amorphous and vague, sliding away before she could crystallise them into a hard image. Even more infuriatingly, the harder she tried to visualise him, the more impossible it became. Instead, the male image that came most easily to her mind's eye was that of Gareth Simmonds.

Frantically Louise took a deep gulp of her wine, keeping a firm grip on it as she searched feverishly through her diary for the photograph of Saul which she always, always kept there.

Louise was clutching the photograph when she heard someone knocking on her door.

Katie… Her sister had changed her mind, cancelled her date realising just how much she needed someone to be with her. Tipsily, Louise lurched towards the door, yanking it open as she cried out, 'Oh, Katie, thank goodness you're here. I…'

Her voice faded away as her visitor stepped grimly over the threshold, firmly closing the door behind him.

'You!' she said shakily as she looked up into the merciless gaze with which her tutor had swept the room before finally coming to rest on her tear-stained face. 'What do you want…?'

'I came to bring you these,' Gareth Simmonds told her, and held some papers. 'You left them on my desk this morning…'

'Oh… I…' Awkwardly Louise reached out to take them from him, forgetting that she was still holding not just Saul's photograph but also a half-full glass of wine.

As she reached for the papers Saul's photograph slipped from her fingers. Immediately Louise tried to retrieve it, accidentally bumping into Gareth Simmonds as she did so, wine slopping from her glass onto both his wrist and her own arm.

Before she could stop him Gareth Simmonds was bending down to pick up Saul's photograph.

'No. Don't...' she began, but it was too late.

As he picked it up he paused, studying Saul's features thoughtfully and then looking from the photograph to her face before declaring ironically, 'He's a very good-looking man, Louise, I'll grant you that. But is he really worth messing up the whole of your future over? He's too old for you, anyway,' he added dismissively.

Louise's temper, rubbed raw during her earlier dressing down at his hands, burst into crazy pain.

'No, he's not...he's...' To her consternation she felt fiery tears beginning to burn the backs of her eyes. Pouring the rest of the contents of her glass down her throat, she gulped rebelliously, 'I'm not a child, you know. I'm a woman...'

The derisive look in his eyes demolished the last of her precarious hold on her temper and pushed her over the edge of caution into reckless fury.

'What is it?' she demanded. 'Don't you believe me? Well, I am, and I'll prove it to you... Saul *would* have wanted me if she—Tullah—hadn't come along...'

'How much of that stuff have you had to drink?' she heard him demanding as he ignored her furious statement and removed from her hand the glass she was still holding to sniff it with an irritated frown.

'Not enough,' she told him forlornly, adding aggressively. 'And give me back my glass. I *need* another drink...'

'No way. You've already had more than enough.'

'No, I haven't...' Angrily Louise reached out towards him, trying to snatch back her glass, but he was holding onto it too tightly, and as he lifted his arm to remove it even further from her reach she lost her balance and staggered heavily into him. His body had all the unyielding hardness of solid rock, only it felt much warmer…warmer and…

Louise blinked as she realised that the heavy thud she could feel beneath her hand was the beat of his heart.

It felt oddly reassuring…*comforting*… Dizzily she started to frown as her alcohol-confused brain tried to assimilate this unacceptable information. She had the most peculiar desire to put her head against his chest, just where her hand was resting, and close her eyes, to let herself be comforted by that steady, sure heart-beat, like a child being soothed by the comfort of its parent.

Experimentally her fingers flexed and relaxed. She could feel the springiness of his body hair beneath the fabric of his shirt. Her eyes widened as she took in this additional information. Louise instinctively let her body start to relax against the warmth of his.

The arm he had raised to steady her when she had first fallen against him was still there, holding her, supporting her. She wriggled closer to his body and closed her eyes. She could smell the man-scent of him—so much stronger than the elusive, hard-to-reach scent that clung to Saul's shirt. This was the real thing, a *real* man. Louise breathed in deeply and ap-preciatively. His hand had moved to her hip, hard and warm through her clothes. She *liked* the feel of it there.

'Louise.'

The sharp warning note in his voice made her open her eyes and focus dizzily on him.

'No, don't go,' she whispered drunkenly. 'Don't go… I want you to stay with me… I want…'

He started to withdraw from her, and she read the stern message in his eyes. She quickly closed her own eyes and reached up with one hand to cup his face. She lifted her head and opened her mouth against his, using her other hand to take his hand from her hip to her breast.

As she felt the hard male warmth of his palm against her breast her body stiffened, quivering in excited expectation. The deep, tremulous breath she took lifted her breast against his hand. She felt his fingers curve into the shape of her body and his touch become a caress. The pad of his thumb stroked her nipple gently, and a quiver of sensual delight ran through her. This was what she had ached for, *yearned* for. Her tongue-tip stroked his lips, urgently demanding entrance, her breathing quickening in passionate arousal.

She had waited so long to be with him like this. Her teeth tugged pleadingly at his bottom lip as desire flooded through her. She could feel his lips starting to part as he gave in to her feminine aggression.

She had been *so* hungry for him to kiss her like this, she acknowledged dizzily as his mouth started to move over hers. She adjusted her body to get closer to him, and felt him shift his weight to accommodate her. A jolt of sensations rocketed through her, her inhibitions obliterated by the powerful force of the rich wine she had consumed. She felt as though she was floating on a high tide of incredible sensation. Her tongue darted wantonly into his mouth. She *wanted* him to touch her without her clothes, to feel his hands on her bare body. She *wanted* to touch him the same way—to absorb every last essence of him.

This was what she had been crying out for, starving for. *Dying for!* This, and *him*.

Against his mouth she cried his name…

'Saul. Saul… Saul…'

Abruptly Louise found herself being set free, *pushed* away from the intimacy of the male body her own craved so badly. Only his hands still held her, manacling her wrists as he shook her.

'Saul,' she protested.

'Open your eyes, Louise,' she heard a harsh and shockingly familiar male voice demanding bitingly. 'I am *not* your precious Saul, whoever he might be…'

Her tutor! She wasn't… This wasn't Saul at all. It was…

Abruptly she opened her eyes, gagging nauseously on the combination of too much wine, too little food and too much man—much too much man, her body told her as she reeled with shock. It was a lethal combination of strong wine mixed with strong emotion.

'I feel sick,' she wailed piteously.

'Oh, God,' she heard Gareth breathe irately, and then the next thing she knew was that he had picked her up and was half carrying her, half dragging her into her small bathroom, where he pushed her down in front of the lavatory—*and* only just in time, Louise realised as her stomach heaved and she started to retch.

It seemed like a lifetime before her stomach had disgorged its unwanted contents, but logically she knew it could only have been minutes.

Cold and shaking, she stood up, clinging onto the edge of the basin, running the tap and reaching automatically for some mouthwash.

She still felt dizzy, confused, not really sure just

what was happening. Clumsily she headed for the bathroom door, only to find herself being taken hold of very firmly and marched into the living room.

'Sit down and eat this,' she heard herself being told, and she was pushed unceremoniously into a chair and handed a plate of hot toast.

'I'm not hungry…' Apathetically she started to turn her head away.

'Eat it,' he ordered. 'My God, what's the *matter* with you? What the hell are you trying to do to yourself…?'

Louise felt her head starting to ache.

'Why don't you go away?' she demanded shakily.

'Not until you've eaten this,' she was told implacably.

Louise looked at the toast. Her stomach started to heave again.

'I don't want it,' she told him stubbornly. 'I just want—'

'Saul…' he interrupted her savagely. 'Yes. I *know*. You've already told me that…remember…?'

Louise blanched as she realised just what he meant. The alcoholic fog clouding her brain was beginning to clear with unwelcome speed. She looked at his mouth. Had she actually…? She could see a small swollen bruise marking his bottom lip, where she had… Quickly she looked away.

'I don't feel well. I…I want to go to bed…'

'Why? So that you can fantasise over your precious Saul?' he derided unkindly.

Louise closed her eyes. She could feel another wave of dizziness surging over her. She tried to stand up and the dizziness increased. She could feel herself starting to black out. She tried to fight it, and then stopped. What was the point? What was the point in *anything* in a life that didn't have Saul in it.

Defeatedly she let herself slide down into the darkness.

When she woke up she was lying, still dressed, in bed, and Katie was sitting on a chair next to it, watching her. Her room had been tidied up and the air smelled fresh with polish and coffee. It was light outside, she recognised.

'What are *you* doing here?' she asked her sister groggily. Her throat felt sore and her head ached dreadfully.

'Professor Simmonds came looking for me. He said you weren't very well,' Katie told her carefully, avoiding looking directly at her.

Professor Simmonds. Louise closed her eyes, her body starting to shake as she remembered what she had done. With appalling clarity and total recall, behind her closed eyelids she could not only *see* the expression on Gareth Simmonds' face, she could even more demeaningly actually *feel* every sensation she had felt when she had…when *she* had…

Groaning, she rolled over, burying her face in her pillow.

'What is it? Aren't you feeling well? Do you want to be sick?' Katie asked anxiously.

'I… I… What did Professor Simmonds say to you about…about me?' she demanded frantically.

'Er…nothing… Well…he just said that you weren't well,' Katie told her, adding hurriedly, 'There's some kind of bug going round. Loads of people have gone down with it. He *did* say that if you wanted to go home immediately, without spending

CHAPTER THREE

ABRUPTLY shaking her head to dispel her thoughts, Louise came back to the present. Her coffee had grown cold while she had been lost in her painful thoughts of the past and she would have to make a fresh cup. As she refilled the kettle and waited for it to boil she picked up one of the collection of smooth polished stones which decorated the open shelves, holding it cupped in her palm and smoothing her fingertips over its cool surface.

It had been a gift to her from her brother Joss. It was one of his most special stones, he had told her solemnly when he had given it to her, and holding it and stroking it would make her feel calm.

He had found it on one of his regular walks with Great-Aunt Ruth, with whom he shared an affinity for the countryside.

Louise smiled ruefully now as she closed her fingers around its comforting strength. It had galled her a little at the time, even though she had refused to acknowledge it, that someone as young as Joss had been so easily able to identify that part of her personality which she herself least liked.

The turbulence of her own nature offended her pride. She liked to think of herself as someone who was totally in control of herself, *and* her reactions. Perhaps because she needed to feel that they *were* under her control, because that was the only way she could reassure herself that the way she had behaved under the influence of her intense adolescent crush on Saul and the things she had done would never, ever happen again.

Joss. Her smile deepened as she thought affectionately of her brother. He had all the virtues that Max, the eldest of them, lacked. She had never met anyone as well rounded, as complete within themselves, as her younger brother. Even as a young child he had exhibited an extraordinary degree not just of sensitivity and awareness of the emotions of those around him, but also a compassion and a wisdom which Louise had always secretly rather envied.

As she replaced the stone her eye was caught by the small print that hung on the wall close to the shelves. It was a sketch of the Tuscany countryside which she had drawn herself while on holiday there with her family. That had been the summer— Biting her lip, she turned away abruptly.

After she and Katie had made up their quarrel over what she, Louise, had seen as Katie's betrayal of her in telling Gareth Simmonds about her crush on Saul, that should have been the end of the matter—and of Gareth Simmonds' involvement in her personal life. But it hadn't been.

Briefly Louise closed her eyes. She had never been back to Tuscany since that summer, although she had spent time in other parts of Italy. Her parents thought it was because she had outgrown the simple pleasures of the family holidays they had spent there, in the large rambling villa which they rented every summer just outside the small, unpretentious little village where they, as regular summer visitors, were on first-name terms with all the inhabitants. But her refusal to return had nothing to do with thinking herself too sophisticated and grown-up for the company of her family.

Tuscany... Even now she could smell the warm, rich scent of the earth, feel the warmth of the sun.

By the time they had arrived at the villa that summer she and Katie had been talking again—*just*—and by a common but unspoken agreement nothing had been said or shown by either of them to their parents, nor the other members of the family holidaying together, to reveal that they had ever fallen out.

If, for the first time since their birth, apart from their choice of university courses, they were opting to do things separately, spend more time apart, then it had been put down to the fact that they were growing up and wanting to become individuals.

While Katie had stayed close to the villa, spending hours in the kitchen with Maria—the second cousin of the family who owned the villa, and who spent her widowhood looking after the villa's visitors—going with her to shop at the local markets and indulging her passion for cooking, Louise had set off in an ancient borrowed Fiat with her sketchpad to explore the neighbourhood.

It had perhaps been inevitable that the Fiat, unloved by the family who owned it and, perhaps more importantly, also unserviced by them, should have decided to stage a protest in the form of refusing to start one hot dusty afternoon, when Louise had returned to it having spent the morning sketching a small shrine she had seen at the roadside.

Recognising defeat when the Fiat had stubbornly refused to start after several attempts, Louise had looked up and down the empty road along which only one single, solitary car had passed that morning.

There was nothing else for it. She would have to walk to the red-roofed villa she could see set in the midst of an ancient grove of poplars lower down the hill.

The walk had taken her longer than she had anticipated, the road winding its way steadily downwards. The villa's wrought-iron gates had been closed, but she'd been able to see a car parked in the driveway. As she'd opened the gates she'd realised that the car had British plates which was a relief, although the thought of appealing to an Italian family for help hadn't particularly worried her. She was fluent in the language after so many holidays spent there.

She'd been perspiring stickily from her walk, and ruefully conscious of her dusty bare legs and sunburned nose as she'd approached the villa.

When no one had answered her knock on the villa's front door she'd walked a little warily round the side of the house, and then stopped.

In front of her had been a sparkling, simple-shaped swimming pool, surrounded by an elegant paved area set out with sun loungers and decorated with huge tubs of cascading flowers.

Someone was using the pool, cutting through the water with an impressively fast crawl, brown arms neatly cleaving the water.

As she'd studied the seal-dark male head turned away from her an odd sensation had gathered in the pit of Louise's stomach, tiny quivers of unmistakable female appreciation running like quicksilver along her veins.

Irritated with herself, she'd turned away, her face suddenly warm with a heat that had *nothing* to do with the sun. The swimmer had obviously seen her, she'd recognised, because she could hear him heaving himself out of the water.

Warily she'd turned to face him, hoping her expression wouldn't betray what she had just been feeling.

'Louise! What…?'

Through the shock of recognising Gareth Simmonds' voice, two startling but totally unrelated facts hit Louise. The first was that he had instantly and immediately recognised who *she* was, even though he could quite easily have been confused as to which twin she might actually be. The second was that now, confronted with him, advancing towards her and sending droplets of pool water showering to the floor, and wearing a pair of black swimming shorts which she was breath-gulpingly sure ought only to have ever been on sale with a stern warning of the effect they might have on a vulnerable female, she knew that odd earlier frisson of awareness had *not* been a mere trick of her imagination. Dizzily she discovered that she was focusing on the exact point where the dark wet arrowing of body hair disappeared beneath the waistband of his shorts.

'My car's broken down. It won't start,' she told him breathlessly. 'I didn't…'

Quickly she fought to get control of herself, demanding aggressively, 'What are *you* doing *here*…?'

The look he gave her made her glower even more ferociously at him.

'What's wrong?' he asked her dryly. 'There isn't, so far as I know, any law that says holidaying professors aren't allowed to inhabit the same turf as their students. And I could, of course, ask you the same question. As it happens, my family own this villa.

They bought it about ten years ago, when they were holidaying here and fell in love with the area. Normally the whole family would be here, but unfortunately this year...'

'The *whole* family?' Louise questioned him, unable to stop herself.

'Mmm... I *do* have one, you know.'

'But they aren't here now...?'

'No,' he agreed.

'Have you got a large family?' Louise asked him, without knowing why she had done so. After all, why should she care?

'Mmm...sort of... I've got three sisters, all older than me and all married with children; they, along with my parents, normally descend on the villa for at least a month during the school holidays, but this year my eldest sister and her husband have taken their three children to New Zealand to see her husband's family.

My second sister and *her* husband and two boys are sailing with friends off the Greek Islands and my youngest sister and *her* husband, who, like my father, is a surgeon—there's a tradition of going into medicine in the family, and in fact I've rather broken with that tradition in electing to go into teaching rather than following my father and sisters into medicine—have gone with my parents to India. My mother is involved with UNICEF in a fund-raising capacity, and they've gone to see some of the work that's being done with the money they've raised.'

He spread out his hands in a dismissive gesture and told her dryly, 'So there you have it, a short, potted history of the Simmonds family. Oh, and I forgot, there's also my grandmother, who is very much in the

tradition of a grand matriarch—though not exactly in
the Italian style. My grandmother's forte lay in bringing up her three sons single-handedly after she was
widowed, and in feeding their appetite for education
rather than pasta—she's a Scot, so that's perhaps
where *that* comes from.'

As he spoke he was reaching for a towel from one
of the sun loungers, and briskly began to rub himself
dry.

He had a surprisingly muscular-looking body for a
university professor. Louise could have sworn that beneath his tutorial 'uniform' of soft Tattersall check
shirt and well-worn cord trousers lay a body as mis-
shapen as the old-fashioned knitted cardigans favoured by many of his older colleagues, but quite obviously she had been wrong.

He had stopped speaking briefly, and as she turned
her head towards him she drew in a small, surprised
gulp of air. He was rubbing his wet hair dry with the
towel, his stance revealing the hard firmness of his
belly and the strength of his upper arms.

Louise had no idea how long he'd been in Tuscany,
but it had certainly been long enough to give his skin
an undeniably warm golden tan.

'You're not feeling faint or anything, are you?'

His sharp frowning question made Louise's face
burn, and she hurriedly averted her gaze from his
body. What was the *matter* with her? She had grown
up in the middle of a large, closely knit extended family unit, where the sight of the male body at every
stage of its development, from babyhood right
through adolescence, young manhood to middle age
and beyond, had been so commonplace that until she
had formed her crush on Saul she had been openly

derisive of other girls' embarrassed and curious interest in the unclothed male form.

And yet here she was, breathing too shallowly and too fast, with a face that felt too hot and a potently explosive sensation low down in her body threatening her composure to the extent that she was having difficulty forming even the most basic coherent thought—and just because she had seen Gareth Simmonds wearing a pair of swimming shorts!

'Look, let's go inside, where it's cooler, and you can tell me exactly where your car is and I—'

'No. No, I'm all right,' Louise started to protest, but it was too late. He was already walking purposefully towards the open doorway to the house, leaving her with no alternative but to follow him inside.

If she had doubted that he might be telling the truth about his family, the number of photographs that crowded the flat surfaces of the heavy solid wooden furniture in the comfortably sized sitting room would soon have put her right. Even without studying them too closely Louise could immediately see the resemblance to him in the happy, affectionately close groups of people featured in the photographs. Her mother's small sitting room and her aunt Ruth's elegant small drawing room were similarly adorned with photographs of her own family, but that knowledge did nothing to alleviate the sense of anxious wariness that had gripped her ever since she had realised just whose territory she had unwittingly strayed into.

'The kitchen's this way,' Louise heard Gareth informing her as he led the way to the rear of the villa and the large, traditional farmhouse-style Tuscan kitchen.

'Sit down,' he instructed her firmly, pulling a chair

out from the table and then beginning to frown as she hesitated. To get to the chair she would have to move closer to him—*too* close to him, Louise recognised. He really had the most sexy and masculine-looking arms. The kind of arms you could just imagine locking tightly around you and holding you…the kind of arms…

'Louise.'

The sharp way he said her name penetrated the totally alien fog of shockingly unexpected feminine arousal that had momentarily swamped her.

What on *earth* was happening to her? It must be the heat or something, Louise decided hastily, still refusing to sit down as she repeated huskily that she was perfectly all right.

'If I could ring my father and explain to him about the car…' she told him.

'It might be easier if I took a look at the car first,' Gareth Simmonds argued, and Louise's face flamed, not with embarrassed confusion at her own inexplicable awareness of him this time, but with quick anger that he should dare to imply that she had not properly diagnosed the problem with the car herself.

'*You* won't be able to start it,' she warned him immediately, but she could see that he didn't intend to let her put him off.

'It's halfway up the hill,' she informed him. 'I'd stopped to sketch the shrine there…'

'Oh, yes, the Madonna. I know where you mean. Look, why don't you wait here, out of the heat, while I go and take a look?'

Dearly as she wanted to go with him, and see his expression when he discovered that she was right and the Fiat wasn't going to start, a small, inner, unexpectedly cautious voice warned Louise that she might be better advised to stay where she was. Even more unexpectedly, she actually found herself not just listening to it but actually agreeing with it as well.

She wasn't sure what malign fate had brought her here to be confronted by the person who, after Saul, she absolutely least wanted to see, but she *did* know that, given her extraordinary reaction to him just now, it would be extremely unwise of her to insist on doing *anything* that kept her in his company.

In fact, she knew that if she could just have summoned the strength to argue with him she would far rather have insisted on ringing her father and begging him to come over to fetch her just as soon as he possibly could.

Once Gareth had gone, having assured her that she was free to make herself as at home as she wished in his absence, she acknowledged that it was a good deal more comfortable inside the pleasant shade of the villa than outside in the full heat of the hot summer's day.

There was a bottle of Chianti on the table, and she was tempted to pour herself a glass, but, remembering what had happened the last time she and Gareth Simmonds and a bottle of wine had come together, she opted instead to pour herself a glass of water.

Taking it with her, she wandered back through the house, pausing to study the photographs in the sitting room. There was one there of Gareth Simmonds as a young boy, flanked by his parents, his grandmother and his older sisters. Hastily Louise looked away from it.

Outside, the water in the swimming pool glittered temptingly in the sunlight. If their own villa had one drawback, it was that it didn't possess its own pool;

they had to share one with two other villas situated close by.

Louise licked her suddenly dry lips. With any luck Gareth Simmonds would be gone for quite some time. He hadn't struck her as a man who could ever give in easily to anything, and she judged that he would be determined not to come back until he could prove her wrong in asserting that the car wouldn't start.

Beneath the cotton fabric of her chino shorts and her top, her skin itched with heat and dust. The swimming pool looked so very, very tempting.

Narrowing her eyes, she looked longingly at it and then, recklessly dismissing the cautious voice that warned her that what she was doing was dangerous—when had that ever put her off anything?—she walked very deliberately towards the pool and quickly stripped off her shorts and top.

The weight she had lost in the months she had ached for Saul had left her looking fragilely fine-boned. Too thin, according to her mother, who had been shocked when she had first seen Louise out of her baggy shirts and in her more revealing shorts and T-shirts. She was certainly too thin for Tuscan male tastes, although she had noticed that that had not stopped Giovanni, Maria's nephew, from making an increasing number of excuses to come up to the villa and flirt heavily with both herself and Katie.

Her skin, nowhere near as tanned or healthy-looking as Gareth Simmonds', was just beginning to lose its British pallor, but was more pale honey than rich gold. Beneath her shorts she was wearing a pair of plain white briefs, and under her top—nothing. Her breasts, firm though they were, were still femininely full, their shape disguised by the looseness of the top she had been wearing. A quick glance around the pool assured her that she had the place to herself. Gracefully Louise dropped into the water, deliciously cool against her hot skin.

Blissfully she floated lazily for a few seconds, and then started to swim. One length and then another, checking at each turn that she still had the place to herself. She was bound to hear Gareth Simmonds returning. The sound of a car engine would carry perfectly on the clear hot summer air.

She did another length, and then another, and then floated again for several seconds before some sixth sense abruptly made her roll over and flounder for a few seconds in the water as she opened her eyes.

Gareth was standing at the end of the pool, watching her. Cautiously she swam to the far side, where she had left her clothes and the towel which *he* had discarded earlier. How long had he been standing there? Not long—he *couldn't* have been.

As she pulled herself out of the water she could see him starting to walk towards her. Quickly she enveloped herself in the wet towel, shivering as it touched her damp skin.

'Take this one. It's dry.'

He was standing far too close to her, Louise acknowledged as she fumbled with the damp folds of the towel wrapped around her.

As she reached reluctantly to take the dry towel from him she could feel the one wrapped around her body starting to slide away. Quickly she made a grab for it, but it was too late. She could feel the heat flushing her face as Gareth's sharp eyed navy blue gaze thoughtfully studied her nearly naked body, but it wasn't her breasts his glance lingered the longest on, Louise noticed; it was her ribs and the narrow over-slenderness of her waist.

'You're still too thin,' he told her curtly, and before she could stop him, much to her chagrin, she felt him swiftly and practically envelop her in the dry, sun-warmed towel which he briskly fastened round her.

'I am *not* thin. I'm *slim*,' Louise retaliated through gritted teeth.

'You're *thin*,' Gareth countered grimly. '*And* you know it, otherwise you wouldn't be so defensive. I take it that your…that Saul isn't here on holiday with your family.'

Louise stared at him, her embarrassment over the fact that he had seen her virtually naked body forgotten as she marvelled not just at his memory but also his tutorial ability to make her remember that she was still his erring student.

'No, he isn't. *Not* that it's *any* business of yours,' she reminded him sharply.

'No? In so much as you are still one of my students—a student whose standard of work has dropped lamentably—it is *very* much my business. You were right about the Fiat. It won't start,' he added, before she could catch her breath to argue with him. 'I'll give you a lift home.'

'There's no need for that,' Louise protested. 'I can ring my father…and…'

'I'll give you a lift home,' Gareth reinforced as though she hadn't spoken. 'Give me five minutes to shower and get changed.'

'You might *think* you're a woman, Louise,' he told her astoundingly as he turned to go. 'But in fact, in many ways you're still very much a child—as you've just proved,' he told her as he glanced from the pool to her towel-wrapped body.

To Louise's chagrin, when Gareth drove up to the villa with her, her parents were standing outside, quite plainly having just returned home themselves. It naturally followed that she had to introduce Gareth to them, and explain not only what had happened to the Fiat but who he was.

'You're Louise's professor!' her mother exclaimed with a smile. 'Oh, poor you, coming all this way and then having your privacy invaded by one of your students.'

'I rather think that Louise believes if anyone is deserving of commiseration for the coincidence, then it's her,' Gareth advised her mother dryly.

Hospitably her mother offered Gareth a drink—but he hadn't had to accept, Louise fumed an hour later, as Gareth was still chatting, apparently quite happily, to her parents while *she* sat in silent resentment beside her mother. That was bad enough. But when her mother invited him to join them for dinner, and Gareth accepted, Louise wasn't sure which of them she disliked the most. However, a welcome diversion was fortuitously provided when Giovanni slouched round the corner of the villa, his face lighting up when he caught sight of Louise.

'Here comes your admirer,' she heard her father warning her. Louise tossed her head, suspecting that Giovanni was even more astonished than her father when, instead of irritably rejecting his unwanted and quite obviously sexually intentioned advances as she normally did, she not only responded to his soft-eyed looks and flowery compliments, but actively encouraged them.

'Oh, dear, Louise, was that wise?' her mother sighed once he had gone. 'Maria was telling us only this morning that his family are trying to encourage a match between Giovanni and his third cousin.'

'I wasn't actually thinking of *marrying* him, Mum,' Louise told her mother meaningfully, adding pointedly, just in case anyone listening—including her wretched and far too watchful tutor—had missed the point, 'He's got the most terrifically sexy body, though, don't you think?'

'Oh, Louise…' Jenny protested, but over her daughter's downbent head she gave her husband a rueful, slightly relieved look, which Louise caught out of the corner of her eye. She knew very well how concerned her family, especially her parents, had been about her crush on Saul, and they weren't to know that her pretence of being physically attracted to Giovanni had nothing to do with Saul but *everything* to do with the impassive and unwanted presence of the man seated next to her mother, silently watching the small piece of theatre being played out in front of him.

'I think I'll just go and see what Maria's planning for supper,' she told her mother airily, standing up to follow Giovanni who had disappeared in the direction of the kitchen and his aunt. 'Suddenly I'm rather… I'm…hungry…'

Tossing her head, she left her startled parents to exchange surprised looks as she stalked ferociously after her prey.

Once inside the kitchen, though, it was a different matter. Under Maria's stern eye, Giovanni's earlier swaggeringly macho display of flirtation quickly turned into bashful silence, and while Louise herself had been happy enough to encourage him while Gareth was looking on—how dared he imply that she was little more than a child?—now she lost no time in making it plain to the young Italian that she simply wasn't interested.

In the days that followed Louise very quickly came to regret not just encouraging Giovanni, who had now taken to following her around at every opportunity, but even more importantly running into Gareth.

An easy, relaxed friendship had very quickly developed between her parents and her tutor—even Joss and Jack seemed to enjoy his company, going off on long walks with him to explore the Italian countryside—and, whereas normally Louise would have been able to give vent to the pent-up irritation his almost constant presence in their family circle was causing her to Katie, there was a certain amount of distance between her and her twin still, a small and as yet not totally healed sore place from the quarrel they had had at Oxford—the quarrel of which Gareth himself had initially been the cause.

When her cousin Olivia, her husband and their little girl came to join her own family the situation, at least in Louise's eyes, became even worse.

Like Gareth, Olivia's husband Caspar was a university lecturer, and the two men very quickly hit it off, so that while technically Gareth was the one who was the outsider in their family group it was Louise who often felt on the outside of the comfortable closeness that everyone else was enjoying sharing.

Part of the reason for this was that she couldn't

quite bring herself to forget that Olivia was a close friend of Tullah's. Tullah, who had taken the place in Saul's heart and Saul's life that she, Louise, had so desperately wanted for herself. And, worse, Olivia had been there on that ill-fated evening when she, Louise, had behaved so stupidly and so…so dangerously, tricking Tullah into following her into the maze and leaving her there so that she could spend the evening with Saul. Only it hadn't worked out like that, and instead…

Watching Olivia and Caspar sitting with her father and Gareth in the sun one afternoon, Louise couldn't help wondering if Olivia had told *Gareth* about what she had done.

'Lou, why don't you come and join us?' Olivia called out cheerfully. 'I could do with some female support among all these men.'

For a moment Louise was tempted. She had always liked Olivia and, yes, even admired her—and, oddly, perhaps, for someone with her relatively competitive and ambitious nature, Louise had a very definite soft spot for small children, especially Olivia's little girl, Amelia. Louise had often gladly given up her own free time to occupy Amelia so that Olivia and Caspar could have some time alone. But today, seeing the way that Gareth broke off his conversation with Caspar to look at her, she fibbed quickly, 'I can't…I…I'm seeing Giovanni. He's taking me out for a drive…'

'Giovanni?' Olivia gave her an old-fashioned look, and Louise could see that she was surprised.

'Careful, Lou,' Caspar teased her. 'These young Italians can be hot stuff, and they aren't—'

'Will you all please stop telling me what to do and

trying to run my life for me?' Louise interrupted him
angrily, her anger caused in reality far more by the
fact that Gareth was an unwanted witness to Caspar's
teasing than what Caspar had actually said.

'First you tell me to keep away from Saul, and now
you're telling me to keep away from Giovanni. I *am*
over eighteen, and who I choose to…to be with is *my*
affair and no one else's,' she finished in a fierce voice,
before turning on her heel and starting to walk away.

She was almost out of earshot when she heard
Caspar saying, 'Phew…what did I do?'

'She still must be feeling very…sensitive about
Saul,' she heard Olivia telling him. Bunching her
hands into angry fists, Louise almost ran the rest of
the distance to her bedroom.

No doubt by now Olivia and Caspar would be re-
galing Gareth with the full details of her wretched
stupidity. Her cheeks burned, and to her chagrin she
discovered that hot angry tears were splashing down
her face.

Why, oh, why had she had to bump into Gareth
like that? And why did he have to keep on coming
round here? The rest of her family might have made
him welcome, but surely he could see that she…

Since she didn't, in reality, have a date with
Giovanni and since in reality dating him was the last
thing she wanted, she was forced to spend the afternoon sulking in her room hoping that no one would
realise that she was there.

CHAPTER FOUR

IT WAS during the last week of their stay in the villa that things finally came to a head.

Caspar and Olivia had already returned home. Katie, with whom Louise had still not totally made her peace, had gone out for the afternoon with the rest of the family, who had wanted to visit the local monastery, so that Louise was on her own. Even Maria was having a day off, which was no doubt why, she realised later, that Giovanni had decided to pay her an unexpected and unwanted visit.

She was lying on the sun-baked patio when he arrived, her bikini top untied and her eyes closed as she soaked up the hot sun and the even more welcome peaceful solitude.

The first intimation she had that Giovanni was there was when she heard his liquid voice asking if she would like him to put some suntan oil on her bare back.

Startled by his presence, she immediately turned over, and realised her mistake when she saw the way he was staring appreciatively at her naked breasts.

Immediately she reached for her bikini top, telling him at the same time that his aunt was not there and that he had better leave.

'I know she is not here, *cara*,' he told her crooningly. 'But that is why I am here. So that we can have some time together alone. I have wanted to be alone with you for a very long time, and I know that it is the same for you. Your eyes have told me so,' he teased her.

His own eyes were liquid with something that Louise judged had been ignited more by physical lust than tender emotion, but either way she was simply not interested.

'Giovanni…' she began warningly as she scrambled to stand up, but either he had misread the tone of her voice or he had decided to ignore it, because instead of giving her some distance he made a grab for her.

Thoroughly outraged, Louise tried to break free of his hold, but he was a strongly built young man, much taller than her and much, much heavier, and it suddenly struck her with a sharp thrill of fear that if he should choose to do so he could quite easily physically overpower her.

'Giovanni,' she began again, but this time, as she was all too uncomfortably aware, her voice sounded rather more hesitantly pleading than firmly assertive.

'Louise…what's going on?'

Never had she thought she would be so grateful to see Gareth Simmonds, Louise admitted as Giovanni immediately released her and started to say something to Gareth that she felt too shaky to catch.

Her hands, as she reached down for the skimpy top of her bikini, were trembling so much that it was impossible for her to fasten it, and instead she could only hold tight to it while wrapping her arms protectively across her naked breasts as Gareth told Giovanni curtly that he wanted him to leave.

'You *do* realise what could have happened, don't you?' he asked Louise sharply, once the noise of Giovanni's battered Vespa had died away.

Both his expression and his tone of voice immediately set Louise's back up. He was behaving as though he were her father, or her brother, as though he had a *right* to tell her what to do, to bully and correct her.

'Yes, I do,' she answered, her voice shaking as she added, completely untruthfully, 'And, for your information, I *wanted* Giovanni to make love to me...'

'To do what?' Gareth's voice dripped with cynical contempt. 'I doubt that *love* had very much to do with what he'd got in mind...' he told her derisively.

Louise's chin tilted dangerously.

'So he wanted to have sex with me. Is that so wrong?' she challenged him, tossing her head. 'After all, I've got to lose my virginity somehow, become the woman you're so keen to tell me I'm not. And since, as I'm sure you're now very well aware, thanks to my cousin and my loving, loyal sister, I can never share that experience with the one man...the *only* man I...'

Pausing, Louise bit down hard on her bottom lip. Why on earth had she got involved in this conversation, embroiled in this situation? Just thinking about Saul had made her heart ache, and filled her eyes with treacherous tears. Fiercely she fought to suppress them.

'It doesn't matter to me who the *hell* it is—who *he* is any longer.' Louise virtually spat at him. 'I just don't care...'

She had said more, far more than she had ever intended to say. Much more...too much, she acknowledged shakily. But instead of taunting her for her immaturity, instead of talking down to her as he had been doing all these last unbearably long weeks, she heard him saying in a voice that shook almost as much with anger as her own had done, 'Are you *crazy*? Have you *any* idea just what you're saying? Of course it damn well matters.'

'Not to me it doesn't,' Louise told him savagely. 'Why should it?'

Before he could stop her she turned on her heel and ran through the villa, up to the bedroom she shared with her twin.

From its windows it was possible to see the village, with its red-tiled roofs and the hillside beyond, but it wasn't the view that held Louise's attention, her eyes widening as she realised that Gareth had followed her upstairs and was now standing just inside her room.

'You dropped this,' he told her gruffly, handing her her discarded bikini top.

Automatically she reached out to take it from him, and then stopped as she saw the way he was looking at her.

'Keep away from Giovanni, Louise,' she heard him advising her grimly. 'He isn't…'

'He isn't what?' she demanded, anger flaring again. 'I don't *care* about what he isn't. I only care about what he *is*… He's a man, isn't he…a male? And he can… I'm tired of being told I'm still a child…not a woman. What does it take to make me a woman? As if I didn't know.

'I just want to have sex,' she told him defiantly, 'and I don't care who it's with…not if I can't have Saul…If I can't have Saul then it might as well be anybody…'

'You don't mean that,' she heard him contradicting her flatly. 'You don't know what you're saying…'

'Stop patronising me…' Louise was practically

howling at him now, so driven by the combination of her own feelings and his resented, unwanted presence that her reactions were no longer fully under her own control. 'I do mean it…'

'Oh, no, you don't,' Gareth was telling her sharply. 'And I'll prove it to you.'

Before she could even guess what he had in mind he had slammed her bedroom door closed and was standing between her and it—her and freedom. An ominous sense of things having gone too far began to trickle like icy water into her veins, but Louise wasn't going to give in to it and risk losing face in front of him.

'*I* lost *my* virginity to a friend of my youngest sister,' she heard him telling her coolly as he started to unfasten his shirt. 'She was twenty; I was just seventeen.'

Louise couldn't take her eyes off his body, his shirt…his hands… In appalled, paralysed fascination she watched as he finished unfastening it and shrugged it off. Calmly he started to reach for his belt.

Nervously Louise moistened her suddenly dry lips.

'What's wrong?' she heard Gareth taunting her. 'Having second thoughts…?'

'You…you can't mean this. You don't know what you're doing…' she whispered shakily.

'Yes, I can, and yes, I do. You said you wanted to lose your virginity. *You* said you didn't mind *who* you lost it to. I'm here, and I can promise you, Louise, that I'm perfectly willing and able to assist you. After all, it might as well be me as Giovanni, mightn't it…? *You* don't mind which of us it is, after all, do you? And forgive me, but it is quite some time since I've had sex, as the sight of your extremely attractive naked breasts has just rather forcefully reminded me.

'Men are *like* that, you know,' he continued conversationally. 'There's something about the sight of a pair of pretty, pert bare breasts that just naturally turns a man's thoughts to how those same breasts would feel filling his hands, how they might taste when he could get to suckle on them, how the *woman* they're a part of might react if he showed her…'

When he heard Louise's small shocked gasp he asked her quietly, 'What is it? I'm not embarrassing you, am I, Louise? After all, *you* were the one who said that it didn't matter *who* you had sex with, and, like I've just said, I'm more than willing to oblige you… *More* than willing… Here, feel,' he commanded, reaching out for her hand.

Louise stared at him in horrified fascination. What on earth did he think he was *doing…saying…*? He was her *tutor*. He was… She closed her eyes and then flicked them open again as, shockingly, she had a sudden explicitly clear mental image of him the way he had been that first day she had seen him climbing out of the pool at his own villa. Then she had been very much, if unwontedly, aware of the fact that he was not *just* her tutor but also very, very much a man, and now, suddenly and inexplicably, she was aware of it again.

'Did you…did you love her…your sister's friend?' she managed to ask him jerkily as she tried to drag her appalled gaze from his face. She did not *dare* to look at his body now that he had removed his shirt and was, it seemed, in the process of removing the rest of his clothes as well.

'I dare say I *believed* that I did,' he told her coolly.

'But at seventeen…I was *just* seventeen. What's wrong…? Louise, have you changed your mind…?'

Oddly, despite the fact that he had been talking to her for several minutes, he had still not unfastened his belt, and yet it had taken him no time at all to unfasten and remove his shirt.

Just for a second Louise was tempted to give in and admit that, yes, she had most certainly changed her mind, but her pride, always one of her own worst enemies, refused to let her. Give way, give in, and to him…? No… No… Never… And besides—besides, she knew perfectly well that he was only bluffing, and that he would never… Well, *she* could play that game just as well as him, and probably even better.

Her confidence returning, she gave a small toss of her head and told him firmly, 'No. I haven't.'

She pursed her lips and forced herself to make a thorough visual inventory of what she could see of him, determinedly lingering as long as she dared on the bare, bronzed expanse of his torso before quickly skimming over the rest of his, thankfully, still clothed body and returning her gaze to his face, saying, as disparagingly as she dared, 'You aren't as…as macho as Giovanni, but I suppose you'll still do.'

She saw at once that she had touched a raw nerve. A muscle twitched warningly in his jaw, but she willed herself to ignore it.

'By rights I ought to put you over my knee and…'

Widening her eyes, Louise willed herself not to blush as she asked him provocatively, 'Ooh, is that some special kind of position? I don't have your experience, of course, and—'

'You really are asking for it, Louise,' she heard him warning her, but she wasn't going to give in.

Shrugging, she told him tauntingly, 'Well, yes, I suppose I am… You needn't worry about me getting pregnant, by the way—I *am* on the pill…'

Her doctor had prescribed it several months earlier, when her emotional trauma had begun to have a disruptive effect on her normal monthly cycle.

'Very practical of you,' she heard Gareth commending her curtly. 'No doubt that was for Saul's benefit, was it? You do surprise me. I should have thought that deliberately encouraging, if not inciting the kind of ''accident'' that would have forced his hand and made him offer you and his child the protection of his name would have been more in keeping with the high drama of your infatuation with him.'

Louise's face blazed with angry colour.

'How *dare* you?' she breathed taking an impulsive step towards him. 'I would *never* try to trap a man like that,' she told him with fierce pride—and meant it.

'Louise,' she heard him saying almost wearily as he raised his hand and cupped the side of her face. To tell her what? Something she really didn't want to hear, she was pretty sure of that, and so far as she knew there was really only one sure-fire way to stop him.

Without stopping to consider the consequences of her actions, desperate only to silence him and have him stop dragging up the still raw pain of her loss of Saul, she quickly closed the distance between them, placing her mouth against his as she whispered, 'Save the lecture, Professor; *that* isn't what I want. What I want—'

She never got to finish her sentence, because suddenly and totally unexpectedly she heard Gareth groan deep down in his throat, and the next minute she was being dragged tightly against his body by his free hand as his mouth opened over the prim closed shape of hers and he proceeded to kiss her in a way she had previously only experienced at second hand, via the television screen.

She had known, of course, that people did, *must* kiss like this—had even dreamed and fantasised about Saul kissing her with just this kind of intimacy and hard male heat—but the reality of having a man's body pressed up hard against her own, the bare flesh of his torso hard and firm and hot against the nakedness of her breasts while his hand cupped her face and his mouth moved against hers with devastating expertise and determination, was like comparing watching someone else screaming through the air on some wild fun-park ride with being the one sitting there in the seat feeling that experience for oneself.

But no big-dipper ride, however terrifying, appalling and thrilling, could come anywhere near making her feel what she was feeling right now, Louise acknowledged as she felt her whole body submit to an avalanche of feeling—of sensation—of reaction—she had *never*, ever guessed it *could* possibly feel.

She couldn't even control her body's urgent, hungry response to the skilled sensuality of his kiss, never mind do anything about the way her breasts, her nipples were already aching so tormentedly for the kind of caresses and intimacy he had described to her only minutes earlier.

Briefly, bravely, Louise tried to fight what she was feeling, to withstand the dizzying surge of hormone-drenched arousal that swamped her, but it was a lost cause, her brain no match for the clamouring hunger

of her body. Weakly she clung to the only solid thing
she could find to cling to, her nails digging unwittingly into the hard muscles of Gareth's upper arms
as she hung onto him for support.

'Louise.'

She heard Gareth protesting warningly against her
mouth, as though he could feel what was happening
to her and was urging her to resist it, but Louise
couldn't resist it; she didn't *want* to resist it and she
didn't want him to tell her to.

'No. No-o-o…' she moaned, pressing tiny pleading
kisses against his lips, his jaw, his throat.
'No…Gareth… No, don't stop. Don't stop now…'
she begged him, lost to everything. 'No, you can't.
You can't…'

And to prove her point she pushed her body even
closer to his, moving frantically against him, bestow-
ing eager, feverish kisses against whichever bit of him
she could reach.

'Louise. Louise… No. You…' She could hear him
protesting, but at the same time his hand was reaching
out to cup her breast.

Louise shuddered wildly in sensual delight as he
touched her, urging him huskily, 'Do what you said
you would do before… You said you wanted to taste
me…them…' she reminded him, her voice sensually
soft and slurred, her eyes bright with shocked passion,
dilating in betrayal of her need as she focused blindly
on him. And as she saw him hesitating she moved
invitingly against him, arching her body against his,
showing him the need she could feel pulsing so
strongly through her veins and her senses.

The rest of the villa was empty, silent, the air in
her room hot and languid from the afternoon sun.

Louise could see a tiny bead of sweat forming on Gareth's throat. She watched it in fascination as he tensed, his throat muscles rigid. Each second—each breath she took—seemed to stretch out for ever. Time itself felt as though it was standing still. She could see, hear, almost feel Gareth trying to swallow; the small bead of sweat moved. She reached out with her fingertip and caught it, holding his gaze with her own as she very deliberately transferred it to her tongue.

His whole body seemed to be caught up, galvanised by the fierce shudder that racked him. His hands cupped her breasts; his mouth covered hers. Louise shuddered in intense pleasure as wave after wave of sensual response flooded over her.

She could feel Gareth's hands, firm, broad, his fingers long and supple, shaping her as they slid down the silky hot flesh of her back before coming to rest on the rounded curves of her bottom. He bent his head, his hair brushing against her naked skin softly, in the most tenuous and spine-tingling kind of caress. She could feel the heat of his breath against her breast, and the delicate shivers of sensation down her spine became fierce, gut-wrenching, arousal-drenched waves of female need. He was caressing her breast with his mouth, gentle, slow, deliberately explorative kisses that drove her into a fury of impatience and longing.

Overwhelmed by her own need, she moved frantically against him. His mouth brushed her nipple, stiff and aching with the hunger that he himself had conjured up with his shockingly explicit verbal descriptions earlier.

She felt him hesitate, and her frustration boiled up,

bursting past what was left of her self-control and ability to think and reason logically.

Her hands found his shoulders, the flesh hot, and stroked the muscles and bone beneath, and their sensory message of his alienness, his total maleness, made her groan deep down in her throat—the same kind of feral yearning sound a hunting lioness aching for a mate might have made.

Her hands reached his back, strong and sleek, and urged him down towards her body. She felt the heat of his expelled breath against her nipple and shuddered uncontrollably beneath its impact. So might the hot peaks of a desert sand dune feel, when lashed by the scorching burn of the hot sirocco wind, the sensation both at once an unbearable aching pain and the promise of an even more intense and untenable pleasure.

'Do it… Do it…'

Not even hearing herself breathing the thick, urgent, guttural words had the power to shock or silence her, and the sensation that rolled through her as he gave in to her female command was not one of triumph or any kind of cerebral pleasure. Rather it was a form of relief so exquisite that she felt as though her whole body, her whole self was being drenched in a sensation so acutely intense that it was almost beyond her to bear it.

Rhythmically she moved herself against him, her hands going out to hold his hand as he drew her nipple deeper into his mouth, his earlier delicate, tentative suckling giving way to a fierceness, an urgency, that sent her delirious with reciprocal pleasure.

'Yes. Oh, yes… Yes…' she heard herself beginning to chant as her body writhed helplessly, no longer within her own mental control but totally and completely responsive to the male allure of his.

She was the one who reached for the fastening on his belt, and it was *she* too who urged and demanded that he remove the rest of his clothes.

'I want to see you, all of you,' she insisted to him. 'I want…' And then her voice and her body, her hands, grew still when she saw that he had given in to her pleas. Her whole body stiffened, a massive visible shudder running right through it as she gazed wide-eyed at him, slowly absorbing the visual reality of his body.

No need to question whether or not he wanted her; she could see perfectly well that he did. Tentatively she reached out and let her fingers slide down the soft arrowing of hair that neatly bisected his body. When she reached his stomach she could feel his muscles start to clench, but he didn't try to stop her.

The hair around the base of the shaft of his manhood was thick and soft. It clung to her fingers as though wanting to encourage her touch. Gravely Louise allowed herself to linger there a while, exploring the springy strength of the dark curls. Above her downbent head she heard him groan, and her naked breasts, her inner, secret womanhood throbbed urgently in a silent echo of the need he was expressing.

Her hand trembled slightly as she reached out to touch the hard, erect strength of him—her tremor wasn't caused by any feeling of trepidation or apprehension, it was simply her body's warning to her that it was as close to losing control as his low, raw groan told her that his was.

Delicately and slowly she explored the full length

of him, her lips parting on a soft, heavy breath of concentration.

Beneath her fingertips his flesh burned, his body rigid and hard. The sensual scent caused by the heat of their bodies filled the small, hot room, making her feel dizzy with longing.

Drawing back from him, she looked towards the bed and then at him, but before she could say anything he was removing her hand from his body and telling her thickly, 'You *know* me now, Louise, and now it's my turn to know you.'

Like someone trapped in a dream, without the power to move her limbs, Louise simply stood there while he removed her bikini bottoms. The sensation of his hands sliding down her thighs to remove them and then moving back up over them far more slowly and exploratively made her feel as though she was melting from the inside out. As she closed her eyes he stood up and picked her up in his arms, carrying her over to her bed. Laying her carefully on it, he started to touch her, caress her, licking her breasts. First one and then the other was given the moist attention of his tongue, and then his lips, suckling gently at first and then far more urgently on her nipples while she writhed and protested incoherently that what he was doing to her was too pleasurable for her to bear.

Slowly he kissed his way down the length of her body, his hands firmly parting her legs so that he could kneel between them, his fingertips stroking gently up the inside of her thighs. A soft, tormented moan escaped from Louise's throat, and her whole body started to tremble eagerly, helplessly snared in the unbreakable grip of her own arousal.

When his hands cupped her sex, and slowly and very deliberately started to explore it, laying it bare, not just to his touch but to his sight as well, Louise closed her eyes. Not because she felt self-conscious or inhibited, but simply because the sexual excitement exploding through her was almost too much for her to bear.

Within its intensity she could sense not just her own desire to push back the boundaries of her sexual knowledge and experience, but also her extraordinarily powerful female anger against herself, against Saul, against nature itself almost. Anger and love, love and anger—which of them was the stronger? Her body quivered feverishly beneath his touch, so delicate and yet at the same time so…compulsively needed, so…so addictive to her senses.

Inside her the desire tensed and coiled. Urgently she opened her eyes. He was bending his head towards her. She could feel herself hovering on the edge of a precipice, carried there, *hurled* there by the ferocity of her own need. Frantically she reached for his shoulders, whispering thickly, the words almost lost against his chest, 'Yes…oh, S… Now…now… I want you now.'

Her body was already quivering in the grip of its first pre-climax spasm of warning, and she whimpered beneath the force of it. He was moving onto her, *into* her, slowly—too slowly, her aroused senses recognised, and her flesh surrounded him with eager complicity, the jerky movement of her hips setting a fast and urgent rhythm that she could feel him trying to resist. Her hands slid down his back, urging him to thrust deeper within her. She felt him pause, resist almost, but her body wouldn't let him. Moist and ur-

gent, more erotic and arousing, more *irresistible* by
far than any practised sensual persuasion, it finally
overcame and overwhelmed his attempt to hold back
from her, and he began to move far more deeply and
strongly within her.

It was like hearing her favourite, most emotion-
arousing piece of music, looking out of her bedroom
window at home on Christmas Day to see the countryside deep in an unexpected blanket of snow; eating
her favourite food; having her emotions and her
senses touched in every single way that aroused them,
and all at the same time. It was all those things and
more. All those things intensified a thousand—no, a
hundred thousand times over, a sensation, a feeling, a
being so, so intense, so perfect, almost beyond her
capacity to bear its delight, that she thought when the
fiercely strong climactic contractions surged through
her body that the relief would cause her to break apart.

Afterwards, lying in Gareth's arms, crying and
clinging to him as she fought for the words to tell him
how magical, how mystifying, how awesomely un-
believably wonderful she had found the experience in
between her emotional tears she could hear him telling
her hoarsely that it was all right, that she was safe,
that he was sorry. Somewhere between registering
what he was saying and trying to respond to it she
fell asleep, and when she woke up it was dark and
Gareth was gone, leaving her tucked up in her bed,
her bikini neatly folded on her chair beside her.

Downstairs in the villa she could hear her parents'
voices, and then Katie came rushing into the room
calling out urgently, 'Lou, wake up. We've got to
pack. There's been some sort of emergency at home

and we've got to go back. Dad's got us an early-morning flight…'

'An emergency… What…?' Louise demanded groggily, her thoughts automatically turning protectively to Saul.

'I don't know. None of us do. All I know is that Mum was on the phone to Maddy for simply ages.'

In the rush to pack up everything and make it to the airport to catch their flight, Louise simply didn't have the time to dwell on what had happened with Gareth, and anyway her lethargic, sensually sated body felt too complete and satisfied at that stage, too well pleasured and indolently disinclined to take issue with her mind about what had happened for her to do anything other than secretly luxuriate in the aura of sensuality that still clung to her senses, anaesthetising her against any need to analyse what had happened or why.

That came later, once they were back at home—hours of endless soul-searching and self-cross-examination while she went over and over what had happened, half inclined to give in to the temptation to comfort herself by believing that she had simply dreamed the whole thing. Dreaming about Gareth Simmonds in that way would have been bad enough, but of course she knew it was no dream.

The crisis which had brought them back to Haslewich, as Louise had guessed, involved her grandfather, who had developed a severe chest infection, and Maddy had rushed up from London to be with him.

'Mum is over with Gramps and Maddy. Maddy doesn't look very well herself, though Gramps is over the worst of it now. Joss was very worried about him.

You know what he's like?' Katie said, a few days after their return.

'Don't I just?' Louise agreed darkly.

Her brother had caught her off guard only the previous day by asking her if she had heard anything from Gareth Simmonds since their return.

'No. Why should I have heard anything?' she had demanded, red-faced. '*I* wasn't the one who kept on encouraging him to come round to the villa… *I* wasn't the one who went on long, boring walks with him.'

'They weren't boring,' Joss had contradicted her affably. 'He knows almost as much about the countryside as Aunt Ruth. He told me that when he was my age he used to spend his holidays in Scotland, with his grandmother. Anyway,' he had added, returning to her earlier question, 'he is *your* tutor.'

Was. Louise had been on the point of correcting him, but she'd stopped herself just in time. She had already made up her mind that she was going to change courses. The thought of going back to Oxford and having to face Gareth Simmonds now after what had happened made her break out in a cold sweat and shudder with self-loathing. How *could* she have behaved like that…?

While she and Katie were still talking the door opened and Joss came in.

'Could either of you drive me over to Gramps,' Joss asked winningly. 'I thought I'd go and see if there was anything I could do.'

'Why do you want to go over there?' Louise asked him curiously.

'I thought I could go and play chess with Gramps and give Maddy a bit of a break, so that she can go out and do some shopping or something to cheer herself up a bit…buy herself a new dress,' he added, with male vagueness.

'But Mum's over there with her,' Katie pointed out.

Joss shook his head. 'No, she isn't,' he told them. 'She had a meeting of the mother and baby home committee at three. She was just going to call and see Maddy on the way.'

'I'll drive you,' Louise told him, springing up and busying herself looking for a jacket, so that neither he nor Katie would see the emotional sheen of tears in her eyes brought there by the sudden awareness of just what kind of man her younger brother was going to turn out to be.

As she had promised herself she would do, Louise transferred to a different course and a new tutor once she was back at Oxford. Ironically her twin attended Gareth Simmonds' lectures herself now, but every time Katie mentioned him Louise very determinedly changed the subject and blanked her off, telling her quite sharply on one occasion, 'Katie, if you *don't* mind, can we *please* talk about something else, or *someone* else?'

'You don't like Professor Simmonds, I know—' Katie began.

Louise interrupted her, laughing harshly as she told her, 'It isn't simply that I don't like him, Katie—I *loathe*, detest and abhor the man, totally, completely and utterly. Do you understand? I loathe him. *Loathe* him…'

But she still dreamt of him at night that first term of the new year, and into the next—bewildering, confusing dreams involving a kaleidoscope of emotions and feelings from which she awoke in the early hours, her body shaking and drenched in perspiration and her eyes wet with tears.

The phone rang sharply, piercing her thoughts and bringing her back abruptly to the present. Quickly Louise went to pick up the receiver.

'Ah, so you are back. Why have you not returned my call?'

As she listened to the plaintive voice of Jean Claude, Louise reminded herself that she was no longer nineteen, and that she had come a long, long way from the girl who had cried out to Gareth Simmonds to make her a woman.

'When will you be free to have dinner with me?' she heard Jean Claude asking her.

'Not this week, I'm afraid,' she told him firmly.

'But *chérie*, I have missed you. It has been so long…'

Louise laughed.

'Stop trying to flatter me, Jean Claude,' she warned him, ignoring his mock-hurt protests. 'Look, I know very well that there are scores of women besides me in your life, so don't try to tell me that you've been spending your evenings alone and lonely at home…'

She could almost feel his ego expanding as she spoke. Despite his intelligence, Jean Claude was a particularly vain man, and Louise had already discovered that it was always easy to appeal to him through his vanity. That vulnerability in him, though, didn't mean that he couldn't be extremely shrewd and perceptive on occasion. He had already challenged her to disprove to him that the reason she had not, so far, gone to bed with him was because emotionally there was another man in her heart, if not in her life. But she wasn't going to resurrect *that* particular argument right now.

'My boss has a big meeting in the morning, which could drag on, and then there's a formal dinner at night...'

'The committee which is to look into the fishing rights of the Arctic seas—yes, I know,' Jean Claude acknowledged. 'Our governments will be on opposite sides on this matter, I suspect.'

Louise laughed.

'Perhaps we shouldn't see one another for a while, then,' she teased him. 'Just in case!'

To her surprise, instead of sharing her laughter, Jean Claude's voice became unusually grave as he told her, 'This is an extremely serious matter for us, *chérie*. Our fishermen need to be able to fish in those waters. Yours...'

Louise could almost see him giving that small Gallic shrug he so frequently made.

'Yours have an area of sea—of seas—to fish which far exceeds the land mass which is your country...'

'A legacy from the days when Britannia ruled the waves,' Louise joked ruefully, but Jean Claude continued to remain serious.

'Such colonialist views are not considered acceptable in these modern times *petite*', he reminded her. 'And if you would accept a word of warning from me I would suggest that you do not voice them too publicly. There are many nations based here in Brussels who consider that they have good reason to resent what they view as British tyranny and oppression...'

It was on the tip of Louise's tongue to point out mildly that the French, along with the Dutch, and the Portuguese, come to that, had all been equally vigorous at some stage of their history in pursuing the acquisition of new colonies, lands and seas over which they staked ownership, but Jean Claude's serious tone prevented her, and besides, as she had often noticed, sensationally handsome and attentive though he was, for her tastes the Frenchman lacked one vitally important virtue: he had virtually no sense of humour.

'It's going to be next week before I can see you, Jean Claude,' she told him instead.

'Very well…then I shall ring you next week. Although we could always be together later…after your dinner is over…' He started to purr meaningfully.

Louise laughed.

'Spend the night with you, you mean… *Non. Non, non…*'

'Now you say *non*, but one day soon you will say *oui*, and not just to spend the night with me,' he warned her, and she could hear the smile of satisfaction in his voice as she laughed and said her good-byes.

'You're wrong, Jean Claude,' she murmured to herself as she replaced the receiver. Attractive though he was, she was in no danger of being tempted to join his long list of lovers.

'Oh, but you are so cold,' he had complained the last time she had refused him. 'Cold outside, but I think *very*, very hot inside. Very, very hot…' he had whispered as he had attempted to deepen the passion of the kiss they were sharing.

'Why so bashful?' he had added when she had gently, but firmly, disengaged herself from him. 'You are a woman of very great attractiveness, Louise, and

I cannot be the first to tell you so—nor the first man to take you to bed…'

'*You* haven't taken me to bed,' Louise had felt bound to remind him.

'Not yet,' he had agreed, adding wickedly, 'But I shall…and very soon.' His voice had deepened as his hand reached out to stroke her breast.

Deftly Louise had manoeuvred herself away from him and opened the door of his car.

He was right about one thing. He was not the first to have wanted to take her to bed, but…

'Oh, no… *No*,' Louise told herself fiercely. 'I'm not going through all that again. I'm not travelling down that road…thinking *those* thoughts…'

Wasn't it one of the first signs of long-term spinsterdom when one started talking to oneself…?

Spinsterdom… It was an old-fashioned, very non-politically correct and out-of-favour word, with all its unkind connotations and in-built prejudices. But a spinster was, after all, what she was, and what she was likely to remain…

By choice, she reminded herself fiercely. By *choice*. By the expression of her *free will* because… because…

'Stop that,' she told herself sternly, reminding herself mundanely, 'You've got to be up early in the morning!'

CHAPTER FIVE

'LOUISE. Good!' her boss greeted her as she hurried into Louise's office. 'I'm glad you're here early.'

'I thought you'd want me to brief you on the possible legal complexities of this proposed change in fishing rights.'

'Yes, yes, I do,' Pam Carlisle agreed. 'But I also want you to accompany me to this morning's meeting. Things have changed rather a lot since we first discussed the matter. For a start, there's been a good deal of political argument brought up by some of the other committee members over the fact that the proposed Chair, Gareth Simmonds, is British, and of course the existing fishing rights are also British.'

'Yes... Yes, so I understand,' Louise agreed tensely, keeping her face averted from her boss as she fiddled with some papers on her desk.

'You know? But how?'

'My sister told me, and as it happens Gareth Simmonds was on the same flight as me. I... He was my tutor for a while when I was up at Oxford,' Louise explained brusquely. There—it was said...out...over and done with.

'Oh, you know Gareth, then.' Pam beamed at her. 'We're most frightfully lucky to have had him agree to accept the Chair, and, as I've already pointed out to the other committee members, they simply couldn't have a chairperson who could be less biased. Well, if he was your tutor *you* must know that. He really is the most— It's just as well I'm a very happily married woman,' she told Louise frankly, with a wide grin. 'I can tell you, Louise, when he smiled at me I could practically feel myself melting. His students must have fallen for him like ninepins, poor man…'

'Poor man? *Why* poor man?' Louise asked, rather more sharply than she had intended, she could see, as Pam gave her a puzzled look.

'Oh, dear, Lou, have I trodden on an Achilles' heel?' She asked, with amusement. 'Did you have a bit of a thing for him while you were an undergrad?'

'No. I most certainly did not,' Louise denied vehemently, her colour suddenly very high and her eyes spitting sparks of anger. 'If you want the truth…' She paused, only too well aware of the danger she was running into.

'Yes…?' Pam prompted.

'Oh, nothing,' Louise hedged. 'Look, I've produced a list of possible points that may be raised, and, of course, there's always the chance that we're going to have that old accusation of colonialism thrown at us…'

'Colonialism…?' Pam raised her eyebrows. 'Well, I suppose you *could* be right, and it's certainly best to be prepared for everything.'

Louise, who knew the situation equally as well as her boss, nodded. 'It's going to be my job to persuade the committee that we need to keep fishing quotas down and retain as much control over our fishing rights as we can. It's not going to be easy…'

'No,' Louise agreed. 'I've read up as much as I can on maritime law, and, of course, all the other legal facts that cover the situation. I've prepared several briefs for you on the subject, and I'm also getting hold of translations of the law and legal histories that the other committee countries are likely to be using as counter-arguments.'

'Mmm…looks like I'm going to be doing an awful lot of reading.'

'Well, I'll condense as much of it as I can, and, of course, if a point is raised that needs further exploration…'

'You'll deal with it. Yes, I know you will, Lou. Have I told you recently, by the way, what a treasure you are? When Hugh first recommended you to me I admit I *was* rather dubious…but he convinced me that you would be up to the job and he was more than right.'

Hugh Crighton was Saul's father, her grandfather's half-brother. Initially a barrister, and now a semi-retired judge, he lived in Pembrokeshire with his wife Ann, and it was from living in a coastal area that he had become acquainted with the European MP Pam Carlisle, for whom Louise now worked.

Originally, when she had been offered the job, Louise had resentfully assumed that this was her uncle Hugh's way of getting her out of his son's life. But at a family gathering Hugh had taken her on one side and told her gently, 'I know what you're thinking, Lou, but you're wrong. Yes, I *do* think it's a good idea for you and Saul to have some distance between you, and for Tullah and Saul to be allowed to build their new life together, but I also happen to think that you're ideally suited for this kind of work. You've got the right kind of fighting spirit it needs.'

'I wanted to be a barrister,' Louise had reminded him.

'Yes, I know,' he had acknowledged. 'But, my dear Lou, you're too hot-blooded and—'

'Too hot-tempered,' she had supplied angrily for him.

'Spirited,' he had amended. 'A crusader...a leader. You need the kind of challenge this work specifically will provide.'

And, of course, he had been right, and if she was honest, the thought of practising law in the dry, dusty courts of the European legal system did not appeal to her any more.

'You just want to be a barrister so that you can prove to Gramps that you're better than Max,' Joss had commented calmly at that same gathering. 'But it's all right, Lou,' he had told her in a kind voice. '*We* all know that you *are* better...'

Better... What did that mean? she wondered now. What had happened to the young woman who had declared that if she couldn't have Saul then all she wanted in compensation was to be materially successful, to make her mark in the world? Why was she suddenly beginning to feel that there might be something missing from her life, that there might be *someone* missing from it?

'Lou? Are you all right...?'

'Yes. Yes, I'm fine,' she assured Pam Carlisle, swiftly gathering up the papers she would need as she prepared to follow her out to the waiting car.

En route to their destination, Louise studied their surroundings absently through the car window. Brussels, despite hearsay to the contrary, was, in fact, a beautiful city; but it was true it *was* a majestic and very proper kind of rigid beauty that perhaps could not always be easily appreciated. But beautiful it was, nevertheless, Louise acknowledged as the driver brought the car to a halt and got out to open the doors for them.

Several of the other committee members and their assistants had already arrived. Louise knew most of them by sight if nothing else. Brussels' political circles were surprisingly small, in view of the number of politicians and ancillary workers and diplomats who worked at the commission.

She was grimly amused to see that the French representative had with him a particularly aggressive and highly qualified legal adviser big-wig, who Louise suspected was far more used to running his *own* committees rather than sitting in a back seat capacity on someone else's. She had never actually met him before, but knew of him by reputation, and, as she whispered discreetly to her boss, it proved how seriously the French were taking the issues that they should have supplied their representative with someone so very senior.

'This is a very serious political issue for them,' Pam Carlisle agreed. 'Even more so in many ways than it is for us. But it's the Spanish contingent we should expect to have the most trouble with.

'Oh, look, there's Gareth Simmonds just walking in,' Pam told her, but Louise had already seen him.

His dark, impeccably tailored suit emphasised the masculine power of his shoulders—and their breadth. Beneath the pristine crispness of his shirt Louise could see his chest rising and falling as he breathed. Was it still bisected by that same dark arrowing of soft, finger-magnetising dark hair? Did he still…?

Angrily, she turned her head away.

'I'd like to have a word with him, but I've been

warned to be especially careful. We can't afford to take any risks of having him accused of favouritism,' Pam commented.

'Strictly speaking he shouldn't be in a position to favour *anyone*,' Louise reminded her dryly. 'The issue is to be resolved by sticking to the *law*.'

From the past Louise could almost hear Gareth Simmonds' voice as he lectured them on the finer points of European law, his tone becoming increasingly passionate as he pointed out to them that the way ahead lay not so much in the British law courts, but in those of the new European parliament.

'New community laws will be written which will supersede the old, nationalistic laws, and the responsibility for making those laws could well lie in your hands…'

The meeting was being called to order. Out of the corner of her eye Louise watched Gareth. He was deep in conversation with a stunning blonde whom Louise recognised as one of the phalanx of legal advisers attached to the German embassy—Ilse Weil. From her body language, it was quite plain that it wasn't just Gareth's attention as the chairperson of the committee she was courting, Louise decided derisively. And, what was more, Gareth Simmonds didn't seem to be doing anything to put a less intimate distance between them.

Abruptly, she turned away. If Gareth Simmonds chose to respond to another woman's sensual come-on, then that was no business of *hers*. No business at all. Nor was there any way she would ever want it to be.

'Thanks, Lou… I appreciate the way you handled everything. We were faced with some pretty tricky questions, and I could be wrong, but I've got a gut feeling that one or two people were quite definitely caught off guard by the answers you were able to come up with.'

'Mmm… I wouldn't be *too* optimistic,' Louise warned her boss, adding dryly, 'We *are*, after all, dabbling in pretty murky waters…'

'Murky, maybe, but hopefully legally within our territory,' Pam responded with a grin. 'You haven't forgotten we've got this wretched dinner tonight as well, have you?'

Louise shook her head.

'I must say that I'm not particularly looking forward to it—all that boring small talk. *Why* is it that diplomatic small talk is even worse than any other kind?'

Louise laughed. 'Cheer up,' she consoled her boss. 'Only another few days and then you'll be going home.'

Her boss had some leave she was due, which she had decided to take to coincide with her husband's early retirement from the local government department he headed.

'Once Gerald has retired, at least we'll be able to spend a bit more time together. Although I'm not sure how well he's going to adapt to living here in Brussels,' she confessed.

Louise suspected that it wasn't so much Brussels her boss was concerned about her husband adapting to as the fact that he would be living there rather in her shadow.

The nature of her job meant that Louise rarely worked normal office hours, and so she had no qualms about her plan to head straight back to her apartment now the meeting was over. She had some reading up she wanted to do, and one or two other things. A couple of points had been raised at the meeting that she wanted to check up on, and then, she decided luxuriously, she would probably go for a swim. The apartment block where she lived had its own gym and in-house swimming pool facilities, which Louise used as regularly as she was able.

Ilse Weil had collared Gareth Simmonds again, she noticed as she started to collect her papers together. Much as it went against the grain for her to have to admit it, he *had* chaired the meeting extremely well. She had almost been able to see the committee members' respect for him growing as he'd dealt courteously but firmly with some of their more outrageous claims and counter-claims.

From a legal point of view, of course, his grasp of the subject would be absolutely first class.

Out of the corner of his eye Gareth watched Louise turn to leave.

He had known, of course, that she was working in Brussels, and it had been perhaps inevitable that they should run into one another. It hadn't been altogether welcome news for him to discover that the British representative on the committee had Louise working for her as her assistant, but by then it had been too late for him to back out.

Seeing her on the plane had been a shock that he hadn't been expecting, and he could still feel the after-effects of the jolt that had hit him like a surge of electricity when he had stood up and seen her.

Ilse Weil was still talking to him. He bent his head towards her and smiled politely. She had long blonde hair and good skin. Beneath the fine wool of her top he could see the firm jut of her breasts, her nipples discreetly outlined. Male instinct told him that she would be far from cool in bed, but his body refused to be impressed—or aroused.

Louise… She had had her hair cut short, a gamine crop. It suited her, revealing the perfection of her delicate bone structure, making her look somehow more feminine and fragile than she had done with it long. Her clothes, unlike Ilse's, did not reveal the curves of her breasts, and there was certainly no suggestion of any tempting thrust of an aroused nipple beneath the shirt she was wearing under her suit jacket. He had seen the flash of dislike in her eyes when she had seen him earlier, just as he had seen it on the plane. She had quite obviously still not forgiven him for what had happened that summer in Tuscany.

'Gareth?'

'I'm sorry, Ilse. I missed what you were saying.' He was forced to apologise as she placed a smooth white hand on his arm. Her nails were painted an immaculate glossy dark red. They were long and elegantly manicured. Louise's nails were short and unpolished, or at least they had been that summer in Tuscany. But they had still been long enough to leave long, raised, passion-driven weals in his skin, on his arms and his back where she had raked him with them in the frantic intensity of her sexual passion—but not for him. *Her* passion had not been for him. His mouth hardened. Had it been deliberate, the way she had tangled his name with another man's as she'd pleaded with him to satisfy her, to take her, to…?

'I'm sorry, Ilse. I really must go.' He interrupted his companion.

Immediately she pouted, her finger curling round the cloth of his sleeve.

'Oh, but I hadn't finished… But then I shall see you tonight at the dinner.' She gave him a flirtatious look. 'Perhaps I might even arrange for you to sit next to me…'

'I rather think the other members of the committee will have something to say if they think I'm paying you too much attention,' Gareth told her gently, before retrieving his arm.

An affair with a woman who threatened to be as tenacious as Ilse was obviously the last thing he wanted. An affair with *anyone* was the last thing he wanted… He closed his eyes for a moment and leaned against the wall. What he *wanted*…what he wanted was, ironically, what his mother and his married sisters were continually telling him he *needed*. A wife, children…a family… Louise!

All of those things, those life fulfilments, were denied to him, though, and had been denied to him since that fateful summer's day in an Italian villa when he had wilfully, stupidly, and for ever and ever, heart-achingly, life-challengingly allowed his emotions to overrule his intelligence.

Now, for him, there could be no happy-ever-afters. How could there be when he knew, had known, from the moment he touched her, that any other woman than Louise could only and for always be second best? And that any children he might have with her, no matter how much loved, would always stand in the shadow of the children he might have had with Louise.

He had known, of course, all along, that she had not shared the explosive, mind-shattering moment of stark truth and self-knowledge he had been forced to endure, that for her there had been no savage, searing pain of recognition for the emotional significance of what was happening, no realisation that here was something that wasn't going to remain hidden by the anger he was using to mask it, and that he was deluding himself by trying to convince himself that his reaction to her was merely physical.

He had been under no illusions; she had simply been punishing herself, trying to destroy her love for another man in the fierce heat of what they had shared. She had not emerged from the inferno of their lovemaking with her emotions transformed, transmuted, from the base metal of lust into the pure gold of love—but he had. Oh, yes, he most certainly had.

He had tried to contact her the following day, telling himself that it was the right thing to do, the responsibly aware thing to do, but when he had initially telephoned and then called round at the villa he had found it empty. It had been another day before he had been able to make contact with Maria and discover that an emergency had taken the family home.

On his own return to Britain he had tried again—telephoning Louise's home in Cheshire. Jenny had answered the telephone, her voice warm with recognition as he'd explained that he had learned from Maria that they had had to leave before the end of their holiday.

She had thanked him for telephoning and had written down his number when he had proffered it—'just in case Louise wanted to have a chat with me before the new term starts'.

There had been a brief but very significant pause before Jenny had told him a little uncomfortably that Louise had told her parents she had decided to change courses.

He had known then, of course, that what had happened between them was something that Louise didn't want to pursue. And he had told himself firmly that he was a mature, thinking man and that he would somehow get over what he was feeling.

And in a way he had. He no longer woke up every morning longing for her, and the memory of the time they had spent together was something he only allowed himself to relive very, very occasionally—or at least it had been.

His family thought the reason he hadn't married was that he was too choosy...too dedicated to his work.

'If you're not careful, you're going to end up a lonely old man,' they had warned him as, last Christmas, they'd plucked a miscellany of small children and large animals from his prone body.

'If you're not careful I shall be a *grandmother* before you're a father,' his eldest sister had told him direfully.

Since her eldest child, a girl, had not yet reached her teens, Gareth had felt impelled to deny this statement, but the truth was that, much as he would like to be married, to have for himself the obvious happiness and contentment that existed for his sisters with their partners and their families, there was one vital component missing from his life that made this scenario impossible.

He needed to find *someone* he could *love*—someone who would love him in return. He was a long way past the age when the excitement of mere sexual lust, no matter how strong, was enough to convince him that it was a sound basis for a long-term relationship.

'Please don't blame Lou for…for… She can't help it,' her twin sister Katie had told him, her voice trembling slightly as though she could feel an echo of her sister's pain. 'It's because she's in love.'

In love… Oh, yes, Louise had been in love…!

'If I can't have Saul then it might as well be anybody…' she had told him passionately, when he had pointed out to her the consequences of her flirtation with the young Italian nephew of the villa's housekeeper.

Anybody… Even *him*… Wearily Gareth bowed his head. There was pain and then there was guilt, and of the two of them…which did he find it hardest to bear? The knowledge that he couldn't control his emotions, or the knowledge that he couldn't control himself? Both were spirit-crushing, heart-numbing emotions, but of the two… He looked again at Louise, and for some reason she stopped what she was doing and looked back at him. Even at this distance he could see the rejection and the dislike in her eyes. What would she say, he wondered, if he were to go over to her and tell her…take her…?

Having watched Gareth lever his shoulders away from the wall on which he had been leaning, Louise looked abruptly away from him. When she picked up the last pages of her notes she saw that her hand was trembling. Stuffing the pieces of paper into her case, she warned herself that she couldn't afford to give way to her emotions.

She hated the knowledge that he had about her, the fact that she could *never* take back the power she had given him over her, the fact that she could *never*, ever forget or wipe out what had happened between them. Even now there were times when she came awake from her dreams with his name on her lips, when she could hear an echo, the sound of her own voice calling out to him in the throes of her agony of sexual need. She had been a virgin, and yet, in the space of those few hours, her body had flowered, burst into full womanhood in a way that had left her feeling as though she hardly knew herself at all.

All her dreams of sex with Saul had centred on the thrill of finally having him to herself, of *his* desire for *her*, *his* arousal, *his* need. Naively she'd visualised him begging her to allow him to touch her body. It had simply never occurred to her that *she* might be the one doing the begging, that *her* emotions, *her* desires might be the ones that were out of control, that *she* might...

But in the end it hadn't been Saul who had heard those shaming cries, who had seen...felt...*known* her body's urgent need for fulfilment.

She could feel her body starting to grow hot, and she had an urgent desire to run out of the building and away from Gareth Simmonds just as fast as she could. But of course she couldn't give in to such a childish temptation. Instead she held her head high and walked as calmly and quickly as she could towards the exit.

'I'll see you tonight,' Pam told her when the car stopped outside Louise's apartment building.

'Er...yes,' Louise agreed, before climbing out of the car.

Her telephone was ringing as she let herself into her apartment. Picking up the receiver, she was surprised to hear her twin's voice on the other end of the line.

Their mother's habits of good housekeeping and thriftiness had, as Katie had once ruefully confided to Louise, proved almost as beneficial in her career as her Oxford degree, her boss at the charity for whom she worked being profoundly impressed by Katie's firm grip on their departmental budget. As Louise was well aware, Katie was not given to making expensive overseas telephone calls merely for the self-indulgence of hearing her sister's voice.

Knowing this, her response to her twin's warm greeting was coloured by a little bit of anxiety as she asked her, 'What is it? Why are you ringing? Has something happened to Gramps or…?'

'No. Everything's fine.' Katie quickly reassured her. 'I just wanted to make sure you'd got back all right and that everything was…er…okay.'

There was a photograph of her sister, of both of them, in fact, in their university gowns, on the table just in sight of where Louise was standing, and she frowned suspiciously into her twin's smiling features now as she quickly mentally ran over all the various interpretations that could be put on Katie's comment.

'Why did you leave it until my flight to tell me Gareth Simmonds would be in Brussels?' she demanded quietly.

'I *wanted* to tell you,' Katie admitted guiltily. 'Don't be cross, Lou,' she coaxed. 'I just didn't want to spoil the weekend. Are you angry?'

Louise closed her eyes and then opened them again.

'What's to be angry about?' she asked as carelessly

as she could. 'With any luck I shan't have to have very much to do with him.

'How much longer are you working on your current project?' Louise asked her twin, firmly changing the subject and at the same time trying to banish from her mind the annoying image that would keep on forming there of Gareth's dark head inclined attentively towards Ilsc's bright blonde one.

'I'm not quite sure,' she heard Katie telling her.

'Well, don't forget you promised you'd try to get over here soon if you can.'

'I will try,' Katie agreed. 'It was lovely seeing everyone at home—so much has happened while I've been away working in London that there was simply masses for me to catch up on with everyone. What with Tullah and Saul's new baby—and I couldn't get over how much Olivia and Caspar's two have grown—and Mum and Aunt Ruth have done wonders with their fund raising for their mums and babes. Mum told me that she and Aunt Ruth are going to try to buy an older house for conversion into flatlets for single mothers.

'Aunt Ruth was saying that the stable block at Queensmead would make a wonderful potential conversion, and that its setting would be perfect…'

'Gramps would never agree to anything like that,' Louise laughed, her face breaking into a wide grin as she pictured her irascible grandfather's reaction to the news that his sister wanted to turn the stable block of his large mansion into homes for the area's single mothers and their babies.

'No, I know, and so, of course, does Aunt Ruth. I sometimes suspect that the only reason she pretends to Gramps that she's serious about it is because she knows how much he loves to have something to get angry over and to fight about. He's just not been the same since Uncle David disappeared…'

'No. He hasn't,' Louise agreed, and for a second both of them were silent as they thought about their father's twin brother.

'Do you think we will *ever* hear anything from him again?' Katie asked Louise slowly, eventually.

'I don't know. I suspect that for Gramps's sake, if nothing else, Dad hopes that he will get in touch, and it must be strange, too, for Olivia. Her mother has another man in her life, and Olivia only sees her when she and Caspar go down to Brighton to stay with Olivia's grandparents. David doesn't even know that Caspar and Olivia are married, never mind that they've got two children.'

'I know… I can't imagine what it would be like not to have Mum and Dad, can you?' Katie asked.

'No. I can't,' Louise agreed.

Katie suddenly interrupted their discussion about their family life to ask her with unexpected urgency, 'Lou… It isn't bothering you *too* much…about… about Gareth Simmonds being there in Brussels is it?'

'No. Of course it isn't,' Louise denied. 'Obviously I would have preferred *not* to have had him working in the same arena, but because the Commission is so closely interwoven the fact that he *is* working here would have meant that we would have been bound to run into one another sooner or later, even if he hadn't been heading the same committee that Pam is on. After all, why *should* it bother me? I don't like him, it's true, but I can live with that.'

There were some things too private to discuss even

with someone as close to her as her twin was, and her real feelings about Gareth Simmonds and his presence in Brussels was quite definitely one of them.

'Look, I've got to go,' she told Katie. 'There's a big official dinner this evening, and I've got some reading up I need to do.'

These official Commission dinners, which in the early stages of her new job had filled her with such trepidation and seemed so daunting, had now become boringly familiar.

The dinner-table talk would be all the usual gossipy stuff, unleavened by anything genuinely worth talking about, Louise decided later, as she quickly showered and got herself ready, automatically pulling on the first of her wardrobe's three smart black dresses which she and Katie and Olivia had chosen on a weekend shop in London before Louise had taken up her new post.

The dresses, two of which had been bought as a bargain from a designer shop in Bond Street in its end-of-season sale, had more than paid for themselves, and in fact drew compliments every time she wore them. In matt black jersey, they were easy to wear and even more practical. They could actually be washed—a bonus indeed in view of the number of times Louise had to wear them. The one she had chosen to wear tonight was sleeveless, with a wide slashed neckline, the fabric fitting sleekly to her body and draping flatteringly over one hip.

Her urchin-short haircut needed little attention other than a fiercely expensive reshape every few weeks, and she had never favoured more than a minimal amount of make-up—eyeshadow in subtle smoky shades to emphasise the shape and depth of her eyes, blusher, and lipstick which discreetly played down the fullness of a mouth that caused members of the male sex to stop and look again with speculative interest.

Both she and Katie had inherited their father's lean, elegant frame. Louise had never minded being tallish, but she had on occasions during her teens wished that her body was a little more curvaceously rounded. Time had granted her that wish, and although she was still enviably slender, according to her female friends, she had the kind of distinctly feminine curves that made the black jersey cling to her body with loving fervour.

Black shoes and a handbag large enough to hold a small notebook and a pen—things she never went anywhere without—and she was ready, with five minutes to spare before the car arrived.

Irritatingly her last thoughts as she stepped into the waiting car were not of her recent conversation with her twin, and Katie's promise to fly over to Brussels, or even of the conversational pitfalls she might be called upon to face regarding this morning's committee meeting at tonight's dinner, but instead were focused ominously and exclusively on the man who had headed that committee meeting.

Gareth Simmonds. Hadn't she *already* wasted enough, indeed far too much emotional energy on him?

One of the first things she had done when she had originally come here to Brussels to work was to tell herself that she was not going to allow any events from her past to cast dangerous shadows over her new life—and one of the darkest and most dangerous shadows in her life then had been the one cast by her ex-tutor…her ex…

Her head jerked up as she instinctively fought to deny even allowing herself to mentally frame the word 'lover'. They had *not* been lovers. Not in the true sense. Not as she interpreted the word.

Was there a woman in his life now? Pam, her boss, had made mention of the fact earlier that he was a single man, and as such would no doubt be in great demand socially.

'And not just single either,' Pam had commented admiringly. 'He's stunningly attractive and hunky with it…'

'Is he?' Louise had retorted in a clipped, short voice. 'I really hadn't noticed…'

Not noticed. When her brain had already faultlessly recorded and remembered the sheer thrill of female awe she had felt that first time she had seen him fully naked.

The car had stopped and the driver was, she realised belatedly, waiting for her to get out.

CHAPTER SIX

HOLDING her hand over her still half-full glass of wine, Louise shook her head at the circulating waiter, refusing his offer of a fresh glass.

It paid to keep a clear head at these affairs, and she had never been very good with alcohol.

Formal affairs such as this reception and the dinner which would follow it were really very much more Katie's strong suit than her own, and it had been brought very sharply home to her, not long after her original arrival in Brussels, that despite the fact that everyone close to her, including herself, always thought of *her* as being the stronger and more independently minded of the two of them it was Katie who had that nice degree of social confidence and easiness. She, as her twin, had developed the habit of allowing Katie to attend to all the social niceties that attended such conventional gatherings for *both* of them.

It had brought her rather sharply down to earth and humbled her a little to recognise how much she had depended on her twin in formal social situations, and indeed how much she had abused Katie's willingness to chat politely to ancient aunts, indeed to anyone whom she personally had deemed dull or boring, leaving her free to behave with unrepentant selfishness and very much please herself as to who she talked to and who she didn't.

A few months in Brussels had very quickly changed all that, and now Louise was adept at simulating interest in even the dullest of subjects—which didn't mean that she enjoyed it any more, she acknowledged ruefully as she directed a polite social smile towards the Commissioner paying her heavy compliments before excusing herself by saying that she thought her boss would be looking for her.

Louise made her way over to where Pam was deep in conversation with a fellow British Euro MP.

'Hello, Louise.' Pam welcomed her to her side.

'How is your aunt Ruth keeping, Louise?' the man Pam was in conversation with asked warmly. 'The last time I saw her she gave me the most fearful lecture on the damage she believes is threatening the British countryside from the volume of articulated lorries we're getting.'

Louise laughed. She knew John Lord quite well, since, in addition to being a Euro MP, he was also one of their close neighbours.

'Aunt Ruth is campaigning vigorously for a bypass for Haslewich, and she does have a point,' she conceded. 'The new business park outside the town *has* brought in an increased volume of traffic.

'I was just at home for the weekend, and my younger brother, Joss, was full of the fact that an Italian lorry driver had missed his road and got his artic stuck right in the middle of town, wedged solidly in between two listed buildings. Apparently it took the police five hours to unblock the traffic and get things back to normal.'

'It is a problem, I know,' John Lord agreed. 'The town does need a new bypass, and under one of the new EC agreements community funds should be provided to help pay for it.'

The conversation moved on and Louise excused

herself to go and circulate. It wouldn't do any harm to pick up as much feedback as she could after this morning's meeting.

Ten minutes later, just as she was discreetly checking her watch to find out how much longer it would be before they went in for dinner, she heard a familiar and very sensual voice behind her.

'Aha, there you are *chérie*…'

'Jean Claude.' She turned round immediately to smile up at him. He really was the most wickedly handsome-looking man, but oddly enough his almost film starish good looks did very little for her in any personal sense. Jean Claude was the kind of man who, while laying siege to one woman, would always be secretly looking over her shoulder to check out another potential victim. Louise suspected that her knowing this, realising that for him sex, seduction, relationships were all simply part of a very enjoyable but never serious game that he revelled in playing, automatically protected her, and prevented her from taking him too seriously.

'When are we going to get together?' he whispered to her as he skilfully drew her slightly away from everyone else. 'I have some leave owing to me. We could spend it together,' he suggested meaningfully. 'I could take you to Paris, show you things that only a person with experience could show you.'

Louise laughed and shook her head.

'Impossible, I'm afraid…'

'Ah, you are no doubt busy rushing to find laws to protect your cold northern seas. They are almost as cold as your heart, *chérie*…'

'And *both* are very well protected,' Louise informed him firmly, then smiled at him. This situation

over fishing rights had never been one it was going
to be easy to resolve, but she knew better than to
respond to the lure that Jean Claude was trailing in
front of her.

He might be a man who very much wanted to take
her to bed, but he was also a Frenchman, with a vested
interest in seeing his own country increase its allo-
cation of the existing fishing rights. *She* wasn't powerful or important enough to influence the outcome of
the newly formed committee in any shape or form,
but it would be very easy for a woman who was emotionally vulnerable or not quite wary enough to be
tricked into giving away information which *might* be
useful to an opposing party, and Louise was very
much aware of that fact.

Several yards away Gareth, who had been adroitly and
very determinedly annexed by Ilse Weil virtually from
the moment he'd arrived, frowned as he saw the way
Jean Claude's hand lay possessively on Louise's arm,
his body language making it plain that he would per-
mit no other man to break into their intimate conversation.

Ilse, following his glance, raised her eyebrows.

'Oh, dear, I see Jean Claude is up to his tricks. It
is well known here in Brussels what he is about,' she
told Gareth with a dismissive shrug. 'And it is also
rumoured that one of the reasons the French are so
well informed is *because* of Jean Claude's skill in
persuading his lovers to confide in him.'

She gave Gareth an arch look and made a purring
sound deep in her throat as she told him, 'I'm afraid
when *I'm* in bed with a man I lose myself so com-

pletely in the sex that the last thing *I* want to do is to talk politics…'

'I know what you mean,' Gareth agreed gravely. 'I too have a rule about never mixing business with pleasure…'

He was saved from having to say any more by an announcement requesting everyone to go in for dinner. Louise, he couldn't help noticing, seemed particularly reluctant to end her conversation with her companion.

'Louise.'

Louise tensed as she heard Gareth saying her name. The dinner had finished ten minutes ago, and she had hoped to slip away early, but now Gareth was bearing down on her, making it plain that he wasn't going to allow her to escape until he had said whatever it was he wanted to say to her.

'Gareth.' She acknowledged him curtly, glancing politely at her watch and then at the door.

'I saw you talking to Jean Claude le Brun earlier,' Gareth informed her, equally pointedly ignoring her attempts to show him that she was anxious to leave. 'You may not be aware of it, but it seems that he has something of a reputation in Brussels.'

Louise stared at him, her hackles immediately starting to rise as she caught the drift of Gareth's warning.

'A reputation for what?' she challenged him angrily. 'For being a good lover? What *is* it *exactly* you're trying to ask me, Gareth? Whether or not it's well deserved?'

'What I was trying to *warn* you against was the danger of putting yourself in a position where you might inadvertently discuss certain sensitive subjects,' Gareth corrected her grimly.

Louise's eyes widened and then darkened, first with disbelief and then with anger, as she drew in a sharply outraged breath.

'Are you *seriously* trying to suggest that Jean Claude is trying to lure me into some kind of sex trap, like…like someone out of a James Bond film?' she demanded scornfully. 'How ridiculous and how *typical* of you, Gareth. There *are* men who want to go to bed with me simply for the pleasure of doing so,' she informed him with angry scorn. 'They aren't all like you, and—'

Abruptly she stopped, mentally cursing herself for allowing her emotions to get the better of her. But it was too late. Gareth had quite obviously heard her and equally obviously wasn't going to let her escape.

'They aren't all like me and what?' he challenged her silkily.

Furious with herself, and with him, Louise immediately took refuge behind the ploy of quickly changing the subject.

'My private life has absolutely *nothing* whatsoever to do with you,' she informed him, and then added for good measure, 'You have no right, no right at all, to dare to suggest to me that—' She broke off, and then continued furiously, 'How would *you* like it if I suggested to you that *you* should take care not to be lured into bed by Ilse Weil? After all, *your* position as head of the committee into the fisheries question surely makes you far, *far* more vulnerable a target for someone to try to influence your decision than me.'

She had a point, Gareth had to admit, but what he couldn't admit—at least not to her—was the fact that it wasn't merely concern for matters of diplomatic delicacy that had prompted his warning to her...

'You have no right to dictate to me *how* I live my private life,' Louise continued fiercely. 'You're not my tutor now, Gareth. You have *no* control over my life or my future. You might have been able to punish me for what you decided...for loving Saul, but—'

'To *punish* you?' Gareth interrupted her sharply. 'Louise, I promise you I—'

'You what?' she interrupted him shakily. 'You weren't responsible for the fact that I didn't get my first? It wasn't because of you that I—'

'You're not being fair.' He stopped her quietly. 'And neither are you being very logical. I wasn't your tutor and I—'

'No, you weren't,' Louise agreed. 'But...' She stopped. How could she admit to him that it had been because of her confused feelings for him, her fear of what those feelings actually were, that she hadn't been able to give her full attention to her work for her remaining time at university—that her thoughts of him had come between her and her work, that the sheer effort of denying them had drained her of the energy she needed for her study?

She was, she discovered, shamingly close to tears. The sheer intensity of the anger she was feeling was unblocking memories she had thought locked safely away.

Not once during her years at school had it occurred to her that she wouldn't always be the praised, clever student, and the shock to her pride and her self-esteem, never mind her plans for her future, when her work had been criticised had been very hard for her to come to terms with.

Yes, maybe *now*, with hindsight in a very small corner of her mind, she was just about beginning to admit that the life she was making for herself, the cut and thrust of the European scene, was far better suited to her passionate nature than the much more sterile atmosphere of the upper echelons of the British legal system would have been. But it was a very, very reluctant admission, and certainly not one she was prepared to share with Gareth Simmonds.

'I'm sorry if I said the wrong thing,' Gareth began quietly. 'I was simply trying to warn you.'

'Why warn me? What makes you think that *I'm* particularly in need of that kind of warning? Or can I guess? Just because I made the mistake of…of loving the wrong man…' She stopped and swallowed, and then told him bitingly, 'The relationship I choose to have with Jean Claude—*whatever* that relationship is—is no one's business but mine.'

'In one sense, no,' Gareth agreed. 'But in another… You don't need me to tell you that Brussels is a hotbed of gossip, and—'

'No, I don't,' Louise agreed tautly.

She had had enough of listening to Gareth lecture her. More than enough. Abruptly she turned on her heel, walking smartly away from him before he could say or do anything to stop her.

She was still seething over her run-in with him over an hour later, back in her flat, as she read through some notes while preparing for bed.

What right had he to dare to question the wisdom of her relationship with Jean Claude?

But it wasn't so much his assumed right to warn her that was making her so furiously angry—and not just with him but with herself as well—as the thinking she knew lay behind it. No doubt *he* was remembering her as the girl who had fallen so foolishly in love with a man who didn't want her, and who had then recklessly compounded her folly by inciting another man, who *also* didn't love her, to relieve her of her virginity—another man whom she had realised too late that she—

Those memories, that knowledge, and seeing Gareth, had reminded her of that hurt, and of her own foolishness.

Waking up early, unable to get back to sleep, Louise went down to the basement of the apartment complex which housed the gym and the swimming pool. At this hour of the morning she had the pool to herself, and the energy it took to make herself complete a punishing sixty lengths thankfully robbed her brain of the ability to concentrate on anything other than gritting her teeth and forcing herself to meet that target.

The last five lengths hadn't been a very sensible idea, she acknowledged when she eventually tried to haul herself out of the pool and discovered that she was too weak to do so. Instead she had to swim tiredly over to the steps and then climb them on legs that trembled with over-exertion and exhaustion.

Her short hair clinging sleekly to her scalp, her eyes momentarily closed as she willed herself not to give in to the jelly-like urging of her legs to simply sit down and rest, she was unaware of the fact that she was no longer alone in the pool area until she heard an unwontedly familiar voice demanding curtly, 'Louise? Are you all right…?'

Gareth Simmonds. What on earth was *he* doing here? Or was she simply hallucinating, dreaming him up in some insane desire to inflict even further punishment upon herself?

Groggily she opened her eyes. No, she *wasn't* dreaming. Despite the fact that the pool area was almost tropically heated, her skin suddenly broke out in a rash of goosebumps, and she started visibly to shiver. Gareth was standing less than a yard away from her, wearing a pair of businesslike black swimming shorts. The rest of his body…

Louise swallowed and gulped, then tried to draw extra oxygen into her suddenly starved lungs, a hot flood of perspiration drenching her skin despite the fact that she was actually trembling as though she was icy cold.

The sight of him brought down an avalanche of memories for which she was totally unprepared, against which she had absolutely no defences, and she could feel her knees starting to buckle under their crushing weight.

In Tuscany he might have been more tanned, but so far as she could see nothing else had changed. His body was still the same male powerhouse of energy and sensuality, and, yes, he *did* still have that same arrowing of dark hair, so very masculine and dangerous to look at, but so soft and sensually stirring to touch.

'Louise…'

She could feel the strength starting to leave her legs as the blood roared in her head and her heart pounded with sickening force.

'No.'

Automatically she put out a defensive hand as she saw Gareth coming towards her, but he ignored it, catching hold of her by the shoulders, his face, his eyes, expressing an unexpected and unfamiliar look of concern as he demanded urgently, 'What is it? What's wrong? Are you feeling ill…?'

'Let…let me go,' Louise demanded, frantically struggling to pull herself free of his grip, but the tiled surround of the pool felt slippery beneath her wet feet, and she could feel herself starting to lose her balance, so that instead of pushing herself free of Gareth she had, instead, to cling onto him for security. This close she could smell the heat of his body—not, this time, as strongly musky as it had been on that fateful Tuscan day—and mingling with it a hint of lemon freshness from his soap…or aftershave…?

Louise wasn't even aware she had asked such a question until she heard him reply, his voice disconcertingly close to her ear, 'Shower gel. My eldest niece's choice—a Christmas present.'

'In Italy you smelled of…'

What was she saying…thinking…betraying…? She cursed herself mentally in desperation, but it was too late; Gareth was already holding her slightly away from him so that he could look down into her face, her eyes…

Louise blinked and tried to look away from him, but it was impossible. She felt her breath rattle in her lungs as their glances locked, clung, refusing to let go, like lovers' bodies.

'In Italy *you* smelled of sunshine and heat and of being a woman,' Gareth told her softly, as though he knew exactly what it was she had been about to betray herself by saying.

Louise opened her mouth to protest that what he was saying was wrong, that he was speaking the unspeakable, the unimaginable, the forbidden, but no words came out, and instead she discovered that she was focusing blindly on his mouth, studying it, staring at it as though she was starved for the…

'Louise…'

Afterwards she would ask herself why on earth her brain interpreted the way he said her name as an invitation to do what she did—to close the gap between them and to press her mouth against his, not so much in a kiss, more in a compulsive, instinctive response to a hunger that demanded far, far more than the mere meeting of their lips.

What she was doing was wrong, crazy…insane. But it was too late. She had already done it and Gareth… Gareth…

Heavily she closed her eyes as she heard him repeating her name over and over again, before he started to kiss her.

Her body trembled violently beneath his hands, but she made no move to stop him when he wrenched down the top of her swimsuit, baring her breasts to his touch. Against her body she could feel the hardness of his, and her own flesh leapt in immediate response, immediate recognition of its first…its *only* lover.

Heedlessly, ruthlessly, it laid waste to all the barriers she had painstakingly erected between herself and…and this… And instead of repudiating him, as she knew she must, Louise heard herself moaning his name, sobbing it aloud almost as she hung helplessly in his arms, her body no longer her own to command or protect, responsive only to what he might tell it or arouse within it.

She could feel the heat of his chest against the naked dampness of her breasts, and it was as though their first coming together had only been yesterday. As though she had learned *nothing* in the time since— as though all the resolutions she had made for herself in those long, agonising weeks and months afterwards, when she had finally realised just what was happening to her, just what *had* happened to her, had never been. As though this man had never caused her so much pain that she had sworn she would *never*, ever forget the agony of the lesson she had learned through him.

A sound, a long, tortured, aching sob of need and longing, tore at her throat. Beneath Gareth's hands she felt her body tremble and burn; beneath his mouth she felt herself melt, yield, yearn, until the intensity of her own hunger threatened to devour her.

All sense of place or time had long since left her. They could have been anywhere; she really didn't care. All that really mattered, all that was actually real, was what she could feel. Eagerly she pressed herself against Gareth, and felt the answering hardness in his own body.

Somewhere in the distance a door slammed, and abruptly Louise came back to reality. Immediately she pulled back from Gareth, covering her exposed breasts with her hands and then turning her back to him as she frantically struggled with the straps of her swimsuit.

'Louise.'

She could hear him saying her name urgently, but she shook her head in denial of whatever it was he might want to say to her, not even daring to turn round, knowing she couldn't allow herself to look at him as she denied him fiercely. 'No. No! Just leave me alone, Gareth… *leave me alone.*'

And without giving him the chance to stop her she started to walk away from him, and then to run.

Silently Gareth watched her go. What was there, after all, that he could say? What explanation, apology could he make for what he had done? To admit that he had momentarily lost control would make matters worse rather than better, and as for pointing out to her that she had been similarly vulnerable...

To see that tormented hurt in her eyes, to feel the need coursing through her body, to sense the longing she was so obviously struggling to repress and to know that she was repressing it because she still wanted, still loved another man, a man she could not have, had been like receiving a death blow, which was ironic when he had long ago assured himself—and believed those assurances—that he had come to terms with the knowledge that she loved someone else.

In Italy he had told himself initially that it had been anger, irritation, impatience with the way she was so wantonly and childishly destroying the pleasure of sharing herself with a partner who genuinely cared about her that had driven him to do what he had done. But he had known the moment he touched her that he was lying to himself, that he was just as guilty, just as burdened by inappropriate emotions for someone who did not want him as she was herself.

He might not have called those emotions love—not then—but he had known for sure what they were when he had held her in his arms and heard her cry out another man's name while *he* loved her.

Gareth closed his eyes. The Louise he had fallen in love with had been a mere girl, and he had derided himself for having done so, telling himself it was the classic tale of the mature tutor falling for his youthful pupil, hoping to recapture his own youth through her. But they were tutor and pupil no longer, and Louise was now a woman in *every* sense of the word. And his feelings hadn't changed, merely deepened, strengthened. But then he hadn't needed anyone to tell him that. He had known it the moment he saw her on the plane. Had known it even before then.

Had known it at Christmas, when his family had teased him about his lack of a wife and children of his own. Had known it and ached for it as he'd held his youngest nephew in his arms and known beyond any kind of doubt that the only mother he wanted for *his* children was Louise. How had it happened? He didn't know. And when? Before Italy? What did it matter now? All that mattered was that quite obviously for Louise nothing had changed, and she still loved her cousin Saul.

Even though she had had a hot shower to warm her cold body, and drunk a mug of coffee, she was still shivering, still shaking with reaction to what had happened down by the pool, Louise acknowledged. And no amount of water, no matter how piping hot, could wash away the scent of Gareth that still clung somehow to her own skin, which had embedded itself for ever in her vulnerable senses.

Gareth.

When had she known just how she really felt about him? In Italy, when she had fought to deny it with a ferocity that should have warned her just how frightened she really was? At home that Christmas when everyone had tiptoed around her, afraid of mentioning Saul's name or the fact that he and Tullah had now set a date for their marriage, when in reality Saul and what she had once felt for him had paled to the faintest of shadows?

Gareth.

She had denied for as long as she could what had happened to her, telling herself that she was just over-reacting, that it was the classic virgin's response to her first experience of sex to imagine she was in love with the man who had been her partner, reminding herself with bitter scorn of how pathetically trite it was for a student to fall in love with her tutor.

You don't even like him, she had told herself over and over again. You're just transferring your feelings to him from Saul… He doesn't really mean anything to you, and you certainly don't mean *anything* to *him*.

The last part of that statement might have been true but the rest of it certainly hadn't.

And so she had transferred to another course, had told herself bitterly that she was *glad* that Gareth no longer taught her, had done everything and *anything* she could to make sure that she never came into contact with him. But, while she might have been able to control her daytime waking thoughts and responses, at night in her dreams it had been different. At night in her dreams she'd ached for him, yearned for him, clung to him while her body desperately tried to relive the pleasure he had given it.

The pain, the agony of waking each morning to the reality of knowing that he didn't want her, that he *wasn't* a part of her life, had shown her more clearly than anything else just how childish and adolescent her feelings for Saul had actually been.

With Gareth there had been no question of her trying to pursue him, to convince him that he really wanted and loved her, no adolescent fantasising that against all the evidence to the contrary she could make him love her.

Finally, she had grown up.

She was still shivering, and her head had started to pound with sick intensity, a sure sign that she was about to suffer one of her fortunately rare migraine attacks. It was pointless even thinking about trying to go to work. Dizzily she picked up the phone and dialled her boss's number.

'A migraine!' Pam exclaimed when she had explained how she felt. 'Don't even *think* of trying to come into work. I know how bad they can be.'

By now the pain was so intense that it was all Louise could do to croak a disjointed response before she replaced the receiver and somehow managed to drag herself into her bedroom.

Gareth Simmonds. Why had fate so cruelly brought him back into her life? Why?

CHAPTER SEVEN

LOUISE woke up abruptly. Her migraine had gone and someone was knocking very loudly and impatiently on her apartment door. Pushing back the bedclothes, she swung her legs onto the floor, grimacing as she realised she had gone to bed still wearing her swimsuit.

As always in the aftermath of one of her migraines, she felt mercifully pain-free, but somehow slightly unfocused and not quite together, her body and her brain both working slowly as she reacted automatically to the continued knocking and went to open the door.

'Joss! Jack! What on earth are you two doing here?' she exclaimed as she saw her younger brother and cousin.

Whoever she had expected to find outside her door it had certainly not been them.

'Lou, Jack isn't feeling very well,' her brother announced urgently, ignoring her question as he put a comforting, protective arm around his cousin's shoulders and ushered him into Louise's apartment.

'He was sick during the Channel crossing and...'

'Sick...'

As Louise inspected the slightly green and heavy-eyed face of her younger cousin she recognised that he was indeed looking extremely unwell.

'Jack...' she began in concern.

But he shook his head and told her wanly, 'I'll be fine... I just need to lie down for a while...'

'The bedroom's this way, Joss,' Louise informed her brother, leading the way as Joss guided his cousin across her small living room and into the inner hallway that gave on to the apartment's single bedroom.

Quickly straightening the bed before Jack virtually fell down on top of it, Louise frowned. What on earth were the two boys doing here?

Jack, Olivia's younger brother, had made his home permanently with Louise's parents following his father's disappearance some years earlier, and was now looked upon by Louise as more of another brother than a cousin.

His mother, never particularly maternal and suffering from an eating disorder, had announced that the last thing she felt capable of doing was single-handedly looking after a teenage boy—and one, moreover, who had already spent far more of his time with her brother-in-law and his wife than he had with her—and Olivia, his elder sister, while more than willing to give him a permanent home, had allowed herself to be persuaded by Jenny and Jon that it was in Jack's best interests for him to remain where he was, living under their roof, instead of being subjected to even more changes.

It was an arrangement which worked very well. At fourteen, Joss was two years younger than Jack, and they were not just close in age but close in other ways as well—more so than if they had actually been brothers, Jenny often said. And to Louise and Katie, growing up in their parents' comfortable family home, Jack had simply been accepted as though he were an extra sibling.

There had been some talk of Jack going to Brighton to live with his mother and his maternal grandparents once his mother's health had recovered, but when offered this option Jack had declared very firmly that he wanted to stay where he was.

An extra mouth to feed, an extra child to love and nurture was, as Louise knew, no problem to her parents, and if anyone had ever asked her she herself would have said quite honestly that she'd never thought of Jack as being anything other than a very close member of her intimate family, and she knew that her twin would have said exactly the same.

Within the family Joss and Jack were known collectively as 'the boys', just as she and Katie were referred to as 'the twins', but she hadn't missed the way that Jack had withdrawn from her just now, when she had gone to give him the same swift and automatic hug of greeting she had given to Joss, nor the way he hunched his body away from her as he lay on her bed as though somehow in rejection of her.

As she closed her bedroom door she beckoned to her brother to follow her into her small kitchen, where she automatically filled the kettle with water and, much to her own wry amusement, heard herself taking on a role which she had hitherto assumed belonged exclusively to women like her mother as she asked him, 'Are you hungry. I don't have much in, but I can rustle up some sandwiches, I expect.' And then, without waiting for a response, she continued firmly, 'What on earth is going on, Joss? What are you doing here? Mum never rang to say you were coming. I don't even have a spare room to—'

'Mum doesn't know.'

Louise, who had been just about to start slicing some bread to make him some sandwiches, stopped what she was doing and turned to face him, putting the knife down on the breadboard.

'What do you mean, Mum doesn't know?' she demanded suspiciously. There was a small silence while her brother looked down at his feet and then at the kitchen wall.

'That's one of the sketches you did in Tuscany, isn't it?' he asked her. 'I—'

'Joss.' Louise warned him.

'I've left them a note…explaining.'

Louise's eyebrows rose.

'Explaining what?' she asked warily.

'Well, I couldn't tell them what we were doing— they would have stopped us.'

'Oh, now, surely not,' Louise protested dryly. 'I mean, why on earth should she? You're only fourteen. I can't think of any reason on earth why the parents should possibly object to the pair of you doing a disappearing act…'

Joss gave her a sheepish look.

'I know. I know…' he conceded. 'But I had to come. If I hadn't…I tried to persuade Jack that it wasn't a good idea, but he just wouldn't listen, and the mood he was in I was afraid he would just up and leave anyway. At least this way I was able to come with him and persuade him that we should come here to you. He didn't want to, and it took me ages to persuade him that you might be able to help…'

'To help with what?' Louise demanded, exasperated.

'He wants to find David…his father,' Joss told her simply.

There was a brief silence while brother and sister looked at one another, and then Louise picked up the bread knife and reached for the loaf, telling Joss quietly, 'I think you'd better tell me the whole story.'

Ten minutes later, when she and Joss were sitting opposite one another in the small sitting room, Joss biting appreciatively into the sandwiches she had just made, he told her with a grin, 'Do you know, you sounded just like Mum back there in the kitchen?'

He was growing up fast, Louise recognised as she studied his lanky frame. Once he filled out a bit more he would probably top Max's six-foot frame, and maybe even grow taller than the Chester cousins, the shortest of whom was a good six feet two.

'Mmm…maybe. But don't expect me to listen as indulgently to whatever piece of mischief the pair of you are up to as she would,' Louise warned him, adding, 'You're lucky I was here. I *should* have been at work. If I hadn't had to go back to bed this morning with a migraine…'

'Yes, it was lucky,' Joss agreed, happily munching on another sandwich. 'I *was* a bit worried about how I was going to persuade Jack to hang around if you weren't here. When we hitched a lift from the ferry terminal he was all for going as far as Spain before we stopped.'

'Spain?'

'Mmm…He said that Uncle David once sent Gramps a card from there. Jack saw it when he went round. It was on Gramps' desk, apparently, although he couldn't get a proper look at it, and he says that when he went back to try and read it *properly* it had gone.'

'To read it *properly*? He had no right to be even thinking of doing such a thing,' Louise told him severely, wisely forgetting all the times she had been guilty of attempting to read her school reports upside down on her father's desk.

'Uncle David *is* his father,' Joss pointed out with unanswerable logic.

'Yes. I know,' Louise agreed. She started to frown. What she had initially assumed was just some boyish prank was beginning to take on a much more ominous perspective. So far as she knew, Jack had been happy—very happy—to make his home with her parents. She couldn't remember ever having heard him *mention* his father, never mind expressing a desire to see him. Olivia, she knew, had very ambiguous feelings about both her parents, and had once remarked to her that she found it was much, much easier to think charitably of them now that they were not a part of her day-to-day life.

'I know that Uncle David is Jack's father,' Louise repeated. 'What I *don't* understand is why Jack should have decided he needs to see him so urgently that the pair of you have to set out to do so without first discussing it with Mum and Dad. Has there been a problem at home—a row about something…bedrooms not being kept tidy, homework not being done, that kind of thing?' Louise asked, mentally casting her mind back to her own adolescence and the areas of contention between herself and her parents then that might have led to her taking the same kind of action. Although, to be fair, she couldn't actually remember ever having wanted to leave home.

'No, it's nothing like that.' Joss shook his head, his answer so immediate and so positive that Louise knew he was telling her the truth.

'Then what *is* it?' she asked him.

'Not what, but *who*…' Joss corrected her, explaining, 'It's Max. He was in a foul mood when he was home last time. I think he must have quarrelled with Maddy because I saw her crying in the kitchen. Max had wanted Dad to play golf with him, but Dad said he couldn't because he'd already promised to take Jack fishing. Max probably wanted to borrow money off him anyway—you know what he's like.'

'Go on,' Louise encouraged him when he paused to wolf down the last of the sandwiches. She would have to go out and buy some extra food. There was no way she had enough in her meagre store cupboards to fuel a pair of appetites like her brother's and her cousin's.

'Well, I don't know exactly what Max did say to Jack, but…' Joss pulled a face. 'All Jack would say was that Max had called him a cuckoo in the nest, unwanted by his own parents, and asked Jack if he had any idea how much his school fees were costing Dad. Not that it's—'

'He did *what*? Do the parents know about any of this?' Louise asked her brother acerbically.

Joss shook his head. 'No. I wanted to tell them but Jack wouldn't let me. I think he's a bit afraid that Max might be right and that—'

'Right? Of course he isn't right. Mum and Dad look on Jack as one of us,' Louise protested indignantly. 'They'd no more begrudge the cost of Jack's school fees than they would yours. Less…'

'No, I know that. But you know how Max is about money…'

'Yes. I do know,' Louise agreed. It was an unfathomable mystery to her how she and the rest of her siblings, her cousins, could ever have come from the same gene pool as Max.

'I suppose one of the things that makes Max so horrid is that, deep down inside, he must know that no one likes him,' Joss suggested.

Louise gave him a surprised look.

'If only! If you're trying to drum up my sympathy for Max you're wasting your time—and putting the cart before the horse. The reason no one likes *Max* is because he is the way he is, not the other way around. Look at the way he treats poor Maddy—'

Louise broke off, wondering belatedly if her mother would approve of her discussing such a subject with her younger sibling. But Joss didn't look in the least disconcerted by her comment.

'Aunt Ruth says that Maddy is a bit like a sleeping beauty, and that she doesn't do anything because she hasn't woken up to her own true potential yet. Aunt Ruth says one day she will, and that when she does Max had better watch out,' Joss told her simply.

'Jack says that he doesn't want to be a burden on the parents any longer,' he added, 'and that he intends to find his father and make him repay Dad for everything that he's spent on him. *And* he says that if he can't then he'll have to forget about university and get a job so that he can earn some money to repay them himself…'

'Oh, Joss,' Louise protested emotionally. 'That's the last thing Dad or Mum would want him to do. Why on *earth* didn't he talk to them about this instead of…?'

'He said he couldn't because he knew that they would deny everything,' Joss told her.

'They would deny it because it simply isn't true. They love him just as much as any of us,' Louise protested.

'I *know* that,' Joss agreed. 'But I don't think that Jack does. It must be hard for him, though, because in a way Max was right about one thing. Uncle David and Aunt Tania didn't really want him and Olivia... Not like Mum and Dad want us.'

Louise bowed her head, knowing that there was nothing she could say.

'Different people have different ways of loving,' she informed her brother gruffly. 'Just because Uncle David and Aunt Tania weren't as good at parenting as the folks, that doesn't mean that Olivia and Jack weren't loved and wanted.'

Joss looked steadily at her. 'Aunt Ruth says that having truly loving parents is like having a hundred fairy godmothers—only better!'

Louise gave her brother an old-fashioned look.

'All right, now I know why Jack is so determined to find his father—although how on earth he hopes to do so when Dad's tried without success I *don't* know. But what I don't fully understand is exactly what *you* are doing with him...'

'I couldn't let him go on his own,' he told her simply. 'Anything could have happened to him. So I thought if I could persuade him to stop off here with you, you could...'

'I could *what*?' Louise prompted, firmly ignoring the sharp tug of emotion she had felt as she listened to him. Her brother had enough admiring fans already without her adding herself to the list.

'Well, I told Jack that you might be able to find something out for him...what with Brussels being the headquarters of the European Union and everything, but...'

'I understand what you're saying, Joss,' Louise

agreed. 'But you do know, don't you, that Mum and Dad will *have* to be told where you are, and that they'll insist that the pair of you go straight back to school?'

'Yes, I know.'

Louise looked at him. She had a pretty shrewd suspicion that Joss had known exactly what would happen in stopping off to see her, *and* she suspected that he had deliberately manipulated events so that a full stop would be placed on Jack's expedition before it took them too far from home.

'You stay here with Jack,' she told him. 'I need to go out and do some shopping if I'm going to be able to feed you. When I come back I think a telephone call to home would be in order, don't you?'

Gareth paused in the foyer to the apartment block. He had had to call in to see Pam Carlisle earlier in the day, to check on a couple of points she had raised in the committee, and during the course of their conversation she had happened to mention that Louise had been struck down with a bad migraine. He would be the last person she would feel like seeing. He knew that, especially after this morning. But it hadn't been difficult getting her apartment number from her boss, though he had to admit he had felt a small stab of guilt over the way he had described himself to her as an old friend of the family.

'Oh, really? Louise never said,' she had responded, obviously rather puzzled.

'It probably slipped her mind,' Gareth had responded.

No, *she* wouldn't want to see *him*, but he wanted…*needed* to see her. This morning… He closed his eyes. Damn it, his body still ached unbearably for her, but that was *nothing* compared with the agony of deprivation and loss that was affecting his emotions.

Joss answered the door to his knock, recognising him straight away and welcoming him in.

'Louise's just gone out for reinforcements… food…' he explained with a warm smile.

'I was just going to make a cup of tea for Jack,' he explained as he led the way to Louise's small kitchen. 'He didn't feel very well on the ferry and he's lying down. Can I make one for you?'

Gareth smiled his acceptance, his attention briefly caught by Louise's sketch of Tuscany.

'Louise drew it,' Joss remarked as Gareth studied the sketch of the small shrine on the road to his family's villa.

'Yes,' Gareth agreed, without removing his attention from the sketch.

'She's not the world's best artist,' Joss elaborated. 'Strictly speaking her perspective could be improved upon.'

'Strictly speaking,' Gareth agreed urbanely.

'But of course I expect *you* see it with rather different eyes,' Joss commented simply.

Gareth swung round to look properly at him.

He had got to know Louise's family well during the summer in Tuscany. Joss had been rather younger then, of course, but Gareth had very quickly picked up on the fact that within his family he already had the reputation of being something of a prophet and a seer, and was blessed with, if not exactly foresight, then certainly twenty-twenty emotional vision. Bearing in mind all this, Gareth resisted the temptation to probe more deeply into the reasoning behind his statement and said calmly instead, 'Yes. I believe I do. Are you and Jack planning a long stay with your sister?' he asked conversationally, determinedly changing the subject.

'Er…no… The thing is, she wasn't *really* expecting us at all. She's only got one bedroom…'

Gareth had enough experience from dealing with his nieces and nephews, not to mention his students, to know when someone was being evasive, and it wasn't very long before he had managed to coax the full story out of Joss.

'What makes Jack believe his father might be found in Spain?' he asked him, when he had finished.

Half an hour later, when Louise eventually returned to the apartment, weighed down by several bulging carrier bags, it was to discover that not only had Gareth apparently made himself very much at home in her apartment, but that it had additionally been arranged that her brother and her cousin were going to be staying with him, and not, after all, with her.

'Gareth says he doesn't mind, and since he's got a spare bedroom it seemed the sensible thing to do,' Joss informed her as the three of them deftly relieved her of her heavy shopping.

On the point of informing Gareth in no uncertain terms that there was absolutely no need for him to involve himself in what, after all, was a purely personal family affair, Louise looked across her small and now very crowded sitting room, which seemed to be filled with very big males, and hesitated.

'I promise you, they'll be perfectly safe,' Gareth informed her quietly.

Louise frowned as she looked from his clear, intent gaze to her brother and then her cousin who was now out of bed and looking better, correctly interpreting the message both in Gareth's words and his expression that he knew what was going on.

While she had been rushing round the supermarket snatching up food she had acknowledged that the first thing she needed to do was to speak to her parents— something it would be very difficult for her to do with Jack in the apartment with her. If Gareth took both boys back to *his* apartment with him she would at least have the opportunity to speak openly to her mother and father, and she knew, too, that they would both be safe in Gareth's hands, that she need not worry that he would somehow allow Jack to do a disappearing act on them. In fact, if she was honest, it was almost a relief to have Gareth there, if not to take charge then certainly to play a supporting role in the small mini-drama which had erupted into her life.

A relief to have *Gareth* there? She could feel herself starting to stiffen with inner apprehension at the thought, but oddly, instead of telling him that his help most certainly wasn't needed, she found herself turning instead to Jack and asking him gently, 'Are you feeling okay now?'

'Yes,' he responded. 'It was the ferry and then the jolting of the lorry ride…it made me feel really sick.'

'I told you you shouldn't have eaten that curry,' Joss remarked severely.

'I was hungry,' Jack countered. 'And anyway, *I* wanted to go straight to Spain, not come here first and—'

'Look, why don't we argue out the pros and cons of this later?' Gareth interposed, pushing back his sleeve to look at his watch as he announced, 'It's almost six p.m., and I don't know about everyone else, but I'm getting hungry. What do you say to you two coming round to my flat with me, where you can have a shower and get yourselves sorted out, and then, say at seven o'clock, we'll come back for Louise and the four of us can go out for something to eat?'

Louise opened her mouth to object, to say that she was perfectly capable of making her own arrangements, not just for the boys' welfare but for her own supper as well, but quite unaccountably she discovered that she was closing it again without a word of protest being uttered.

Both boys had brought haversacks with them, and with truly amazing speed Gareth soon had them and their belongings organised and marshalled at the door of her apartment.

'Is seven o'clock all right for you?' he asked Louise as Joss opened the door.

'Yes…it's…it's fine,' she agreed. The close confined space of her small hallway made it impossible for her to move away from him. Was it really only this morning that he had held her in his arms and she had…? Shakily she closed her eyes, unable to bear the burden of the memories she was reliving.

'Are you all right? Is it your migraine…?'

Her *migraine*… How did *he* know about that?

Louise's eyes opened abruptly.

'I'm fine,' she told him curtly. How would it feel to be the woman Gareth loved, the woman he wanted to cherish and protect, to spend his life with, to have his children with? She could feel herself starting to tremble deep down inside, and it was several minutes after they had gone before she felt able to walk to the telephone and dial her parents' telephone number.

Her mother answered the phone almost immediately, and Louise could hear the anxiety in her voice as she did so.

'It's all right, Mum ,' she told her quickly. 'They're here with me.'

'They're *what*?' She could hear the astonishment in her mother's voice. 'But what…? Why…?'

Quietly Louise outlined the details of the story Joss had told her.

'Oh, no,' her mother protested when she had finished. 'I can't believe that Jack could ever think we felt like that. Neither your father nor I have ever…' Her mother stopped speaking for a moment as her emotions overwhelmed her.

'And you say Joss told you that it's because of what Max said to him that Jack has decided that he's being a burden on us…?'

'Well, yes, at least according to Joss. But I was wondering, Mum…' Louise paused and nibbled thoughtfully on her bottom lip. 'He's at a very sensitive age, and no matter how much you and Dad love him you *aren't* his mother and father. There are bound to be times when he wonders about them, when he feels angry and hurt and rejected by what they've done, and perhaps…'

'Yes. I understand what you're saying,' her mother agreed quietly. 'Olivia and Ruth both think that we…that all of us might have been over-compensating to him for the fact that David and Tania aren't here, and I think they're probably right. Thank goodness Joss had the good sense to come to you…'

'Mmm…' Louise agreed, and then added warningly. 'I don't want to sound pessimistic, but it seems to me that this isn't something that's going to go away very easily. All right, *this* time he's here, but…'

'I know what you mean,' her mother acknowledged swiftly. 'And it isn't even a matter of ensuring that he doesn't take off to go looking for his father again. There are quite obviously some very important issues concerning his parents troubling Jack. Issues which he no doubt thinks can only be resolved by discussing them with his father face to face. Right now Jack needs David, and I only wish it was possible for him to have him here. Since he disappeared your father has tried very hard to trace him, but without any success. Your grandfather has received the odd card from him, just telling him that he's safe, but that's all. Where are the boys now, by the way?' her mother asked.

Louise hesitated.

'Well, actually, they're with Gareth Simmonds,' she told her, trying to sound as casual as she could, but horridly aware that her voice sounded just a little too high-pitched and strained. 'You remember him, don't you, Mum? He was in Tuscany when—'

'Gareth? Of *course* I remember him,' her mother agreed. 'Katie said that he was working in Brussels, and I wondered if the two of you would bump into one another.'

'Well, he has an apartment in the same block as me, and since he has a spare bedroom, and I don't, he's offered to put the boys up there. I was glad, really, because it's given me an opportunity to ring you and speak to you without Jack being here. You'll have to let me know what arrangements you want me to make for sending them home—always supposing that Jack can be *persuaded* to go home voluntarily...'

'Mmm. I know that could be tricky. Look, let me speak to your father, and to Olivia as well. After all, Jack is her brother. Can I ring you back later?'

'Yes, that would be a good idea. Gareth and the boys are coming round for me at seven, and we're going out for something to eat.'

'Well, give them both our love, and thank Gareth on our behalf for being so helpful, will you, please, Lou?' her mother asked, before ringing off.

Thank Gareth for being so *helpful*. Oh, yes, and perhaps her mother would like her to fling herself into his arms and give him a big kiss as well...

Involuntarily Louise discovered that she was curling her toes into her shoes, her whole body threatening to tremble with aching longing.

It had been several years now since she had forced herself to make a constructive critical analysis of herself and to recognise certain self-destructive personality traits, chief among which had to be her self-willed stubbornness—the stubbornness which had kept her locked in the belief that her teenage crush on Saul was the kind of love that made them matched soulmates and him the only man she could ever love or want.

By the time she had learned that real love was a far more complex and sometimes less easily recognised emotion it had been too late. The damage had been done.

Now, with the benefit of hindsight, it seemed incredible to her that she had never stopped to question just why she had been so determined, so eager, to go to bed with Gareth. Simply to shed the burden of her virginity? No! Oh, no. Somewhere all along, even though she had refused to recognise or acknowledge it at the time, among the anger, the resentment, the sense of furious anguished pain, there had been something else, something which had not merely been sexual curiosity or even physical attraction.

It hurt her to acknowledge even in the privacy of her own most secret thoughts that a part of her had wanted, needed, ached for Gareth all along—for Gareth himself, not just as a substitute, any substitute, for the intimacy she'd been denied with Saul. And of course Gareth himself must surely, at some level, have recognised that fact—he was, she suspected, far too intelligent not to have done so, which no doubt explained why he had been only too pleased for her to distance herself from him.

After all she had learned from her unwanted pursuit of Saul, she had been proudly determined she was not going to repeat that mistake with Gareth. She was not going to offer her love, *herself*, and be rejected—but oh, how she had ached for him to want her, to love her, and to show and tell her so. Stupid, impossible dreams of course!

'Gareth telephoned...' her mother had said, shortly after their return from Italy, and her heart had stood still while she fought to stop her body's physical reactions from betraying what she was feeling, from giving away any trace of that huge, weakening surge of need and longing that had swept over her.

'Mmm...' her mother had continued. 'He'd heard from Maria that we'd been called back unexpectedly, and he was just ringing to see if everything was all right...'

To see if everything was all right... Not to see if

she was all right, not to speak to her…not to say, to ask… Fiercely she had swallowed back her tears, clenching her hands into tight fists.

Please God, not again…not a second time. This time she was not going to make a fool of herself by showing her feelings… This time…this time she was a woman, Louise had recognised painfully. This time she was not going to cry for a man who didn't want her, like a child crying for a denied need. This time she wasn't even going to let herself acknowledge her feelings. What feelings? She had no feelings—at least not where Gareth Simmonds was concerned. Why should she have? After all, he had no feelings for her!

'Anyone want more coffee?'

To Louise's initial chagrin, it had been Gareth who proved to be the more knowledgeable about the city's restaurants, despite the fact that she had lived there for much longer.

'I'm only going on what I've been told,' he had volunteered when Louise hadn't quite been able to conceal her reaction to his expertise.

The square where they had eaten was surrounded by streets on which fish vendors and restaurants displayed their wares on open stalls.

Predictably, it had been the more visually unappealing species of fish—to Louise's eye at least—which had caught the boys' enthusiastic attention.

'Ugh…it looks horrid,' Louise had objected when Joss had drawn her attention to a particularly vicious-looking glassy-eyed monster.

'Mmm… I don't know whether or not it's a sign of getting old, but I must say that these days I prefer not to be able to recognise the food on my plate in its original life form,' Gareth had calmly responded to the boys when they had derided her for her squeamishness. But Louise had been ruefully amused to notice that neither of the boys had taken the restaurateur up on his offer to go and choose their fish as they swam in their tanks.

The streets around the square were busy and bustling, creating an almost holiday-like atmosphere— which must be the reason she was feeling so dangerously happy, Louise decided as both boys declared themselves satisfactorily full in response to Gareth's question.

The ambience of the square was one of relaxed enjoyment and a warmth that one might more readily have associated with Paris rather than Brussels, with its unfairly 'staid burgher' reputation. Because of its present-day association with the Common Market and modern politics, one sometimes forgot that Brussels was a city with a long and distinguished history.

Louise also shook her head in response to Gareth's offer of more coffee. The evening had gone surprisingly well. It had amazed and, yes, if she was honest, piqued her just a little to see how quickly Gareth had re-established a very strong rapport with both her brother and her cousin.

Of the four of them she was probably the one who felt the most self-conscious and wary, she recognised, and that was because… She bent down to reach for her purse, determined to ensure that she paid for her own and the boys' meal.

There had been moments during the evening when she had found herself joining in with the boys' laughter as Gareth told them a particularly funny story about his own family, but her laughter had quickly been replaced by a feeling of envious sadness. *She* would never be a part of his life. *She* would never be special to him, as his sisters and his nieces and nephews so obviously were. He would *never* love her the way he loved them; his eyes would *never* light up warmly when he spoke of her, thought of her. If he had cared he would never have ignored what had happened between them—and ignored her!

'Well, if everyone's ready, I think we'd better be going,' Gareth announced as he glanced at his watch.

To Louise's relief he made no objection to her statement that she intended to pay their bill.

Jack, she was relieved to see, was looking much happier than he had done at the beginning of the evening. Louise ached to be able to reassure him that whatever Max had said to him, however hurtful it must have been, could never be a true reflection of what the other members of their family felt, but she could sense that he would close up on her if she did, and that he was still feeling too sensitive for the subject to be easily broached. And besides, she guessed intuitively, it wasn't so much *her* reassurance he craved and needed, nor even that of her parents, but rather that of his own parents, and most especially his father.

As they left the restaurant Louise discovered that the boys were walking ahead of her while Gareth fell into step beside her. Instinctively she started to walk a little bit faster, but Gareth kept pace with her. In her haste to make sure that she wasn't left on her own with him, she almost stumbled.

Immediately Gareth's hand shot out to steady her, his body offering a bulwark for her to lean into while she got her balance. Weakly Louise closed her eyes.

The evening air was heavy with the scent of the traffic and the city, but stronger by far was her awareness of the sensual warmth of Gareth's body, its scent dizzying her, robbing her of the ability to fight her desire to move closer to him, her illusion that he *wanted* her to move closer.

To her chagrin she discovered that her hand was resting against his chest. No, *clinging* almost to his jacket, she recognised, her head inclining helplessly towards his shoulder.

'Are you all right? Your migraine hasn't come back, has it?' she heard him asking her, his voice almost short and terse, as though… As though he was uncomfortable with the way she was practically leaning against him, Louise decided. But when she struggled to pull herself away he wouldn't let her. The boys had stopped several yards ahead of them to study a sculpture in the centre of the small square they were walking through, their faces absorbed.

'It must have been a shock for you to have the pair of them turn up on your doorstep so unexpectedly,' she heard Gareth saying to her as she weakly allowed herself to relax back into the warmth of his body, and the arm he had placed so securely around her. 'I must say I think you've handled the situation very well.'

'Er…thanks for stepping in the way you did,' Louise responded. 'My parents said to give you their thanks as well, by the way. I spoke to my mother after you'd gone. She's going to ring me back later to discuss what arrangements they're going to make to get the boys home…' She paused, and looked worriedly across at her brother and her cousin.

'Has…? Did…? Jack wants to find his father… and—'

'Yes, I know.' Gareth interrupted her gently. 'I take it that no one does know where he is?'

'Dad's tried to find him,' Louise told him, 'but without any success. Oh, I could wring Max's neck. He must have *known* how upset Jack would be by what he said. He really is the most selfish, thoughtless…'

'Unlike the rest of his family, who, from what *I've* seen of them, are extremely caring and concerned for one another,' Gareth told her.

It was impossible for her to see his expression properly now that it was dark, but Louise could hear an intensity of emotion in his voice that surprised her.

Gareth looked down at the top of her head. Protecting one another obviously came easily and naturally to most members of the Crighton family.

He could still remember how determined to protect her twin her sister Katie had been, when she had explained to him just why Louise was skipping so many lectures.

'Louise…about this morning…'

Immediately he could feel her tensing, and starting to withdraw from him.

'I don't want to talk about it,' she told him quickly. 'I…it shouldn't have happened. I…'

Cursing himself under his breath, Gareth immediately let her go. What a fool he was. Just because for a few moments she had relaxed in his arms, that didn't mean… Mind you, he derided himself inwardly, it was probably just as well she *had* put some distance between them. Another few seconds of standing close to her like that and she would surely have discovered exactly what kind of effect she was having on him.

He saw the way she was studying Joss and Jack and, guessing what she was thinking, tried to comfort her.

'Try not to worry,' he advised her. 'I'm sure your parents will find some way to reassure him.'

'I hope so,' she agreed. 'But they can't...they aren't... I was thinking earlier, when we were in the restaurant...trying to imagine how *I* would feel if I were Jack. It must be hard for him, and I can understand *why* he would want to find Uncle David.'

'Yes,' Gareth agreed quietly, 'but there are other, more effective ways of doing so than giving up his studies and hitch-hiking all over Europe...as I'm sure your father will be able to explain to him.'

It was an odd and very disconcerting experience to have Gareth trying to comfort her instead of criticising her. Somehow it had been a lot easier to try to cope with her feelings when they were antagonists.

At Gareth's insistence he and the boys saw her back to her own apartment, and Gareth even insisted that she open the door and go inside before they left her.

Impulsively Louise turned to hug first her brother and then Jack.

'Thanks for everything, Lou,' he told her gruffly, returning her hug with teenage embarrassment.

'There's nothing to thank me for,' Louise told him, ruffling his hair. 'You're my...you're family.'

Quickly blinking back the tears she knew he would be embarrassed to see, she turned to thank Gareth once again for his help, and then gasped back a small sound of shock, as instead of keeping his distance from her, he was actually taking her in his arms and hugging her just as fiercely as Jack had done. But the sensations she felt in *Gareth's* arms were a world apart from those she had experienced when hugging her cousin.

'Gareth—' she started to protest, but he was already dropping a light kiss on her forehead, and then a far less light, breathtakingly intimate and far too brief one on her startled parted lips.

'Goodnight,' he whispered against her mouth. 'Sleep well and don't worry… They'll both be safe with me and I'll bring them over in the morning.'

He had turned to go, marshalling the boys in front of him, before she could say or do anything.

Her hands, she discovered as she locked and barred the door after them, were trembling slightly, and her heart was racing as though she had just sprinted a hundred metres.

Why had he kissed her like that? Simply as an automatic reaction following the boys' example? But *his* kiss had not been… His kiss. His *kiss*. She closed her eyes and felt her face start to burn.

In the sitting room her telephone had started to ring. Quickly she pushed the memory of Gareth and the unexpected, heart-jerking, sweet tenderness of his brief kiss out of her mind, and went to answer its summons.

CHAPTER EIGHT

'LOU, it's me,' Louise heard Olivia announce herself. 'Your mother's told me what's happened. Where are the boys now? Are they…?'

'Gareth has taken them back to his flat with him for the night. I don't know whether or not Mum mentioned to you that he's working here in Brussels now, and—'

'Yes, yes, she did.' Olivia interrupted her quickly. Louise knew that Olivia would have remembered Gareth from Tuscany, and guessed that her cousin was far more anxious to talk about her brother than to discuss past acquaintanceships. She knew that she was right when Olivia cut across her to ask her worriedly, 'Lou, how is Jack? Is he…?'

'He *seems* fine,' Louise told her cautiously. 'He was sick after the travelling, but he's over that now, and he seemed chirpy enough this evening. The four of us went out for a meal—my apartment isn't really equipped for any serious cooking, but…' She hesitated.

'But what?' Olivia pressed her.

'Well, he *seems* okay, Livvy, but, easy as it would be to put all the blame for his upset on Max's shoulders, I can't help thinking that there's more to the situation than that. Jack is a sensible enough boy. He knows how Max is, and he knows as well how much my parents love him. I can't help wondering if this desire to find your father is perhaps something he's been brooding on in secret for some time.'

'You've just put into words exactly what *I've* been thinking,' Olivia agreed. 'I feel *so* guilty, Lou. I should have seen…*guessed*. But I've been so tied up in my own life, the girls and Caspar. And Jack seemed so happy, and well adjusted to the fact that Dad and Mum were no longer on the scene, that I'm afraid I just assumed that he felt the same way about the situation as I do. But of course I was an adult when it all happened. Jack was only a child.'

Louise knew, without her cousin having to explain, what she meant by 'when it all happened'. She was referring to the disappearance of her father.

Louise's own father had tried to trace him, and so too had Olivia and Jack's mother, who was now divorced from him and remarried.

'Mmm… I was thinking about…everything…this evening while we were out,' Louise told her. 'Do you think, Livvy, that by trying to protect Jack from the truth we've perhaps made the situation more difficult for him to cope with? He's an intelligent boy, and from what Joss has let slip I get the impression that the pair of them have a pretty good idea of what actually happened. Of course your father's disappearance is bound to have left Jack with an awful lot of unanswered questions—and an increasing number of them, perhaps, as he grows up. After all, looking at it from Jack's point of view, he perhaps feels that when your father disappeared he took with him the answers…'

'You're very perceptive, Lou,' Olivia told her. 'I must admit I hadn't put myself in Jack's shoes and tried to see things from his point of view. When Dad took off, to be blunt, I was so shocked and traumatised by the discovery that he had virtually stolen someone else's money that I was glad he'd disappeared. I don't know *how* I would have dealt with the situation if he hadn't… By going he relieved me of the necessity of having to do anything other than let your father and Aunt Ruth clear up the mess that he had left behind.'

'I think you're being too hard on yourself, Livvy,' Louise protested. 'I don't know how I would have coped in your shoes. I have to admit that I can't help sympathising with Jack, though. I know that *this* time we've managed to nip his plans in the bud, but—'

'But what happens next?' Olivia interrupted her wryly. 'That's what's been worrying me…'

'Well, I've had a thought,' Louise began hesitantly. 'And it *is* only a thought, that's all…'

'Go on,' Olivia commanded.

'Well, perhaps if Jack felt less isolated, if my father could involve him in his own enquiries to try and locate your father… If Jack could be *involved*, somehow, that might at least stop him from bunking off school and help him to feel he has some say, some control in things.'

'I hear what you're saying,' Olivia told her. 'And, yes, I think you could be right. I'll talk to your father about it, *and* to Jack. Which reminds me. The reason I'm ringing is to tell you that Saul will be flying over to collect both boys. He was due to come over on business anyway, apparently, and he says it's no trouble for him to bring Joss and Jack back with him.'

'What…when will he be arriving?' Louise asked her quietly.

'He's advanced his meeting and he's leaving first thing in the morning; he says his business should be over by mid-afternoon. Look, I must go; I can hear Alex crying. Thanks again, Lou…I'm *so* grateful to you. It was such a shock when your mother rang to tell me what had happened.'

'I know what you mean.'

Olivia paused. 'Lou, it won't be a *problem*, Saul coming to collect the boys, will it?' she asked tentatively.

'Not in the least,' Louise replied promptly and truthfully—meaning it.

'No…that's what Tullah said,' Olivia agreed after another small pause, and Louise knew that it was a measure of how far she had come that she felt not the least degree of chagrin or resentment at the thought of her cousin and Saul's wife discussing her.

Another measure of her maturity, she acknowledged with far less pleasure, was that she did not have the least inclination to confide to Olivia just *why* it was that she knew so positively that her feelings for Saul were no more than those of a cousin—and had been for a very long time. Since Tuscany, in fact…

Louise opened her eyes abruptly. She had been asleep, dreaming about Gareth. In her dream she had been trying to reach out towards him, to hold him and kiss him, but every time she'd tried to do so he'd moved away from her.

A glance at her alarm clock warned her that it would soon be time for her to get up. Not that she particularly *wanted* to go back to sleep. Not if she was going to have *those* kind of dreams.

After a quick breakfast, she rang her boss at home, explaining to her what had happened and asking if

she might have the day off to look after the boys until
Saul arrived to collect them.

'By all means,' Pam Carlisle assured her. 'How's
the migraine, by the way?'

'Gone,' Louise told her. 'Fortunately.'

After she had finished talking to Pam she cleared
away her breakfast things, wondering what time
Gareth would bring the boys round, and what she was
going to do with them until Saul arrived.

She had just finished tidying up the kitchen when
she heard Gareth and the boys arrive. Going to the
door to let them in, she was relieved to see that Jack
was smiling.

'Thank you for giving them a bed for the night,'
she said to Gareth as he followed them into her flat.

'I've been on the phone to the parents,' she informed both boys as she ushered them into her living
room, a little disconcerted to realise that instead of
leaving Gareth had closed the door and joined them.
'And Saul will be calling round later to take you both
home.'

'Saul?' All three of them repeated his name with
varying degrees of emotion, but it was Gareth's quick,
sharp demand that overrode the other voices as they
made eye contact and she saw the critical condemnation in his look.

She could see that Jack was beginning to look
slightly uneasy, and quickly she reassured him.

'It's all right Jack,' she told him. 'Mum and Dad
do understand. You should have told them that you
wanted to find your father,' she pointed out gently to
him, and when she saw that he might still be determined to head off for Spain, added, 'And maybe Dad
has been a little at fault in neglecting to keep you

informed of…things. He *has* tried to find your father, you know, and—'

'Is it true that Dad will have to go to prison if he comes back to England?' Jack blurted out, his face going scarlet as he focused anxiously on Louise.

'Who on earth told you that?' Louise asked him, shocked.

Jack shook his head.

'No one…at least not in so many words. But Max…'

'Max is a trouble-maker. He's like—'

'Like my father,' Jack interrupted her.

Louise bit her lip in consternation. Gareth was still there and showed no sign of planning to leave, but this was not a conversation she particularly wanted to have with him as an observer—a critical observer, no doubt, she decided irritably.

'So far as I know, Jack, your father *has* never been, *was* never motivated by malice, which I have to be honest and admit Max very often is. But it's true that your father and Max do share certain personality traits…'

'Uncle Jon once told me that the reason Dad was the way he was is because…because Gramps spoiled him…' Jack told her uncertainly.

'Gramps *did* spoil him,' Louise agreed. '*And* he has spoiled Max too…given him…given them both the impression that they have the right to put themselves first.'

'Uncle Jon told me as well that no one should blame Dad completely, because Gramps' expectations of him had put him under a lot of pressure…'

'Yes, Gramps does have very, very high expectations of his favourites,' Louise agreed dryly.

'Dad can't have loved *us* very much, me and Livvy, can he?' Jack asked her huskily. 'Not and have done what he did. Uncle Jon would *never* disappear and leave all of you…'

'I'm sure that he *does* love you, Jack,' Louise contradicted him. 'The fact that he disappeared isn't a reflection on you, you know, and it *certainly* doesn't mean he doesn't *love* you. In fact, I expect that one of the reasons he left was because he *does* love you both, very, very much.'

She saw the look that Jack was giving her, and explained quietly, 'By leaving, he probably thought that he was helping to protect you.'

'Do you really think so?' Jack questioned her uncertainly.

'I'm sure of it,' Louise confirmed, sure now that Jack would return to Haslewich, and the loving family awaiting him.

'What time's Saul arriving?' Joss interrupted.

'He has some business, which will take him until after lunch, so I doubt that he will be here until late afternoon,' Louise informed him. 'Is there anything that either of you would like to see or do while you're here? I've taken the day off work so…'

'Gareth's going to take us to this place where we can surf the net,' Joss informed her excitedly.

Louise opened her mouth to point out that Gareth had no right to make any such arrangements without checking with her first that it was all right, and then closed it again.

'You can come with us if you want to. Can't she, Gareth?' Joss added.

'Gee, thanks,' Louise drawled as she looked across at Gareth, half expecting to see him sharing her amusement that Joss should think she might consider this a high treat.

But instead of smiling Gareth was frowning, his voice curt and terse as he demanded, 'I take it it was *your* idea that Saul should be the one to come for the boys?'

Louise looked at him.

'No, as a matter of fact, it wasn't—' she began.

But before she could finish he cut across her and said sarcastically, 'I see. So it was just a fortunate coincidence, was it?'

Louise looked across to where Joss and Jack were too deep in a highly technical discussion about some new computer technology to be aware of what was going on between Gareth and herself.

'I don't know *what* you're trying to imply,' she began in a heated, low-pitched voice, 'but for your information Saul is—'

'I know *exactly* what Saul is to you,' Gareth interrupted her savagely. 'My God, haven't you—?'

He stopped abruptly as Joss looked across at them both questioningly.

'I'd better get my coat,' Louise informed Gareth. 'How far is this place? Can we walk, or…?'

'No. I'll drive us there in my car,' Gareth informed her brusquely.

'If you've both finished, I think we ought to be heading back to the flat,' Louise informed Joss and Jack as she glanced quickly at her watch. Gareth had insisted on taking them for a late lunch at a small trattoria close to where they had spent the morning, and now, as they all stood up, Louise gave him a dismissive smile and told him, 'There's no need for you to drive us back. I'll get a taxi.'

All day she had been conscious of a very definite brooding hostility in his attitude towards her, and despite her determination not to let either him or the boys see how much it was affecting her the strain was beginning to take its toll.

She already knew, of course, that he neither liked nor approved of her, but the contempt she could feel emanating from him today had brought home to her just how very vulnerable she was where he was concerned.

'We can't go home without going to Gareth's flat to collect our stuff,' Joss reminded her practically.

Louise's heart sank. But he was right, of course. However, when they arrived at the apartment block, a little to Louise's consternation they discovered that Saul was already waiting in the foyer for them.

'Saul, I'm so sorry,' she apologised. 'I didn't think you'd be here until later.'

'Don't worry,' Saul reassured her as he smiled at her, and then looked thoughtfully towards Gareth. 'My business was completed earlier than I expected.'

'You must be Gareth.' Saul smiled, extending his hand towards the other man. 'I'm Saul Crighton, Louise's cousin...'

'And ours,' Joss added.

'Yes, I know,' Gareth acknowledged tersely, ignoring Saul's outstretched hand and turning instead to the two boys, reminding them, 'Your things are still in my apartment. I'll—'

'Oh, yes. You'd better go with Gareth now and get them,' Louise interrupted him quickly, seizing the opportunity to ensure that she had a few moments of privacy with Saul to put him fully in the picture just in case Olivia hadn't already done so.

Over the boys' heads Gareth sent her a corrosively contemptuous look. Her face burning, as much with unhappiness as anger, Louise looked away from him.

'Not exactly the friendly type, is he?' Saul commented dryly once he and Louise were on their own.

'You mean Gareth?' Louise asked, fumbling with the key as she started to unlock her apartment door. 'It's my fault… He… I…'

She stopped.

'He thinks I'm trying to manipulate the situation so that I can have some time on my own with you,' she told Saul with painful honesty as she pushed open her apartment door and beckoned to him to follow her inside.

'He…he was my tutor that time when…the time of the masked ball, and…' She stopped. 'In a way he's right I *did* want to have some time on my own with you, but not for the reason he suspects. I wanted to have a private word with you about Jack, Saul. I don't know how much Livvy has told you.'

'Not much at all…only that Jack has taken it into his head that he wants to find David.'

'Yes, that's right, he does. I've tried to talk to him, but I'm worried about him, and I wondered if perhaps you… He *needs* someone to confide in, someone he can talk to who he can trust.'

'I'll do my best,' Saul promised her gravely.

'He thinks his father didn't love him.'

Saul was starting to frown, and to her chagrin Louise suddenly felt her eyes fill with tears.

When he saw them Saul's frown deepened with concern.

'Lou…' he began. But she shook her head trying to smile as she told him huskily, 'Saul, I'm sorry… It's just… I can't understand why I'm such a fool. You'd think after the lessons I learned through having that fearsome crush on you that I'd know better than to risk loving a man who doesn't love me back. But…'

'A man who doesn't love you back… Are we talking about your extremely unfriendly friend and ex-tutor Gareth Simmonds, here?' Saul asked her dryly.

Louise shook her head, but it was no use; the strain of the last twenty-four hours was having its effect on her, and the next thing she knew she was in Saul's arms, her head pressed firmly against his shoulder while he comforted her in much the same way he had done many years ago, when she had still been a child suffering from the pain of a scraped knee. But broken skin could in no way be compared to the agony of a broken heart, and she wasn't a child any more but a woman, Louise reminded herself.

'I'm being an idiot. I'm sorry,' she apologised, blowing her nose firmly on the handkerchief he proffered as she gave him a frail smile.

She was still smiling up at him, and still held securely in his arms, several seconds later as the sitting-room door burst open and Joss and Jack, followed by Gareth, came in.

The sight of Louise in Saul's arms was plainly of no interest to either Joss or Jack, both of whom, in their different ways, were anticipating their return journey to Britain in Saul's charge with a certain amount of trepidation.

Gareth, though, reacted completely differently, coming to an abrupt halt only feet away from them and saying with open contempt, 'I'm sorry if we're interrupting something…private.'

Automatically Louise started to move away from Saul, but to her consternation, instead of letting her go, Saul kept a firm hold on her arm, his other hand giving her a small warning pinch out of Gareth's sight as he countered dangerously, 'Yes, so am I.' He turned his back on Gareth, so that his view of Louise's face was blocked as he told her tenderly, 'I meant what I said the last time we met, you know. You'll always be very…special to me, Lou…'

Louise gawped at him. What on earth was Saul trying to do? He must know the interpretation that Gareth would put on his comments after what she had just told him, and now here he was, quite deliberately, or so it seemed, adding some volatile and combustible material to the flames fuelling Gareth's suspicions.

'Come on, you two,' he instructed the boys, in a much firmer tone of voice, before turning to Gareth and telling him formally, 'It seems I owe you a debt of thanks…' And then, to Louise's bemusement, he lifted her hand to his mouth and gently kissed her fingers, before very firmly and expertly drawing her into his arms and holding her there intimately for a few long seconds.

Louise didn't offer to go down to the foyer to see Saul and the boys off; her legs felt as though they wouldn't carry her as far as her own front door, never mind the foyer.

What on *earth* had got into Saul to make him behave so…so outrageously? It must have been as obvious to him as it had to her that Gareth was not in the least amused by his behaviour. Shakily she closed her eyes and put her hand on the back of her small sofa to steady herself as the apartment door banged shut behind them all.

CHAPTER NINE

'HAVE you gone completely out of your mind? He's a married man, for God's sake, and no matter how much he might feel like having a bit of sex on the side with you, right now I'll bet that's *all* he's got on his mind. Have you stopped to *think* that if he really wanted you, if he *really* cared…if he *really* had the least degree of respect or affection for you, he would never…?'

'Gareth.' Weakly Louise opened her eyes. 'I thought you'd gone. What…?'

'For God's sake, Louise. He *might* be your cousin…you *might* still love him, but—'

Louise had had enough—more than enough.

'No, I don't,' she corrected Gareth flatly. 'Or at least I don't love him in the way that *you're* trying to imply. And even if I did…' She pushed her hand tiredly into her hair.

'If you don't love him then what the hell were you doing in his arms back there?' Gareth demanded furiously.

'He was just holding me…comforting me…' Louise told him wearily.

'Comforting you? Oh, my God, now I've heard everything—'

'That's right,' Louise interrupted him. 'You *have*. Or at least you've heard all you *are* going to hear and if you want the truth, Gareth, what I've *heard* is too much…much too much from *you*. I want you to

173

leave,' she told him. 'You have to leave,' she added with quiet desperation. 'You have to leave, Gareth, because if you don't…'

She stopped, unable to say any more as one bright tear and then another filled her eyes and splashed down onto the hand she had lifted to wipe it away.

'Oh, God, Louise, how *can* you love a man who…?'

'Who doesn't love *me*?' Louise supplied for him, when, instead of obeying her command, Gareth took a determined step towards her.

'A man who isn't *worthy* of your love,' Gareth corrected her gruffly. 'I know how you feel about me, Lou. I know how much you dislike and resent me…'

He stopped as Louise gave a small strangled yelp of mingled pain and laughter deep in her throat.

'No, you don't,' she told him bravely. 'You don't know how I feel at all…because if you did… Gareth, please, I just can't *cope* with this. You *have* to leave,' she begged him.

But inexplicably, instead of obeying her, he was suddenly reaching out for her and taking hold of her and telling her hoarsely, 'I may not know how *you* feel, Lou, but I certainly know how *I* feel, and how I've felt for one hell of a long time. It's tearing me apart, thinking about you wasting your love, your life, on someone who…on a man who… I *know* he's your cousin but…'

'For the last time, Saul is *not* the man I love,' Louise told him, her self-control finally deserting her. 'You are that man, Gareth. *You* are the man I love, the only man I have *ever* properly loved, and the only man I am *ever* likely to properly love. The reason Saul was holding me in his arms when you and the boys walked in was because I had just been telling him about you, and—'

'Gareth! Gareth! Let go of me,' Louise demanded breathlessly as she lifted her hands to push him firmly away from her.

But it was too late, and besides, Gareth quite obviously had absolutely no intention whatsoever of letting her go. Instead he was demanding thickly, 'Say that again… You love *me*…? When…? How long…? Why…?' he began, and then stopped, closing his eyes and taking deep breaths before muttering something under his breath that Louise couldn't quite catch.

When he opened his eyes Louise felt her heart lurch dangerously against her chest wall as she saw the way he was looking at her.

'We can *talk* later,' Gareth informed her softly, barely breathing the words so that she automatically had to move even closer to him to hear what he was saying.

'Right now there's something far more important I need to do…far more important and far, far more pleasurable…'

'Gareth…' Louise protested weakly, but it was too late. His mouth was already moving over hers and she was responding to him, her body melting against his as his mouth moved more determinedly over hers, his tongue tracing the shape of her lips and then gently probing them apart.

'No,' Louise whispered, but the word was more a soft sigh of pleasure than any kind of real denial.

It was the longest, sweetest, most loving, cherishing kiss she had ever known, Louise decided dreamily as Gareth continued to caress her lips, his hand cupping her face, stroking her skin, his heartbeat thudding

fiercely beneath the hand she had originally lifted to
fend him off and which had now stayed to curl possessively into the front of his shirt. She felt dizzy,
light-headed almost, with a mixture of desire and disbelief, unable to comprehend properly that this was
actually happening, that *she* was *here* in Gareth's
arms, that *he* was holding her, kissing her, loving her,
as though he actually meant it.

'Have you any idea just how much I've been wanting to do this?' he was whispering against her mouth.
'How much I've *ached* to touch you…kiss you…*love*
you, Louise?'

'I thought you despised me…disliked me,' she
whispered back.

'Despised *myself*, disliked *myself*, yes. But *never*
you,' Gareth groaned. 'When I came to the villa that
morning…the morning after and found that you'd all
left…I thought at first that it was because…that
I'd…that you'd been so affected by what had happened, that your parents… But then Maria told me
that there was some problem at home.'

'I *was* affected by what…what we did. But not in
the way you mean,' Louise told him truthfully, shivering in delicious pleasure as his lips started to caress
the soft curve of her throat.

'I knew that I'd…enjoyed…what happened, and
that you'd made me feel things…do things…I'd no
idea I could feel or do. But it wasn't until the following Christmas that I realised what had happened to
me. I'd told myself that I hated you, that I was glad
you weren't my tutor any longer and that there was
no contact between us. I even managed to persuade
myself that I was still in love with Saul, that I had

simply transferred what I felt for him into a physical response to you…'

'Well, you certainly had *me* convinced,' Gareth interrupted her hoarsely. 'You called out his name when I…'

'I didn't even know I had…it must have been a protective reflex,' Louise told him softly, achingly. 'A way of trying to pretend to myself that you weren't…that I wasn't…' She stopped, and her eyes widened in fierce response as he ran his fingertip around the neckline of her top and her breasts immediately started to ache wantonly for his touch.

'Last time, when I went home, Saul and Tullah were both there. Everyone was tiptoeing around me as though I was an unexploded bomb. I admit I had been dreading seeing them myself, but when I did…' She looked up into his eyes. 'He was just Saul again,' she told him simply. 'Just my cousin. There was *nothing* else, and I couldn't really understand how I had ever thought…felt…wanted…

'Ever since Tuscany I have been having these dreams about you… Dreams when I…we… I thought it was simply because you were the one who…' She paused, flushing, and then laughing as she shook her head. 'I was so naive…naive and stubborn. I didn't *want* to admit the truth to myself, but I looked at Saul and I ached for you so badly…wanted you so badly…'

As her eyes filled with tears at the memory of the shocking fierceness of the pain, Gareth's eyes darkened in protective love.

'I was thinking about *you* as well,' he assured her. 'Wondering what you were doing…and who you were with…wishing it was me and wishing to hell that I hadn't been stupid enough to give way to feelings that I knew then were dangerous…'

'But you didn't *love* me when we…when you… You didn't *love* me. Not then,' Louise protested.

Gareth looked steadily at her.

'You're right. You *were* naive,' he told her huskily. 'Of course I damned well loved you. You don't think for a single solitary moment that I would actually have…that a man who didn't love…? You couldn't really have believed I could be so unprincipled as to…?'

'I thought you did it because you were angry with me,' Louise told him simply. 'I thought it must be a male reaction thing.'

'"A male reaction thing."' Gareth laughed huskily and closed his eyes. 'Oh, it was certainly that, all right,' he assured her. 'A *very* male reaction thing. The kind of male reaction thing that happens when a male, a *man*, falls deeply and passionately in love.

'I could have killed you when you told me that you were planning to lose your virginity with Giovanni. Do you know that?' he asked her lovingly.

'Well, you certainly made it plain that you didn't think it was a very good idea,' Louise agreed demurely. '*When* did you fall in love with me…?'

'It started one afternoon in my rooms. You were arguing passionately about something. I can't remember what. I looked at you and suddenly…' He paused and shook his head. 'It just happened. I told myself not to be a fool. I even reminded myself of all the reasons why it wouldn't work. And then you started skipping lectures, getting Katie to sit in for you instead…'

'Katie *said* you knew about that.'

'Of course I knew,' he told her lovingly, adding wryly, 'And so, too, did my body. It never reacted to Katie the way it did to you. And then, when I found out that you were in love with someone else…' He paused and shook his head. 'That day when I came to your room and found you there half-drunk…'

'I felt so humiliated that you'd seen me like that,' Louise whispered. 'And then you turned up in Tuscany…'

'I wasn't too pleased either. I'd gone there hoping to get things in perspective, to get my emotions under control, and instead…'

'Why didn't you *say* something…tell me how you felt?' Louise asked him.

'How *could* I when you'd already told me that the only man you could ever love was your precious Saul?'

'I knew in Tuscany that it was just a silly crush that had burned itself out, but I'd made such a big drama out of it that I couldn't bring myself to let it go. And then you took me to bed and I realised that you were right…that I had just been a girl…but after our afternoon together I woke up a woman, and it was as a woman that I began to realise that I loved you,' Louise told him softly.

'I couldn't repeat all the mistakes I'd made with Saul…I couldn't embarrass you and humiliate myself by putting you through all the stupid things I'd done to try and get Saul's attention—I didn't even *want* to. I could see just how ridiculous…how selfish and, yes, childish in many ways my behaviour had been. I knew then how different real adult love was from my teen-age fantasy of what love was, which I had woven around my feelings for Saul.

I'd believed that if I just tried hard enough I could *make* Saul love me. With you… With you I *knew* that the only way your love could be mine was if you gave it to me freely, and I knew you would never do that…'

'You knew wrong, then, because you already had it,' Gareth whispered rawly to her. 'Oh, Lou, when I think of the time we've wasted, the days, the years, the nights we've spent apart when we could have been together.'

'Especially the nights,' Louise agreed wickedly, her mouth curling up at the corners, but she still blushed a little bit as she saw the way he was looking at her.

'It's been a long time,' he told her huskily. 'And there hasn't been anyone else for me since then, Louise…'

'There hasn't been anyone else for me either,' Louise told him a little shyly, adding shakily, 'What you…what we did…the way I felt, was so…so good…so right…that I couldn't…I didn't… I was afraid of spoiling the memory of it, because I knew no one else could ever make me feel the way you had done.'

'No one else?' Gareth quizzed her gently. 'Not even Jean Claude…?'

Louise burst out laughing.

'No one else,' she confided. 'And *especially* not Jean Claude…'

'Gareth, what is it? What are you doing?' she demanded as he suddenly turned away from her and reached for the telephone, quickly pushing the buttons and wrapping his free arm around her to stop her from moving away from him as he started to speak into the receiver.

'Paul, it's Gareth Simmonds here. Look, I'm not going to be around for the next few days—an urgent family matter… Yes… Well, the committee doesn't have another meeting until next month, I know… Can you check through my diary and cancel all my appointments for the next week, please? Oh, and by the way, can you ring the airport and book me two seats on the first available flight for Pisa? You can ring me back on this number,' he added quickly, giving Louise's telephone number and then replacing the receiver before she could say a word.

'Tuscany,' she said, her eyes starting to shine.

'Tuscany,' he agreed.

'But Pam…'

'No buts. Pam will be able to manage without you for a couple of days.' Gareth informed her masterfully, and then groaned as he added ruefully, 'I'm not quite sure how *I'm* going to manage to keep my hands off you until we reach the villa… You do realise, don't you, that it's a good two-hour drive from the airport and—?'

'The *villa*… But it might not be empty, and you could—'

'If it isn't empty then I shall bribe whoever is staying there to move out,' Gareth informed her determinedly. 'And besides…*my* family's villa *is* empty at the moment. It might not be quite the same—'

'*Your* family's villa? With the pool…' Louise interrupted him. 'The pool where I saw you swimming that day the Fiat broke down…?'

'Uh-huh…the very same one.'

Louise closed her eyes and gave a small, femininely ecstatic sigh.

'I want to go *there*,' she told him happily. 'Oh, yes,

I want to go *there*, Gareth. I want it to be *there*…
please…'

'Of course… But why…?'

A small smile curved her mouth as, leaning forward, she whispered to him, 'Because that's where I realised for the first time just what a very, very sexy man you are, and that's where, when I saw you getting out of the pool in those trunks, I couldn't help wondering just how you'd look without them, and that's where…'

'Okay, I think I get your drift,' Gareth told her softly.

'Well…?' Gareth asked Louise lazily, smiling sexily at her as he leaned over her sun lounger to kiss her awake.

'Well, what?' she asked him, sitting up and taking the drink he had brought her.

They had arrived at the villa in the early hours of the previous morning. Louise had wanted to go straight to bed, but Gareth had demurred.

'Let's wait until this afternoon,' he had suggested meaningfully, and, her stomach knotting with sharp, sensual excitement, Louise had agreed.

It…*he*…had been worth waiting for…*more* than worth waiting for, and today her body still felt relaxed and softly heavy with sensual satisfaction.

'Well, do I look just as good without my shorts as you hoped?' Gareth teased her.

Louise laughed.

Last night Gareth had persuaded her to go skinny-dipping with him, and afterwards they had made love beside the pool in a tangle of damp limbs and soft, warm towels.

'Oh, every bit as good…' she confirmed. 'But you can always prove it to me again if you want to,' she teased him provocatively.

'Oh, I *want* to,' Gareth assured her.

'I hope everything is going to work out all right for Jack,' Louise murmured, her eyes darkening a little as she thought about her young cousin. 'I feel that we've *all* been guilty of not realising how much his father's disappearance has affected him.'

'It *must* have been difficult for him,' Gareth agreed sombrely. 'But you handled the whole situation very well. You're going to be a very good mother, Lou…'

'But not yet,' she told him. 'Or at least not until we're married…'

'No, not until we're married. You'll make a lovely winter bride with your colouring…'

'A winter wedding…' Louise murmured.

'I have to warn you that I have at least a dozen nieces who will all want to be bridesmaids…'

Louise giggled. 'Oh, not a dozen, surely!'

'Well, four,' Gareth amended. 'You *do* want to marry me, don't you, Lou?' he asked her, his face and voice suddenly very serious.

'Oh, yes,' Louise assured him huskily. 'Oh, yes, Gareth. Yes…yes…yes…' she moaned, as his mouth covered hers and the sun lounger rocked perilously beneath their combined weight.

'Louise is going to marry Gareth Simmonds,' Joss informed his great-aunt Ruth solemnly as he sat in her drawing room eating the fresh scones she had just baked.

'So I understand,' she agreed, smiling over his head at her American husband, Grant. They had only been married a few years themselves, even if their love went back over several decades.

'I like him. He understands things...' Joss told them seriously. 'Maddy was crying again yesterday, when I went to see Gramps. Why does Max have to be so horrid to her?'

Ruth sighed as she looked at him.

'I'm afraid that Max is just like that, Joss,' she informed her great-nephew sadly. 'Some people are, and when they are I'm afraid it takes a miracle to change them.'

'But miracles do happen,' Joss pointed out gravely. 'Look at you and Uncle Grant.'

'They do, yes,' Ruth agreed.

'I hope one does happen to Max...for Maddy's sake,' Joss added.

Ruth looked at him calmly.

'I shouldn't build your hopes on it, Joss,' she warned him. 'Not where Max is concerned.'

'I still can't totally believe it,' Katie told her twin, shaking her head slightly. 'You and Gareth in love and getting married...'

'What Mum finds harder to believe is that I'm going for the whole traditional wedding bit, complete with dress and bridesmaids,' Louise informed her sister wryly. 'We're getting married Christmas week, and spending Christmas Day at home with the family. Then New Year in Scotland, with Gareth's family, before we go off on honeymoon.'

Katie was in Brussels with Louise, and Gareth had promised to take them both out for dinner.

'You like his family, then?' Katie asked her twin.

'Oh, yes,' Louise confirmed enthusiastically. 'A

small part of *me* still can't quite believe it, either, Katie, I feel so…so special…so…so lucky… so…'

'So loved?' Katie suggested gravely.

Louise frowned. Was that a small shadow she could hear in her twin's voice, see in her eyes, and, if so, why?

'Katie…' she began, but her sister was already getting to her feet and picking up their empty wine glasses.

'It's six o'clock,' she warned Louise. 'We're going to have to start making a move if we're to be ready for Gareth when he calls for us at seven-thirty.'

'You are going to be there, aren't you?' Louise demanded as she followed her into the kitchen. 'At the wedding, I mean… No last-minute trips to the back of beyond to inspect some irrigation scheme or anything…'

'It's documents that I inspect, Lou, not irrigation schemes,' Katie reminded her lightly. 'And, yes, I shall be there.'

She was glad that she had been alone when she had taken Louise's ecstatic telephone call to tell her that she and Gareth were going to be married. Louise had put her silence down to the fact that she had been so surprised by her news… Well, she *had* been surprised, but…

Louise wasn't the only one who could love inappropriately and unwontedly. Not that Katie had ever imagined that Gareth might feel something for *her*, but then neither had she suspected that he was actually in love with her twin.

Anyway, whatever foolish dreams she might once have had had been packed away quietly and for ever now, along with all the other things that belonged to her childhood and the past. And, yes, of course she would be at their wedding, and she would smile for them and *with* them. How could she not? How could she not be happy for her twin? And how could she not grieve a little for herself?

'We'll never be alone, Katie,' Louise had once told her. 'We'll *always* have each other.'

But Louise had been wrong and now she *was* alone. Alone and lonely and hurting.

'You know that Gareth actually knew right from the start when you attended his lectures in my place that you weren't me?' Louise burbled happily as Katie quietly washed her used glass. 'He could tell the difference between us because he loved me...'

'Yes, you told me,' Katie acknowledged calmly, her hand trembling a little as she put the clean glass down.

'I love him so much, Katie,' Louise told her sister softly. 'I just wish that you... I want you to be as happy as I am...I want you to have someone to love and be loved by.'

'I'm happy as I am,' Katie told her, and promised herself that one day, very soon, it would be true.

*   *   *   *   *

The Perfect Father

CHAPTER ONE

'THAT was some game you played over the weekend, Sam. I certainly never expected to see the Corporation's gold trophy go to a woman…'

'Sam isn't a woman, women are small and cute and cuddly, they stay at home and make babies…. Sam… even her *name* isn't womanly…'

Samantha Miller drew herself up to her full height—an inch over six feet—which was an impressive four inches above the man who had just so publicly and cruelly criticised her.

'You know your trouble don't you, Cliff,' she drawled affably. '*You* just don't know a *real* woman when you see one. Seems to me that a man isn't so very much of a man if the only kind of woman he can handle is the kind you've just described, and as for making babies…' She paused for emphasis, well aware of the fact that she had the attention of their fellow employees who had happened to be in the large airy open-plan office with them, 'I'm woman enough to have a baby any time I want one.'

Only now was she revealing the true extent of her anger at the way Cliff had insulted her; her eyes flashing challenging sparks, her voice trembling a little with the force of her feelings.

'*You* have a baby…' her antagonist jeered angrily before she could continue. 'Who the hell would want to impregnate a woman like you? No way. Your only chance of having a child would be via some med student's sperm and a syringe…'

Enough of the people standing around broke into laughter for Samantha to recognise that no matter how publicly she might be accepted by her colleagues, an uncomfortable proportion of them seemed to share Cliff Marlin's views.

Faced with the same situation another woman might have burst into tears or lost her temper but not Sam. You learned young when you were as tall as she was that crying didn't look cute, and besides…

Looking down from the advantage of her extra inches Samantha bared her teeth in a totally false smile and gave a dismissive shrug.

'You're entitled to your opinion, Cliff, but gee, it's a shame that you're such a sore loser. Mind, if *I* played golf as badly as you do, I guess I might be a tad sore about it, too. And as for making babies…*how* many times did you miss that putt on the eighth…'

Now it was Samantha's gibe that earned a responsive titter of amusement from around her.

Without giving Cliff the opportunity to retaliate she turned on her heel and walked quickly away, her head held high.

What did it matter that she knew the moment she was out of sight and earshot that the others would be talking about her, gossiping about her, the six foot Amazon of a woman who, in all the time she had been with the Corporation, had never attended any of its social events with an escort; the only one of her admittedly relatively small group of female peers in what was essentially a very male-biased industry who had not, at one point or another, confided the details of her private life to the others.

Now, at just over thirty, Samantha was well aware that she had entered a decade which might prove to be one of the most productive and fast-paced of her whole life. It was also a decade which would see the chance of her meeting a man, the man…the man she would be able to fall in love with, the man she would want to spend the rest of her life with, the man with whom she would have the babies she craved so much, sharply declining.

There would be men of course…were men… masses of them, men who didn't want to commit, men who didn't want children, men who did want children, but who most definitely did not want a wife, men who were already married…men who… Oh, yes, the list of men to avoid was endless and the choice narrowed even further when one was as picky as her.

'Why don't you at least have a date with him?' her twin sister Roberta had demanded the last time she had been over visiting her family in the States from her new-found home in England. Their mother had been complaining to Bobbie about Sam's obduracy in not accepting a date from the man who had been pursuing her at the time.

'There isn't any point. I already *know* he isn't the one,' Samantha had told her fatalistically. 'It's all very well for you to take Mom's side,' she had complained to her twin later when they were on their own. 'You've *found* your man, your perfect "one and only," and when I've seen how special what you and

Luke have together is, how happy *you* are, how could *I* possibly settle for anything less.'

'Oh, Sam.' Bobbie had hugged her contritely. 'I'm sorry, you're right, you *mustn't* but I have to say I hope you find him soon. Oh dear,' she had then apologised as she'd started to yawn, 'I do feel tired.'

'Tired, I'm not surprised,' Samantha had laughed, and then unable to stop herself she glanced with rueful envy at her twin's heavily pregnant body—not with twins as Bobbie had first hoped, though. This was another single pregnancy. Seeing the look in her eyes Bobbie had asked her gently, 'Have you *never* met anyone you could love, Sam? Has there *never* been anyone you have loved?'

Samantha had thought for a moment before shaking her head. Her blonde hair, unlike her twin's, was cropped into a mass of short tender curls that framed her perfectly shaped face making her large blue eyes seem even larger and darker than Bobbie's.

'No. Not unless you count that crush I had on Liam way back when he first started working for Dad... I must have been all of fourteen at the time and Liam pretty soon made it clear that he wasn't interested in a juvenile brat with braces on her teeth and her hair in plaits.'

Roberta had laughed. Liam Connolly was their father's most senior assistant and it was no secret in the family that Stephen Miller was encouraging him to run for the position of State Governor when he himself retired.

'Yeah, well I guess to a man of twenty-one, especially one as good-looking as Liam, the idea of having a fourteen-year-old adoringly worshipping him doesn't hold that much appeal.'

'Believe me, so far as Liam was concerned it didn't have *any* appeal,' Sam had returned feelingly. 'Do you know he even refused to kiss me one particular Thanksgiving. Can you believe that—and me his boss's daughter…'

'Yeah, that could have been a real bad career move,' Bobbie had agreed tongue-in-cheek, '*and* an even worse one if Dad had found out Liam was encouraging you.'

'Mmm…and Liam has always put his career ahead of everything else.'

Bobbie had raised her eyebrows a little at the critical note in her twin's voice, inviting an explanation of Sam's acidic one.

'Oh, come on, Bo Bo, there's been a succession of women in his life—and his bed—but even Dad's commented on the fact he's never come anywhere near making a serious commitment to anyone. Lordy, he hasn't even allowed any of them to move into his house.'

'Perhaps he's still looking for Ms. Right…'

Samantha had given her sister an old-fashioned look.

'If he is, then all I can say is that he surely is having one hell of a good time with an awful lot of Ms. Wrongs first!'

Now, all too well aware of what was likely to be being said about her behind her back in the general office, Samantha headed for the elevators. So what if officially she wasn't due to take her lunch break for another full half an hour? Right now she needed to breathe fresh clean air and not the stale rancid stuff she had just been forced to endure, contaminated as it had been by Cliff's malice and envy. Because that *was* what had sparked his attack on her, Samantha knew that... He had been riding her hard for the last six weeks—ever since she had been offered the promotion he himself had wanted.

She had a month's leave coming up soon, thank goodness, and she had already made arrangements to spend most of it in England with her twin.

Her father's term as State Governor had only a little more time to run, otherwise he and her mother would have been joining her.

Theirs was a very close family, made all the more so because of its history. Her mother had been born illegitimately to Ruth Crighton, the unmarried daughter of the Crighton family of Haslewich in Cheshire, England, at the time when unmarried girls of Ruth's class simply did not become pregnant or certainly were not supposed to.

It had been during the Second World War. Ruth had fallen deeply in love with Samantha's grandfather but, due to a misunderstanding and the disapproval of her own father who had a bias against Americans, Ruth had erroneously believed that Grant had lied to her about being single and actually already had a wife and a child in the States. Pressured by her family, Ruth had given her baby, Samantha and Roberta's mother, up for adoption.

By one of those quirks of fate that always seemed too far-fetched to be possible, Ruth's baby had been feel secure and it reinforces their instinctive beliefs that…'

'…that what? A married man is a better Governor than an unmarried one?' her father had asked dryly. But he still had to concede that Sarah Jane had a point.

'Well, Liam certainly isn't short of suitable candidates for the position of his wife,' her father had admired, immediately looking a little shamefaced as her mother had expostulated.

'Stephen Miller, I do believe you are envious of him!'

'Envious. No, of course I'm not,' he had protested.

'Well, I should think you should look a mite ashamed,' her mother scolded mock severely. 'Otherwise I might start to believe that you don't appreciate either me or your family.'

'Honey, you know that just isn't true,' her father had responded immediately and so tenderly that tears had filled Samantha's eyes.

How could she ever accept second-best when she had before her not just the example of her twin's fervently happy marriage, but that of her darling, wonderful parents and, of course, her grandparents who were still just as much in love with one another now as they had been that fateful war-torn summer they had first met.

Only she seemed unable to find a mate for herself, a mate who would love her and father the children Cliff had so hatefully taunted her that no man would want to give her.

Oh, but *what* she would give to prove him wrong, to walk into that general office not just with her wonderful Mr. Right on her arm but with her stomach triumphantly, wonderfully big with his child...his children... As yet Bobbie hadn't followed in the Crighton family tradition and conceived twins. She had hoped earlier on in her current pregnancy she might have done, but her routine scans had shown that there was only one baby, although now in the late stages of her pregnancy Bobbie was grumbling that she felt large enough to be carrying quads.

Twins!

Twins... They ran through the history of the Crighton family like an often-repeated refrain and yet, oddly, despite all the new marriages which had taken place these last few years amongst her cousins—first, seconds and thirds—no one had, as yet, produced the next generation of double births.

Samantha closed her eyes. She could see herself now, leaning a little heavily onto the strong supporting arm of her love, her smile beatific, her body weighed down by the twin babies she was carrying perhaps, but her spirits, her heart, buoyed up with love and excitement.

'Sam.'

The sharp warning note in her twin's voice was so clear, so real, that Bobbie could almost have been there beside her.

Guiltily she opened her eyes and then realised that someone *had* actually spoken to her but that that someone was most definitely not her beloved twin sister.

Exhaling warily she looked up into the silver-grey eyes of Liam Connolly.

Yes, looked *up* because Liam, thanks, or so he said, to the Viking ancestry he claimed he possessed through his mother's Norwegian family and in spite of his quite definitely un-Nordic very dark hair, was actually a good three inches taller than she was herself, taller even than her own father—just.

'Er, L—Liam…' Why on earth was she stuttering and stammering like a child caught with her fingers in a forbidden cookie jar? Samantha wondered.

Liam indicated the busy road in front of them and told her dryly, 'I *know* you like to *think* you're superhuman but somehow I don't think the right way to try to prove it is to cross the freeway with your eyes closed. Besides, we have a law in this state against jaywalking, you know.'

As Sam heaved a small rebellious sigh, she had no idea what it was about Liam that always made her feel as though she was still fourteen years old and hot-headedly troublesome with it, but somehow or other he always did.

'Dad says you've agreed to run for State Governor when he retires,' she announced, trying to change the subject.

'Mmm…' He shot her a perceptive look from those incredible eyes that sometimes could seem so sexily smoky and smouldering and at other times could look so flintily cold that they could turn your heart to ice and your conscience to a clear piece of Perspex with every small sin clearly visible through it.

'I take it you don't approve?'

'You're thirty-seven. New Wiltshire County practically runs itself. I should have thought you'd want something you could get your teeth into a little more.'

'Like what? President?' Liam drawled. 'New Wiltshire County might not mean much to *you,* but believe me it's got a hell of a lot going for it. Do you realise that we're well on our way to passing new state legislation which will actually have our people voluntarily giving up their guns? Did you know that *we* have one of the lowest rates of unemployment in the entire union and that our kids have one of the *highest* overall pass out grades from high school? Did you know that our welfare programme has just been applauded as one of the finest in the union and that…'

'Yes…Yes, I *do* know all those things, and I'm not knocking the county. It's my home, after all, and I love it. My father is its Governor and…'

Fixing his steel-grey gaze on her, Liam ignored what she was saying, demanding seriously, 'Did you know that the gardens surrounding the Governor's residence have been declared a tribute to our Governor's lady's taste and knowledge of—'

'Oh, but *I* designed those,' Sam began and then stopped, glaring accusingly at him.

'Oh, all right, you got me there,' she acknowledged ruefully, her own mouth curving into a reluctant smile as she saw the humour in the curl of Liam's mouth.

'New Wiltshire County is a wonderful place, Liam, I know that. I just thought you might prefer something a little bit more…a little bit less parochial,' she told him dryly, unable to resist adding, 'After all, you seem to spend an awful lot of time in Washington.'

'With your father,' Liam replied promptly before

adding, 'but if I'd realised that you were missing me...'

Sam gave him a withering look.

'Don't give *me* that,' she warned him. 'I know you—remember... I don't know what all those girls you date see in you Liam—' she began severely.

'No?' he interrupted her swiftly. 'Want me to show you?'

To her own irritation Sam could feel herself starting to colour up a little.

She knew perfectly well that Liam was only teasing her. She ought to; after all, he had been doing it for long enough.

'No thanks,' she responded automatically. 'I prefer exclusivity in my men. Exclusivity and *brown* eyes,' she told him mock musingly. 'Yes, there is quite definitely something about a man with brown eyes.'

'Brown eyes... Mmm... Well, I guess I could always keep mine closed—or wear contact lenses. What were you thinking about when I saw you just then?' he demanded, completely changing tack.

'Thinking about?'

Samantha knew perfectly well how he would read it if she was to tell him. He would be even more disapproving and dismissive than her twin sister.

'Er...nothing...not really,' she fibbed, then as she saw him start to frown and guessed that he wasn't going to let her answer stand without some further questioning, she added quickly, 'I was thinking about my upcoming visit to Bobbie.'

'You're going to England?'

Samantha shot him an uncertain look. He was

frowning and his voice had sharpened almost to the point of curtness.

'Uh-huh, for a whole month. More than long enough I guess for Bobbie to put her matchmaking plans into practice,' she told him flippantly.

'Bobbie's trying to matchmake for you?'

'You know what she's like.' Samantha shrugged. 'She's so besotted with Luke that she wants to see me equally happily married off. You'd better watch out, Liam,' she joked, 'You're even older than me. She could be matchmaking for you next! Mind you, perhaps she's right. England could be the place to find a man,' Samantha mused, her eyes clouding as she remembered Cliff's taunt. 'There is something deeply attractive about English men.'

'Especially when they've got brown eyes?' Liam asked in an unfamiliarly hard voice.

'Umm…especially then,' Samantha agreed unseriously. But Liam, it seemed, was taking the subject much more seriously than she was because he looked away from her and when he looked back his eyes were a particularly cold and analytical shade of grey.

'It wouldn't be *one* specific brown-eyed Englishman we are talking about, would it?'

'One specific…' Samantha was lost. 'Well, gee, I guess one would be enough,' she agreed, putting on her best country-cousin hill-billy voice. 'At least to start with, but then… What are you getting at, Liam?' she asked him, dropping the fake accent as she saw the way he was watching her.

'I was just remembering the way Luke's brother was watching you at Luke and Bobbie's wedding,' he told her coolly. '*His* eyes were brown, if I remember correctly.'

'James…' Samantha frowned. She couldn't quite remember what colour his eyes had been and most certainly James had been a real honey, seriously good-looking and seriously open about his own desire to settle down and raise a family, no commitment phobia there and most definitely no bias against tall independent women. No sirree.

'Mmm…you're right, they *were*,' she agreed, giving Liam an absent smile.

'Of course, we'd have brown-eyed babies.'

'*What* did you say…'

Vaguely, Samantha looked at Liam. She had just had *the* most wonderful idea.

'Brown-eyes genes dominate over blue, don't they?' she asked him, not expecting a response.

'Sam, just what the hell is going on?'

Liam grabbed hold of her upper arm, not painfully but firmly enough for Samantha to recognise that he wasn't easily going to let go of her.

She gave a small sigh and looked up at him.

'Liam, would *you* say that I was the kind of woman who couldn't…who a man wouldn't…' She stopped as her throat threatened to clog with tears, swallowing them down fiercely before continuing gruffly, 'Someone told me today that I'm not woman enough for a man to want her to…to…to become a mother. Well, I'm going to prove him wrong, Liam… I'm going to prove him so wrong that…

'I'm going to go to England and I'm going to find myself a man who *knows* how to love and value a *real* woman, the *real* woman in me and he's going to love me and I'm going to love him so much that…

'Let me go, Liam,' she demanded, aware that he'd tightened his grip on her. 'I've already overrun my lunch hour and I've got about a million and one things I have to do…'

'Samantha,' Liam began warningly, but she'd already pulled free of him and was walking away. Her mind was made up even if rather ironically it had taken Liam of all people to point her in the right direction and there was no way she was going to let anyone change it. In England she would find love just as her twin had done. Why on earth hadn't *she* thought of that…realised that before? English men were different. English men weren't like Cliff. English men… One Englishman would love her as she so longed to be loved and she would love him right back.

Already she was regretting having told Liam as much as she had. Oh, that wilful impetuous tongue of hers, but she certainly wasn't going to tell anyone else—not even Bobbie. No, her quest to find her perfect Mr. Right, the perfect father for the babies she so longed to have, was going to be *her* secret and hers alone.

Her eyes sparkling with elation, Samantha walked back into her office building.

CHAPTER TWO

'JUST think, in a little over a week I shall be in Haslewich with Bobbie.'

Samantha closed her eyes and smiled in delicious anticipation, looking more like the teenager she had been when Liam had first met her than the sophisticated, independent career woman she now was.

On the opposite side of the elegant mahogany dining table, which was a family heirloom and which her mother had insisted on bringing with them from the family residence in the small town which her husband's family had virtually founded to the Governor's residence where they now all lived together, Sarah Jane Miller smiled tenderly at her daughter.

'I really do envy you, darling,' she told her. 'I just wish that your father and I were coming with you but it's impossible right now.'

'I know, but at least you'll be getting to spend Christmas with Bobbie this year. Dad's term of office will have finished by then.'

'Mmm... I must admit I shan't be sorry,' her mother responded, and then looked apologetically across the table to the fourth member of the quartet.

Over the years Liam Connolly had worked for her husband the two men had become very close and Sarah Jane knew it was no secret to Liam that she preferred the elegant New England home she had shared with her husband to the rather less intimate atmosphere of the Governor's residence which was also home to the state's small suite of administration offices.

'Oh, Liam, it's not that the house isn't...' She stopped and laughed, shaking her head. 'What am I saying,' she chuckled ruefully. '*You* know all too well that I can't wait to get back to our own home. I hope that when you do decide to marry that you'll warn your wife-to-be just what she's going to have to take on...when she moves in here...'

'It isn't a foregone conclusion that I'll get elected to the governorship,' Liam reminded her dryly.

'Oh, but I hope you do,' Samantha's mother insisted. 'You're so obviously the very best man for the job.'

'Sarah Jane is right,' Samantha's father cut in warmly. 'And I can tell you, Liam, that I've heard on the grapevine that the New Wiltshire and even some Washington hostesses are already preparing their celebratory dinners for you.'

Dutifully Samantha joined in her mother's amused laughter but for some reason she couldn't define, she didn't find the idea of Liam being vetted by the sophisticated women of Washington as pleasantly amusing as both her parents did.

'There is one thing you are going to have to consider though, Liam,' her father was continuing in a more serious vein. 'I'm not saying that your election to the governorship is dependent on it, but there's no getting away from the fact that as a married man you would significantly increase your appeal to the voters.'

Very carefully Liam put the pear he had been peeling back on his plate. He had, Samantha noticed, unlike her, managed to remove most of its skin without either drastically altering the shape of the fruit or covering himself in its juice. But then, Liam was like that. She had seen him remove his suit jacket to set about lending a hand to some mundane task requiring the kind of muscle power so very evident in his six-foot-four broad-shouldered frame and complete the job without even managing to get a speck of dirt on his immaculately clean shirt. She, on the other hand, couldn't so much as open a fridge door without knocking something over.

'It's only a matter of months before voting takes place,' Liam reminded her father dryly. 'Somehow I feel that the voters would be less than impressed by a hasty and a very obviously publicity-planned marriage.'

'There's plenty of time before your first term of office would begin,' her father pointed out. 'I knew I wanted to marry Sarah Jane within days of first meeting her.'

Across the table Samantha's parents exchanged tenderly loving looks. Sam looked away. Her parents were so very, very lucky.

Fiercely she worried at her lip. As a teenager her mother had once told her gently, chidingly, 'Samantha Miller, if you keep on doing that, that poor bottom lip of yours is going to be permanently sore and swollen.'

'Mom's right,' Bobbie had hissed teasingly at her when their mother had left the room. 'But my, oh, my, how sexy it's going to look. Boys are just going to die wanting to feel how it is to kiss you.'

'Boys…yuck…' Samantha had protested. Who wanted boys when there was *Liam?* What would it be like to be kissed by him? He had the sexiest mouth she had ever seen. Just thinking about it, never mind looking at it, made her shiver all over.

'I understand what you're saying,' Liam was admitting to her father now, 'but personally I don't believe that getting married is necessarily going to make me a better Governor. In fact,' he added wryly, 'it would probably be more likely to have just the opposite effect. Men in love are, after all, notoriously unable to concentrate upon anything other than their beloved.'

'Perhaps it's just as well then that you are in love with your career,' Samantha suggested, adding before Liam could comment, 'You have to admit that you've always given it far more attention than you have any woman.'

'Sam…' her mother objected, but Liam simply shook his head.

'No wonder you're no good at chess,' he taunted her, 'making a move on your opponent is no good unless you keep yourself protected and have the next move already planned. *I* could point out that you are equally bereft of a partner and that you, too, would appear to have sacrificed your most personal intimate relationships in favour of your career.'

'Not in the way that you have, I haven't,' Samantha objected hotly. 'You deliberately pick women who you know you're going to get bored with. You don't want a serious relationship. You're a commitment phobic, Liam,' she told him dangerously. 'Secretly you're afraid of giving yourself emotionally to a woman.'

'Oh, then it seems to me that we have something very much in common.'

'What do you mean?' Samantha asked him challengingly.

'It's so obvious that the kind of man you need is one who'd keep you earthed, provide a solid base to offset your own more tempestuous one, but instead you always go for the same type, emotionally unstable, manipulative, lame dogs. My guess is you feel more passionate about them as a cause than as men.

'You accuse me of being afraid of giving myself emotionally to a woman, Samantha. Well I'd say that you are very much afraid of committing yourself, of giving yourself wholly and completely, sexually, to a man. Excuse me.' Without giving her any opportunity to either defend herself or retaliate, he stood up, politely excusing himself to her parents.

'I've got some work I really need to do. I'll see you in the morning Stephen and I should have those figures you were asking me for by then.'

As he walked around the table and gave her mother a brief kiss on the cheek Samantha wondered if her face looked as hot with chagrin as it felt. How could he have said something like that to her, and in front of her parents? It wasn't true, of course, how could it be?

It wasn't, after all, as though she was some timid, cowering virgin who had never known physical intimacy. She had lost her virginity in the time-honoured way as a sophomore at college with her then boyfriend whom she had been dating for several months. And if the experience had turned out to be more of a rite of passage than the entry into a whole new world of perfect love and emotional and physical bliss and euphoria, well then she hadn't been so very different from any of her peers, from what she had heard.

True that, unlike Liam, she didn't have a list of sexual conquests as long as her arm. True, her own secret, somewhat mortifying view of herself was as a woman to whom sex was never going to be of prime importance, certainly nothing as important as emotional intimacy or as the love she would have for the children she would bear. But was that so very wrong? Did putting sex at the top of one's list of what was important in life truly make for a better person? Samantha didn't think so and she was certainly not going to pretend to either a sexual desire or a sexual history she did not possess simply because it might be expected of her.

'You know, it's at times like this that I wonder if you're actually a teenager or really in your thirties,' Samantha heard her father remark ruefully as he, too, stood up.

Imploringly she looked at her mother.

'That's not fair, Mom. It was *Liam* who started it and…'

'Your father does have a point, darling,' her mother interrupted her gently. 'You *do* tend to ride Liam rather hard at times.'

'*I* ride *him!*' Samantha objected indignantly, and then she suddenly felt her face flooding with scarlet colour, not because she felt guilty about what she had said but because she had suddenly realised the sexual connotations of her mother's comment.

Liam…sex…and her? Oh no! No… She had outgrown *that* particular folly a long time ago.

'He deserves it,' she told her mother fiercely. 'He can be so damned arrogant. If he ever gets to be Governor he's going to have to develop a far more human and gentle way of dealing with other people. When it comes to figures or logic Liam may be the best there is, but when it comes to his fellow human beings…'

'Sam. Now you *are* being unfair,' her mother chided her firmly. 'And I think you know it. If you'd only seen the way Liam reacted to and spoke with the children at the Holistic Centre the other week.'

She paused and shook her head.

'I could have sworn I saw tears in his eyes when he was holding that little boy,' she commented to her husband as he prepared to leave the room. 'You remember the one I mean, the autistic boy they had there for assessment.'

'Yes, Liam told me himself that if he gets elected he intends to make sure that the centre gets the very best of funding and help he can give it.'

The Holistic Centre was one of Sam's mother's pet charities—the establishment and support of charities was very much a Crighton thing on the other side of the Atlantic. The series of special units Ruth, Samantha's grandmother and Sarah Jane's mother, had established were unique in the facilities they provided for single parents and their children and all the Crighton women were tireless in their fund-raising work for a diverse range of good causes.

Out of all the charities her own mother supported, the Holistic Centre, which treated children with special needs, was Samantha's own favourite and whenever she could she gave her spare time to helping out there and working to raise money for it.

'I didn't know that Liam had visited the centre,' she commented sharply now.

'Mmm… He asked if he could come with me the

last time I visited,' her mother explained. 'And I must say, I was impressed with the way he related to the children. For a man without younger siblings and no children of his own, he certainly has a very sure and special touch with kids.'

'He's probably practising his baby kissing techniques to impress the voters!'

'Samantha!' her mother objected, quite obviously shocked.

'Samantha? Samantha what?' Sam demanded shakily as she got up. She knew she was overreacting and perhaps even behaving a little unfairly but somehow she couldn't help herself. Right now *she* was the one who needed her parents' support, their complete and full approval...their understanding. Cliff's cruel comments had hurt her very deeply, shaken her, disturbed her, uncovered a secret ache of unhappiness and dissatisfaction with herself and her life.

'You always take Liam's side,' she accused her bewildered parents, her eyes suddenly brilliant with tears. 'It's not fair...' And then, like the youthful teenager her father had accused her of resembling, she turned and fled from the room.

'What on earth was all that about?' Stephen asked in confusion when she had gone. 'Is it one of those women's things...?'

'No. It's not that.' Sarah Jane shook her head, her forehead pleating in an anxious maternal frown.

'I'm worried about Samantha, Stephen. I *know* she's always been inclined to be a little up and down emotionally—she's so passionate and intense about everything—but that's what makes her the very special person she is... But, well...this last year...' She paused, her frown deepening. 'I'm glad she's going on this visit with Bobbie. She never says it, but I know how much she misses her.' She paused and gave him a wry smile.

'Do you remember when they were growing up how it was always Sam who played big sister to the other kids on the block and how, when Tom came along she fussed over him like a little mother? We always said then that Sam would be the one to get married first and have children and that Bobbie would be the career girl.'

She saw that Stephen was looking a little nonplussed.

'What is it you're trying to say?' he asked her.

'I'm not sure,' she admitted. 'I just know that something's upsetting Samantha.'

'Well, she and Liam have never exactly seen eye to eye.'

'No, it isn't Liam,' Sarah Jane told him positively. 'Poor Liam, I do feel for him.' She gave a small chuckle. 'I rather suspect that if he hadn't been sitting at our dinner table there was a moment this evening when he might definitely have reacted more forcefully to Sam's remarks.'

'Mmm… He and Sam have never got on,' her husband agreed.

Sarah Jane's eyes widened.

'Oh, but…' she began and then stopped. 'Do you think he'll seriously consider getting married in order to strengthen his position in running for Governor?'

'Not purely for that,' Stephen announced positively. 'He's far too honest—and too proud—to stoop to those kinds of tactics, but like I said earlier, he is thirty-seven and, despite all the hassle Sam gives him about his girlfriends, he's never given me the impression that he's the kind of man who needs to feed his ego with a constant stream of sexual conquests—far from it.'

'Mmm... I think you're right. In fact—' She stopped. 'With his ancestry it's entirely feasible that Liam's rational exterior could hide a very emotional and romantic heart indeed. In fact I think that Liam, contrary to what Sam said, *is* looking for love and commitment—he just hasn't found the right woman yet, that's all.'

She got up from the table and dropped a loving kiss on her husband's cheek as she walked past him.

'I'd better go up and see if Sam's okay.'

A week later Samantha gave a small sigh of achievement and relief as the clasps on her large suitcase finally responded to the pressure of her weight on top of the case and snapped closed.

'Thank goodness,' Sam muttered under her breath.

She would be way over the weight limit, she *knew* that, but what the heck. A series of long excited conversations with her twin over the intervening week had elicited the information that there were a series of social events coming up in both Chester and Haslewich which Bobbie intended to have her twin join in.

'There's the Lord Lieutenant's Ball at the end of your stay. We've already got tickets for that. It's going to be especially wonderful this year as the current Lord Lieutenant is stepping down. You'll need a proper evening gown for that, and then there's the charity cricket match and the strawberry tea afterwards. The bad news, though, is that Luke has three very important court cases pending so he could be called away at short notice. And of course with the baby due soon I shan't be able to do as much as I would have liked. However, once he or she arrives, you and I are going to do some serious fashion shopping, I'm so tired of maternity clothes.'

'Mmm…' Sam had enthused. 'I've read that Milan is *the* place to shop right now, the prices are really keen and you know how I love those Italian designers.'

'Mmm… Which reminds me, don't forget to bring some clam diggers, will you, and some jeans. They just don't do them over here like they do back home. Oh, and dungarees for Francesca and shirts for Luke and for James…'

'How is James?' Samantha had asked her twin coyly.

'He's fine and he's certainly looking forward to seeing you,' Bobbie had taunted her.

Samantha had laughed back. Bobbie had taunted her mercilessly at the time of her own wedding that James had fallen for her, but then Samantha had simply thought of him as a very nice soon-to-be in-law and member of the large Crighton clan.

Now, though, things were a little different.

Milan wasn't the only city to boast fine designer shops and *she* had paid an extended visit to Boston prior to doing her packing. The resultant purchases were all designed to underscore the fact that being tall did not in *any* way mean that was not wholly and completely a woman. A satisfied smile curled Samantha's mouth as she contemplated the effect of her new purchases on her intended victim. James, she knew instinctively, was the kind of man who preferred to see a woman dressed like a woman.

Her smile was replaced by a small frown as she studied her closed suitcase. Closed it might be, but it still had to be gotten downstairs and there was no point in calling the man who helped with the garden to assist her. Hyram was a honey, but he was close on seventy and there was no way he could lift her case.

Nope… There *were* occasions when being tall and healthily muscled were an advantage—and this, she decided, was one of them.

She negotiated the suitcase to the top of the stairs so that she could leave it in the lobby ready for her early morning flight and had just paused to take a rest, muttering complainingly at the overstuffed case as she did so. Her face felt hot and flushed and the exertion had made her hair cling in silky strands to the nape of her neck and her flushed cheeks. Turning her back towards the stairs, she eyed the suitcase.

'It's not just my clothes,' she told it sternly. 'It's that sister of mine and…'

'What the…'

The unexpected sound of Liam's voice on the stairs behind her caused Samantha to jump and turn round, forgetting that she had momentarily balanced the case precariously on one of the stairs whilst she leaned against it to hold it in position.

The result was inevitable.

The suitcase, disobligingly ignoring her wailed protest, slid heavily down the stairs, past Liam, bouncing on the half landing before coming to a halt against a solid wooden chest where the combined effect of its speedy fall and its heavy weight caused the clasps to burst open and the contents of the case to tumble out all over the stairs.

'Oh, there now, see what you've done,' Samantha accused Liam angrily. 'If you hadn't crept up on me like that…'

'I rather think, more to the point, *you* shouldn't have overpacked the thing in the first place,' Liam corrected her dryly, turning his back on her as he headed down the stairs, hunkering down on the half landing as he proceeded to gather up the case's disgorged garments.

It was, as Samantha later seethed to herself in the privacy of her bedroom, revoltingly unfair of fate to have decreed that the stuff which had fallen out of her case wasn't the sturdy, sensible jeans she had bought for her sister, nor the dungarees for Francesca, her niece, nor even the shirts requested by her brothers-in-law, but instead, the frivolous bits of silky satin and lace items of underwear *she* had recklessly bought for herself on her shopping spree in Boston.

Creamy satin lace-trimmed bras with the kind of boning that meant that the kind of things they did for a woman's figure were strictly seriously flirtatious. And, even worse, there on the carpet beside them were the ridiculously unfunctional French knickers that had helped swallow up a large portion of her pay cheque. Add to that the equally provocative garter belt and the silk stockings and combine them with the incredulous disdain with which Liam was looking from her scarlet face to the fragile pieces of feminine lingerie he was holding in his hands and it was no wonder that she was feeling uncomfortably hot and embarrassed, Samantha reflected.

'I guess you aren't planning to do much sport in Cheshire,' Liam commented laconically. 'Or—' his eyebrows shot up as he gave her a very thorough look

'—perhaps I'm wrong…' He continued silkily, 'Thinking of going hunting are you, Sam? If so…'

'They aren't mine, they're a present for Bobbie,' Samantha lied feverishly, hurrying down the stairs to snatch them away from him.

'Mmm…. Well, if you'll take my advice…as a man…something a little simpler and less structured would serve your purpose much better. These,' he told her with a contemptuous look at the boned demi bra he was holding, 'might be exciting for boys, but men…real men, prefer something a little more subtle and a lot more tactile… A sexy slither of silk and satin with tiny shoestring straps, something silky and fluid that drapes itself softly over a woman's curves, hinting at them rather than… There's nothing quite so sexy as that little hint of cleavage you get when a woman's strap slips down off her shoulder…'

'Well, thank you *very* much for your advice,' Samantha snapped furiously at him. 'But when I want *your* opinion on what a man finds sexy, Liam, you can be sure I'll ask you for it. And anyway—' She stopped abruptly.

'Anyway what?' Liam asked her mildly as he bent down again to retrieve a pretty silk wrap which was lying under the suitcase.

Samantha glared at him.

How could she tell him that when you were a woman with breasts as generously rounded and full as hers were, the type of silky clingy unstructured top *he* was describing was quite simply a ''no-no'' unless you wanted to stop all the traffic on the freeway.

'This isn't for Bobbie,' he told her positively as he handed her the wrap.

'What makes you say that?' Samantha demanded.

'It's not her colour,' he told her simply. 'Her skin is paler than yours and her eyes lighter. *This* is your colour, but coffee or caramel would suit you even better.'

'Thank you *so* much,' Samantha gritted acidly as she snatched the wrap from him.

As she bent to try to stuff her possessions back into her suitcase, Liam knelt down beside her.

'You need another case,' he told her calmly. 'This one, *if* you get it as far as the airport, will probably break the baggage conveyor belt. That's if it doesn't burst open again first.

'You're wrong, by the way,' he added mystifyingly as Samantha tried to ignore the reality of what he was telling her.

'It isn't only women with tiny breasts who can go braless. You've got far too many hang-ups about your body, Samantha, do you know that?'

'Is that a fact? Well. I'll thank you to keep your opinions on my hang-ups and my…my breasts…to yourself *if* you don't mind,' Samantha gritted hot-faced at him, wondering how he had followed her embarrassed train of thought.

'Of course, when it comes to bouncing around the tennis court, I agree that a woman needs a good sports bra,' Liam was continuing as if she hadn't spoken.

Samantha shot him a wary look. *She* played tennis in the residence's court most mornings with her father and she *always* wore a sports bra—so what was Liam implying?

'Look, why don't *I* carry this back to your room for you so that you can repack it in two cases,' Liam was offering.

To Samantha's chagrin, as he picked up the case

she could see that he was able to carry it far more easily than she herself had been able to do—carrying it not downstairs where she had intended to take it, she recognised, but back in the direction she had just come—to her bedroom.

As he elbowed open the door and dumped the heavy case on the floor, Samantha followed Liam into her room.

'I *was* taking that downstairs...' she began to up-braid him and then stopped abruptly.

Standing with his feet apart and his hands on his hips, Liam wasn't watching her but instead was focusing on the pretty upholstered chair beside the window.

The chair—an antique—had been a gift from her grandmother, a pretty early Victorian rocker which Samantha had had recaned and for which she had made her own hand-stitched sampler cushions. But it wasn't the chair or the cushions which were holding Liam's attention—Samantha knew that and she knew too exactly what he was looking at.

'Mom made me keep him,' she began defensively, pushing past Liam and rushing over to the chair, protectively picking up the battered and slightly thread-bare teddy bear who was seated on it.

'She says it reminds her of when we were little. It was her bear before us and then Tom had him, too, and... Oh, you don't understand,' she breathed crossly. 'You're too unemotional. Too cold...'

'You should run for government office yourself,' Liam told her sardonically. 'With your mind-reading talents you'd be a wow.'

'Mind-reading,' Samantha breathed heavily. 'Oh you...'

'For your information I am *neither* unemotional *nor* cold and as for Wilfred…' Ignoring Samantha he walked up to her and deftly took the bear from her unresisting grasp.

'I had one very like him when I was young. He came originally from Ireland with my grandfather. He was just a boy then…'

Samantha's eyes widened. Liam rarely talked about his family—at least not to her. She knew he had no brothers or sisters and that his grandparents, immigrants from Ireland, had built up a very successful haulage business which Liam's father had continued to run and expand until his death from a heart attack whilst Liam was at college.

Liam had sold the business—very profitably—with his mother's approval. From a very young age he had known that he wanted to enter politics and both his parents and his grandparents when they had been alive, had fully supported him in this ambition, but it was from her mother that Samantha had gleaned these facts about Liam's background, not from Liam himself.

'Why does he never talk to me…treat me as an adult?' she had once railed at her mother when Liam had pointedly ignored some questions she had been asking him about his grandparents. She had been at college at the time and working on an essay about the difficulties experienced by the country's immigrants in the earlier part of the century and she had hoped to gain some first-hand knowledge and insights into the subject from Liam's memories of his grandparents.

'He's a very proud man, sweetheart,' her father had responded, hearing her exasperated question. 'I guess he kinda feels that he doesn't want his folks looked down on or…'

'Looked down on… Why should *I* do that?' Samantha had interrupted him indignantly.

'Well, Liam is very conscious of the fact that his grandparents came to this country with very little in the way of material possessions, just what they could carry with them in fact, whilst…'

'He thinks that *I'd* look down on him because your family arrived with Cabots and Adamses and all those other "first families" on the *Mayflower* who went on to form the backbone of North American early politics, wealth and society,' Samantha had protested hotly. 'Is that what he really thinks of me?'

'Sweetheart, sweetheart,' her father had protested gently. 'I'm sure that Liam thinks no such thing. It's just that he's as reluctant to have his family background put under the public microscope as your mother would be hers. Not out of any sense of shame—quite the reverse—but out of a very natural desire to protect those he loves.'

'But Gran is still alive whilst Liam's grandparents are dead,' Samantha had objected.

'The principle is still the same,' her father had pointed out gently.

Now, some impulse she couldn't name made Samantha ask Liam softly, 'Do you still have it…the bear…?'

His austere features suddenly broke into an almost boyish grin and for one breath-stopping moment Samantha actually felt as though something or someone was physically jerking her heartstrings. Impossible, of course, hearts didn't have strings and if hers had then there was no way that one Liam

Connolly could possibly have jerked them. No, it was just the mental image she had had of him as a small boy listening solemnly to his grandfather whilst he related to him tales of his own Irish upbringing.

'Yes.'

'You'll be able to keep it for your children and tell them the stories your grandparents told you,' Samantha told him impulsively.

Immediately his features changed and became formidably harsh.

'Don't you jump on the bandwagon,' he told her grittily. 'Everyone seems determined to marry me off. I've even had Lee Calder giving interviews stating that a single, childless Governor won't understand the needs of the state's parents. My God, when I *think* of the way he's been trying to cut down on our education.'

Lee Calder was Liam's closest contender for the governorship, a radical right-winger whose views Samantha's father found totally unsympathetic. Lee was an overweight, balding man in his mid-forties, twice married with five children who he had overdisciplined and controlled to such an extent that the eldest, a boy, was rumoured to have shown his unhappiness by stealing money from his parents and trashing the family home with a group of friends one summer when the family were on vacation without him.

No matter what her *personal* opinion of Liam might be, Samantha knew that her father was quite right when he said that Liam would make an excellent Governor. Highly principled, firm, a natural leader, the state would flourish with Liam at its helm.

Lee Calder on the other hand, despite cleverly managing to package himself as a devoted family man and churchgoer, had a string of shady dealings behind him—nothing that could be proved, but there was something about the man. Samantha vividly remembered the occasion at an official function when he had grabbed hold of her and tried to kiss her.

Fortunately she had been able to push him away but not before she had seen the decidedly nasty glint in his eyes as she rejected him.

She had been all of seventeen at the time and as she recalled his second wife had been pregnant with their first child.

'Don't accuse *me* of trying to marry you off,' she challenged Liam now.

'No. By the looks of what you've got in that case you're more interested in changing your own single status,' Liam agreed derisively.

'I've *told* you, *those* are for Bobbie,' Samantha insisted.

'And I've told you if *you* really want to catch yourself a man, the best way to do it is by…' He stopped when he saw her frown, then continued. 'You know that I'm driving you to the airport in the morning, don't you?'

'Yes,' Samantha agreed on a small sigh. She had a very early start and had been quite prepared to order a cab but her father could be an old-fashioned parent in some ways.

'No, sweetheart, you know what you're like for getting yourself anyplace on time.'

'Dad,' Samantha had protested, 'that was years ago…and an accident…just because I once missed a plane doesn't mean…'

'Liam's driving you,' her father had announced,

and Samantha had known better than to argue with
him. 'As it happens, he's picking someone up, as
well.'

'Someone… Who?' Samantha had asked her father
curiously.

'Someone from Washington. I want him to take her
on board as his campaign PR, she's very good.'

'She?' Samantha had raised her eyebrows, her
voice sharpening slightly. 'You wouldn't be doing a
little matchmaking would you, Dad?'

'Give your sister our love, remember,' he had answered her obliquely, 'and tell her we can't wait to
see them all….'

CHAPTER THREE

SAMANTHA checked a sleepy yawn as she ruffled her fingers through her still-damp curly crop. Despite the invigorating shower she had just taken her body was protestingly aware that it was only just gone three in the morning.

Still, she could sleep during the flight, she promised herself as she slicked a soft peachy-pink lipstick across her mouth and grimaced at her refection.

Not bad for a woman who'd slipped over thirty. Her skin was still as clear and fresh-looking as it had been ten years ago and even if there was now a deeper maturity and wisdom in her eyes than any twenty-year-old could have, a person was going to have to stand pretty close to her to see it.

James was in his mid-thirties but he had that boyish look about him that a few Englishmen have. Although equally as tall and strongly built as his elder brother Luke and just as stunningly handsome, James had about him a certain sweetness of nature which more austere men like his brother, and to some extent Liam, too, lacked. James was, in short, an absolute honey. He would be very easy to love, a wonderful husband and father…and an equally wonderful lover? The kind of lover she knew instinctively a man like *Liam* would be.

Samantha put down her lipstick and frowned. Now what on earth had put *that* thought into her head?

Liam as a lover…! Her lover? No way at all!

She glanced at her watch. Time she was downstairs. Liam would be picking her up in five minutes and he was very hot on good timekeeping.

Even though she had said her goodbyes to her parents the previous evening, she wasn't totally surprised to have them rush downstairs minutes before she left to hug and kiss her and reiterate their messages of love to her twin as well as the rest of the Crightons.

'Don't forget that your grandparents should be arriving in Haslewich during the time you are there,' Samantha's mother reminded her.

'How could I forget anything involving Grandma Ruth?' Samantha teased her mother.

Ruth Crighton, as she had been before her late marriage to Sarah Jane's father, was affectionately known as Aunt Ruth to virtually all of the Crighton family and so had become Grandma Ruth to Bobbie, Samantha and their younger brother.

Blissfully married at last to the American soldier she had first met during the Second World War, Ruth divided her time together with her husband between Haslewich and Grant's beautiful American house.

'Better not keep Liam waiting,' her father counselled as they all heard the knock on the door.

She went to let him in and he thanked her before going over to her mother to give her a very easy and natural almost filially warm hug. Samantha acknowledged grudgingly that there was no way she could ever fault Liam's behaviour towards her parents. He might deliberately rub *her* up the wrong way, inciting her to open rebellion and sometimes even outright war, but no one could have faked the look of very real warmth and affection he was giving her folks.

'I see you took my advice about the suitcases,' was

his only comment to her once they were inside his car and he had loaded her two cases into its trunk.

Samantha scowled at him.

'My decisions to repack had nothing to do with you,' she told him loftily and a mite untruthfully. 'Mom wanted me to take some extra gifts over for the family.'

The derisory look Liam was giving her silenced her.

'Dad said you were picking up a Washington PR expert from the airport,' she commented, deliberately changing the subject.

'Mmm…'

'You surprise me, Liam,' she told him. 'I thought you were far too confident to feel you needed any image polishing or manipulating.'

'*I* don't,' Liam assured her, 'but some of your father's supporters are concerned that Lee Calder could be planning to market himself as the family's champion and they want to start up a damage limitation exercise.'

'By what, marrying you off to this PR woman?' Samantha asked flippantly before adding, 'Wouldn't it be simpler just to marry your current date… whoever she is…'

'There *is* no current date,' Liam told her. 'And to be frank, Samantha, I'm getting rather tired of this image you keep trying to push of me as some kind of serial lady-killer. For your information—' He broke off, cursing as a truck suddenly swerved out of a side street in front of them.

Samantha was far too glad of the diversion to reintroduce the same topic of conversation once the truck had gone. Much as she enjoyed baiting Liam, she also knew when it was wise to back off a little.

'I could say much the same thing to you, you know,' Liam murmured, turning his head to look directly at her as she turned towards him, warily waiting for what he was going to say.

'If you're as keen to prove to your colleagues as you said that you are woman enough to be a mother, then there are far easier ways of doing so than going looking in England for a man to father your child.'

'What are you suggesting—artificial insemination. No way!' Angrily Samantha turned away from him, staring in silence out of the car window.

Liam was a good driver and long before they had crossed the state line Samantha had dropped off to sleep, her body angled towards Liam's, one hand resting under her face.

After he'd safely overtaken a truck, Liam turned his head to look at her. She had to be one of the most breathtakingly stunning women he had ever seen. Her sister Bobbie was beautiful but where Bobbie exuded an air of relaxed self-control, Samantha was a bundle of quicksilver fieriness, impulsive, impatient, almost too sensitive for her own good at times, proud and...

Liam cursed under his breath. As *he* knew all too well, there were almost no lengths Samantha would not go to to prove her point if someone hurt her pride. And he knew better than most, having watched both girls grow up, that despite all the positive influences they had received from their parents and family, both of them, but especially Samantha, were privately a little sensitive about their height.

Liam could remember overhearing a much younger

Samantha telling her mother in a low voice choked with tears, 'Mom, the other girls at school say that I should have been a boy because I'm so big…but I'm not a boy, I'm a girl and…'

'They're just jealous of you, darling,' her mother had reassured her quickly. 'You are indeed a girl, a very beautiful, clever and lovable girl, a very feminine girl,' she had reinforced, and Liam had watched as Sarah Jane had very cleverly and with maternal love and concern, made sure that her daughters learned how to focus on the very feminine aspects of their personalities, to hold their heads up with pride and grace.

They *were* tall, and as a teenager Samantha especially had gone through a phase when she had been all gangly limbs, a little lanky and perhaps almost boyish, but that had been as a teenager. Now she was all woman… Oh, yes…now she was very definitely all woman!

Waking up beside him, Samantha wondered what had caused that sudden burst of fire to ignite the darkness of Liam's eyes. Whatever it was, whoever it was… Was it a whoever rather than a whatever? Samantha suddenly wondered. The new PR woman perhaps? She gave a small, quick, sharp intake of breath. Liam might be prepared to bow to the fears of the more conservative lobby and do the conventional thing, marry in order to improve his public appeal, but there was no power on earth that could ever force her to do the same thing. Her principles, her need of her own self-respect, were far too strong, but Liam of course, was far too pragmatic to understand such a sensitive point of view. Cousin James in Chester was very sensitive. She had noticed that in him the moment they had met, and had been touched and warmed by it and by his concern for her.

James.

She was *already* beginning to feel a very definite tingle of excitement at the thought of seeing him again. The Crighton men made wonderful fathers, even the family's erstwhile outcast Max had totally and unexpectedly shown that he possessed the loving Crighton gene when it came to parenting.

'He seems more thrilled about this new baby they're expecting than Maddy is,' Bobbie had confided to her sister when she had passed on to her the news that Max's wife Maddy was pregnant with their third child.

'A reconciliation baby,' Samantha had commented. 'Well, I hope it works—for the new baby's sake.'

'Mmm… I can't get over how their relationship has turned around,' Bobbie had continued. 'Max seems to have completely given up his old ways. He's based himself in Chester now and he and Luke have developed a rapport I would have thought completely impossible at one time.

'It's Maddy who's changed the most, though. I thought that with Max back at home, recovered from the vicious attack he suffered in Jamaica and so completely repentant and determined to make their marriage work that Maddy would have reverted to her previous role of full-time wife and mother—after all, it's no sinecure, not when you think of what running a house like Queensmead entails, and the fact that she's also got Ben living with them.

'I know she thinks the world of him and him of her, and of course Max has always been his favourite grandchild, but that doesn't alter the fact that he can be very irascible and that he holds very strong and old-fashioned views. But no, instead, she's not only kept on the work she was doing for Grandma Ruth's mother and children charity, but she's actually got even *more* involved. Luke told me the other day that Max had admitted that he sometimes felt as though he needed to make an appointment in order to get Maddy's undivided attention these days.'

'Mmm…well I certainly noticed how much she's blossomed the last time I was over,' Samantha had agreed.

Previously she had found that Maddy, with her self-effacing timid ways, although sweet-natured and gentle, wasn't someone she felt particularly drawn to, but on her last visit she had been not just amazed and intrigued by the change in her, but she had also discovered how interesting and entertaining Maddy was to talk with.

'She certainly has. Her latest thing is that she's instituted a bi-monthly women's night out when we all get together and leave the men in charge of the babes. We all host the event in turn and it's amazing the different things everyone comes up with. It's my turn next and I was wondering if we could bribe the men into extending their child-minding so that we might have a weekend in New York.'

Recalling their conversation now, Sam remembered, too, how she had felt just that little bit envious of her sister's almost idyllic lifestyle. Her own friends, the girls she had grown up with and then met at college, were scattered all over the States and beyond them, some married, some not, and whilst they all kept in sporadic touch there was not the close-knit sense of community, of family, between them that

Bobbie had become so much a part of in her life in England.

Samantha knew enough of small close-knit communities from her childhood in New England to be aware that sometimes they could be restrictive and even stultifying but… But the pluses were greater than the minuses in the balance sheet of life, at least in her opinion, and the teasing affectionate friendships which she had witnessed existing between her twin and the other members of the Crighton clan were something she couldn't help contrasting with her own sense of alienation and separateness from her own work colleagues.

They were approaching the airport now, the freeway increasingly busy. What was she like, Liam's new PR? Intelligent? Sparky? Glamorous? All of those and very probably a whole lot more, Samantha decided. Her father had certainly sounded impressed by her.

Was that why she was experiencing these unfamiliar little tickles of antipathy and this disobliging sense of not wanting to like the other woman? Samantha wondered ruefully.

Liam had parked the car and was opening his door.

'I'll get you a trolley,' he was informing her.

'For goodness' sake, Liam,' she snapped. 'Stop smothering me. I'm perfectly capable of getting my own trolley. I'm a big girl, remember…'

'Maybe, but I'm an old-fashioned man,' he reminded her almost tersely. 'Wait here…'

'Wait here!' Samantha opened her mouth to snap angrily that she would do no such thing but it was too late, he was already striding determinedly to where the baggage carts were stacked.

Typically she discovered when he returned with one, unlike her he had managed to find one that wheeled smoothly and easily.

'Liam,' she protested fiercely when he insisted on pushing it for her.

'What *is* it with you?' he demanded grittily. 'You know your trouble, don't you, Samantha?' He answered his own question without allowing her any time to make her own response. 'You're afraid of being a woman. You're afraid of…'

'I'm no such thing,' Samantha interrupted him furiously. 'I…'

'Yes, you are,' Liam taunted her. 'Look at the way you even prefer to be called Sam instead of Samantha.'

'That's not because…it's just easier for people to say…quicker…'

Liam's eyebrows lifted.

'Quicker maybe, but nowhere near as sexy.'

'Sexy!' She glared at him.

'Mmm… Samantha…' He said her name slowly, drawing out each syllable. 'Samantha is a woman's name and like a woman should be lingered over and enjoyed the way a man…'

'Thanks for the psychoanalysis,' Samantha snapped fiercely, 'but I've got a plane to catch, remember, Liam? So, if you want to do some lingering I suggest you wait until you've picked up your new PR. *She* might be more impressed than…'

'See, you're doing it now,' Liam stopped her softly. 'What is it you're really afraid of, Samantha…? I'll take a guess that it isn't not being enough of a woman…it's being *too* much of one.'

Samantha stared at him, for once completely lost

for words. His soft-voiced comment had struck un-
nervingly close to home, too close… To have someone, *anyone,* see so deeply and intimately into her
most private self was a disturbing enough act on its
own, but when that someone was *Liam,* a man who
she had dismissed as someone too prosaic…too practical…too unemotional to…

'I need to check in,' she told him, making a grab
for the trolley only too relieved to have an excuse for
both changing the subject and escaping his presence
and her own thoughts.

'Mmm…'

Instead of relinquishing the trolley handle Liam
kept hold of it so that her hands were resting close to
the warmth of his and then, before she could guess
what he intended to do, Liam moved with surprising
swiftness, covering her hands with his own and keeping her captive, his head bending over hers in the
same half beat of time that she lifted her face towards
him in irritable surprise.

'Li—,' she began but got no further than the first
syllable of his name before his mouth was covering
hers.

He had only kissed her very occasionally before,
brief non-sexual courtesy kisses on her cheek and so
she was completely unprepared for the reaction the
hard determined pressure of his mouth evoked from
her now.

Her pulse gave an unexpected shock-cum-thrill little flutter that left her feeling breathless and light-
headed. Or was it the increasingly firm pressure of
Liam's mouth that was doing that? An unexpectedly
delicious and temptingly enjoyable firm pressure, the
kind of firm pressure that made her sigh softly and

lean responsively into him, her own lips starting to part on what just might have been a give-away small sound of heady pleasure.

It was, of course, the bright lights of the airport that were making her close her eyes and then open them slowly again to focus hazily and wonderingly on the deep smouldering depths of Liam's—of course it was. Languorously, Samantha felt her lips soften against his… Mmm…but it was such a lovely kiss, such a sensuous, nerve-skittering, heart-thrillingly sexy kiss that she would have to have been made of stone to resist it.

But…

Abruptly she stiffened, realising just where her thoughts were heading, and firmly she pushed him away.

'Thank you, Liam,' she told him sweetly. 'That was very nice but shouldn't you be saving it for someone more…appreciative…'

His eyebrows rose as he released her.

'Much *more* appreciation and they'd have been hauling us up for indecency,' Liam drawled back.

'Indecency…' Samantha shot him a fiercely indignant look, preparing to do battle, and then stopped, her face flushing as she saw the brief, oh so wryly explicit look he was giving her body.

There was no need of course for *her* to look down at her T-shirt-clad breasts to see just how tautly erect her nipples now were. *She* could feel it…them.

'That's just—' she began defensively.

Liam stopped her, shaking his head as he told her dryly, 'You don't need to tell *me* what it is, hon,' he drawled. 'In fact—'

'They'll be calling my flight,' Samantha told him, desperate to escape.

She knew her face must be flushed because her body felt hot. Her mind was burning with questions and her instinctive need was simply to escape just as fast as she could, to avoid any kind of confrontation. *Not* with Liam, no, it was *herself* she didn't feel able to confront, her *own* inexplicable behaviour and re-actions. Grabbing hold of the trolley, she started to walk away from Liam as quickly as she could, refusing to give in to the temptation to turn round and see what he was doing—how he was looking.

The girl at the check-in desk gave her a calmly professional smile as she checked her travel documents and indicated that Samantha was to put her luggage on the conveyor.

Samantha could feel a prickling sensation running jarringly up and down her spine. She just *knew* that Liam was still there watching her. Unable to stop herself, she turned round, her mouth opening in a small O of disbelief when she couldn't see him. He had gone already. Aggrieved she double-checked the area where she had left him, muttering beneath her breath as she did so, 'Well, thanks very much…'

It was typical of him, of course, to behave in such an outrageously high-handed manner and then simply walk away without any explanation. No doubt if she had asked him for one he would have responded with something unflattering.

The check-in girl was indicating that she was to go through to the departure area. Briefly Samantha hesitated but there was still no sign of Liam. No doubt he was far more interested in meeting this new PR person than he was in seeing *her* off.

A little forlornly Samantha went through into the departure lounge.

From his vantage point, well away from the busy main concourse, Liam watched as Samantha set off on her journey. Kissing her like that had been a mistake and mistakes were something that Liam did not normally allow himself to make. It wasn't good policy for an ambitious young politician. Ambitious…young… Liam gave a semi self-derisory little smile.

Young he most certainly no longer was—and as for ambitious? Recently he had become increasingly aware that he had absorbed much more from working with Samantha's father than the mere mechanics, the bare bones of what the governorship of their small state actually involved.

Stephen Miller was a true philanthropist. Someone who genuinely wanted to improve the lot of his fellow men, to raise their expectations of life and their belief in themselves in ways both temporal and secular. A rapport had developed between them which had touched upon the sensitive and idealistic side of Liam's nature, the Celtic inheritance which believed so strongly in the right of the human race to stand proud and free.

His ambitions now no longer centred on Washington or the personal goal of high office. In stepping into Stephen Miller's shoes, he would be granted a unique opportunity to build on foundations so secure and true that ultimately they could support a society as near to perfection as man with his inherently flawed nature could ever get. Their health care programme, their record for supporting the more needy, especially the elderly, was already being lauded as a model on which other states should base their own programmes.

Their high school drop-out rate was decreasing every year and one of Liam's own goals would be to find a means of motivating the less intellectually gifted and of giving them both a sense of self-worth and the respect of others.

Liam didn't believe in deluding himself. Getting the governorship was but the first very small step in what was going to be a long, testing and arduous journey. There was no space in his life either now or in the foreseeable future for…complications.

Other people might claim that he needed a wife but the kind of wife he had in mind, as he knew very well, the kind of *marriage* he had in mind, was a carefully organised and businesslike political partnership, a marriage where it was automatically acknowledged that his work would come first.

The cool analytical controlled side of his nature agreed with this, the idealistic, passionate Celtic side did not.

He saw the tiny frown, the quickly hidden forlorn look Samantha gave the empty space where he had been standing before turning and walking away.

He could still vividly remember the impact she had had on him the first time he had seen her. A teenager she might have been, but her burgeoning womanhood had still been there for those with the eyes to see it. She might have been shy and a little awkward, blushingly self-conscious about the crush she had had on him, but he had been all too well aware of the powerful strength of the womanly passion she would ultimately own.

Pride and passion—they were a dangerous combination in any woman, but most especially in one like Samantha who also had such a strong maternal yearning.

He had seen the look in her eyes as she held other women's babies, when she played with her twin's little girl. If her pride and her idealism had been less he suspected that she might, long ago, have settled for a mundane marriage to a man who allowed her to control their relationship whilst she gave the full passion of her love to their children, but Samantha wasn't like that. There was no way she could ever allow herself to accept second-best. But now the cruel gibes of her work colleagues had galvanised her into action and she was determined to prove him and them wrong.

Liam frowned. It was time for him to go and meet the Washington flight. Samantha had been more on the mark than she knew with her slightly waspish comments about Toni Davis. Ostensibly she was quite simply joining his campaign in a PR capacity, but Liam was no fool. He knew perfectly well that one of the reasons her name had been put forward was because she would make a perfect political wife. Subtle, discreet, content to remain in the background and to exercise her ambitions via her husband, Toni Davis was the complete antithesis to Samantha who had *never* learned to fully control her emotions and realise that the best way to do battle for her beliefs was not always the most upfront and open way.

He could hear the Washington flight being announced. As he lifted his arm to look at his watch Liam recognised that the scent wafting from his jacket was Samantha's.

CHAPTER FOUR

'SAM…over here….'

Samantha checked and then waved frantically, her face breaking into a wide beaming smile as she caught sight of Bobbie's brother-in-law and her cousin, James Crighton, waiting for her on the other side of the airport arrivals barrier.

'James, what a lovely surprise,' she cried, hugging him enthusiastically. More than one person stopped to admire the attractive picture they made. James, tall, dark and boyishly good-looking, and Samantha, almost equally as tall and stunningly eye-catching with her golden-blonde hair, their arms wrapped around one another as they kissed with genuine affection.

'Mmm…' James murmured appreciatively, a teasing glint in his eyes as Samantha started to disengage herself. 'That was nice…'

'*Very* nice,' Samantha agreed with laughing playfulness, offering him saucily, 'Want another…'

Laughter gurgled in her throat at the look that James was giving her. They had always gotten on well together but where she was all quicksilver reactions and emotions, James was far more laid back and calm which she found blissfully soothing.

'People are watching,' James warned her as his lips touched hers.

'Who cares,' Sam returned recklessly, but he still released her, Samantha noticed. Now Liam would not only have mocked *her* he would also have deliberately and arrogantly ignored everybody else.

Liam! Why on earth was she thinking about him now? It should be James she was concentrating on. Beneath her lashes she flicked him a considering look. It was easy to dismiss and overlook the attractiveness of James's smile, the sheer niceness of him, in favour of the spectacularly smouldering sexuality of his cousin Saul, the austere, exciting sensuality of his brother Luke, the sledgehammer onslaught of the outrageous physical appeal of his other cousin Max, but James, in his own way was every bit as special and sexy as the other Crighton men, even if he came across as being rather more gentle, a little less macho and hormonally charged.

Personally *she* preferred James to the others. His presence was so relaxing and soothing. She loved the calming effect he had on her, so very different from the hostile aggression Liam so often aroused in her. James would make a wonderful father. She could see him now…

'Bobbie said to apologise for not being able to meet you herself. Francesca's had a bit of a chesty cough and she didn't want to leave her.'

'Oh, poor little girl,' Samantha instantly sympathised. 'How is she…? Is she…?'

'It's nothing too serious,' James assured her. 'It's just that she's been a bit fretful.'

'Well, it's very kind of you to make time to meet me,' Samantha thanked him. 'The last time I spoke to Bobbie she mentioned how busy both you and Luke are.'

'Mmm… Well thankfully, since Max joined the chambers the pressure has eased off a little, or at least it was doing but, well I shouldn't complain about the fact that we seem to be attracting more briefs than ever. Aarlston-Becker have been placing a considerable amount of work our way via Saul and increasingly I seem to be finding that I'm spending more and more of my time in the Hague involved in lengthy international cases.'

Aarlston-Becker was the multi-national concern with offices in Haslewich, and Saul Crighton, a member of the Haslewich side of the Crighton family through his father Hugh, her own grandmother Ruth's half-brother, headed the legal team and so it was quite natural that when he needed the expert opinion of a barrister that he should apply to his own family for it.

'Dad was complaining only the other day about how much the legal profession has changed,' James continued. 'Historically, of course, barristers did have specific and special areas of expertise, now these areas have become much more individually defined. We've even been talking about taking on a new member of Chambers due to the amount of medical compensation cases we've been getting.'

'Pity I'm not qualified in that field myself,' Samantha told him doe-eyed.

'*You're* looking for a career move?' James asked her interestedly.

'Sort of,' Samantha responded tongue-in-cheek, her eyes dancing with amusement as she wondered what he would say if she were to tell him in just exactly *what* direction she was envisaging her career moving and why.

'Would you mind if we called on my parents on

the way back?' James was asking her as he guided her towards his waiting car.

'No, not at all,' Samantha responded promptly.

She had already met James' parents and the rest of his family on several occasions and had got on well with them.

She knew from Bobbie that they had just moved to a ground-floor apartment in a recently renovated large Victorian house on the banks of the Dee.

'Henry loves it,' Bobbie had told Samantha, referring to her father-in-law. 'He spent hours wrangling with the builders over the quality of workmanship and Pat says that taking charge of the owners association has given him a new lease of life.

'Luke complains that he can see a lot of his father's stubbornness in Francesca…'

'His *father's* stubbornness,' Samantha had repeated drolly, whilst Bobbie had laughed ruefully.

'Okay, okay, I know, I have my fair share of that particular vice, no need to rub it in. Still, a little toughness won't do Fran any harm, not if she's going to follow family tradition and go into the law.'

'Fran! No way,' Samantha had told her twin robustly. 'She's going to be running the country at the very least.'

The Cheshire countryside in sunshine had to be one of the prettiest sights there was, Samantha reflected happily as she sat next to James in comfortable silence as he drove them towards Chester.

In the distance beyond the fertile neatly checkered fields lay the blue haze of the Welsh mountains. No wonder in centuries gone by there had been so much feuding over the Welsh border. No wonder warring

English kings had needed to build so many strong castles to protect their rich domain.

It was a humbling thought to remember that the Romans had farmed these lands and mined the rich vein of salt from which the town of Haslewich had got its wealth and its name.

Now the salt was no longer mined and the modern legacy that industry had left was one of flooded salt works and dangerously unstable buildings.

As though he had read her mind James commented conversationally, 'We've got an interesting case at the moment. A local farmer is trying to sue Aarlston-Becker because he claims the weight of the company's headquarters is causing subsidence on his land.'

'Oh, and is it?' Samantha asked him interestedly.

'Hard to say, but certainly it's a topic which arouses an awful lot of emotions. It's the classic story of the old guard being suspicious of the new incomers. The case had been given a lot of local publicity. Aarlston has an image to maintain of a socially aware and ecologically sound organisation so, in the end, to protect that image they may have to opt for a one-off payment to the farmer. His land is over a mile away but he maintains that because of the interlinking network of mines and tunnels beneath the ground, the weight of the Aarlston building is being reflected in land subsidence some distance away.'

'Mmm…sounds like a try-on to me,' Samantha pronounced.

'Mmm…indeed,' James conceded, returning the laughing smile Samantha was giving him, his gaze lingering for just a shade longer than was merely cousinly on her face.

A small sensation of happy warmth curled up through Samantha's body. Coming to England had quite definitely been the right decision. What she would give to have Cliff witness that look she had just seen in James' eyes.

They would make the most beautiful babies together. Samantha gave a small contented sigh.

How thoughtful of fate to give her plans an active boost like this. Keeping her voice carefully neutral she told James, 'With her pregnancy and everything Bobbie has her hands pretty full at the moment…'

Deliberately she affected a small downcast sigh. 'I was so looking forward to seeing a bit more of the area, too, and of catching up with the rest of the family.'

'Well, if you need an escort *I'd* be more than happy to offer my services,' James responded gallantly.

Samantha produced a slightly self-conscious look, flapping her eyelashes and exclaiming, 'Oh, James, would you…? That would be so kind, although I didn't mean…'

'It would be my pleasure,' James assured her fervently.

She really wasn't behaving very well at all, Samantha reflected a little guiltily, but it was for the very best of causes and if she hadn't sensed that James liked her…

They were just outside Chester now and Samantha could feel the excitement starting to bubble up inside her. She was so looking forward to being with Bobbie. She gave an exultant sigh and closed her eyes. What would Liam make of Chester, she wondered. He would be impossibly well informed about its long history, of course, with every fact and figure at his fingertips, and whilst *she* fantasised about the romanticism of its history, he would no doubt insist on bringing her down to earth by reminding her of the savagery and bloodshed it must have known.

Angrily Samantha opened her eyes. Liam! *Why* on earth was she thinking about *him?* Just because he had kissed her? Just because she…

'Are you okay?' James was asking her, sensing the tension, his forehead creased in concern.

'I'm fine,' Samantha assured him, but somehow it felt as though a small cloud had been cast over the exultation she had felt earlier. It was stupid of her to compare the warm, affectionate, almost brotherly touch of James' lips to the hard, pulse-dizzying possession of Liam's, and *why* was she doing it anyway? Liam's kiss hadn't meant *anything* to her.

Not cerebrally maybe, but her *body* had certainly responded to it—to *him.*

An accident; an aberration, a faulty bit of sexual programming, that was all that had been.

'You've gone quiet. Are you tired?' James asked her solicitously.

'A mite jet-lagged I guess,' Samantha agreed, gratefully seizing on the excuse he had given her for her lapse in concentration. James was so wonderfully caring and considerate.

'We're here now,' he told her as he swung his small sporty car in through a pair of high wrought-iron gates which opened automatically for them.

The builders who had renovated and converted the large Victorian house into apartments had taken great care to maintain the original facade and to provide well-secured grounds around it. An immaculate expanse of gravel swept round to the front of the building. No parking bays had been marked out on it but James informed Samantha drolly that there was a definite parking spot for each apartment and woe betide anyone who parked in the wrong place.

'I think if he could get away with it Dad would impose ''on the spot'' fines on unwitting miscreants parking in the wrong place,' he told her ruefully.

'It's a magnificent house,' Samantha enthused, automatically reaching for the passenger door handle of the car, but before she could swing it open James was out of the car, sprinting round to the door to open it for her.

There was always a certain formality and protocol attached to being a member of the Governor's family but Samantha couldn't remember the last time a *date* had proved so solicitous towards her.

From its elevated position on the banks of the Dee the house overlooked the river itself and the countryside beyond it and Samantha could well appreciate why James' parents had wanted to move here.

'With none of us left at home Ma was finding the house far too large and with three storeys, each with a flight of stairs, it made sense to move to somewhere more easily manageable.'

As he spoke, James was guiding Samantha towards the main entrance to the building.

A special security card was needed to gain entrance into the inner hallway, coolly elegant in cream marble and illuminated with an enormous crystal chandelier.

'It's this way,' James told her, indicating a pair of handsome carved doors on the left and going up to them to press the bell.

Almost immediately the door was opened by James' mother. Although Patricia Crighton was a very attractive-looking woman, it was from their father that Luke and James had inherited their striking dark good looks.

'Samantha, my dear, do come in,' Patricia Crighton greeted her, kissing Samantha warmly on the cheek.

The drawing room the older woman took Samantha to was filled with the elegant antiques Samantha remembered from their previous home. There was, she noticed, a very recent photograph of her twin sister with her husband Luke and their little girl amongst the other family photographs on top of the elegant Queen Anne side table.

'Is Dad here? I've got those papers he asked me for,' James said to his mother.

'He's in his study, darling,' she responded, adding, 'Oh, and by the way, we've got a visitor.' She stopped, giving James a rather wary look, and then the drawing room door opened to admit her husband and a young woman who Samantha did not recognise.

'Rosemary, what the devil are you doing here?' she heard James demanding sharply, the antagonism so very evident in his voice and his demeanour that Samantha looked at him in surprise. Suddenly he looked and sounded so very much more like his elder brother, so very forcibly a Crighton, and it was obvious from his expression what his feelings were for the girl who had just walked into the room. What on earth had she done to make James, of all people, dislike her so much? Samantha wondered curiously.

Small and red-headed, she had a neat triangular-shaped face with high cheek-bones and huge amber-flecked golden eyes. Although she was wearing jeans and a T-shirt there was no disguising the rounded voluptuousness of her figure. Her waist was tiny,

Samantha noticed, so small that she guessed a man could easily span it with his hands.

'Rosemary, my dear,' James' mother was beginning but the girl wasn't paying any attention to her, instead she was concentrating wholly and completely on James, fixing him with a fulminating look of bitter hostility.

'Oh, it's all right, Aunt Pat,' she announced with an angry toss of her head. 'Far be it from me to point out that since this isn't James' house *he* doesn't really have any right to question my presence here. Your mother has invited me to come and stay with her, James,' she added, baring her teeth in a smile that made Samantha think of an angry and dangerous little cat.

'Rosemary needed a break,' James' mother was saying palliatively. 'She's worked so hard for her finals and now that she's qualified…'

'Qualified?' James interrupted sharply. 'God help anyone who needs…who's desperate enough to need *your* medical expertise, Rosemary. Personally I'd sooner…'

'James,' his mother commanded warningly.

Two brilliant coins of hot colour were now burning in the girl's creamy pale skin and her eyes… Samantha grimaced a little as she studied their furious molten heat. Small she might be, but there was no mistaking the ferocity of her emotions.

'Rosemary has just finished her medical training and qualified as a GP,' James' mother informed Samantha gently. 'And since I'm her godmother I felt that her hard work and dedication deserved rewarding with a small treat, especially since her fiancé Tim is going to be working abroad all summer.'

As James' mother spoke Rosemary lifted her hand, showing off the diamond ring she was wearing, the look she gave James a mixture of defiance and triumph.

'You see, James,' she told him, 'not all men share your opinion of me.'

'You're engaged!' It was plain to see how shocked James was. 'What a masochist!'

'James!' Pat Crighton expostulated sharply.

Grimly James turned towards his father.

'A small treat,' James picked up on what his mother had said. 'So you've invited her to stay here for a few weeks…' His voice full of disgust.

'Here are the papers you asked me for,' he said to his father, turning his back on his mother and Rosemary.

'We must go,' he informed them all. 'Bobbie is expecting us and Samantha's beginning to feel a little jet-lagged.'

'It's probably something to do with a lack of oxygen,' Rosemary chipped in in mock sympathy, something about the acid sweetness of her voice causing Samantha to focus on her more closely. When she did so the outright hostility in the other girl's eyes startled her.

'Rosemary…' she could hear James beginning warningly, but it was becoming clear to Samantha that the redhead had as reckless a hot temper and an emotionally driven streak as her hair colour suggested because she deliberately ignored him and continued.

'It can't be easy inhabiting such a rarefied atmosphere…*or* being so tall…'

Samantha's eyes widened a little. The other girl's

hostility totally perplexed her but cat fights had never been her style...even so...

'Mmm...but it does have its compensations,' she drawled in her best and most laid-back American voice, turning from the girl to James who was standing protectively by her side.

If she stood up on her toes they were almost exactly shoulder to shoulder, face to face, lips to lips.

Very deliberately Samantha looked into James' eyes and then allowed her glance to slide downward to his mouth before touching her tongue tip to her own upper lip.

'Er... I think we'd better leave,' James announced thickly.

Samantha permitted herself a languorous look of superiority in the direction of Rosemary and then checked it as she saw not just bitter fury in the girl's eyes but the hot glimmer of tears, as well.

Tears? For James? But she was wearing another man's ring. Thoughtfully Samantha said goodbye to James' parents and followed him out to the car.

'I don't know what on earth's possessed my mother to invite Rosemary to stay,' James was fuming as he started his car's engine.

'They obviously get on well together and since Rosemary is her goddaughter...'

'Rosemary is a menace...a...' James said. 'But my mother can't or won't see it.'

'She's very pretty,' Samantha offered, trying another tack.

'Pretty...' James stared at her. 'She was a red-haired brat with freckles.'

'Mmm...well, she's *still* red-haired,' Samantha agreed.

'She used to come and stay with us during the school holidays. Her parents worked abroad and she was at boarding school.'

'You didn't get on with her?' Samantha guessed.

'...and the rest,' James agreed. 'She really was the most loathsome little pest. "I'll tell Aunt Pat..."'' he mimicked and then shook his head. 'I know you must think I'm overreacting but she really used to get under my skin.'

He wasn't drawing a very attractive picture of the other girl and given her unwarranted and unprovoked malicious comment to herself, Samantha might have agreed with him but for those unexpected tears. Rosemary's feelings for James were no concern of hers, Samantha reminded herself, and since she had her own plans for James' future...and since Rosemary herself was engaged... Even so she couldn't help wishing that she hadn't seen those tears, that she hadn't for that brief pulse of time felt the other girl's distress.

'Come on then, give me all the news about the family,' Bobbie urged her twin.

They were sitting in Bobbie's comfortable kitchen, James having just left, whilst Francesca played busily around them.

'There isn't that much *to* tell that you don't already know,' Samantha protested. 'Mom and Dad can't wait to get over here to see you all...'

'Mmm...I'm hoping to persuade them to spend more time over here when Dad retires. How's Liam's campaign going, by the way?'

'Dad's convinced he'll walk it but there has been concern expressed over Liam not being married. He drove me to the airport. He was picking up a PR woman they've hired from Washington to project his image.'

'Liam married, how will *you* feel about that?' Bobbie teased her.

Samantha shot her an indignant look.

'Why should *I* care. Just because I once had a teen-age crush on him…'

'Okay, okay…I was just joking,' Bobbie reassured her, but she still studied her twin a little thoughtfully.

Samantha had lost some weight and she looked strained…stressed…

'You know, Bobbie, I do envy you,' Samantha admitted abruptly.

Instinctively Bobbie looked to where Francesca was playing, knowing without it having to be put into words just what it was about her life that her twin envied.

'You're a born mother, Sam,' she told her gently, her expression suddenly changing to one of acute alarm as she demanded, 'You're not thinking of going through with that fool idea you once had of becoming pregnant via a fertilization programme…'

Samantha laughed.

'No,' she reassured her, her face sobering as she admitted, 'I don't want my kids growing up envying yours because yours have a real live daddy and mine don't.'

'So there isn't a prospective daddy anywhere on the horizon?' Bobbie probed.

Samantha looked away from her.

'Samantha!' Bobbie pounced excitedly. 'There *is* someone…tell me… Who is it? Do I know him…? Sam…'

'Oh, no… I'm not saying anything,' Samantha told her, vehemently shaking her head.

'I'm going to phone home,' Bobbie threatened determinedly.

'There isn't any point, the folks don't know any more than you do…'

'So there *is* something to know then…'

'No!' Samantha denied.

There was no way she intended to let Bobbie in on her plan to marry James until she was a lot more certain of her own ground. Sure she and James got on well together but… She *could* love him, Samantha was convinced of it, and he, she was equally sure, could love her.

He would be a *perfect* father. She could see it all now. She closed her eyes blissfully, mentally imagining her own cosy homely kitchen and her own adorable children filling it. She wanted boys, she knew that already, boys with thick dark hair and solemn grey eyes… Grey eyes… Her own flew open. Now where, oh, where, had *that* idea come from? Firmly she recorrected her imagination. Her children, her *twins,* would have eyes the same colour as their father's of course. They would have James' *brown* eyes.

Having finished her game, Francesca stood up and stalked imperiously towards her.

'Did you bring me a present from my grandma in America?' she asked her.

'Francesca,' Bobbie protested warningly.

But Samantha only grinned and asked her twin dryly, 'Wonder where she gets *that* from?'

'Not from me,' Bobbie denied, but her face was pink and she knew as clearly as though she had read Samantha's mind that her twin was remembering an incident from their own childhood when she, Bobbie, had shamingly asked much the same question of their own grandfather.

'Poor Mom was *so* mortified,' Samantha teased her.

'Not half so mortified as I was when she banished me upstairs to my room *and* I haven't forgotten that *you* were the one who told me to ask.' Bobbie said with heartfelt ruefulness.

After they had finished, still laughing, Samantha confided to her twin, 'I've bought her the cutest outfits.'

'Mmm… Well I may as well warn you that if it isn't Barbie doll pink then Francesca won't even *look* at it.'

'No… How can you doubt me?' Samantha responded, grinning at her. 'She'll *love* it.'

'Samantha…' Bobbie warned warily. 'What…'

'I've even got her the matching sparkling pink shoes and…strictly for dressing up, of course,' she assured her stern-faced twin.

'…and for you I made a special trip to Boston. I've got you the sexiest Donna Karan number you've *ever* seen. It dips right down at the back so that… Not that you'll be able to wear it until after the new baby arrives—but still that won't be long now!'

'You have…where…*show me*…' Bobbie demanded excitedly.

The pair of them were still giggling over the clothes-strewn spare room when Luke arrived home over an hour later.

'Auntie Sam brought me pink shoes,' Francesca informed him proudly.

Laughing Samantha shook her head as she kissed her brother-in-law.

'Guess what I've brought you…'

'I don't think I dare,' Luke drawled, looking past her to where his wife, all pink-cheeked and bright-eyed was holding up in front of her a dress that Luke could immediately see would cause a total uproar if she ever wore it in public. Bobbie looked like a little girl clutching on to a much-wanted toy and he already knew there was no way anyone was going to prise it away from her.

'So what have you brought for Luke?' Bobbie asked her twin absently an hour later as they all sat down together for their meal.

Grinning at her brother-in-law, Samantha told him, 'It's a golf club, a new one, I don't believe you can get it over here yet.'

'Not an "iron overlord,"' Luke breathed hopefully.

'The very same,' Samantha confirmed, laughing as he got up and came round the table to hug her and then demand, 'Where is it? I…'

'Not until after you have finished your meal, Luke,' Bobbie mock frowned at him.

By nine o'clock Samantha was ready to concede that her long flight had caught up with her.

'If you're really sure you don't mind if I go to bed…?'

'Of course we don't mind,' Bobbie reassured her.

'What's wrong?' Luke asked Bobbie an hour later as he handed her the mug of chocolate he had just made her.

'I don't know…it's just…Sam's up to some-thing…'

'Like what?'

'I don't know and there's no point in my asking,

she'd just clam up on me, but *something's* going on…'

'Twin telepathy?' Luke teased.

'Something's bothering her, Luke, she's put her guard up to prevent me finding out about it but I *know* it's there… I wish she could find her special some-one… She so desperately wants children…'

'Mmm…now that I did notice.'

'Well, at least I've got lots of things planned to entertain her whilst she's here…'

'Mmm…I'm afraid there's a slight problem on that score,' Luke told his wife quietly.

Bobbie looked questioningly at him.

'Luke…' she began.

'Yes, I know we agreed that I would take time off to look after Francesca so that you would be free to spend time with Sam, but…'

'But *what*…'

'The Dillinger case comes up for trial next week and I'm going to be in court.'

'Oh, Luke, no…' Bobbie wailed.

'Bobbie, I'm sorry, but you know the way things are.'

She did, of course she did, Luke was a barrister and if one of his cases came to court then he had to be there.

'Sam's here for several weeks and with any luck the case should be over in two,' Luke comforted her.

'Well, I just hope that *Sam* understands,' Bobbie told him.

CHAPTER FIVE

'I REALLY am sorry, Sam,' Bobbie apologised to her sister, 'but there's nothing that Luke can do.'

They had just finished eating breakfast and Bobbie had explained to her twin that she wasn't going to be as free to devote her time to her as she had hoped.

To her relief Samantha seemed completely unfazed by her news.

'Don't worry about it,' she told her sunnily. 'Besides,' she added, her voice and eyes softening, 'you and the coming baby mean far more to me than socialising and treats₁ As a matter of fact, James has actually offered his services as an escort should I need one.'

With a shaky smile Bobbie reached out to cover her twin's hand with her own. 'I *am* feeling more tired with this baby, and both my doctor and Luke have insisted that I ought to rest,' she admitted, her face brightening as she added, 'But at least you'll have James to take you about.'

James and Samantha had always got on well together.

'Well, hopefully Luke's case should be over in a fortnight and…'

'Mmm…well that should be long enough.'

Samantha bit her lip as she realised she had spoken her thoughts out loud.

'For what?' Bobbie asked her curiously. 'I…'

'Oh, nothing… I just meant that a fortnight should

261

be long enough for the case to be concluded,' Samantha fibbed airily, quickly redirecting Bobbie's attention by asking her, 'How's Fran doing at school now? You were concerned that she wasn't being stretched enough.'

'Mmm… I was, but Luke says that she is only four and he doesn't want her being pushed too hard and that he'd rather she exercised her own curiosity naturally.'

'Well, he does have a point. Look at the way the pair of us ran wild whenever we went to Gramps, and it certainly didn't do us any harm.'

'No, I suppose not.'

'Olivia's invited us over for lunch today.'

'Has she? How are she and Caspar?' Samantha asked affectionately and within several minutes the sisters were deeply immersed in a detailed update of what was happening within the Haslewich and Chester branches of the Crighton family.

'It's a pity that Grandma Ruth can't be here right now,' Bobbie commented.

'Mmm… I was looking forward to seeing her and Gramps,' Samantha admitted. 'But I can understand why she felt she had to go to Pembrokeshire. How is Ann?'

Ann Crighton, Hugh Crighton's wife, had been involved in an accident which had resulted in her being hospitalised for several weeks.

'Well, she's at home now and the doctors have confirmed that she will make a full recovery, but Hugh's terrified that she's going to try to do too much. She's been forbidden to climb any stairs or to do anything more than walk very slowly and gently until the damage to her back heals properly.'

'It's frightening to realise just how much damage even the slightest car accident can cause.' Samantha gave a small shiver. 'According to what Gran has told Mom, it was just a simple shunt and the car which hit Ann's was hardly moving at all.'

'Yes, I know,' Bobbie agreed soberly. 'It certainly made me feel very wary about taking Francesca out anywhere in the car for weeks afterwards and I can understand, too, why Hugh asked Grandma Ruth for her help in keeping Ann occupied whilst she's recovering.'

'They're such a lovely couple and although Gran never says so, I suspect that she secretly prefers Hugh to Ben, even though Ben's her full blood brother and Hugh only a half.'

'Mmm…but then just because there's a full blood relationship between siblings, it doesn't necessarily mean that they are going to like one another.'

This was said so gravely that Samantha gave her twin a quick look before teasing, 'And what conclusions am I supposed to draw from that, sister dear?'

Bobbie looked at her, her face relaxing into a smile.

'Don't worry, I'm not trying to say I don't like *you*…hate you sometimes, maybe…' she teased back and then, shaking her head, she confided, 'No…it's not us…but…'

'But what?' Samantha encouraged when she fell silent.

'Well, you know how it can be with families sometimes…brothers and sisters, siblings…just don't always get on…'

'Sibling rivalry… Well, we've certainly had our fair share of that in the Crighton family. I mean, if you want a classic example just look at Jon and

Jenny's family. Louise and Katie positively loathed Max at one time, and...'

'Yes, yes, I know what you're saying but it isn't...' Bobbie stopped again and then started to trace an abstract pattern on the wooden kitchen table with her fingertip.

'It's Fran and the new baby,' she admitted huskily after several seconds. 'I think she's starting to get a little bit jealous—even before he or she is born.'

She looked so upset.

'But surely, Bobbie, that's only natural,' Samantha defended her niece immediately. 'She's bound to feel a little bit jealous,' Samantha told her twin robustly. 'Everything will be all right, though.'

'Yes, I know you're right,' she agreed, adding gently, 'You will make such a wonderful mother, Sam.'

Although Samantha laughed, a little later on whilst her twin was on the telephone to Olivia confirming the arrangements for their visit, she couldn't help feeling a small stab of envy. Here was her sister, her twin, talking about having her second baby whilst she didn't even have the means of having her first yet. But, with a bit of luck, she soon would have, she comforted herself.

Everything she had heard and seen of James during the drive back from the airport yesterday had confirmed the decision she had already made. There was no doubt about it. He was *perfect* father material. Add to that the fact that she genuinely liked him and enjoyed his company, the way she could so easily see the two of them meshing together and becoming a very happy and contented couple, and suddenly Samantha was very impatient to see him again and to put her plan fully into motion. Okay, so she hadn't fallen *in* love with him but love, after all, came in very many disguises.

There was nothing *morally* wrong in what she was planning and if she had not been able to see in James' eyes how very easily he could be encouraged to fall in love with her she would not in any way have contemplated going ahead with her plans.

She had made up her mind—it was time to put to one side her dreams of meeting her perfect other half. She might not be headily in love with James in the same way that her twin had been, still was, with his brother Luke, but she liked him and enjoyed his company, he was just so relaxing and pleasant to be with she just couldn't imagine anyone *not* finding him so, other than Rosemary. Heavens, but she had never seen anyone cause such an intense and explosive reaction in him. He really did dislike the girl. Poor Rosemary.

'We'd better make a move,' Bobbie warned Samantha when she had finished her telephone call.

'It's gone ten now and we'll have to be back by two so that I can pick Francesca up on time.'

'Will Olivia and Caspar have any more children, do you think?' Samantha asked Bobbie conversationally half an hour later as Bobbie drove towards Haslewich.

'I don't know. She works full-time now as you know and she and Uncle Jon keep on talking about taking on a new partner, but although neither of them will admit it, the main thing that's holding them both back from doing so is the fact that since its inception the partnership has always only been family members. There's a good crop of young Crightons growing up now who might one day want to qualify as solicitors and join the business, but right now…Tullah, Saul's wife works part-time with them two days.'

'Can't they take someone on as an assistant rather than a full partner?' Samantha queried.

'Well, they could and that's exactly what Max has been urging his father to do. It's looking increasingly as though Jack will opt to train as a solicitor and join the business but that's still several years away and at the moment they are so busy that Jenny's complaining that she hardly ever sees Jon.'

'What about Joss, has he any plans for his future?' Samantha asked her twin.

Joss, Jon and Jenny's younger son, was hotly tipped in the family to become their leading light in the legal world and Samantha knew that Bobbie had a very soft spot for the teenager who had been the first member of the Crighton family she had met on her first visit to Haslewich.

'At least a dozen,' Bobbie grinned. 'He's gorgeous, Sam…such a very special person, so special in fact that it's hard sometimes to remember not to overlook Jack.'

'Mmm… I wonder what happened to Jack's father David. Does Jack ever talk about him?'

David Crighton, Jon's twin brother, was Jack and Olivia's father and whilst recuperating from a heart attack he had simply walked out of the lives of his family and made little attempt to get in touch with them since.

Olivia, Samantha knew, had no real wish for her father to make a reappearance in their lives. Before his disappearance she and Jon had discovered that he had been fraudulently helping himself to money from one of their client's accounts. It was only thanks to

Ruth's intervention that the whole unpleasant matter had been resolved without a scandal and Samantha knew from Olivia's own comments that she had never really forgiven her father for what he had done.

Her mother, who had divorced David in his absence, was now remarried and living in the south of England. Olivia had never been close to either of her parents and Jack had, of his own free will, chosen to live with his aunt and uncle rather than with his mother.

'So, you don't think that Olivia will have any more children, then,' Samantha repeated.

'I think she'd like to and I know that Caspar would—his work allows him to have more time to spend with them than Livvy's does but, to be honest, I suspect it's rather a sensitive issue between them at the moment. They were due to go on holiday this year to visit Caspar's family in the States, but it had to be cancelled because Livvy is just so busy.

'Haslewich has become rather a mini boom town. The extended motorway system has meant that several international industries have moved into the area and, of course, that means extra jobs, which means increased property development. Property prices have risen and on the outskirts of the town they're currently just about to open one of these specialised shopping villages, all designer outlets and very, very smart.

'Not that that was without problems—you ask James. He's just won a very involved case for one of his clients against one of the contractors on the development.'

'I can't imagine James prosecuting. He always seems so gentle and compassionate. Although…'

'Although what?' Bobbie questioned interestedly as she slowed down for the motorway exit to Haslewich.

'Well, we called on his parents on the way back from the airport and there was a girl there—Rosemary. I've never seen James react so antagonistically to anyone…mind you, her attitude towards *him* was extremely…'

'…provocative?' Bobbie suggested.

Samantha looked at her. 'Aggressive, *I* was about to say… Do you know her, Bobbie?'

'I've met her. She was visiting Luke and James' parents last Christmas and I had gone to see them with Francesca. Francesca wasn't very well and Rosemary was absolutely sweet with her. She's just recently qualified as a doctor, you know, and Pat was telling me that she is hoping to specialise in the area of paediatrics within the surgery complex. She certainly has a wonderful way with children.'

'You liked her, then,' Samantha stated.

'Well…yes, I did, but I know what you mean about her and James, they certainly strike sparks off one another. Apparently she spent several months living with Henry and Pat whilst she was a teenager. Her parents were working abroad at the time, Luke wasn't living at home then, but James was, and the two of them just didn't hit it off together.'

'Mmm… Oh, isn't this the most beautiful scenery,' Samantha enthused as she glanced out of the car window to look appreciatively at the gently rolling Cheshire countryside.

'Very,' Bobbie agreed.

'It's so peaceful,' Samantha stressed.

Bobbie laughed. 'It might be now, wait until you get to Livvy's!'

Olivia and Caspar's home was outside the town of Haslewich, a pretty, long low collection of buildings surrounded by a large garden and fields.

As Bobbie brought the car to a halt on the driveway, Olivia was opening the front door and coming hurrying to meet them.

Slim and energetic, her bobbed hair gleamed in the sunshine and a swift smile curled her mouth as she welcomed them.

'Bobbie… Sam…' She hugged each of them in turn and then gestured towards the house.

'I thought we'd have lunch in the garden, it's such a lovely day. I nearly had to cancel,' Olivia confessed as she led the way through the house to the doors which opened out onto the pretty brick patio.

'I was due in court with one of my clients last week and the case was put back originally until today, but the case currently being heard is still ongoing—fortunately.'

'Do you do much court work?' Samantha asked Olivia as they settled themselves in comfortable chairs and Olivia poured them all some coffee.

'An awful lot. I didn't used to but increasingly these days, yes. I'm afraid that it's becoming rather a bone of contention between me and Caspar, primarily because it means I can't always structure my working life to fit in with his.'

'Mmm…and I guess you daren't hire another live-in nanny just in case she runs off with another of your sexy cousins,' Bobbie said teasingly.

All three of them laughed, remembering that Bobbie had worked for a time for Olivia and Caspar when she had first arrived in Haslewich.

'Mmm…well there is always that, but although I've

had help from time to time, Caspar and I both feel that we want to bring the children up ourselves. The trouble is that, right now, Caspar is doing rather more of the parenting than I am and that leads to problems between us. I get jealous,' she admitted ruefully. 'I know it sounds silly and it's certainly very unmodern of me, but I could cry when the children run to Caspar with their scraped knees and their tears instead of to me.'

'Couldn't you lessen the number of hours you work?' Samantha suggested practically.

Olivia rolled her eyes expressively. 'I wish... As it is I'm conscious of how often Jon takes home my workload to allow me to have extra time off. No, we both know that the only real answer is to take on at least one and maybe two qualified solicitors, but the problem is that anyone we take on of the calibre we need would automatically want to become a partner somewhere down the line and, whilst Ben's alive, well even if he wasn't, I guess that both Jon and I are Crighton enough not to want to dilute the partnership.

'Of course we could turn down work but...' She pulled a face. '*That* goes so much against the grain. No, at the moment we're in a strictly no win situation and no matter how many junior assistants we might take on, when it comes down to it, Jon and I are the only senior members of staff. However, today I am having a day off...

'How are your family?' she asked Samantha, changing the subject.

'They're fine. Mom and Dad are looking forward to Dad's retirement later in the year and to their vacation over here, of course.'

'Mmm... We're all looking forward to seeing them,

especially Aunt Ruth of course. How is the divine Liam, by the way.'

Sam's eyebrows rose at this description of her currently least favourite person. Not even to Bobbie had she confided her reaction to that unprecedented and totally unexpected kiss Liam had given her before she had left home.

'He's fine. He'll shortly be running for State Governor.'

'Governor. He'll be the sexiest one the union has ever had.' Olivia rolled her eyes again. She had, of course, met Liam at Bobbie and Luke's wedding—renewing their acquaintanceship when she and Caspar had visited the States some years ago.

'Sexy! Liam!' Sam started to expostulate and then stopped quickly veiling her eyes to conceal her expression. *She* didn't think Liam was sexy, of course she didn't, but the memory of that unprovoked kiss was still lingering disturbingly not just in her mind but on her senses as well.

The telephone was ringing when they walked into the house on their return from their visit to Olivia. Bobbie picked up the receiver and then pulled a face, holding it out to Samantha.

'It's for you,' she told her dryly, eyebrows raised. 'It's James.'

'James,' Samantha exclaimed in a pleased voice as she took the receiver from her twin and deliberately turned her back towards her.

'Tonight…yes…I'd love to…' she agreed. 'What time? Yes, I guess eight will be fine.

'James is taking me out for dinner tonight,' she told her twin after she had concluded her call. 'He says there's a new restaurant opened on the river which is very highly acclaimed.'

Bobbie opened her mouth as though she was about to say something and then closed it again as she surveyed her sister's flushed face and happy eyes.

James and Samantha?

Well, her twin would certainly never find a more easy-going nor indulgent partner than James, and Sam would certainly benefit from someone in her life who would ground her a little, but was James strong enough to match Samantha? Samantha could sometimes get a little carried away with her ideas and plans and didn't always think them through properly from a practical point of view, as Bobbie well knew. She was inclined to be impulsive and idealistic and she was also extremely strong-willed. She needed a man who would not just understand and love her but who would share and match the deeply passionate and intense side of her nature, as well. A pretty tall order, Bobbie knew, but to her mind Sam deserved the best.

James was a darling and nothing would make Bobbie happier than to see him settled and married. He had already suffered disappointments in love and if anyone deserved to be loved, then it was certainly James. But was Samantha the right one for him? James liked order and calm; he liked routine and neatness, as a Virgo he tended to be almost even a little bit overfussy on occasions. His desk, his office, and his home were models of orderliness and pristine neatness.

Sam, on the other hand, could cheerfully live in the kind of chaos that made other people either stare in envy or grit their teeth in despair, depending on their own natures.

She was headstrong, vital, vibrant, swinging from one extreme to another in the space of a handful of minutes. She possessed a joie de vivre that other people either adored or loathed, there were no half measures with Samantha, whereas James epitomised the spirit of compromise. Still, they did say that opposites attract.

'If you're going near the river I'd take a warm jacket with you,' Bobbie warned her. 'It can be quite cool near the water in the evening.'

Predictably Samantha was still upstairs getting ready when James arrived to collect her.

Bobbie let him in and hugged and kissed him lovingly.

'Sam won't be long,' she assured him.

James gave her a small smile.

'Good, I've booked the table for eight-thirty which just leaves us time to drive there and order a drink at the bar before we eat.'

Rather ruefully Bobbie looked away, relieved to hear her twin's feet on the stairs as Samantha came hurrying down.

She had certainly dressed for the occasion, Bobbie reflected as she studied her sister.

The pretty linen wrap skirt emphasised the female shape of Sam's body and the toning effect of cream on cream with the softly draped top she was wearing created an image of soft delicacy whilst Sam's freshly washed tousled curls gave her an appealing youthful air.

'Where's your jacket?' Bobbie asked her as Sam passed her in the hall.

'If I get cold I'll have to borrow James',' Samantha

told her sotto voce, smiling mischievously as she saw her twin's expression.

'You'll need a jacket,' James warned her, unconsciously echoing Bobbie's comment to her earlier.

Samantha hesitated, torn between protesting that she wasn't a child and that if she chose not to wear a jacket then it was *her* choice and allowing herself to bask in the unfamiliarity of James' male concern.

In the end the latter won out and she hurried back upstairs, returning with a soft cashmere wraparound knitted jacket draped around her shoulders.

'Very nice,' Bobbie approved.

'You look lovely,' James told her quietly and sincerely, smiling tenderly at her as he reached out and gently straightened the ruffled edge of her knit so that both sides were equally matched.

Samantha's eyebrows rose but she didn't make any comment.

'We'd better go,' James was informing her. 'We don't want to be late for our table.'

Bobbie, who knew that her twin had raised being late to an art form, forbore to make any comment, but instead mentally crossed her fingers as she wished the pair of them a pleasant evening.

'*Sam* and *James?*' Luke exclaimed later when Bobbie was telling him what had happened. His eyebrows rose and he gave her a droll look. 'You *have* to be joking. James knows to the last pair exactly how many socks he has and where they are. I would be astonished if your sister could find a single item in her wardrobe in less than a week!'

'Mmm…you could have a point,' Bobbie allowed. 'Except that Sam would be more likely to have most of her clothes lying in a heap on her bedroom chair or floor,' Bobbie admitted with a grin.

'I rest my case,' Luke told her mock solemnly.

'Yes, but opposites do attract,' Bobbie reminded him hopefully.

'Mmm…they also have some of the most spectacularly messy and acrimonious divorce cases that ever come to court. Take it from me, I've seen them.'

'Mmm…well, James seems pretty keen…'

'Maybe *now* he does, wait until Sam has dropped ice cream on his suit, lost her purse and locked him out of his own car,' Luke suggested.

Since her twin had on the occasion of her last visit committed all three of those crimes against Luke, Bobbie felt unable to say very much in defence of her sister.

'James would drive Sam mad,' Luke told her more seriously. 'She'd end up resenting or even loathing him.'

'But if they fell in love,' Bobbie protested.

'With the idea of being in love, yes, but with each other—no!'

In the soft shadows of the restaurant's private walled garden Samantha started to put her plan into action. The romantic venue James had chosen for their meal was certainly a good start and she was enjoying having James fuss round her, checking that she was warm enough, that her chair was comfortable, that the menu was to her liking. It felt wonderful to be so thoroughly pampered.

'James, you're spoiling me,' she told him softly as she leaned across the table to cover his hand with her own just fleetingly enough to be subtly intimate without lingering too long or being too obvious.

It would be quite in order for her to kiss James goodnight as a thank you for her evening out she decided judiciously as the waiter took their order—and *when* she did…!

A naughty little smile curled her mouth.

'You know, you frighten me a little when you look like that,' James told her ruefully.

'Me—frighten you!' Sam rolled her eyes wickedly.

CHAPTER SIX

'So, IN your opinion, Toni, your professional opinion that is…' Liam stressed, 'I'm not going to win the governorship unless I have a wife.'

They were seated opposite one another in the privacy of Liam's apartment since Toni Davis had insisted that the subject she wanted to discuss with him was far too vital to the success of his campaign for them to risk anyone else overhearing it.

He watched as she arched an eyebrow and gave him the benefit of her perfect profile whilst making a slightly depreciative moue.

'I couldn't say *that,* but there is no doubt that amongst a certain section of the voters a Governor who has the right kind of wife is considered to be preferable to one who doesn't.'

'The *right* kind of wife?' Liam asked her, his own eyebrows lifting. Toni gave him a small intimate look.

'Liam, I've worked in PR a good while *and* in Washington, we both know that to be successful, a politician needs to have the right kind of partnership support. I'm sure we've *both* seen very able politicians failing to make the grade because of…problems in their domestic lives…

'Your voters feel that a married Governor will be more in tune with their own lives and needs. You and I both know that it takes a very special kind of woman to fully understand the stresses and pressures that go with high office.

'In my view,' Toni Davis continued, 'the very best kind of successful political marriages are those where both partners are working together for a common goal and where both partners understand their roles and one another. For a man in high office it is vitally important that his wife is totally committed to his success and to him.'

'Isn't that a rather old-fashioned point of view?' Liam checked her.

'Old-fashioned it may be, but it works,' Toni told him firmly.

'So you believe that a politician should marry for expediency rather than for love?' Liam challenged her.

'Romantic love seldom lasts and can cause far too many problems. A successful politician doesn't have time to waste on emotion,' Toni told him calmly. 'You're a very sensible man, Liam, and an ambitious man, I know, so I'm sure you understand what I'm saying.'

Liam gave her a thoughtful look.

Oh, he understood what she was saying right enough. From the moment he had picked her up from the airport Toni had made it clear that it wasn't just her professional expertise in public relations she was prepared to put at Liam's disposal. She might not have come right out and said that she would like to be the Governor's wife, but she had certainly made it plenty clear in a number of other ways.

Stephen Miller had told Liam privately that he had heard from a source in Washington that Toni had, for several years, been having an affair with a very high-ranking Congressman.

'He was a lot older than her and his wife was terminally ill. Word is that she was prepared to sit it out and wait to become his second wife but that when, instead of asking her to marry him, he upped and married someone else she vowed that she would find a way of getting even with him.'

'And did she…'

'Well, he isn't a Congressman anymore…'

'Mmm…nice lady!'

'She certainly knows what she wants,' Stephen Miller had agreed.

As Liam watched her gravely whilst she warmed to her theme and started to list the many advantages to the kind of marriage she was proposing, he reflected that there was, in all honesty, something to be said for what she was suggesting and that she would most definitely make an admirable wife for an ambitious politician.

Unfortunately, there were two very good reasons why *he* didn't feel able to take her up on her proposals.

'Well, I take your point,' he interrupted her firmly, 'but I guess I'm the old-fashioned kind myself and I kinda think that I'd be cheating the voters just a little if I married purely to get their vote. I guess you *could* say it was a matter of pride. You see, I'd want to be loved for my *self* both by the voters *and* by my wife,' he told her gently.

She was still staring at him with her face unfalteringly flushed and her mouth open several seconds later as he strolled towards the door and held it open for her.

A little later in the day he had occasion to call at the Governor's house to see Stephen Miller.

'He's in his study,' Sarah Jane told Liam with a

smile, asking him fondly, 'How did your meeting go
with Toni this morning? Stephen says that she's absolutely determined that you'll win the governorship.'

'Well, right now I guess she isn't feeling too
pleased with me,' Liam admitted.

When Sarah Jane waited, he elucidated, 'I can't
marry just to secure the governorship. Toni's insistence that the right kind of wife will secure it for me
may be correct, but...'

As he spoke his glance lingered briefly on a photograph of Samantha on one of the tables in the hallway.

Following his gaze Sarah Jane smiled ruefully. In
it Samantha was wearing her graduation gown and for
once she looked almost a little awed and unfamiliarly
subdued by the gravitas of the moment.

'You know, Liam, there have been times when I
worried that I might be hindering Stephen's career.
It's no secret to you that I'm looking forward to him
retiring.'

'What is obvious to *me* is that Stephen's love for
you and his family means far, far more to him than
being a politician,' Liam told her truthfully.

'Sam used to be passionately resentful of the way
her father's career took him away from us all when
she was younger,' Sarah Jane commented ruefully as
she walked across to her daughter's photograph and
picked it up.

'Yup, I remember, and it wasn't just his *career* she
resented so passionately,' Liam replied dryly.

Sarah Jane laughed. 'Oh dear, yes, she did go
through a phase of blaming you for his absences. She
was jealous of you, of course, because you got to

spend time in Washington with him whilst she couldn't.

'Poor Sam,' Sarah Jane sighed. 'She'd certainly never make a politician's wife. I used to think that once she grew up she'd be less impulsive and… intense…but… I'll go and get Stephen for you, Liam,' she offered, putting the photograph back and walking towards his office.

In her absence Liam picked up the picture of Sam.

Sarah Jane was right, Sam would never make a politician's wife. She would never toe the line, never keep a tactful silence when an issue was raised about which she felt passionately, and she felt passionately about every issue there was. She would never put her husband's career before her own dearly held beliefs, she would never tell her children, *their* children, not to bother their father with their problems because he was a very busy and important man. She would never allow her man, her mate, to get the idea that she could be kept discreetly in the background and she would certainly never, ever, accept the kind of cold clinical and entirely rational relationship which Toni had recently outlined to him.

Oh yes, there were a hundred, no, a thousand reasons why Sam would not make a good politician's wife.

He was carefully replacing the photograph in its original position when Stephen came hurrying towards him, Sarah Jane not far behind.

'Toni's just been on the phone to me,' he began, but Liam stopped him.

'Yes, and I can guess what she had to say but what *I* told her stands. The voters of this country have to want me as their Governor as I am,' he told Stephen

firmly. 'But that isn't what I've come to tell you—
I'm taking a couple of weeks leave.'

Stephen stared at him.

'What! Right *now*, in the middle of the campaign…'

'The campaign can run quite happily without me
for a while. In fact, you never know, the voters might
discover that an undiluted diet of Lee Calder might
give them a craving for a different kind of politician.'

'Mmm… Well, you could be right and you certainly won't get any time to take any leave if you do
get the governorship. Where are you planning to go?'

'Ireland,' Liam told him promptly.

'Ireland…' Both the Millers stared at him.

'I've been meaning to visit over there for a
while…trace my roots, that kind of thing,' Liam told
them vaguely.

'Ireland, but it's only just across the Irish sea from
Cheshire,' Sarah Jane told him enthusiastically. 'You
could perhaps fit in a visit to Bobbie whilst you're
there. I know she'd *love* to see you.'

Liam gave a small shrug.

'Bobbie might, but I doubt that Sam would…'

'Well that could be so.' Sarah Jane paused and then
laughed. 'Although from what I hear from Bobbie,
Sam *is* rather preoccupied at the moment. She's been
seeing rather a lot of James since she arrived.'

As Samantha's parents exchanged smiles, neither of
them saw the way Liam's mouth tightened nor the
look he flashed the silent photograph of their daughter.

Seated in her sister's kitchen Samantha leaned her
chin into her hand and gave a small disconsolate sigh.

So far her plans were not going entirely the way she wanted.

Oh, James was proving to be everything she had anticipated that he would be, a thoughtful and protective escort when he took her out and an entertaining and interesting companion, but no matter how hard she tried she just couldn't seem to advance their relationship to a more intimate level.

Take the first night he had asked her out, for instance. After they had left the restaurant they had strolled alongside the river, the perfect romantic setting. Samantha had leant a little against James, smiling warmly and encouragingly at him when he had stopped walking and turned to face her, but instead of taking her in his arms and kissing her as she had expected, he had started to frown a little and caution her that her knit was in danger of slipping off her shoulders.

She had been so irritated by his overcautious behaviour that later on, when he *had* moved to take her in his arms when he had stopped his car outside Luke and Bobbie's home, she had pretended not to be aware of his intentions, slipping out of the car before he could stop her and then kissing him coolly and distantly on the cheek before bidding him a stiff goodnight outside the front door.

Later on she had regretted giving in to her chagrin and irritation but, of course, by then it had been too late.

The following day, at her insistence, he had taken her to the zoo, but the antics of the animals had quite plainly not been to his taste and he had cut their visit short, suggesting instead that she might like to visit

Haslewich's salt museum which he was sure she would find far more worthwhile.

As Samantha was coming to discover, underneath James' apparent easygoing gentleness there was a markedly determined, not to say stubborn, streak. It wasn't that he was either domineering or dictatorial, it was simply that he could at times adopt a smiling loftiness which irritated her into the kind of rebellious behaviour she thought she had left behind with her teens. And yet he was everything she *knew* she ought to want. She only had to see him with Olivia's children and Bobbie's Francesca, to see what a wonderful father he would make.

An added complication to her plans was Rosemary. Despite her avowed dislike of him and her engagement, she tried to attach herself to them with all the persistence and much the same effect as an unwanted burr.

'Poor Rosemary, I'm afraid she finds it rather dull being with someone so much older than herself,' James' mother had commented indulgently to Samantha the previous day when, for the third time Rosemary had insisted on accompanying them.

If Rosemary was so bored then why didn't she go home to her own life and her own friends? Samantha longed to ask, but she managed to keep her views to herself.

'She and James can't bear one another so why she insists on attaching herself to us I just don't know,' she had told Bobbie furiously the previous evening when, at the last minute, Rosemary had prevailed upon James' mother to ask if she could be included in their outing to an open-air play—one of a series which were held every summer at a pretty local Elizabethan manor house.

Bobbie had given her a telling look.

But at the weekend James was taking her to the Grosvenor for dinner and *that* was an invitation she intended to make sure Rosemary did *not* gate crash.

James lived in the city within walking distance of the Grosvenor, Chester's most prestigious hotel, and Samantha had privately decided to boldly suggest after they had had dinner that James might show her over his home. If *that* didn't give him a hint of what she had in mind then nothing would!

It was not that she was planning to deliberately seduce him. Of course not. And anyway, she had seen from the expression in his eyes when he looked at her that he found her attractive and he had certainly hinted at as much with the compliments he had paid her. No, it was just that she felt their relationship needed a small nudge in the right direction to move it on a little faster than it was presently progressing.

James just wasn't the type to force the pace. He was far too gentlemanly for that, and so *she* needed to make it clear to him that… That what? That she wanted him to take her to bed?

Samantha started to frown. *Did* she? *Did* she want them to become lovers?

Well, of course she did, otherwise how on earth was she going to conceive their child. Ultimately they would *have* to… *Have to?*

'You're looking very pensive.'

Samantha looked at her sister.

'No, not really… I was just wondering what to wear when James takes me to dinner at the Grosvenor on Saturday.'

'Mmm... Well, it should be something smart. The Grosvenor's clientele *is* very elegant.'

'Mmm...' Samantha didn't want to admit to her twin that it was more what she should wear to get the right impression over to *James* than to impress the other diners, that was concerning her.

'Mom rang whilst you were out earlier. You'll never guess what...'

'So tell me,' Samantha invited.

'Liam's in Ireland.'

'Liam's *where?*'

'In Ireland taking a vacation and looking up his roots.'

'But Liam never takes a vacation. *Never.* And what about the campaign?'

Bobbie shrugged.

'*I* only know what Mom told me. Oh, she did say though, that that PR woman has gone back to Washington.'

'Oh... Maybe Liam's gone to Ireland to look for a wife,' Samantha suggested cynically.

'Oh, Sam, you aren't being very fair to Liam.'

'He *wants* to be Governor, you can't deny that.'

'No, but he wants the governorship as much for Dad as for himself.'

Bobbie saw her sister's disbelieving expression and insisted, 'It's true. Liam knows how much Dad wants to have him take over from him, how much it would mean to him to be able to retire knowing that he's leaving the state in safe hands, *and* he knows, too, how much Mom has been looking forward to Dad retiring.'

'Liam is Dad's assistant, you're making it sound more as though he's a member of the family.'

'Well, *isn't* he? You *know* how much Mom and Dad both think of him.'

'Too much if you ask me,' Samantha muttered half under her breath. 'I can certainly remember how often they took his side against me.'

'When? Oh, you mean like that time you wanted to go out with the high school jock and Liam told the folks that he'd got a pretty bad reputation. Liam was just trying to protect you, that was all.'

'To *protect* me…' Samantha rolled her eyes. 'Oh, yeah…'

'You're too hard on him, Sam. I know how much Dad values him and Dad is a very good judge of character. Grandma Ruth and Gramps both think a lot of him, as well.'

'So… That's because he's made sure they've only seen the *good* side of him,' Samantha told her.

'Oh, Sam…' Bobbie laughed and shook her head. 'And when I think of the *crush* you used to have on him.'

Bobbie gave her twin a startled look.

'You *aren't* still holding a grudge against him because he didn't return your feelings, are you? You *must* know how impossible it would have been for him to respond to you, not just morally but just about every which way there is. You were under age, you were his employer's daughter, you were…'

'I was damn near six feet tall and looked more like a boy than a girl and I wore braces. Yes, I know, but he need not have treated me as though…as though…as though I was some kind of joke,' Samantha seethed.

'As though you were some kind of joke. No, he never did that.'

'He did, too,' Samantha told her. 'He laughed at me and he…'

'Samantha, he was just trying to diffuse the situation, to let you down gently. I guess…'

'Anyway, for your information I am *not* holding a grudge against him. As a matter of fact—well, I guess you're right and he *is* the right person to take over from Dad and I hope he finds himself a wife in Ireland,' she added generously.

'You do. Well, you can tell him so yourself when he comes over to visit with us at the weekend.'

'He's doing *what,*' Samantha demanded, staring at her.

'He's coming over to visit with us,' Bobbie repeated calmly. 'Apparently Mom suggested it.'

'Liam here! Liam's coming here, to Haslewich!' Samantha started to worry her bottom lip. She still had disturbing flashbacks to those moments she had spent in his arms when he had kissed her and, illogically and *very* dangerously, they always seemed to surface when she was with James! She forced herself to give a small nonchalant shrug.

'Well, it's a pity but I shall probably miss him. Have you forgotten I'm going to the Grosvenor with James on Saturday.' *Going* to the Grosvenor and *planning* to stay over with James although no one other than her knew about *that* plan as yet.

'No, you won't. He's actually going to be staying at the Grosvenor.'

Samantha felt her heart start to sink. She and Liam might have buried their old differences but…but she had confided in him in a moment of weakness, exposed to him her fears and vulnerabilities and she had no wish now to have him watching superciliously and knowingly whilst she put into action her plans for her future with James.

'In fact, I'm thinking about arranging to have a family lunch party at the Grosvenor on Sunday.'

'If Liam finds a wife whilst he's in Ireland and he brings her over, we could make it an engagement party,' Samantha suggested sarcastically. 'Maybe you ought to order a cake.'

'Uh-huh. And would that be for Liam and his intended or for you and James?' Bobbie demanded teasingly, adding with a sideways look, 'Have you told him about your yen to make love out in the open yet, because…'

'That was just a childish fantasy,' Samantha told her loftily, but her face had gone pink nonetheless. It was true that she had always had a private fantasy of making love out in the open beneath the sky, somewhere private and secret, a sacred almost a special place which would belong to her and her lover alone.

A fantasy was just what it was though. Somehow she could not see James sharing it with her. Fantasies didn't always translate very well into real life.

A little uncertainly Samantha surveyed her reflection in the long pier mirror in Bobbie's guest bedroom.

The seductively feminine underwear she had bought in Boston had seemed like a good idea at the time but now that she was wearing it…surely the silky satin was far finer and provocative than she had remembered it. She frowned as she saw the way it clung to her curves, lovingly outlining every detail of her body.

'Sam… I've just remembered… Wow!' Bobbie came to a full stop as she hurried unceremoniously into her twin's bedroom, her eyes widening as she looked at her.

'The dress I'm wearing is silk jersey and it needs something special underneath it,' Samantha began defensively, but she could see from Bobbie's raised eyebrows and wide grin that she was not convincing her.

'Ever heard of a plain simple serviceable body?' Bobbie asked her dryly.

'They didn't have one in my size. You know how difficult it is getting one long enough,' Samantha defended herself.

'Have I said a word?' Bobbie asked virtuously. 'If you choose to wear sexy underwear then far be it from me... You always did have a penchant for...' She stopped and giggled.

'Remember that fuss you made when you had your crush on Liam when Mom took you to buy a new training bra. You refused to have it and begged her to let you have a push-up padded style instead.'

'That was years ago,' Samantha objected, 'and besides, Mom refused...'

'Well, you certainly don't need any help in improving your curves now,' Bobbie told her forthrightly. 'So where is it then?' she demanded.

'Where's what?' Samantha asked her puzzled.

'The dress...the dress that demands the wearing of such sexy underwear,' Bobbie told her, tongue-in-cheek.

'It's here.' Turning round Samantha walked over to the wardrobe and removed the dress she was planning to wear that evening. Completely plain in heavy vanilla silk jersey, its slashed cowl-necked style made Bobbie's eyes widen in envy.

'Hey if you ever get tired of it, you can junk it in my direction puleeze…'

Samantha laughed.

'Let me see it on,' Bobbie commanded.

Dutifully Samantha took it off the hanger and slipped it over her head.

The soft vanilla fabric settled down over her body as though it had been made expressly for her, the heavy fabric draping perfectly over her curves.

She had chosen the bra, carefully picking one with a low back, knowing that the deep vee of the dress would expose a normal bra.

'It's wonderful,' Bobbie breathed, and then frowned. 'Can you step out of it?' she asked Samantha.

Her sister stared at her.

'I don't know, I haven't tried. Why do you ask.'

Bobbie grinned.

'Well, it's just that there's something seriously sexy about a dress that can be slithered out of. You know the kind that just somehow falls to the floor of its own accord. Although,' she paused and eyed her twin judiciously, 'I suppose there is *something* to be said for one that needs an extra pair of hands to aid its removal.'

'I did *not* buy this dress with…with anything like that in mind,' Samantha told her firmly.

'Anything like "that"… You mean, sex?' Bobbie teased, round-eyed.

'It's six o'clock, James is picking me up at half past,' Samantha warned her, 'and he'll expect me to be ready on time.'

'Okay, okay, I get the message. Subject closed, although…' As she headed for the door she paused and told her thoughtfully, 'if you want my opinion that bit of frivolous sexy nonsense you're wearing is very much more Liam than James!'

'For the last time, I did not choose my underwear with a man in mind…any man…'

'Who says I was talking about your *underwear*,' Bobbie laughed. 'I meant the dress. Very…sexy… very Liam…'

She was still laughing as she closed the door behind herself.

'Very Liam…' Samantha studied her reflection worriedly. She had noticed, it was true, that James seemed to prefer it when she wore more classically styled clothes, clothes which were elegant and perhaps even a little strait-laced rather than discreetly sexy. Only the previous evening she had seen him frowning over the revealing little tank top which Rosemary had been wearing. Bright cerise in colour, it shouldn't really have suited a redhead, but somehow Rosemary had got away with it—just.

'Do you really think you should be wearing something like that?' James had asked her.

'Why not?' Rosemary had challenged him immediately.

'Well, a woman in your position…' James had responded quietly.

'A woman in my position?' For a moment Rosemary had looked baffled and then she had laughed.

'You mean, because I'm a doctor.'

'No, actually I mean because you're engaged,' James had told her stiffly, quite plainly offended by her laughter.

In reply Rosemary had given him a wide taunting smile.

'It just so happens that my fiancé actually bought me this top,' she told him softly.

'I'll be glad when she finally goes back home,' James had fumed afterwards when they were on their own.

It was on the tip of Samantha's tongue to point out that if he disliked Rosemary's company so much, then the easiest way to avoid having to endure it would be to cut down on his visits to his parents whilst Rosemary was there, but then she reminded herself that she was perhaps being a little unfair. On each occasion they had called round to see them James had done so at his father's behest.

'Officially, of course, he's now retired, but he likes to be kept au fait with what's going on,' James had explained to Samantha.

His concern and consideration for his parents was another indication of the kind of man he was, Samantha recognised.

James, she suspected, would never miss a child's sports day or Christmas play. He would always be there to cheer his children on on the sports field and to listen to their problems.

From speaking to Olivia, Sam had quickly guessed that she would like to add to her family.

'The biological urge runs very strongly through the female side of the Crighton line,' Olivia had told Samantha cheerfully. 'So be warned.'

'I wonder if Maddy's pregnancy will be twins,' Bobbie had mused a little enviously.

'If it is, she isn't saying,' Olivia informed her.

'I can't get over how much Max has changed, can you?'

Olivia and Max had never really got on and Samantha could hear the reluctance in Olivia's voice as she agreed.

'He does certainly seem to have undergone a very dramatic metamorphosis. I must say though that I thought Luke and James were very brave to admit him into their chambers.'

'Luke says it's working out extraordinarily well,' Bobbie had told her. 'In fact, he said the other night that he's actually missing Max and that he's really looking forward to him coming back from holiday.'

'Mmm...well, *he* isn't the only one,' Olivia had responded wryly. 'Uncle Ben has done nothing but complain the whole time Maddy has been away.'

In the renaissance of her marriage Maddy had become pregnant, so family gossip had it, and to her husband Max's proud delight. So many fecund fertile Crighton women. Samantha closed her eyes. When she had confided in Liam her desire for a child, in the depths of her misery and despair, the last thing she had anticipated was that he was going to turn up here in Cheshire.

Damn Liam. Why, oh, why, couldn't he have stayed safely and distantly where he was? And her feelings had nothing whatsoever to do with that sharp sizzling fusion of sexual chemistry she had felt so powerfully when he had kissed her at the airport, Samantha reassured herself—nothing whatsoever.

CHAPTER SEVEN

LIAM thanked the porter and tipped him generously as he showed him up to his suite.

The hotel was fully booked and as he quickly inspected the elegant suite of rooms he had been given he could understand why.

In the bedroom the bed was large and comfortably inviting, the closet space was generous and the bathroom, when he pushed open the door and glanced inside, was equipped not just with a large separate shower but with a huge Victorian-style bath, as well.

His small sitting room possessed a sofa and a large deep chair in addition to a good-sized desk and more than enough power points to satisfy even the busiest of businessmen.

Sarah Jane had enthused over the hotel to him, explaining that it was owned by the Grosvenor family. 'That's the Duke of Westminster,' she had elucidated helpfully whilst Liam's mouth had twitched slightly in amusement.

'Gee, a real live duke,' he had teased her a little, assuming a mock air of disingenuous excitement.

'Louise and Katie had their joint eighteenth birthday party there,' Sarah Jane added. 'Bobbie was there. Joss had invited her. Of course none of the family knew who Bobbie was then and she believed...' She made a small moue.

'*Why* am I telling you all this? You *know* the whole story.'

He did, of course. He knew a lot about Bobbie's tracing her mother's roots.

He had been rather less successful in tracing his own family but he had not really expected anything else.

He had little close family left in Ireland and whilst he suspected if he persevered hard enough, he could no doubt find himself a whole clutch of cousins three and four times removed, it was not really a desire to meet his relatives which had spurred him into crossing the Atlantic.

Common sense told him that the urge, the need, the emotions, which had brought him here were, from a practical point of view, ones he would be best advised to ignore, just as he had forced himself to ignore them on countless previous occasions in the past.

He stood at the window looking down into the busy Saturday mill-race of shoppers and tourists flooding past the hotel and then closed his eyes.

Behind his closed eyelids he could see her so easily. Samantha at fourteen, all gangly legs and braces, her face hot with betraying colour every time she looked at him, tongue-tied and mortified by the extent of her teenage crush on him.

A few weeks later she had unexpectedly and disconcertingly suddenly sprouted a pair of eye-catchingly full breasts, the product so he had discovered, of an illegally purchased well-padded bra.

Sarah Jane had confiscated the garment but it hadn't been all that long afterwards that nature had compensated for this blow to Samantha's teenage ego, only this time the softly rounded curves filling out the front of her T-shirts had had nothing to do with any kind of shop-bought padding. Liam's expert eye had very quickly discerned the difference between the initial rigid protruberences and the much more alluring and distracting little bounce that the nature-provided pair possessed.

However, with typical female perversity, far from showing them off Samantha had reacted to their arrival by taking to wearing huge concealing sloppy-joe tops.

'They embarrass her,' Stephen Miller had confided to Liam with a mystified male shake of his head. 'Can you beat that? It's damn near thirty-five degrees out there and she's wearing a thick fleece sweatshirt. She says the sports jocks at school stare at her.'

Liam frowned. He could still remember just how that had made him feel.

The first afternoon he had turned up at the high school to collect the girls, Bobbie had calmly accepted his appearance with a grateful smile as he relieved her of her school books, but Sam had reacted so explosively that people had turned in the street to look at her.

'I'm not a child,' she had told her parents furiously at supper that night, ignoring Liam as she glowered over her meal.

'We were just a bit concerned about you both, hon,' her mother had palliated. There had been a spate of articles in the Washington press about diplomats' children being kidnapped and Sarah Jane had been only too happy to accept Liam's suggestion that he drive over to the high school and pick up her daughters.

Predictably, of course, Samantha had retaliated by getting herself a boyfriend—with a car—and announcing that this spotty, monosyllabic youth would, henceforth, drive her home.

And so it had gone on and with every twist of the emotional knife now sunk deep in his guts Liam had warned himself that what he was doing was wholly and completely self-destructive; that even if she *had* returned his feelings, their relationship would be so intense and volatile that it would leave him with no energy for anything else, never mind a politician's career. Sam was too outspoken, too opinionated, too much her own person to be right for him.

In order to accomplish what he wanted to accomplish, in order to go out and do battle and to win in the hostile minefield that was the political arena, when the smallest careless step, the briefest unguarded word could result in one being thrown out of office as carelessly as the Romans had once thrown their Christian prisoners to the lions, having a home life that was a haven of peace and calm, an oasis of sanity, a place as protective of his ego and his self as though it had been his mother's womb, was as vitally essential as breathing oxygen was for life.

And whilst Samantha could be guaranteed to be fiercely protective of her chosen mate and whilst she most certainly would defend him and the children she bore him with every ounce of her skill and fortitude, a calm oasis and a haven of peace she most certainly was not. The relationship; the marriage he had envisaged for himself was one of mutual respect; mutual coexistence, mutual awareness that their relationship was not the motivating prime force of his life. No way would Samantha ever tolerate that!

And yet, she was prepared to marry a man simply because she considered him to be ideal husband and father material. An Englishman who, in her opinion, would prove to be a far better father than her American countrymen.

And who was *he* to try to prove her wrong? Why should he want to? If he had any sense, what he ought to be doing right now was praying for James to marry her just as fast as possible. But when had a man deeply in love ever exhibited any kind of sense?

A man deeply in love!

Liam opened his eyes.

Too many years of loving the wrong woman had quite plainly addled his senses. It must have, otherwise he simply wouldn't be here… So where should he be instead—in Washington with Toni?

Of course, if Samantha *was* determined to marry James then there was nothing he could morally do to stop her, just as there had been nothing he could do to stop her from dating that adolescent high school jerk.

She was, after all, a woman grown and he…

'Oh, what a coincidence,' Bobbie had exclaimed when he had telephoned to tell her that he had booked into the Grosvenor. 'Sam and James are having dinner there together on Saturday night.'

Dinner together and then what? Or were they already lovers? Liam discovered that he had started to grind his teeth. The thought of Sam's magnificent body sensually entwined with that of another man, *any* other man, evoked the kind of primitive reaction inside him that made him want to throw back his head and howl like a hunting wolf. Somehow he didn't think that the Grosvenor would consider him to be a very welcome guest should he attempt to do so.

He glanced at his watch—four o'clock. Bobbie had promised to telephone him in the morning to arrange a get-together. Right now he needed a shower and he could do with something to eat. Picking up the telephone receiver he proceeded to call room service.

'Liam's staying at the Grosvenor.' James looked pleased. 'Perhaps we should give him a ring when we get there and invite him to join us for dinner.'

Samantha gritted her teeth. Really, James was just too good-natured and polite at times.

'Oh, but I was looking forward to just *us* having dinner together,' she protested huskily, adding for reinforcement just in case he needed it, 'On our own.'

Was she imagining it or was James deliberately avoiding looking at her?

'Er, well, yes, that would be lovely,' James was agreeing, but his voice wasn't very convincing, Sam recognised a little irritably.

What was the *matter* with him? Initially, when she had arrived in Chester he had seemed thoroughly delighted to see her but these last couple of days she had noticed that, although he was meticulous about keeping to the arrangements they had made, he also seemed to be becoming increasingly distant and preoccupied.

Why…? Surely she hadn't been coming on too strong to him? She had made sure that she wasn't pushing things faster than he wanted to go, but both last night and the night before he had said goodnight to her with little more than a dry-lipped fraternal kiss, even though she had allowed her own lips to part invitingly when he touched them.

'How much longer will Rosemary be staying with your parents?' she asked him conversationally as he drove into the Grosvenor's car park.

'Er… I… I'm not sure…' he replied, adding, 'I hope we can find a car parking spot, otherwise I'm going to have to drop you here whilst I park somewhere else.'

'Mmm… Have you met her fiancé?' Samantha asked him. 'She doesn't seem to mention him very often.'

James was frowning and Samantha heard him curse as another driver nipped into the only remaining car park spot ahead of him.

'I'll have to drop you here,' he told her curtly, leaning over to unlock the passenger door for her.

'I'll meet you in the foyer just as soon as I've managed to park.'

It was so unlike him to behave irritably that Samantha had felt a little nonplussed. She was aware, of course, that he and Rosemary did not get on but surely her innocent comment about the other girl was not really responsible for his bad temper?

The Grosvenor's foyer was busy and Samantha guessed from the number of smartly dressed people milling around the area that one or more private functions must be taking place.

It was a good fifteen minutes before James finally appeared and he was still frowning Samantha noticed as he made his way towards her and apologised.

'I couldn't find anywhere to park so in the end I drove over to my parents and I've left the car there. We'll have to get a taxi back there to pick up the car.'

His parents—so that explained the touch of lipstick she could just see smudged against his mouth, Samantha acknowledged. Teasingly she pointed it out to him, touched to see the way his colour rose as he took the tissue she was offering him to wipe it off.

It was his mother's of course, and no doubt he was embarrassed at being kissed by her as though he was still a small boy. Tenderly Samantha reached for his hand, intending to give it a little squeeze and to re-assure him that she personally found the devotion he had for his parents sweet and touching, but to her chagrin as she did so he moved back from her.

Trying not to feel hurt Samantha allowed him to guide her towards the hotel's main restaurant.

Once they were inside it he gave his name to the maître de and then frowned as he removed Samantha's coat for her.

'I do hope you aren't going to be cold,' he told Samantha pessimistically as he eyed her bare back.

The temptation to whisper throatily to him that if she was she would have to rely on *him* to do some-thing about it died unspoken as Samantha looked into his frowning preoccupied eyes.

James, quite obviously, had something on his mind and even more obviously it was not the same some-thing which was currently on hers. So much for her plans for an evening of seduction, she acknowledged ruefully as the maître de led the way to their table.

Instead of bringing her secret longing for mother-hood closer, it seemed instead that it was, in actual fact, receding and becoming even further out of reach.

Bravely refusing to allow herself to get down-hearted, Samantha opened the menu the waiter had handed her.

The Grosvenor boasted an innovative and highly acclaimed chef and after Bobbie's descriptions of the wonderful meals she had enjoyed at the hotel, Sam had been looking forward to hers.

James, though, seemed increasingly ill at ease. In

an attempt to relax him Samantha asked him if everything was all right.

'Yes, of course, why shouldn't it be?' he responded quickly, too quickly, Samantha felt.

They had just finished their aperitifs and were waiting to give their order when the maître de came over to their table to tell James that there was a phone call for him.

In common with a good many other high-class restaurants, the Grosvenor did not allow mobile phones into the dining room.

Excusing himself to Samantha, James got up and followed the maître de into the foyer where a room was put at the use of guests to take their telephone calls.

When the wine waiter approached the table and asked Samantha if she would like another drink she hesitated and then nodded her head. Perhaps a drink would help her to relax a little bit more; she certainly needed to do so, James' tension was beginning to communicate itself to her.

She had almost finished her drink before he returned looking flushed and anxious.

'What is it? What's wrong?' Samantha asked him solicitously.

'Oh, nothing…it was…it was just a client wanting to know when his case is likely to be heard.'

A *client?* How had he known where to find James? Samantha wondered soberly. She was strongly tempted to accuse James of being less than honest with her but she reasoned with herself, she could be wrong. After all, there was no reason why he should lie to her.

The waiter came and took their order. After the

briefest look at the wine list and without consulting her, James ordered the accompanying wine.

That alone was out of character for him. He was normally extremely solicitous about consulting her and almost too fussy about making sure he had chosen a good wine.

The first course came and with it the wine waiter who filled both their glasses.

Samantha had a healthy appetite and enjoyed her food, but watching James pick at his, quite obviously too preoccupied to eat it, destroyed her own desire to eat.

Samantha took a deep breath. Enough was enough. Putting down her cutlery she leaned across the table and began quietly, 'James, something is obviously wrong and...' She stopped, her eye caught by the woman standing in the entrance to the restaurant, a small frown puckering her forehead.

'What is it? What's wrong?' James asked her.

He had his back to the restaurant door but as he saw where Samantha was looking he swivelled round.

Samantha heard the sharp exclamation he made under his breath as he saw Rosemary standing in the doorway.

'James, what...?' Samantha began.

But he was already on his feet, telling her curtly, 'Please wait here, Samantha. I'd better go and see what she wants.'

As he reached the redhead, Samantha saw him take hold of her by her arm and almost march her out into the foyer and beyond her own sight.

The waiter came to ask if they were ready for their main course and Samantha shook her head, instead she allowed the wine waiter to refill her glass.

Sipping on her wine she watched the entrance to the restaurant. Five minutes went by and then ten and then another five. Suddenly Samantha had had enough. Finishing her wine she stood up and, ignoring the enquiring looks of the waiters, she marched purposely towards the foyer.

Initially she was unable to see either James or Rosemary. The foyer was now relatively empty though, certainly empty enough for her to be able to hear their voices coming from the room to one side of the foyer.

Frowning she approached it. By the sound of Rosemary's raised voice, although she couldn't make out *exactly* what she was saying, they were having an argument.

The door to the room was half open. Determinedly, Samantha gave it a push and then gave a small shocked gasp.

Rosemary and James were standing just inside the small room. Rosemary had her back to her whilst James was facing her but he couldn't see her and the reason he couldn't see her was because he was engaged in exchanging an extremely passionate kiss with Rosemary and his eyes were closed. Even so, something must have alerted him to the fact that they weren't alone because, suddenly, he opened his eyes and looked straight at Samantha.

She didn't wait to hear whatever it was he might have to say by way of explanation. What explanation was there, after all, that could serve any useful purpose? She had seen what she had seen and she had certainly seen that James was kissing Rosemary who he purported to dislike intensely, with far more fire and passion than he had ever shown towards her. All right, so they might not be an item; a *couple,* but *that* didn't alter the fact that he had quite deliberately misled her about the true nature of his relationship with the other girl.

Feeling both angry and humiliated Samantha turned on her heel and left, too preoccupied by her own feelings to be aware of the presence of anyone else in the foyer, much less the fact that she was about to cannon into him until the breath was expelled from her lungs with dizzying force and a firm pair of male hands gripped hold of her.

'Liam!' she exclaimed in shock.

'Where's the fire?' Liam joked, and then frowned as he saw her face.

'Sam, what is it? What's wrong…?'

Normally Samantha knew that her pride would never have allowed her to admit to any kind of failure but she was still in shock from what she had just seen.

'I'll tell you what's wrong,' she told him furiously. '*My* date…the man *I* thought would be the perfect father for my children, is back there smooching with a girl he told me he didn't even like.'

'James is here with someone else.'

Liam looked bemused.

'But I thought *you* were going to be having dinner with him.'

'So did I, but he didn't have much of an appetite for food, nor it seems, for *me* and now I can understand why,' she told Liam bitterly, her eyes filling with dismayed tears which she hurriedly tried to blink away. To have caught James, of all men, in a clinch with another woman when he had… When he had what? When he had *not* wanted her!

A sharp shudder speared through Samantha's body.

Perhaps Cliff had been right, after all. Perhaps she *wasn't* the kind of woman…perhaps she wasn't *any* kind of woman enough for a man. Fresh tears smarted her throat.

How *could* James do this to her?

'Liam, what are you doing?' she demanded sharply as she suddenly realised that Liam had guided her towards the lift and had pressed the bell.

'I'm taking you up to my suite so that you can calm down and tell me exactly what's going on.'

'What's going on is that James is a lying perfidious beast who… Oh…' Samantha gave a small soft gasp as the lift arrived and the doors opened, allowing Liam to gently push her into it.

Since several other guests joined them on its upward journey Samantha was unable to protest to Liam that all she really wanted was to be left completely and totally on her own until they were out of the lift and he was guiding her down the carpeted corridor to his hotel room door.

'This isn't any business of yours, Liam,' she told him shortly, 'so please stop trying to interfere… All I want to do is to call a taxi to take me back to Bobbie's.'

'You want to go back to Bobbie, looking like this,' he demanded exasperatedly as he opened the suite door and pushed her in front of the mirror hanging in the tiny entrance lobby.

Whilst Samantha stared in revulsion at her flushed tear-stained face, Liam closed and locked the door behind her.

'Now, come and take a seat, try to calm down and tell me what's happened.'

'What's happened is that James is a lying, cheating

rat,' Samantha told him indignantly, refusing to do as he suggested and instead pacing the carpeted floor in front of the suite's sitting room fireplace. The suite, she observed absently, was quite obviously one of the hotel's best ones, lovingly furnished with either genuine antiques or excellent reproductions, the bowl of flowers on one of the console tables was giving off a softly sweet smell but Samantha was in no mood to appreciate the scent of flowers.

'Rosemary is supposed to be engaged to someone else, she's even wearing a ring, and yet just now, downstairs, well, let's just say it was no brotherly kiss he was giving her,' she told him darkly.

Liam's eyebrows rose but initially he made no comment, waiting a few seconds before suggesting calmly, 'Perhaps she's received some kind of bad news and James was comforting her.'

Samantha gave him a scornful look.

'Comforting her? He looked more like he wanted to…' She stopped, her face flushing as she recognised just *what* it was James had looked as though he wanted to do with the woman in his arms.

Samantha closed her eyes, willing the tears she could feel filling her eyes not to fall.

Suddenly she remembered the lipstick that had stained James's mouth when he had returned from parking his car and his earlier preoccupation. Had he and Rosemary…?

'How *could* he do this to me?' she cried, furiously bunching her hands into protesting little fists. 'How *could* he when…'

'Perhaps he didn't realise just what you had in mind for him,' Liam suggested dryly.

Samantha shot him a bitter look.

'He *lied* to me,' she told him fiercely. 'If I had thought for one moment that he was…that there was…

'What's that?' she demanded suddenly, staring at the ice bucket with its complimentary bottle of champagne which was standing on the coffee table.

'Champagne,' Liam told her unnecessarily. 'Look, about James…'

'You haven't opened it yet,' she pointed out.

Liam frowned as he looked at her. Although not a total non-drinker, Samantha had a notoriously low tolerance of alcohol and for that reason tended to avoid anything more than an aperitif followed by a single glass of dinner wine.

'No, I haven't,' he agreed urbanely. 'And if you're suggesting that you'd like a glass… I don't think that would be a good idea.'

'Why not?' Samantha demanded truculently. 'I'm an adult now, Liam, remember, and if I want to get drunk…' Before Liam could stop her she reached out and removed the bottle from the ice bucket, inexpertly managing to prise the cork free.

The bubbling liquid spilled down over her hands and when Liam took the bottle from her it ran down his own, as well. Eyeing him challengingly Samantha raised her fingers to her mouth and slowly started to lick the spilt champagne off them.

Liam felt as though someone had hit him good and hard in the solar plexus.

'Cut it out,' he told her sharply.

'Cut what out?' Samantha demanded.

Liam shook his head. Did she *really* not know what she was doing to him, what images she was conjuring up inside his head with her actions? Just watching the way her tongue curled delicately over her fingers made him want to…

'Well, if *you* won't give me a drink then I guess I'm going to have to go down to the bar and buy my own,' Samantha was telling him aggressively.

Liam thought fast.

'Okay…okay,' he told her appeasingly, 'hang on a second whilst I pour it for you.'

With any luck she wouldn't even notice that he hadn't done more than half fill the glass, only it seemed she had and what was more she was letting him know in no uncertain terms that she had.

'Sam, I just don't think this is a good idea on an empty stomach,' he warned as she tilted the glass and drank quickly from it.

'No? Isn't it supposed to be the classic reaction to finding out that you've been betrayed by…' She stopped. She couldn't say by her lover because James wasn't that. 'Not, I suppose, that *you've* ever had to drown the pain that loving someone who doesn't love you back has caused you,' Samantha challenged Liam recklessly.

She was beginning to feel oddly light-headed and reckless, as though someone had taken the brakes off her reactions and emotions. It was a heady, powerful feeling and one she decided she could quite get to enjoy. With James the last few days she had found that she was constantly having to watch her words, to be careful and tactful so that she created the right kind of impression on him, but with Liam, none of that mattered. Liam knew already just what she was like. With Liam she could be as outspoken as she wished, there was no need, no point, in trying to convince *Liam* that she would make good wife material.

'Not in alcohol I haven't,' Liam told her sternly.

'You mean, *you* have loved someone who didn't want you?' Samantha asked him curiously. 'Who?'

'You're going to regret this in the morning,' Liam told her wryly as he recognised the effect the champagne was beginning to have on her.

'Champagne doesn't cause a hangover,' Samantha told him loftily.

Liam looked unimpressed.

'Why was he kissing her when he should have been kissing me?' she demanded mournfully as she eyed the champagne bottle.

'I want another drink, Liam,' she told him plaintively. 'No, don't stop me,' she demanded as he started to shake his head.

'I *need* to get drunk. After all, I'm suffering from a broken heart.'

'Don't be ridiculous, Sam, *you* don't love James,' Liam told her acerbically.

Angrily Samantha tried to focus on him, to tell him just how wrong he was but discovered, to her bemusement, that he was simply refusing to stand still and was, for some reason, swaying from side to side in front of her.

No, of course she didn't love James, but she wasn't going to have *Liam* tell her so.

'Don't I?' she demanded, frowning fiercely at him. 'And just how would *you* know that.'

'For several reasons,' Liam informed her softly, 'all of which I'd be more than happy to discuss with you—when you're sober.'

'I'm sober now.'

'No, you aren't,' he corrected her.

'What reasons? Tell me. I want to know. Tell me,

Liam,' Samantha insisted, crossing the floor between them, taking hold of his shirt-clad arm and giving it an angry little shake.

Liam closed his eyes.

This close he could smell the heart-wrenchingly familiar scent of her skin and what was worse, he could feel the way his body was reacting to it and to her. It was just as well, perhaps, that Samantha *was* so tipsy, otherwise she would be able to see just what her presence, her proximity, was doing to him.

'Tell me, Liam,' she was still demanding, her eyes a dark, deep, drownable, fatally alluring heavenly blue. '*What* reasons?'

She was standing so close to him now that— Liam took a deep breath and then another but it was no good, there was no way he could stop what he was feeling.

Almost angrily he took hold of her, pinioning her arms at her side.

'This reason, for one,' he told her grimly as he bent his head and expertly silenced the shocked protest she had been about to make with the firm pressure of his mouth.

Samantha's head was spinning, her thoughts, her reactions, her whole self going crazily out of control. This was Liam who was holding her, *kissing* her, she reminded herself. *Liam* who was just about the nearest thing she had to an elder brother, but her *body* didn't seem to be aware of any barriers her mind was trying to throw up between them. Her *body*... Samantha gave a delicate little shudder as she felt pure female sensual longing pour through her body.

'Mmm...'

Beneath Liam's mouth she made a soft appreciative

sound of pleasure and encouragement, lost in the awesome wonder of what she was feeling.

Liam's lips, Liam's tongue, were expertly prising apart *her* closed lips. Dizzily Samantha leant into him.

'Oh, this is pure heaven…'

'Heaven! It's been hell for me,' she thought she heard Liam muttering. 'Wanting you, knowing…'

Liam wanted her!

Bemused Samantha opened her eyes to their widest extent and then closed them quickly again as she realised that Liam's were open and he was looking straight back at her.

Delicious shivers of pleasure were darting all over her body. Why had she *never* realised before now that being kissed could be such a wonderful sensual experience? The hot pressure of Liam's mouth against her own was doing things to her that she never ever wanted to end.

'Don't say that.' She heard Liam groan against her mouth and realised with a small sense of shock that she must have spoken her thoughts out loud.

Dizzily she recognised that she was perhaps not quite as in control of herself as she really ought to be, but somehow it felt like far too much effort to do anything about it and, anyway, why should she want to when she was having such a wonderful, gorgeous, heavenly time in wonderful sexy Liam's arms?

'Mmm… Why have you never kissed me like this before?' she heard herself asking him huskily.

'If you need to ask *that,* then you really have had too much champagne,' Liam responded thickly.

Dreamily she looked up into his eyes.

'Mmm… Liam, *you* are just so sexy,' she breathed happily.

Abruptly he released her.

'Am I? Not five minutes ago you were telling me that you were in love with James. Isn't he the one you should be…'

Samantha glared at him. Not for *anything* was she going to tell him just how disappointed she felt that he had stopped kissing her or just how much she was wishing that he had done more, much, much, more than merely kissed her. If the touch of his lips could make her feel like that, then what would it be like if he were to—

A tiny tremor of excited fear ran down her spine as she recognised the dangerous route her thoughts were taking.

Liam wasn't the man for her. Liam wasn't her kind of man at all. Liam was far too…too…too *much* of a man for *her* liking. What *she* wanted was someone…someone kinder, gentler, someone much *more* malleable. Someone who would not view her with the kind of cynical detachment she was so used to seeing in Liam's eyes when he watched her. Someone, in short, who could not see into her thoughts quite so easily and dangerously as Liam could.

'I really *wanted* to love James,' she told Liam with the mournful honesty of the just-a-little-bit-too-tipsy.

A muscle twitched at the side of Liam's mouth but she couldn't tell whether it was caused by amusement or disgust.

'It's all right for you,' she accused him defensively. 'You…'

'I what?' Liam challenged her.

'It's different for a man.' Samantha backed down a little.

'Not anymore,' Liam advised her wryly.

'Maybe not in theory,' Samantha was forced to agree, 'but in reality…'

She closed her eyes. In reality as she was painfully beginning to learn, a woman was both gifted and cursed by nature in that it was one of her strongest and most powerful basic instincts to nurture and protect the vulnerable life she gave birth to and that instinct went right back to wanting to give that child the very best she could, *even* before he or she had even been conceived. Even the scientists themselves were agreed, women instinctively and automatically picked the mate who would provide their child with the best start in life, which was why *she* had wanted—

But there was no way she could continue with her plans now. Not after she had seen James with Rosemary. Whatever the truth was about their relationship, what Samantha had witnessed had made it overwhelmingly clear to her that there was unfinished business between them and that James was simply not free to father the children she so much longed to have.

'All I wanted was to give my babies the very best father they could have,' Samantha told Liam passionately. 'A father who would put his or her needs first, a father who would be there for them. I don't want my kids to grow up with only their mommy there, with a father whose career is more important to him than his family.

'I've seen what it does to kids to have an ambitious career-orientated father. It's like they're constantly trying to win his attention—his approval. If *you* ever marry, your kids will be like that, Liam. Oh, no doubt you'll love them, in your way, but your work, your career, will always come first…'

'Things are changing,' Liam told her quietly. 'Men *are* beginning to recognise just what they're missing out on…'

'Not in Washington they aren't,' Samantha told him cynically.

She was beginning to feel very tired, oppressed by the weight of her disappointment. She shivered, wrapping her arms around her body and closing her eyes as a wave of physical and emotional exhaustion swamped her.

She had put so much effort into planning her future with James that now that she was being forced to accept that her plans were not going to be realised, reaction was starting to set in, her mercurial temperament causing her spirits to plummet to the depths of misery and desolation.

All she wanted to do now was to crawl away and hide herself from the world and everyone in it until she had had time to come to terms with her disappointment. She wanted so badly to have a child…children… She had even mentally pictured their cute little faces, their heads of thick dark soft hair and their gorgeous grey eyes. Grey…but James' eyes were brown and… Grey eyes—like *Liam's!* That was the second time these compelling grey eyes had intruded on her dreams about future children.

'What's wrong?' Liam demanded sharply as he saw the way the blood drained from her face as she suddenly opened her eyes and focused on him.

'Er…nothing…nothing… I just…I'm just so tired, Liam,' she admitted. 'Everything has gone so wrong… Why…what is it about me…?' She stopped and shook her head, fresh tears of self-pity clogging her throat. By rights she ought to call a taxi and go home to Bobbie's but the thought of facing her sister whilst she was so emotionally upset, of having Bobbie demand to know what was wrong, was just too much for her.

'I…I think I'll call reception and ask them for a room,' she told Liam drearily.

'They're fully booked,' Liam informed her, frowning as he studied her pale face and defeated expression.

In all the years he had known her he had seen her go through many highs and lows, but he had never seen anything affect her as badly as this.

She felt things so fiercely, so passionately, there were no comfortable shades of grey in Samantha's emotional reactions, only blacks and whites.

She hadn't loved James and in losing him she was not losing a lover she was losing a potential father for her children. It was her pride and her belief in her own judgement that was hurting her now, that and her longing for a child, and it was typical of her that she didn't want to be with anyone, even someone as close as her own twin sister.

He glanced through the sitting room of his suite to the closed bedroom door and then looked at Samantha.

'You could always stay here,' he offered.

'Here…in your room.' Samantha frowned. 'But…'

'It isn't a room, it's a *suite,*' Liam pointed out. 'You can sleep in the bedroom, I'll sleep in here on the sofa. It's only for one night, after all…'

He was right, Samantha could see that. The effects of the alcohol she had consumed were wearing off now but she still felt tired and heavy-headed.

'Well, if you're sure you don't mind. Only, *I'll*

sleep on the sofa,' she told him firmly, adding, 'It makes much more sense, Liam, after all, you are much bigger than me and it *is* your room.'

Much bigger. How often did she get to say that to a man? Samantha wondered ruefully, but in Liam's case it was true. He was a good few inches taller than her *and* he had the physique to match his height.

It was a mystery to her how he managed to keep so fit given the demands of his career. She knew he played tennis and that he enjoyed walking. Whenever he could he back-packed into the mountains.

'You should try it sometime,' he had teased her once when she had shuddered over the lack of civilised amenities his vacations involved.

'What, without a proper bed or a shower...or anything.' She had grimaced fastidiously. 'No thanks.'

'What do you mean, no showers,' Liam had objected with a wicked glint in his eyes. 'Nature provides some of the best ones there are. Believe me there is nothing but nothing to compare with standing under a cool mountain waterfall and then swimming in a lake so clear that you can see the bottom...'

'Yeah, and having to share it with coyotes and bears and heaven knows what else, as well,' Samantha had objected. 'Like I just said, no thanks.'

'You don't know what you're missing,' Liam had told her softly. 'There's nothing like the cool clean feel of mountain water over naked skin...nothing like cooking out in the open air.'

'Skinny-dipping and barbecues might be your scene but they most definitely are not mine,' Samantha had informed him censoriously.

Liam had still been laughing as she walked away from him, head held high.

She had been much younger then, of course.

Her head was really beginning to ache. Wearily she stifled a jaw-stretching yawn and then a second one.

'Come on. You're exhausted,' Liam told her. 'I guess there'll be some spare bedding in one of the closets, I'll go find it whilst you use the bathroom....'

CHAPTER EIGHT

SAMANTHA woke up and gave a small grunt of pain. The sofa, pretty though it was, had never been designed to be used as a bed and certainly not by a full functioning woman of six foot plus. She winced as she sat up and her contorted muscles howled their protest.

She looked at her watch. She had been asleep for less than two hours.

Now that the alcohol had cleared from her head she was depressingly aware of the failure of her mission.

What were her chances, she wondered, of persuading Saul Crighton to give her a job with Aarlston-Becker thus saving her from the humiliation of having to return home and face Cliff?

She closed her eyes. They felt dry and gritty and her lips, when she touched them with her tongue tip, felt sensitive and faintly swollen—a legacy from Liam's kiss?

That had been such a dangerous thing for her to allow to happen. Now, with her head clear of the effects of the wine and champagne she had drunk she could see just how her behaviour must have looked to Liam. He would have been less than human if he hadn't... If he hadn't what? Taken her to bed? Certainly nothing she had done or said would have given him the impression that she wasn't willing—anything but!

Go to bed with Liam... What a thought... He was the last person... Abruptly Samantha tensed.

Go to bed with Liam... Seduce Liam into giving her a child... Liam, as she already knew, was a very highly sexed man—look at the number of girls he had dated—and anyway, anyone could see just by looking at him how sexy he was. With Liam there would be no need to coax or coerce him into responding; no need to be delicately guarded or femininely passive. Go to bed with Liam. It was impossible. Conceive Liam's child... No, she couldn't, it was totally out of the question, just a mad thought conjured up by her despair and the loneliness of the night.

What she was thinking, contemplating, was total and absolute madness. Was it? Wasn't she, in seducing Liam into impregnating her, merely following the deepest instinct of her sex? There could be no doubt that genetically Liam was an A1 choice. He was highly intelligent, physically strong, with the kind of skills that any child would rejoice in inheriting.

Maybe so, her sterner and more cautious inner self argued, but he was not a man who could be a father to her child in all the ways that were so important to her.

Did such a man exist? her other more emotional self protested. She had thought she had found the perfect husband in James and look how wrong she had been.

But, to have a child outside marriage and by Liam...her parents...her family... Bobbie would... Never mind her own strong feelings about shared parenthood.

Did any of them need to know? She could always pretend that the baby, her baby, was the result of a coolly taken clinical decision and an equally coldly clinical non-sexual act—an act which she had already vigorously denied to Bobbie that she could ever contemplate. And then there was Liam himself. But she wouldn't be the first woman to *choose* to be a single mother.

Liam, with his political ambitions to consider would probably be only too happy when faced with a fait accompli and her pregnancy confirmed to keep his own role in her baby's conception a secret, a small inner voice tempted her dangerously.

No, what she was thinking was totally inconceivable. Tears filled her eyes. She so much wanted to be a mother. But, if she was going to pretend to the world that that was how her child had been conceived then why not do so, why take the risk of being rejected yet again, of having Liam turn away from her as James had done?

Why indeed, but in having Liam father her child she would have the security of knowing just what her baby's genetic inheritance was. She owed it to her child, too, and as for Liam rejecting her, well there was only one way she was going to discover whether or not he would.

In place of the night wear she did not have, she had wrapped herself in one of the hotel's complimentary towelling robes after having undressed and showered and now, as she pushed aside the covers on her makeshift bed and stood up, its soft folds settled warmly around her body.

He wanted her, Liam had told her earlier, and even through the fog of alcohol her brain had retained those words, that admission, and when it came to wanting…

As she walked unsteadily towards the bedroom

door Samantha felt her pulse start to rise and her breathing become fast and uneven. Perhaps those teenager longings and desires she had thought so transient had had far deeper roots than she had imagined and were not quite dead, after all.

Very gently she opened the bedroom door and walked into the room. Now that her eyes had accustomed themselves to the darkness she could easily see Liam's sleeping form on the bed. A quick hot tug of excitement pulled at her heart, accompanied by a sharp sense of the awesomeness of what she was contemplating, but there was no hesitation or reluctance in the way she moved swiftly and softly towards the bed, waiting until she was close enough to lean over him and whisper his name against his lips before she said anything.

At her husky slightly tremulous 'Liam,' Liam woke up instantly, his body tensing, his eyes probing the darkness.

Samantha was leaning over him, her face, her mouth, so close to his that if he breathed a little deeply her lips would be touching his. He had no idea what she wanted but he knew, all too well, what *he* did. His body was making its needs all too urgently clear.

He lifted his arm to switch on the bedside lamp but Samantha stopped him, clasping his forearm and digging her nails a little into his skin in her urgency.

Liam closed his eyes. God, did she have the slightest idea what she was doing to him? He could smell the warm scent of her skin and her robe was so loosely knotted that he could see the full soft swell of her breasts.

The temptation to reach out and push the cloth aside to fully reveal her body, to slide his palm against the heavy fullness of her naked breast and tease the dark burgeoning flesh of her nipple into an aching peak so that she begged for him to take it in his mouth, was so strong that he had to grit his teeth to prevent himself from telling her rawly and explicitly what he wanted to do to her, how he wanted to make her feel…react…need and want him the way he did her. Under the bedclothes his own body was reacting to his thoughts as urgently as though he had actually put them into action.

Swallowing hard, he demanded shortly, 'Sam, what is it…what do you want…?'

He had fed her the perfect line, Samantha recognised. All she needed now was the courage to take it…use it…

Beneath her fingertips the silky hair-covered flesh of his forearm felt so secure and steady. She guessed that, if necessary, it…*he*…could take the whole of her weight and support it… support her, without flinching and certainly without letting her fall…in any way…

The idea of Liam representing any form of security was a novel one and it made her eyes open a little wider in bemused recognition that she was standing on the brink of an unexpected discovery, but there wasn't time to explore such thoughts right now. Right now…

She took a deep breath. Liam was still waiting for her answer. Using her free hand to unfasten the loose tie of her robe, Samantha deliberately slid it free of her shoulders, releasing his arm and leaning ever further towards him as she told him softly, murmuring the words in his ear, 'What I want, Liam, is you…' Then taking her courage in both hands, before he could say or do anything, she turned her head and placed her mouth very delicately and deliberately over his.

For a second the shock of what she was doing held Liam rigid and completely unable to move, but then, almost automatically, he reached out to grasp her shoulders so that he could push her gently away, the strong core of responsibility that was so much a part of his personality overriding the predatory male instincts of his aroused body.

Samantha tensed as she felt his lack of reaction but she was not about to give up now, not without a fight. Reaching out she clasped his face with her hands and proceeded to deepen the intimacy of her kiss, probing the hard shuttered line of his mouth with her tongue, willing him with every ounce of her willpower to respond to her and then, just when she thought she was going to have to give up and admit defeat, she felt the shudder of reaction that ripped through his body, the dry hard heat of the closed line of his lips suddenly giving way as he turned from rejection to responsiveness. Her own body shuddered in relief and then, even more intensely, in almost shocking pleasure as his hands started to knead the tense muscles of her shoulders, his fingers spreading over her skin, massaging and stroking her flesh.

It must be her relief that was making her so responsive to him, Samantha decided dizzily as she twined her arms around him, eagerly opening her mouth to the probing force of his tongue.

He was the one controlling their intimacy now, his hands sliding down her arms and then gripping hold of her as he rolled back onto the bed, lifting the upper half of her body over him as he did so.

Delicious shivers of sensation were washing all

through her as his actions brought the full weight of her breasts in tantalising close contact with his bare chest. The soft friction of the silky dark hair that covered it moving against her nipples as he kept on kissing her with ever-increasing intimacy made Samantha long to move closer to him, to press her body against him so that the tormentingly delicate friction became a soothing closeness that would take away the ache flooding through her body. She was lying half on and half off the bed, supported by Liam's hands and totally vulnerable to whatever he chose to do to her, she recognised with a small thrill of sensation which she realised in bemusement was actually excitement.

She was the one supposed to be seducing Liam, she reminded herself severely, and not for the physical satisfaction of having sex with him, but for a more important and serious purpose, a purpose which did not necessitate the kind of long drawn-out sensual foreplay she sensed that Liam was now about to indulge in.

But, for some reason, instead of short-cutting events, Samantha discovered that she was actually encouraging them.

If Liam wanted to tantalise her by only just allowing the aroused peaks of her nipples to brush against the wonderful sensual stimulation of his chest then she guessed she might as well do a little tantalising of her own, perhaps by running her fingertips and then her nails along one smooth hard sloping shoulder, just oh, so lightly raking the skin there.

As she felt him shudder in response, Samantha smiled secretly to herself. His lower body and hers might be separated by the thickness of the bedclothes but her woman's instinct told her that he wanted her.

A glorious sense of triumph and happiness filled her, a sense of strength and power, of freedom to be completely and totally herself. Joy bubbled up inside her and along with it a soft gurgle of laughter.

'What's funny?' Liam demanded as he heard it.

'Nothing,' Samantha whispered back honestly against his mouth, lifting her head to rub her face tenderly against his as she told him, 'I just feel *so* good…so…so *happy*…'

As he heard what she was saying Liam veiled his eyes with his eyelashes. Had she *any* idea just what she was saying to him? If *he* had any sense he would stop this right now before it got any further.

'Liam…'

In his hold, Samantha gave a small wriggle of impatience and then determinedly caressed his throat with her mouth, lingering deliberately over the hard swell of his Adam's apple until she felt him swallow in reaction to the sensuality of what she was doing. The words of soft denial he had been about to utter were lost, drowned out by the groan of longing that thundered in his chest. His hands slid from her arms to her breasts as he caressed them as he had imagined doing not just once, but a thousand, no a hundred thousand times in the years since she had reached maturity.

Lifting her further above him, he caressed the smooth warm swell of her breast with his mouth and then opened it over the dark ripe temptation of her nipple.

Samantha moaned sharply out loud as her body reacted to the swift suckling movement of his mouth, with a surge of pleasure so intense that it shocked her.

Her nails raked the warm flesh of Liam's arms. Her

hips writhing frustratedly against the thick muffling barrier of the bedclothes.

'Liam, Liam…' She tugged impatiently on his hair, shuddering as explosions of pleasure racked her body when he continued to caress her breasts. It was like being lapped by an inner tide of feeling, a tide which grew increasingly strong with every surge it made, a tide whose swift undercurrents she could already feel tugging deeper and deeper at the most private core of her being.

'Liam.'

Frantically she pulled at the bedclothes, desperate to wrench them away so that she could get closer to his body, to the wonderful maleness of him, to the completion, the satisfaction, the *oneness* her body craved and which she knew instinctively only his could soothe and satisfy.

Logical reasoning had long since been abandoned. She was operating on instinct alone now, driven and possessed by it and by her need—a need that only Liam could satisfy.

'I want you… I want you… I want you so much, Liam,' she told him, frantically whispering the words against his hair, his throat, just any part of him she could reach out for and touch. When she felt him rolling her over onto the bed beside him she reached towards the bedclothes, fiercely pushing them out of the way, her fingers meshing with Liam's as he did the same thing. Her eyes attuned fully now to the darkness quickly picked out the shape of his naked body as he pushed aside the duvet. Sharply she drew in her breath.

Watching her, Liam reflected that a man would have to be a saint not to react to the look he could see gleaming in her eyes as she studied him, so totally absorbed in visually drinking in every detail of him that she reminded him of a child unwrapping her Christmas presents.

Without the slightest hint of self-consciousness she reached out and traced the length of his arm, her eyes never leaving his body as she explored the flatness of his belly, but then as her fingertips touched the thick darkness of his male body hair she suddenly tensed and raised her gaze to his.

'What is it?' he asked her gruffly.

Samantha looked at him, her face slightly flushed.

'You're just so *beautiful*,' she told him softly. She could see the way his whole body shook with laughter.

'*I'm* beautiful…!'

Still laughing he reached up and took hold of her.

'I'll show you what's beautiful,' he told her huskily. 'This is beautiful.' He kissed one nipple slowly and tenderly. 'And this…'

Samantha trembled as he kissed the other one oh, so lingeringly.

'…And this…' His mouth was caressing the soft warmth of her belly. 'And these…'

He reached down and stroked his hands up over her knees and along her thighs and Samantha made a soft anguished sound of tormented pleasure.

'And this…'

All the breath in her lungs wheezed out of her in shock as Liam turned her on her back and slipped between her legs, his fingers gently probing the secret of her sex, his mouth slowly caressing it.

The undercurrent to the tide she had felt earlier had

now become an inescapable force that threatened to swamp and flood her.

'*You* are beautiful…more beautiful than any woman has any right to be, more beautiful than any other woman could ever possibly be,' she heard Liam telling her thickly as he slowly gathered her up in his arms and covered her with his body.

As he wrapped his arms around her and kissed her, Samantha was conscious of only one thing and that was her need to complete the magical cycle that they had begun, but as she moved to wrap her legs around him, Liam moved his body away from her, kissing her briefly as he whispered, 'Stay there…'

'Stay there!' Confused Samantha watched in disbelief as he got off the bed and padded towards the bathroom. Her whole body was on fire for him, aching for him, so much so that she was actually beginning to shiver as pitifully as a drug addict caught up in the agony of deprivation because he wasn't there.

In the bathroom Liam searched feverishly through the basket of complimentary toiletries for the discreet package he had seen tucked there earlier. The hotel, it seemed, intended to make sure that their guests practised safe sex, which was just as well because his current lifestyle certainly did not include carrying the means for doing so around himself.

Samantha was lying still, curled up in a bundle of rejection, her eyes closed against her pain—why had he disappeared, left her like that?—when he returned.

'Liam,' she began shakily as he touched her and then stopped as he wrapped her in his arms and proceeded to kiss her whispering, 'Sorry, something I had to do.'

Her relief at his return and at the fact that he still

wanted her prevented her from asking a question. Her body already aching with longing for him quickly caught fire from the hungry caress of his hands and this time it was Liam who moaned out loud as he held her hips and she arched her body towards his in invitation and abandonment.

As he entered her, Liam felt the universe turn full circle around him. They fitted together so well they might have been made for one another. He could feel her body responding to every movement of his own, welcoming each powerful thrust, caressing and holding him so lovingly that he could feel his eyes smarting with tears of emotion.

Samantha's eyes were starting to burn with her own shocked, emotional tears. Nothing had prepared her for the intensity of what she was experiencing and it wasn't just the sensation of Liam's body drawing hers to the edge of the precipice which would ultimately throw them both over to free fall through time and space as though they were immortal, that was arousing her almost too unbearably. No, it was the sure strong knowledge that this was her destiny and Liam her mate—that being with him like this now was the most powerful pivotal moment of her whole life.

'Mmm…' Lazily, her eyes still closed, Samantha reached out for the wonderful male warmth she had sensed had been there beside her in bed whilst she slept. But it *wasn't* there any longer. Anxiously she opened her eyes and then as she came fully awake her awareness of what had happened the night before brought her bolt upright in bed, panic, disbelief and denial all clamouring for supremacy in her overloaded brain.

Vaguely she was aware of another external noise overriding the frantic buzzing of her confused thoughts. Someone was knocking on the outer door of the hotel suite.

The bathroom door opened and Liam strode into the room, his hair wet, a towel wrapped discreetly around his hips.

'Mmm…good morning,' he murmured, coming over to the bed and leaning down, obviously intending to kiss her. Nervously Samantha leaned out of the way.

'The door, Liam,' she told him.

'It must be the waiter with our breakfast,' he told her, adding throatily, 'I don't know about you but I sure worked up an appetite doing *something* or other last night!'

Silently Samantha watched him walk into the suite's sitting room. Last night she had seduced Liam into making love to her—not that he had needed much persuasion, she defended herself quickly.

How *could* she have done such a thing? She closed her eyes. She knew only too well how… How many, many times in the past had she cursed the impetuosity of her volatile nature, the need for action, which sometimes overrode all the cannons of common sense and caution. She had done some mighty foolish things in the past, but *nothing,* not one single one of them had come *anywhere near* beating the magnitude of the folly she had committed last night.

Lost in the painful mental interrogations she was subjecting herself to she was only vaguely aware of Liam answering the impatient summons to open the suite door.

But it *wasn't* the waiter with the breakfast he had

ordered he was admitting to his suite, Samantha recognised with a sharp thrill of horror, it was Bobbie and her mother-in-law Pat.

'Oh, Liam, thank goodness you're here,' she heard Bobbie exclaiming worriedly. 'You haven't seen anything of Sam, have you? She never came home last night. She and James were to have dinner here at the Grosvenor and, at first, when she didn't come back I thought... But then when James rang this morning asking for her—'

As she heard her sister's voice becoming clearer and clearer, Samantha stared transfixed at the bedroom door which Liam had left partially open. Perhaps if she moved now she might just make it to the bathroom where she could conceal herself, but even as she frantically wondered what to do she heard her twin's sharp in-drawn breath of shock as she came into view standing in the open bedroom doorway staring stupefied at her.

'Samantha...' she breathed jerkily, whirling round to look pink-faced at Liam exclaiming, 'Oh Liam, I...'

'Bobbie, I can explain,' Samantha called out protestingly but her sister was already discreetly hurrying her mother-in-law away from the open bedroom door. Samantha could hear her apologising to Liam, explaining, 'Liam, I'm so sorry, I had no idea...no one, *Samantha* never said...but I suppose I should have guessed. The two of you always did strike sparks off one another... Oh, but the folks will be so pleased.'

Bobbie's shock was quite obviously giving way to excitement and suddenly she reappeared in the open doorway calling out to Samantha, 'Sam, I'm going to give the both of you one hour to get yourselves downstairs so that we can all celebrate. Fancy not even giving *me* a hint. Oh, my...just wait until I tell Luke...'

'Bobbie. *No.* You don't understand,' Samantha started to protest in panic but her twin was already ushering her bemused mother-in-law towards the suite door.

'Liam, I *am* sorry if we appeared at an inappropriate moment.' She could hear Bobbie laughing. 'But you really have only yourselves to blame. I know what it's like when you're freshly in love and you just want to keep the whole thing to yourselves, but Sam might have given me some kind of hint. And to think that *I'd* almost got her paired off with James.

'Well, Luke is quite definitely going to say "I told you so" to me. He's maintained all along that Sam and James would never suit...and Pat is convinced—' She broke off, giving Pat a rueful smile before her mother-in-law tactfully left, and then turned back exclaiming, 'Oh, Liam...'

In the hallway to the suite Bobbie flung her arms excitedly around Liam and hugged him.

'I am just *so* pleased for you both. I know that Sam has always maintained that she was over her teenage crush on you but I've always had my doubts—and who can blame her. If I didn't love Luke so much...' Bobbie laughed and hugged Liam a second time. 'Oh, I can't wait for Mom and Dad to come over now. This family is just going to have so much to celebrate—Pop's retirement, your inauguration *and* a wedding...'

As she heard the suite door close behind her sister, Samantha slid down beneath the bedclothes, hugging them protectively around her.

As soon as Liam appeared in the still open doorway she demanded accusingly, '*Why* did you let her in…?'

'I didn't have much choice,' Liam retorted calmly, 'and besides…'

'…and why didn't you tell her the truth?' Samantha shrilled furiously at him. 'Why did you let her go on and on like that about us being a couple…in love…? Now she thinks that we're about to get married and…'

'Is that such a bad idea,' Liam interrupted her quietly, quickly seizing the opportunity fate had so unexpectedly given him.

Samantha stared at him. She *had* to be hearing things.

'Us…get married…you and me…' She started to shake her head and then stopped as the appalling truth hit her.

'You *planned* this, didn't you,' she accused him in a shocked whisper. 'You *planned* it. You *deliberately*…' She closed her eyes and gulped. 'Oh, but I've been such a fool,' she told him angrily. 'I can see it all now… Miss Washington PR turned you down and so you targeted *me*. After all, what better wife *could* you have than the daughter of the retiring Governor… I'm the perfect wife, for you aren't I, Liam…and more importantly, my father is the perfect father-in-law… Oh…'

'What the hell are you saying?' Liam interrupted her sharply, his original rush of exhilaration turning swiftly to angry pain. 'You've got to be joking.' But he could see from her face that she wasn't and that she honestly believed the accusations she was hurling at him. He had expected her to be slightly withdrawn from him this morning, to feel a little shy and hesitant, but this… Of course it was unfortunate that Bobbie had seen Samantha in his bed and jumped to the natural conclusion, but…the very idea that Sam could honestly believe that he would stoop so low as to deliberately trick her into a compromising position was so crazy that he ought to be laughing at her, but he couldn't. The way she was reacting rubbed raw against his pride…and against his heart. He had genuinely thought that last night could be the start of— of what?

He had been a fool to let his hopes get out of hand like that and even more of a fool to let his needs get even further out of hand.

Samantha was throwing back the bedclothes and scrambling for the robe she had discarded the night before.

'I need to speak to Bobbie…' she was telling him frantically, almost gabbling the words in her fury. 'I need to tell her the truth…'

'The truth…'

Liam could feel his own anger rising to match hers. 'And just *what* exactly might that be?' he demanded bitingly, his eyes turning an ominous shade of dark stormy grey.

'What are you going to tell her Sam…? Are you going to tell her how you crawled into my bed and begged me…'

'No.'

Angrily Samantha placed her hands over her ears to shut out his shaming words.

'No?' In two strides Liam was across the floor, wrenching her hands away from her ears.

'*You* can tell Bobbie what lies you choose, Sam,

and I can't stop you, but the truth is that last night you wanted me…you begged me…you…'

'I *wanted* to get pregnant,' Samantha railed back at him, her face hot with the intensity of her emotions. 'I *wanted* you to give me a child.'

Immediately Liam released her hands and stood back from her. His face had gone white, his jaw clenched tight. Samantha had never ever seen him looking so angry and for a moment she felt almost afraid of him, shivering as she anticipated the cruelly destructive lash of his tongue as he lacerated her pride with his condemnation of her, but instead, as he turned his back on her and stared out of the window he was motionless and silent for so long that Samantha didn't know how to react. Her own shock-induced anger was beginning to ebb away, now leaving her feeling both ashamed and vulnerable. It was her own sense of shame at being discovered in his bed by her twin that had led her to react so horribly to him. She knew that she owed him an apology.

And then, just when she thought he simply wasn't going to speak to her at all, he began to do so but so quietly that she had to strain her ears to catch what he was saying.

'For your information,' he told her with his back still to her, 'the reason, the only reason, I didn't correct Bobbie's misunderstanding of the situation was because *I* wanted to protect *you*—and not just you, Sam, but your family, as well. Do you really think if I wanted a wife so badly, that I couldn't find one?' he challenged her as he swung round, adding in savage indictment, 'And I'd sure as hell have to be desperate to pick you, despite what you seem to think.

'I can't *think* of a single woman out of all the

women I know who is *less* emotionally and mentally equipped to take on the role of Governor's wife. You epitomise every characteristic that no politician in his right mind wants in a partner. You're impulsive, you leap to implausible conclusions and, even worse, you act on them as though they're known facts. You're stubborn to the point of totally illogical wrong-headedness, you won't listen to reason, you…'

To her chagrin Samantha discovered that tears were pouring down her face.

'…and as for what you said about going to bed with me so that you could get pregnant…'

To Samantha's shock he threw back his head and laughed harshly.

'What is it? What's so funny?' she demanded. 'Why are you laughing?'

'I'm laughing my dear, dear Samantha, because if you'd told me at the start just why you wanted to go to bed with me, there's no way you'd have ever got me there, and if you don't believe me then try asking yourself just why I took the trouble to make sure that you were protected—to make sure that there *were* no consequences…'

'"No consequences,"' Samantha repeated dully. She stared at him her anger rising again. '*No* consequences…' She thumped the bed in furious indignation. '*My* baby is not a *consequence,* I'll have you know, Liam Connolly. *My* baby…'

'*Our* baby,' Liam corrected her grittily. '*Our* baby, that's what he or she would have been, Sam. Not *your* baby but *ours* and there's no way I'd ever allow my child to be brought up by a woman who's got the kind of half-baked ideas that you…'

They were off again, arguing, accusing and

counter-accusing whilst Samantha struggled to take in what he had told her. That visit to the bathroom which she had dismissed merely as a frustrating interruption of their lovemaking had had a purpose she hadn't even guessed at.

'I hate you,' she told him passionately as her eyes clouded with fresh tears.

'I don't feel too hot about you, either, right now,' Liam told her grimly, 'but that still doesn't alter the fact that in less than an hour's time you and I are going to have to put on a convincing show of being idyllically in love.'

'What!' Samantha's jaw dropped.

'You heard me,' Liam told her curtly. 'Right now your sister believes that you and I, having spent an illicit night of passion in one another's arms, are about to swear eternal love to one another.'

'I'm going to tell her the truth,' Samantha reminded him shakily.

'Are you?' Liam shook his head. 'I don't think so,' he told her firmly. 'Have you thought about what this could do to your parents, Samantha? How they're going to feel knowing that you took me to bed purely to get yourself pregnant.'

Samantha opened her mouth and then closed it again.

'I… I won't tell them about that. I'll say it was just…just…'

'Just what? A moment of passion, and have them think that *I* seduced their daughter. Oh, no. No way are you going to put me in that kind of bind,' Liam told her softly. 'Oh, no, right now the only way you and I have of getting out of this with our reputations intact is to play along with Bobbie's belief that we're deeply in love and truly a committed couple.'

Deeply in love...*committed*. *Her* and *Liam*... Samantha opened her mouth to object to what he was saying and then closed it.

'Yes,' Liam challenged her tersely. '*If* you've got another solution then I'd sure like to hear it.'

Dumbly, Samantha shook her head. His mention of her parents had brought her sharply and painfully down to earth. She knew just how shocked and upset they would be if they heard the truth, how hurt and saddened by her behaviour—and Liam's. They already thought of Liam almost as a son and the news that he was to be their son-in-law would delight *both* her parents, but most especially her father.

'But I can't marry you,' she whispered painfully. 'You're going to be Governor and I don't... I can't...'

'Who said anything about *marriage?*' Liam derided her.

Uncertainly she looked at him.

'All I'm saying is that for now, for *everyone's* sake, you and I have to play along with Bobbie's assumptions and allow everyone to believe that we're in love and planning to get married.'

'But we aren't *going* to get married,' Samantha repeated, keeping her gaze fixed on Liam's face.

Immediately he shook his head.

'Oh, no. No way,' he told her savagely. 'No way would I ever marry a woman who only wanted me for the children I could give her.' He looked at his watch.

'We've got half an hour to get downstairs, unless of course you want your sister to think we're so passionately in love that we've gone back to bed, that we simply *can't* keep our hands off one another.'

Flinging him an indignant look, Samantha immediately hurried towards the bathroom. How *dare* he suggest anything of the kind. Just because last night she had seemed to…to want him… She had already told him the reason for *that.*

Once inside the bathroom with the door locked safely between them, Samantha tossed her head indignantly. *Her want Liam*… That was ridiculous…totally and absolutely ridiculous…wasn't it? And the minute she had Bobbie to herself she was going to tell her.

With the water from the shower cascading noisily behind her, Sam bit her lip. She was going to tell Bobbie what? That she and Liam had… She gave a small hurting swallow, the words 'had sex' almost physically hurting her as she tried to force herself to frame them mentally and discovered that, for some reason, the words she actually wanted to use were 'made love.'

But she and Liam had *not* made love. How could they when they did not love one another, when Liam did not love her?

Sam could feel shock zigzagging down her spine in sharp ice-cold splinters of pain just like the ones that were embedding themselves in her heart.

Tears welled up in her eyes. Angrily she blinked them away. What she was crying for was simply the loss of her childhood ideals, her belief that only within the loving intimacy of a committed relationship could she truly experience the physical fulfilment she had had with Liam last night, that only with a man she loved utterly and totally could she want to conceive a child…*his* child.

What had happened to her and to those beliefs that she had been willing to trample on them and to ignore them?

She *deserved* to be in the situation she now found herself in, she told herself uncompromisingly.

As she stepped into the shower, her mouth twisted in a small sadly wry smile. Well, at least no one who knew them was likely to be too surprised when she and Liam decided that their relationship wasn't going to work and that they wanted to go their separate ways.

And there was another aspect to the situation which Liam had not mentioned but which she was uncomfortably aware of.

Whilst Bobbie got on very well with her in-laws, Sam knew that her own mother had always felt a little bit uncomfortable with people because of the circumstances surrounding her own birth.

In the Crighton family, Ruth was treated with the respect she thoroughly deserved and even the realisation by other members of her family that she had borne the illegitimate daughter of her wartime lover and then been forced by her family to give up that baby for adoption had not changed her family's love or admiration for her. And nor, of course, should it have done. The story of Ruth's love for Grant and the trauma of her having to give up their daughter, Sarah Jane, was an extremely harrowing one, but now the whole family was reunited, Ruth and Grant were married, but still their daughter had never totally overcome her insecurity about being harshly judged by others because of the circumstances of her birth.

Her mother, Sam knew, would be very upset to think that Patricia Crighton had seen Sam in a compromising situation with Liam and might in consequence judge her daughter poorly.

No, for her mother's sake as much as anything else Sam knew that she had to go along with Liam's suggestion—go along with, maybe, but if Liam thought for one moment that she was about to be *grateful* to him for doing the gentlemanly thing…

Angrily Sam stepped out of the shower and started to vigorously towel herself dry.

She had just about finished when she heard a firm rap on the bathroom door.

'I'm nearly through,' she called out curtly to Liam.

'Open the door, Sam,' she heard him demanding, ignoring her response to his knock.

Pulling on her robe she opened the door and told him waspishly, 'There, I've finished and…'

She had stopped abruptly as she saw the parcels Liam was carrying and started to frown, 'You've been out to the stores, but…'

'Trousers and a top,' he told her laconically, handing over two of the shiny bags to her. 'I think I've got the size right…'

Sam stared at him, eyes widening.

'I didn't think you'd want to meet with everyone wearing the same dress you had on last night.'

He was right of course, that had been a strictly-for-a-sexy-date dress and was hardly suitable for a family lunch. Even so, for some reason, the knowledge that Liam had actually taken the trouble to go out and shop for her was making her feel not just surprised but ridiculously over-emotional.

She could feel the tears starting to burn her eyes

and in an effort to conceal them from him she lowered her head over the bags and told him grumpily, 'They probably won't fit.'

'Try them,' Liam advised her coolly.

Leaving the bathroom free for him, Samantha hurried into the bedroom.

Inside the larger carrier was a small one which she opened curiously before removing the tissue-packed trousers it contained. Inside the small carrier, also tissue wrapped, was exactly the kind of elegant plain underwear she normally favoured. Even the colour of the semi-nude bra and briefs was exactly the shade *she* would have chosen and she realised with a small sense of shock the size was exactly right, as well.

Now, how on earth had Liam known that? Either he had made a very inspired guess or he knew her much better than she thought. At a pinch, she guessed, she could have shopped for him and got everything in the right size but men were notorious for getting underwear measurements wrong. This bra he had bought for her was exactly right and the briefs were even in the style she favoured for wearing under trousers.

Quickly checking that the shower was still running she closed the bedroom door and slipped them on. She had been feeling rather unhappy about the idea of donning last night's worn things—one of the virtues or vices, depending on how you looked at it, of inheriting half of your genes from a strictly traditional New England family was a near obsession with cleanliness.

A little curiously she removed the trousers Liam had bought for her from their tissue wrapping. From the carrier bag she knew he had bought them from an extremely expensive local store and the label on the caramel-coloured fine wool pants confirmed their quality—Ralph Lauren no less—and as she held them up in front of her Sam knew that they would be a perfect fit.

Like the cream silk shirt he had bought her to go with them and the suede loafers she found in the third bag, everything was so very much in her own style that she could quite easily have bought them herself.

When she turned up downstairs wearing these clothes, Bobbie would automatically assume that she had.

She had just finished brushing her hair when Liam returned to the bedroom, one eyebrow raised as he asked her questioningly, 'Everything okay?'

'They fit fine,' Sam agreed grudgingly, and then her natural sense of fair play and honesty forced her to add, 'They're exactly what I would have chosen for myself. You'll have to give me the bills for them.'

'There's something else,' Liam told her, ignoring the latter part of what she was saying and going over to the coffee table in the suite's sitting room to pick up a small bag Sam had not noticed before.

'I guess if we're going to do this, we'd better go all the way,' he told her mystifyingly as he opened the small shiny dark green bag and removed an even smaller square jeweller's box.

Samantha's heart gave a shocked-bound thudding against her chest wall.

Liam had bought her jewellery…a ring?

'Give me your hand,' she heard him demanding calmly.

Her mouth had gone too dry for her to be able to utter the denial she wanted to make but her whole body trembled as Liam took hold of her left hand, giving her a slightly grim look as he warned her, 'This is no time to start being dramatic, Samantha. You can be sure that right now, whoever is downstairs is expecting us to emerge as a blissfully happily committed couple.'

'No,' she denied quickly. 'Why should they? Bobbie won't have said anything…'

Liam's eyebrows lifted.

'Maybe not in normal circumstances,' he agreed, 'but she wasn't on her own when she saw us. She had Pat with her,' he reminded Samantha, and although he didn't want to provoke another row with Sam he had seen the look of relief in Bobbie's eyes when neither of them had denied their love for one another.

James' parents, whilst welcoming Bobbie to their family were a slightly old-fashioned and very traditional couple. Neither of James' sisters had lived with their now husbands before their marriages and both of them had lived at home whilst attending university in Manchester. Even though it was over an hour's drive away, and whilst there was no way that he was dependent on Sam's father's goodwill to further his political career, he liked the older man far too much to want to cause him any embarrassment or pain— A mutually broken off engagement would be far easier for Sam's parents to accept than a mere one- night stand—not that he ever had any intentions—but his intention, his hopes and needs, had to be put on hold right now, especially with Sam reacting as she was doing.

Concentrating on digesting the unpalatable truth of what Liam was saying, Samantha did not at first pay much attention to the ring he was removing from its box until the white flash of diamonds not so much caught as regally demanded her attention.

When she did look at the ring he was coolly slipping onto her finger she couldn't prevent herself from giving a stunned betraying gasp.

The central flawless sapphire was the deepest densest blue she had ever seen and just about as close to the colour of her own eyes as it could possibly be, whilst the diamonds which surrounded it were sharply white, perfectly clear glittering stones.

It was, Samantha recognised, the kind of ring any woman would be thrilled to receive. Surely only a man deeply in love would choose a stone that so exactly matched his adored one's own eye colour and he would certainly have to be totally besotted to spend the amount of money Samantha guessed *this* ring must have cost Liam.

'What did you do,' she joked shakily, 'hire it for the day…'

The look of hauteur Liam gave her made her feel even more shaky.

'Liam, it's…it's…' She shook her head, unable to find the words to tell him what she thought of his quixotic impulse. 'It must have been so expensive,' she told him weakly. 'What on earth will you do with it…afterwards…'

'Concern—for me?—*that* must be a first,' Liam told her dryly as he closed the box with a firmly businesslike air.

'Hopefully in the fuss over our "engagement" surprise, the way in which our relationship was exposed to the light of day will be overlooked,' he told her sardonically.

'Engaged.' Samantha shook her head. 'But Mom and Dad…'

'…will understand when I explain that it was only the discovery of how much I was missing you and what I stood to lose that prompted me to act impetuously and rush over here to propose to you,' Liam told her calmly.

'Lovers seldom act rationally…so why should we be any exception? I proposed, you accepted, and of course, I couldn't wait to show the world that you're mine by waiting until we got home to get you a ring. After all, it isn't as though I have your ability to trace my family back to the Pilgrim Fathers and beyond and there are certainly no family heirlooms waiting in bank vaults to be handed over to my wife-to-be,' he told her grimly.

Samantha gave a thoughtful look. She knew of Liam's family history and how, as immigrants, they had arrived in America with virtually nothing, but his words brought home to her again how sensitive Liam felt about the subject.

'You can't think that if I were in love it would matter to *me* who my partner's antecedents were,' she challenged him.

'No, but surely you'd want to know what kind of genes you were passing on to your kids, wouldn't you?'

'If I loved someone then I would want my child—our child—to have his genes,' she reiterated firmly.

Liam gave her a cynical smile.

'Well, let's hope the voters ''love'' *me* enough to overlook my lesser heritage,' he told her wryly.

Samantha frowned. 'You don't honestly think that people would be put off voting for you because of that?' she demanded before telling him passionately, 'It's obvious that you're the best man for the job, Liam, and any voter who can't see that for themselves doesn't, in my view, deserve to be allowed to vote.'

'Very democratic,' Liam told her, his expression lightening to one of rueful amusement. 'You really are an all-or-nothing person, Sam, you either love or hate, there's no halfway house with you, no middle ground.'

'Just because I have strong beliefs, that doesn't mean that I can't see another person's point of view,' Samantha objected. 'I'm not intolerant, Liam.'

'No, just passionately opposed to anyone who doesn't share your point of view,' Liam responded with another smile, glancing at his watch and then warning her, 'Come on, we'd better go down and face the music.'

CHAPTER NINE

'COME on, in you go.'

'Oh!'

Samantha gave a small exclamation of stunned disbelief as Bobbie, who had been waiting for them in the hotel foyer, gave her a little push and stood to one side in the open doorway of the hotel's private function room.

Instead of half a dozen or less people Samantha had expected to see, the room seemed full of a sea of expectant faces. For a moment she was tempted to turn tail and run but as though he knew how overwhelmed she felt Liam stepped up behind her, his arm curling supportively around her as he drawled to Bobbie, 'Seems like someone's been busy…'

Samantha heard Bobbie laugh, her initial panic subsiding as she realised that in truth the room only held a relatively small proportion of their many relatives, around a dozen or so, all of them smiling at her in loving happiness and expectancy.

'Well, I just *had* to ring Jenny to give her the news because I knew that she'd already arranged a family lunch here today because Katie's at home and she'd invited Max and Maddy to join them with the children and so I said why didn't we all have lunch together. You don't mind do you?' she asked Samantha. 'Only I'm just so excited for you, Sam. It's like a romance story come true, you falling for Liam in such a big way all those years ago, worshipping him from a distance and having the biggest crush in the world on him,' she teased. 'And now, all these years later the two of you falling for one another as equals. And now,' she added expressively rolling her eyes as she gave them both a merry look, 'Liam must love you to pieces to have followed you right across the Atlantic. She'll make the world's worst Governor's wife, Liam,' she added warningly.

'Oh, thanks,' Samantha told her twin grimly.

'It's true,' Bobbie laughed. 'The first time there's a march outside government house you'll be the one leading it. Do you remember when she organised that protest march against hunting, Liam?' she asked him.

'Will I ever forget it,' Liam responded ruefully. '*I* was the one who had to go get her released from the police cells...'

'Yes, and you were the one who, when we got home, told me I'd have to shower in the backyard just in case I'd picked up...something...' Samantha gave a deep shudder at the memory his words had evoked. Perhaps it was true that she *had* reacted rather recklessly and dangerously, but surely Liam had *over*reacted in his furious cold anger to her when he had come to bail her, cruelly telling her that some of her co-marchers may not be too particular about their personal hygiene.

Whether or not he had been right had never been proved. It had been enough that she had spent the whole night lying awake wondering if every tiny little scalp itch was the forerunner of some unpleasant and unwanted cohabiters.

First thing in the morning she had taken herself off to the hairdressers where she had had her long hair cropped.

She could still remember how her mother had cried when she had seen her and she could remember, too, the look of cold disgust in Liam's eyes as he studied her boyishly barbered short hair. She had grown it long again, but now preferred her hair cropped although in a much more feminine version of her original cut.

'That was when you had your hair cut,' Bobbie added, almost as though twin-fashion, she had followed Samantha's own train of thought.

'Do you remember, Liam?' she asked. 'Poor Mom cried.'

'Yes,' Liam said. 'I remember.'

How terse and angry Liam sounded. Samantha turned her head to look at him and then stood completely still in the circle of his arm, their onlookers forgotten as she saw the look in his eyes.

'Your lovely hair... I didn't know whether to throttle you or...' Liam was telling her softly. 'Not that it didn't suit you short then or now...'

Suspecting that he was trying to sound diplomatic and lover-like because Bobbie was listening Samantha was just about to try to reply in a way that was equally pseudo lover-like when, to her disbelief she heard Bobbie chiming in, 'Oh, yes, I can still remember how chagrined I felt a while back when I overheard Liam telling someone that he thought your cropped curls were just the most alluringly sexy tease on a woman with such a sensationally curvy body.'

Her eyes rounding, Samantha stared at him.

'You said *that*,' she questioned faintly, 'about *me*...'

'I suppose I should have guessed then,' Bobbie was saying as she determinedly ushered them into the

Grosvenor's private function room and called out to the assembled throng, 'Here they are everyone. The Crighton family's latest formally accredited "couple."'

Out of nowhere a waiter suddenly appeared circulating the room with trays of bubbling champagne, or so it seemed to Samantha as she and Liam were engulfed by the excited and enthusiastic members of her family who were waiting to congratulate them.

'I thought you said just a quiet family lunch,' Samantha complained to her twin.

'Well... It's what Mom would have wanted,' Bobbie told her virtuously.

'Mom...! You haven't...' Samantha began but Bobbie shook her head.

'No. I'm leaving *that* to you—and Liam—not that... Oh...'

'What is it?' Samantha demanded hearing the surprised and excited note in her sister's voice as she looked towards the doorway.

'It's Gran and Gramps!' Bobbie exclaimed leaving her sister's side to hurry over to the doorway where Ruth and Grant were standing together with one of Ruth's nephews, Saul Crighton, his wife Tullah, and their children.

It was Saul's parents Hugh and Ann who Ruth and Grant had been staying with in Pembroke and as she stared at them Samantha shook her head and told Liam, 'I just don't believe this. All it needs now is for Mom and Pop to walk in through the door.'

'Well, I doubt that *that's* going to happen, but I think we ought to go over and make our explanations to your grandparents—or rather, I ought,' Liam told her ruefully.

Samantha shot him a surprised look. She could actually hear a faint note of almost boyish uncertainty in Liam's voice and there was quite definitely a slightly sheepish look in his eyes as he looked towards the group of people surrounding her grandparents. It was so unlike Liam to betray anything other than total self-confidence that such an unexpected display of vulnerability caused her to move closer to him and put her hand on his arm in a gesture that was almost protective.

'Gran will understand,' she told him. 'After all, she and Gramps…'

Abruptly Samantha stopped. What on earth was happening to her? Just for a moment it was almost as though she actually *was* Liam's fiancée, as though they *were* actually two very newly committed lovers catapulted into a very public arena they had never expected to have to enter at such an early stage in their newly discovered love. But it was too late now to withdraw from Liam. At the touch of her hand he had moved closer to her and she could see the way the others were regarding them. Infuriatingly Samantha discovered that she was actually blushing and, even worse, that she was more than happy to have the solid bulk of Liam to lean a little shyly into as he started to guide her across the floor to where her grandparents were waiting.

'So, it's finally happened! The two of you have stopped fighting long enough to fall in love.'

Samantha blinked as she heard the loving approval in her grandmother's voice and saw the happiness in her eyes.

'Liam, I just hope you know exactly what you're

taking on,' Ruth was saying to Liam. 'You're *never* going to change her.'

'There's no way I'd want to,' Liam was replying in true lover-like fashion.

And, looking into his eyes heart-jerkingly for a breathless space of time, Samantha could almost believe he meant it.

The afternoon passed in a haze of hugs and kisses and congratulations, the Grosvenor rising to the occasion with true aplomb produced a buffet luncheon fit for the most discerning diner. Dizzily Samantha listened to the various conversations humming in the air around her, the younger ranks of the family were entertaining themselves in one corner of the room whilst another group which included Jon and Jenny had formed around Ruth and Grant, whilst Bobbie, Luke, Tullah and Saul were also busy exchanging reminiscences of their childhoods and of their own early days as couples.

Of them all only Katie was partnerless. A calm very private person, Katie, according to her mother Jenny, was dedicated, not perhaps so much to her job but to the cause it served.

Like Ruth, Katie had a very strong philanthropic caring streak. Her work in the legal department of a large charity might not be going to bring her either fame or fortune but it had to give her a great deal of satisfaction, Samantha acknowledged.

Not that Katie looked particularly happy right now though, she admitted, or was it simply that the very coupledness of everyone else there underlined the fact that Katie was on her own.

When Saul and Tullah came over to congratulate

them, Tullah remarked teasingly, 'Perhaps you're going to beat us to produce the first set of our generation of twin births, after all...'

'Twins... With Liam running for the governorship I doubt they're going to have time to conceive one child never mind two,' Saul told his wife outspokenly. Mortifyingly, whilst the other three laughed, Samantha could feel herself starting to blush as though she were, in reality, in love with Liam.

'When will you get married?' Tullah was asking. 'After voting or...'

Liam gave Samantha a warning squeeze of her hand, answering before she could say anything, 'We haven't settled on a date yet.'

'Well, I guess that means the end of your visit over here,' Bobbie commented ruefully several hours later when everyone else had gone bar Bobbie and Luke and their grandparents, Luke's parents having taken Francesca home with them for the night to give Bobbie some extra time to spend with her twin. She continued before Samantha could say anything,

'I know Liam can't stay over here very long and, of course, you're going to want to go back with him. When are you going to tell the folks?'

As Bobbie had already confided to Luke, the fact that Sam and Liam were lovers had proved to her how much her twin must love Liam.

'Sam has always been so picky—and never ever casually intimate with men in any kind of way—for her to have committed herself to Liam like this proves how much she loves him.'

'I don't need convincing,' Luke had responded knowingly. '*I* knew she and James wouldn't suit.'

'We're going to ring them just as soon as we can,' Liam answered for them both now.

'Well, I know that Sarah Jane won't be too surprised,' Ruth confounded Samantha by commenting. 'I know from what she's told me that she did have hopes…'

Her mother had *hopes…hopes* of her and Liam… How on earth could she have done? Samantha wondered bemusedly whilst Liam veiled his eyes.

He was not entirely surprised that Samantha's mother had guessed how he felt about her daughter. Mothers were, after all, notoriously very insightful in that way. Samantha herself, thank the Lord, was far less intuitive.

As he looked sideways at the ring glittering on Samantha's left hand he could almost taste the bittersweet flavour of the sharp cruelty of the gulf between the relationship the two of them were pretending to and reality.

He was still searingly aware of the double blow Samantha had given him in firstly accusing him of trying to use her to improve his chances of winning the vote—how could she think him capable of that kind of underhandedness?—and of secondly and even more hurtful telling him that she had cold-bloodedly decided to have sex with him because she wanted not *his* child but *a* child. That revelation hadn't just hurt him it had shocked him, as well.

The closeness of the Miller family had appealed to an idealism within Liam that he tried to keep hidden and protected and that Samantha, the woman he loved, should be prepared to deny her own child the kind of upbringing she herself had been so lovingly nurtured in was something he was finding hard to un-

derstand. And what he was finding even harder to understand or forgive was his own dangerous awareness
that given a second opportunity to furnish Sam with
the child she so much wanted, he doubted that he
would be able to resist the temptation to do so; that
way at least he'd have some kind of permanent tie
with her...through their child.

As Samantha listened to her grandparents she acknowledged that her grandfather and Liam had always
got on well. Grant's family was from the Deep South
and he and Liam, in common with her father, shared
a belief that it was of vital importance to find a way
of integrating the diehards of both the Southern states
and the Northern ones in a common purpose that
would benefit everyone. Ruth and Liam had immediately taken to one another so that now, as the whole
family, including Luke, began a passionate discussion
about the increasingly urgent need to give those
young people of both countries the incentive and the
help to free themselves from what western journalists
were currently referring to as 'the poverty trap,' momentarily Samantha felt somehow as though she was
excluded from a particularly charismatic and exclu-
sive circle.

Her views were not that much out of accord with
those of the others, she recognised, it was just that she
favoured a much more direct and possibly contentious
method of putting them into operation.

'I guess it looks like we're going to be having dinner here,' Grant commented jovially at one point.
'We'd better book a table.'

Whilst the others were all eagerly assenting, only
Liam hesitated, looking at Samantha and asking her

in a quiet voice, 'You're very quiet, would you prefer to do something else?'

Samantha's eyes widened, a very definite tug of emotion dragging on her heart, a very real sense of warmth and happiness enveloping her. Liam at least had noticed that she wasn't joining in the others' enthusiastic discussion and he had felt *concerned* enough about her to ask what she wanted to do.

A small fluffy euphoric cloud materialised out of nowhere to wrap itself around her and cushion her. Instinctively she moved closer to Liam, virtually snuggling into his side without realising what she was doing. Not even the comforting strength of his arm going around her as he drew her even closer warned her of the danger she was courting or the vulnerability she was exposing, something which she later put down to the fact that she had, over the course of the afternoon, become so steeped in her role of newly affianced woman that playing that part had become second nature to her.

'Uh-huh…it looks to me like she would,' Bobbie teased her unmercifully, forcing Samantha to realise what she was doing and to push herself away from Liam as she denied fiercely, 'No…dinner here will be fine by me.'

'Well now, here's a thing,' Grant chuckled. 'It looks to me, Liam, like love is already taming our firebrand. She's even learning the art of tactful social fibbing. Perhaps she's not going to make such a bad Governor's wife, after all…'

'For your information,' Samantha began indignantly, her eyes flashing warning storm signals. But Liam silenced her quickly, leaning forward to kiss her briefly on the lips.

The dizziness that flooded her must be because she hadn't eaten much of the buffet, Samantha decided as she forced herself not to give in to the disturbing urge to wrap her arms around Liam and return his kiss—with interest—with very passionate interest.

'She's going to make a wonderful Governor's wife,' Liam told Grant throatily without taking his eyes off Samantha's face. 'And certainly the only wife that *this* potential Governor is *ever* going to want…'

Surrounded by the others' laughter Samantha tried to tear her gaze away from Liam's and discovered that she couldn't. She felt as though she were drowning, melting, as though her whole body was on fire… dissolving, aching, so much so that right now…

Her whole body went hot with mortified colour as she recognised just what direction her thoughts were taking and there was no use kidding herself, the urgent desire she had just felt flooding her body had nothing whatsoever to do with any maternal desire to make a baby. What was happening to her? When had acting the part of being in love with Liam, of having to pretend there was nothing she wanted more than to be alone with him…having to pretend that there was no one she wanted more than him, had right now become so easy, so natural, so *necessary,* that it was as automatic as just breathing?

Whilst the others fussed over practicalities Samantha sat in bemused silence.

'My, oh, my,' Grant commented jokingly at one stage later in the evening when Samantha hadn't even responded to the very obvious lure he had been trailing for her. 'I know they say that love changes a person but…'

To Samantha's surprise it was Liam who came to

her rescue, shaking his head and saying firmly, 'Samantha's and my beliefs, our ideals, have never been as far apart as some folk like to think, it's just that my way of instituting them is a little less assertive than Sam's…'

Whilst the others were still laughing, he turned to her and picked up her left hand and carried it to his lips, kissing her ring finger in a gesture that was simple and loving and so totally without any kind of self-consciousness that Samantha felt her eyes smart with sharp tears. What would it be like if Liam really *did* love her? Previously her dreams of loving a man and being loved by him had all revolved around the family they would have. It had never occurred to her that she might feel such an overwhelming sense of bliss and security nor such a profound sense of belonging, of knowing that she could totally relax and allow someone else to carry her just for a little while.

Bemusedly she looked up into Liam's eyes. He was watching her with a mixture of gravity and an expression she couldn't define. All she knew was that it set her pulse rate rocketing and made her whole body go hot and sensitive just as though he had suddenly touched and caressed it.

Whilst the others were ordering their food he leaned towards her, closing the gap between them, and then whispered against her mouth, 'Keep on looking at me like that Samantha Miller and I might just forget all the reasons why this engagement of ours isn't for real and I might forget, too, just why those precautions I took last night so as not to get you pregnant were the right thing to do…'

And then he kissed her. Not just an ordinary little old kiss, either, but a long, slow, deeply passionate this is my woman and I love her kind of kiss, right there at the restaurant table with nearly all her family looking on. And, much as she loved them, just for a second Samantha wished very passionately that they weren't there and that Liam would do exactly what he had just been whispering to her that he wanted to do and that they were alone, upstairs, in his suite and that…

'You never did tell me what happened to James last night,' Bobbie announced, breaking the dangerous spell holding Samantha entranced.

'James…'

For a moment Samantha actually had difficulty in remembering who her sister meant. 'Oh, yes…well, he had…' She stopped, not sure how much she should say about just what had happened. After all, Rosemary was engaged to another man and she and James were supposed to thoroughly dislike one another.

'Er…there was a phone call,' Samantha fibbed in the end, 'and he said he had to leave.'

'It must have been fate,' Bobbie told her with a broad smile before adding in a semi-audible whisper, 'By the way, have you told Liam yet about you know what…'

'"You know what"?' Samantha frowned. 'I don't know what you mean,' she began, but Bobbie stopped her, shaking her head and reminding her wickedly, 'Remember when you and I had our joint confession fest and I told you about my water fantasy and you…'

'Oh…yes…that…' Samantha headed her off quickly. There was no way she wanted Liam to hear about that idiotic sensual fantasy of hers about making love out of doors, not when they were not really a couple, not when he didn't, couldn't, really love her, but it was no use rolling an anguished look in her twin's direction and whilst Luke and their grandparents were engaged in their own conversation, Bobbie proceeded to inform Liam in a soft undertone just what Samantha's secret fantasy actually was.

'Bobbie, that was a teenage thing,' Samantha hissed, totally unable to bring herself to look at Liam to see how he was reacting to Bobbie's confidences.

'So were your feelings for Liam and now look what's happened,' Bobbie teased her unrepentantly.

It was late when they finally called the evening to an end, Luke and Bobbie leaving first and then Ruth and Grant following them within minutes.

'We'll talk tomorrow,' Bobbie had promised her sister before she left, adding, 'I know you'll want to fly back home with Liam but at least, with the two of you planning to get married it won't be very long before we're all together again.'

It was gone midnight when Samantha and Liam walked through the foyer towards the lifts.

'The hotel's emptied out a little now,' Liam informed her quietly as he buzzed for the lift, 'so I've been able to book you your own room.'

Her own room… Samantha tried to look appropriately appreciative. Bobbie had thoughtfully returned home before the lunch and she had discreetly handed over to Samantha a large holdall containing some of her clothes and toiletries.

With the old-fashioned courtliness that had so often caused her to rebel against him in the past, Liam insisted on walking Samantha to her hotel room door and unlocking it for her. As she stepped past him into the room Sam had a wild longing to stop and turn straight into his arms.

The depth of her own longing unnerved her. What was happening to her? Surely she wasn't so easily suggestible that, less than twenty-four hours of playing at being Liam's lover and wife-to-be had made her feel so wrapped up in the role that she couldn't divorce herself from it and return to reality. She actually had to grit her jaw to stop herself from whispering to him that she wanted to spend the night in his room, in his bed, in his arms, and not just because she wanted his child—no, not just for that at all. What she wanted, she realised shakily, was Liam himself.

'We'll ring home in the morning,' Liam was saying to her.

It was as much as Samantha could trust herself to do to simply shake her head. If she opened her mouth, if she looked at him, if her body even thought that he might make the smallest move in her direction… Even after he had closed the door behind himself it was still several seconds before Samantha could trust herself to move; her fingers shook as she locked the door. The ring Liam had given her caught the light. Despite its weight she was barely aware of wearing it; it was almost as though it had always been there. Reluctantly she took it off. Her hand felt bare…naked…

It took a long time before she finally managed to drop off to sleep and even then she didn't sleep very well. The bed felt uncomfortable and empty without Liam in it…

Liam… Liam… Liam…

She sat upright, drawing up her knees and wrapping her arms around them. What was happening to her? What *had* happened to her? She had *never* been any good at pretending to feel or be what she did not. Never…and yet today, pretending to be in love with Liam had come so easily and naturally to her that—

Abruptly her body tensed as the unpalatable truth struck her. Perhaps the pretence had been easy because, in reality, it was no pretence at all.

But how could that be? How could she possibly have been in love with Liam without knowing it?

Perhaps she *had,* at some deep level of her subconscious, known it. Perhaps that was why she had responded to Liam the way she had. Perhaps that was why she had been so consumed by the desire to conceive his child. Nature worked in complex and not always totally clear ways.

But she couldn't love Liam. *He* didn't love her. She had had to learn that as a girl…and although she had never admitted it even to Bobbie, accepting that he didn't return her feelings had been one of the hardest and most painful lessons she had ever had to bear. Her feelings for him might have been those of an adolescent girl rather than a woman, but that hadn't made them any the less real. But Liam had made it stingingly clear that there was no way he was going to allow her to dream hopeless dreams about him and her pride had done the rest. Now she knew she was going to need that same determination, that same pride, again.

'Remember how very different you feel about all the issues that are important to you,' Samantha warned herself, but listening to Liam this evening as he discussed his altruistic ambitions and hopes for the State she had been forced to acknowledge that, idealistically, they were not so very far apart, after all.

But what was she thinking? Even if by some miracle, Liam actually came to return her love, *she* would never in a million years ever make the kind of wife he was going to need. Even her own family were agreed on that although they seemed to think that she would change...compromise...but Samantha knew that she couldn't, not and still be true to herself.

She unclasped her knees and lay down again, silent tears dampening her pillow as she cried for the man she knew she could never share her life with and the babies they would never make together.

CHAPTER TEN

'SWEETHEART, isn't it exciting, the *Washington Post* is predicting that Liam is definitely going to win. Sam… what's wrong?' her mother asked anxiously as her comment failed to bring the reaction she had expected from her daughter.

'You're not still worrying about becoming the Governor's wife, are you?' she asked Samantha gently. 'Oh, but that's my fault. If I hadn't disliked it so much…' She paused and shook her head. 'But, Samantha, you are so much stronger than I am and even though you won't admit it, you *love* the kind of challenges you and Liam are going to be facing. People are already predicting that you're going to be the most progressive couple to ever hold state governorship, and your father is so very, very proud of you both.'

Samantha couldn't bring herself to look at her mother. Ever since her return with Liam some weeks ago it had been the same. Both her parents had been thrilled with their news and, despite the demands on her time with her father's impending retirement, her mother had still thrown herself into excited preparations for Samantha's wedding.

'We want to wait until after…after the inauguration,' Samantha had protested as she fought down the panicky feeling that was filling her but it seemed that the news of their engagement had started a roller coaster, a tidal wave of reaction, which once set in motion there was no way of stopping.

There had been rallies and meetings, interviews, TV chat shows and such, a whole host of calls upon her time that Samantha in the end had had to concede that her father was right when he had advised her that she was going to have to put her career temporarily on hold at least until after the vote.

One unexpected consequence of her engagement had been the fact that Cliff had started to fawn over her in a way that she found totally nauseating, but now she had far, far more important things on her mind to worry about than him.

The stress she was under was beginning to tell. She had lost weight and the sparkle had gone from her eyes. Now the sapphire on her left hand looked a much deeper blue than they did. She and Liam hardly ever managed to get any time together such was the build-up towards the vote and so they had simply not had a chance to discuss how and when they were going to break the news that they had decided, after all, that they did not love one another.

Samantha closed her eyes. And that was another lie she was going to have to learn to live with. Liam might not love her but *she* certainly loved him. Oh, how she loved him. Her eyes burned with anguished tears.

'Sam, sweetheart, what is it?' her mother begged anxiously as she hurried over to wrap her arms around her.

'It's nothing,' Samantha fibbed. 'I guess every-thing's become so pressured and…'

'…and Liam isn't here and you miss him. Honey, I *do* know,' her mother consoled her. 'But never mind, he'll be back this weekend and the two of you should be able to get some time on your own. Oh, and by the way, I thought we might fly into New York the weekend after and check out some wedding gowns.'

Wedding gowns. Samantha's heart gave a frantic bound. There was nothing she wanted to do more than walk down the aisle on her father's arm and to have Liam waiting there at the altar for her. Nothing… But that was just an impossible dream…a totally impossible dream.

When Liam rang her later that day, for once she was on her own and able to tell him quickly, 'Liam, we've got to talk.'

There was a small pause and she guessed he was probably not on his own by the guarded tone in his voice as he responded, 'Uh-huh…is something wrong?'

'Mom's talking about us going to New York the weekend after next to look at wedding gowns,' she told him, hoping he would be able to decode the message contained in what she was saying. 'She thinks we ought to be discussing which of the Crighton cousins we will be having as attendants and she wants me to go upstate to visit with Dad's family there to see what furniture we might want to get out of store. You know when Dad's folks passed away that Bobbie and I were left some antique furniture and that it's still in store.' She was starting to babble, Samantha recognised as she forced herself to take a deep calming breath.

There was a family business in New England, as well, that her father intended returning to.

Liam, although he never really discussed it, having sold his father's business, was a comfortably wealthy man, probably even more wealthy than her own parents, but money for its own sake had never interested Samantha.

One of the innovative measures Liam wanted to bring in if he was elected was a special form of scholarship for young people who otherwise would not have been able to afford to go to college and he had told Samantha that he intended to underwrite such scholarships himself from his own private means.

The political gap between them was closing with what for Samantha was a heart-wrenching speed. Now she could not even cling to her ideals as a reason to stop loving him.

'I'll be home at the weekend,' she heard Liam saying quietly in response to her call. 'We can talk then.'

The weekend. Wearily Samantha replaced the receiver. That was two whole days away yet. So, for two more whole days, forty-eight hours, she was still going to be Liam's wife-to-be. After that… After that she would need to go as far away from him as she could…to go somewhere where she could hide away and learn to live with her loss and her pain.

A forlorn look darkened Samantha's eyes as she studied the photograph in the article she had just been reading. It depicted her and Liam. They were seated together in the library of the Governor's house, Liam's arm resting tenderly around her shoulders whilst she was turning slightly towards him, her lips gently parted as though in anticipation of his kiss. It was a photograph of two lovers, two people who couldn't wait to be alone together, and it had been taken to accompany the article alongside it in which

Liam had been interviewed about his plans for the state should he be elected into office.

And they said the camera didn't lie. Since her telephone conversation with Liam the previous day Samantha had been mentally rehearsing just what she was going to say to him when he returned. Being Liam, he would be bound to demand to know why it was so urgently imperative that their pseudo engagement was brought to an immediate end and, of course, there was no way that she could tell him, so she would have to invent a reason and so far she had not managed to come up with one which she knew would convince him.

So why not tell him the truth? Quickly she got up and walked across her room and stood staring unseeingly down into the garden that her mother loved so much.

She had got up early this morning and left before breakfast, having told her mother the previous evening that she needed a little time on her own and promising that, yes, she would go and look over the furniture stored in the depository whilst she was here in her father's home town, the same New England town that her parents intended to come back to when his term of office had ended.

This house was old by New England standards, although in Crighton terms it would no doubt have been termed relatively new. She and Bobbie had grown up in this quiet traditional town and their family was a part of it. If she were to go into the town now people would stop her and ask her not just about her parents but about her sister and her sister's child, as well. They would ask after her brother Tom, currently at college and destined to take over the family business from her father when ultimately he stepped down from its overall control—in the time whilst her father had been State Governor he had had to appoint a deputy to take care of the day-to-day running of the business but he had still retained overall responsibility for it.

Tell Liam the truth! How simple it sounded but how totally impossible that would be. Even if she could bear to expose herself to the humiliation of actually telling him that she loved him…him a man who never could and never would return those feelings, how could she be sure that in telling him she wasn't somehow subconsciously trying to put emotional pressure on him to feel sorry for her, to take pity on her and to… To what? To marry her because she loved him? *No!* Immediately she shrank from the very thought. *No! No.* That was the last thing she wanted. If only she had a less volatile and more phlegmatic personality she might be able to contain her feelings a little better, to simply stoically wait out things until after the election, but the day-to-day effect of playing a false role was beginning to rasp so painfully on her nerves that she knew she couldn't trust herself to somehow betray the truth.

No, their engagement would have to be brought to an official end with a proper public announcement that they had both decided that they had made a mistake.

Out of the corner of her eye she saw a car turning into the drive to the house. Her heart started to hammer heavily as she recognised it.

It was Liam's.

Liam!

What was he doing *here?* There was still another twenty-four hours to go before he was due back.

Quickly she started to hurry downstairs, dragging open the heavy front door just as he reached it.

The house, although not presently lived in, was cleaned twice a week but it still had that sad lonely air to it that unlived-in homes possess, Samantha reflected as she closed the door behind Liam and demanded shakily, 'Liam, what are you doing here? You said you wouldn't be back until tomorrow.'

'I know but…you didn't sound too good when we spoke and when I rang this morning and your mother told me that you'd left early to come over here, I decided to cancel the rest of my meetings and drive over.'

'You cancelled your meetings because of *me.*' Samantha looked at him in surprise. Although Liam's ambition was more of the steely determined sort than the aggressive go-getting type, she was still surprised that he had been concerned enough to behave so impulsively.

'Your mother says you aren't eating…'

'I've got a lot on my mind,' Samantha told him defensively. 'I guess I just don't feel that hungry. Liam…I…' She stopped and then took a deep breath, turning away from him so that she wouldn't have to look at him whilst she told him, so that he couldn't look at her and see the truth in her eyes, because she knew that if he did she couldn't bear to see the corresponding pity in his.

'I can't go on with this… It's got to end. The longer we leave it the worse it's going to get. Mom's already making plans for our wedding and Dad…' She stopped and swallowed.

'They're going to hate me for us not getting married. I never realised...' She stopped again. 'We've got to tell them that we've changed our minds, Liam, and that it's over.'

He was silent for so long that in the end she had to turn round and look at him, but although she searched his face for some clue in his expression that would tell her what he was feeling and thinking she could see none.

'It would never have worked out anyway,' she told him, forcing herself to try to make a joke of it. 'Can you really see me as a Governor's wife?'

'Yes, as a matter of fact I can.'

Open-mouthed, Samantha stared at him, unable to conceal her reaction from him.

'But you've always said how impossible I would be and...'

'No. *You've* always said how impossible you would be,' Liam corrected her. 'And maybe twenty, even ten years ago you would have been right. The restrictions imposed on *you* to ensure *my* success *would* have been impossible for you to bear and such that no one would have had the right to want to impose them on you, but things have changed Samantha and are still changing.

'We're living in a new world, a world that's coming to not just see but to welcome and embrace all manner of different kinds of thinking and all manner of different views. We're a strong, braver people now, and we no longer feel threatened by new ideas or innovative ways of dealing with problems. The kind of Governor I intend to be would never have been tolerated a decade ago. The men and women we'll be representing are people like ourselves, the men know that their roles have to be interchangeable with those of their partners and, men and women alike, they recognise that the old style of a woman ''standing by her man'' has gone, that now both partners in a relationship have the right to expect support from the other, that *both* partners are equal and mutually supportive of one another, that a woman has as much right to expect her man to stand by her as he does her.

'We're on the threshold of a new era, Sam, and I predict that it's one that will allow people to coexist in harmony as individuals and that the old straitjackets which required people to conform to certain rigid patterns will be swept aside as people overcome their fears and prejudices to accept one another as they are, to respect them as they are...

'No, you may not have made a good *traditional* Governor's wife, the kind that was always there two steps behind her husband and faded into the wallpaper, but that isn't the kind of wife *I've* ever wanted. I want a wife who will be my partner in every sense of the word and she'll be standing there right alongside me and sometimes I guess, right in front of me,' Liam concluded, almost humorously.

For a moment Samantha was too moved to speak. Everything he had said had touched her so emotionally that she knew she was frighteningly close to breaking down and telling him exactly how she felt about him. How could she *not* love him now, after what he had just said.

'Do the voters know about all this?' she managed to joke shakily.

'The voters have no role to play in my private relationship with you, Sam. Besides,' he added quietly, 'it may have been true that I did once think of you as a woman too individual by far to conform to being a politician's wife, but I was wrong. It wasn't you who needed to change your thinking but me who needed to change mine, and I have done, Sam. I don't just love you, I admire and respect you, as well. There's nothing about you I could ever want to change—not one single thing—apart, of course, from changing your name to mine!' Liam told her in a slow smoky voice that made her stomach tie itself in knots and her heart turn somersaults inside her chest.

Oh, why, why was he doing this to her…? Why couldn't he just agree with what she had said and walk away from her?

'Uh…but we don't *have* a private relationship,' she told him huskily. 'It's just pretend, Liam…it's…'

'Is it?' he challenged her, and then the next minute she was in his arms and he was holding her, kissing her gently at first and then when he felt the soft tremulous response of her lips and the betraying shudder of pleasure that racked through her with a fierce hungry passion that had all Samantha's objections dying unspoken. All she could do, all she *wanted* to do was to simply cling to him; respond to him, *give* him all the love in her that was bursting to be expressed.

'If the voters can't see what an asset you'd be, what a *gift* you are, then that's their loss,' she could hear Liam saying thickly to her as he cupped her face and looked down into her eyes with such a blaze of love in his that Samantha felt as though its heat was going to melt her right through to her toes.

'And their loss isn't going to be mine. Rather than lose you I'd step down from the race.'

Samantha's eyes widened. She could see in his

eyes, hear in his voice, that he meant exactly what he was saying.

'You'd do *that*…for *me*…' she whispered.

'For you *and* for us,' Liam told her softly. 'If that's the only way I can convince you that you mean more to me than anything or anyone else…'

'Oh, Liam…' Tenderly Samantha touched his face with her fingertips. 'I guess that must mean that you love me,' she told him dreamily, her tears falling on his skin.

'Just why the hell else would I come racing across the Atlantic like a complete fool,' Liam challenged her gruffly. 'Have you *any* idea what it did to me to hear you telling me that you were going to go get yourself an English husband…an English *father* for your kids…'

'But I didn't *know*. You *never* said.'

'*You* never *wanted* me to say,' Liam retorted. 'You treated me like…like I might have been your brother.'

'That was because…well, when you first came to work for Dad you made it plain that you were strictly off limits and…'

'You were still a kid…a baby…' Liam interrupted her. 'And then, later, when you grew up, you just didn't seem to want to know.'

'I didn't know,' Samantha admitted, 'not until…' She stopped and blushed a little and then laughed. 'I guess I had to go to bed with you to find out just exactly what I *do* feel for you.'

'Uh-huh… So it *wasn't* just to get me to help you make a baby then,' he reminded her.

Samantha shook her head.

'I guess I had to tell myself it was because I was so shocked by what I had done, but deep down inside

I think I must always have known...have felt... That Sunday at the Grosvenor when all the family were there it felt so good, so *right*—us being together. I missed you so that night.'

'Nowhere near as much as I missed you,' Liam groaned as he took hold of her.

As he started to kiss her she snuggled closer to him, eagerly responding to his rising passion, but then suddenly she pulled away from him and demanded softly, 'Liam, is there really nothing you wouldn't do for me...?'

'Nothing,' he responded. 'Why, what is it you want...?'

'Well, this time...' She stopped and flushed prettily. 'This time when we make love, could I have...could we... I want your baby, Liam,' she told him.

'Liam!' she protested as he started to kiss her with devastating intensity, running his hands possessively the length of her torso, cupping her breasts and then pulling her so tightly into his own body that she could feel the powerful throb of his arousal.

'What*ever* you want from me you can have, *whenever* you want it,' he told her rawly. 'But when it comes to making babies...' He cupped the back of her head and massaged the flesh, looking deep into her eyes.

'I think we both know that that's something we want to happen *after* we're married and not because of what anyone *else* might think but because we want *our* kids to grow up knowing that we loved and respected one another to want to give them that security.'

'Oh, Liam…' Samantha sighed blissfully as she melted into his arms. 'Oh, Liam…'

The house was fully furnished with beds in every room, but Samantha knew that, right now, it wouldn't have mattered *where* they were, so compellingly and urgent was their need and their hunger for one another. Just the touch of Liam's breath on her bare skin was enough to send her body into tiny shivers of almost orgasmic pleasure and as for *his* reaction when she touched and kissed him.

'So, you want to hold out until we're married,' she teased him at one point, and in the end they both admitted it was a very near-run thing.

Their wedding took place three weeks before her father's official retirement and six before Liam's inauguration as the state's new Governor and, of course, during her father's speech there were several jokes about him losing a daughter but gaining a Governor's wife in the family.

Later, when she stood next to her mother, her sister and her brother as their father received the thanks of the state officials for what he had done for the state and then, later still when she stood beside Liam whilst her father spoke of his pride in knowing just what Liam would achieve, she was filled with such pride for the man she had married that she felt that her heart would burst with it. But her most special memory of all as she listened to Liam giving his acceptance speech and discreetly patted the still flat smoothness of her stomach and whispering to their growing child to listen to its daddy, she was thinking not of the future but of the very special and private occasion when the baby growing inside her was conceived.

'You'll love it,' Liam had insisted when she had made a face and exclaimed in horror when he told her that their brief honeymoon was not to be in some idyllic tropical paradise, but a back-packing trip into the mountains.

But the few days they had spent there had proved to be far more memorable than any luxury surroundings could ever have been, especially the first night they had made camp in the small secret glade Liam had taken her to right beside a spring-fed small mountain pool. They had swum there together naked, the water icy cold against the heat of their skin, and then they had made love beneath the stars with their benign silvery glow the only witness to Samantha's soft cries of pleasure as their bodies merged together and created the new life she was now carrying.

The whole family had come over for the wedding, every single one of them, including Bobbie proudly bearing her newborn son, and Samantha had noticed again how withdrawn and quiet Katie had been.

'Jenny is very concerned about her,' Ruth had told them. 'She works so hard, too hard, Jenny thinks. I've suggested that she ought to try to persuade Katie to move back to Haslewich. They could do with her help in the family-run practice.'

Samantha, who had seen the hopeless, helpless look in Katie's eyes whenever they rested on her twin and her husband, wasn't so sure that it was just hard work that was affecting Katie but she kept her thoughts to herself. The family suspected that Louise might be pregnant, but nothing had been said yet. Samantha couldn't imagine anything worse than to love one's twin's man. She couldn't imagine how she would have coped if, for instance, Bobbie and Liam had fallen in love. Just to have the thought form inside her head was enough to make her go dizzy at the thought of the pain such a situation would bring.

James, too, had attended their wedding looking slightly sheepish and keeping his distance from her. Not that he had any need to do so, she had no right to demand an explanation from him for that kiss she had seen him and Rosemary exchanging. But Rosemary's fiancé certainly did. Now Samantha looked across the room to where Liam was working at his desk and then got up and walked over to him, taking up a teasing provocative pose as she perched beside him, swinging the long length of her legs.

'Well now, Mr. Governor, sir,' she breathed sexily, 'they say that power is a very sexy aphrodisiac and that powerful men are very, very sexy in bed.' As she spoke she was reaching across and starting to unfasten his shirt. 'Would you say that that was true…'

Liam leaned back in his chair and closed his eyes and then teased her, 'Well, I guess there's only one way you're going to know,' before getting up and taking hold of her hand and asking her, 'Have I told you today how much I love you, Samantha Connolly?'

'Mmm…not since breakfast,' Samantha responded.

'Mmm… Well I do…and I always will.'

'*Always*…even when I'm hugely pregnant,' Samantha asked him.

'Especially then,' Liam told her softly. 'Oh, yes, most especially then.'

It was perfect. Life was perfect. Their love was perfect. Liam was perfect. The perfect man, the perfect husband…the perfect father…and she loved him more than she would ever, ever be able to find all the words to say.

*   *   *   *   *

A Perfect Night

CHAPTER ONE

As Seb drove past the sign that read, Haslewich—
Please Drive Carefully, he was aware of a dispiriting
grey cloud of self-criticism and disappointment dulling what, if life mirrored fiction, by rights should be
his triumphal return to the place of his birth.

He was thirty-eight years old, virtually at the top
of his career ladder having just been headhunted by
the international drug company Aarlston-Becker to
head their research team. No small feat surely for man
who, as a boy, had been sneeringly dismissed by one
of his teachers as 'just another hopeless by-product of
the Cooke clan.'

He had money in the bank accumulated by hard
work and shrewd investment, a family who even if he
hadn't seen much of them in recent years were by all
accounts more than willing to do the modern equiv-
alent of roasting a fatted calf to welcome him home,
and he was about to take a kind of professional post
that many among his colleagues would have given
their eye-teeth for; all of which surely must be pretty
heavyweight pluses on anyone's balance sheet of life.

But then he *needed* some heavyweight assets to balance out the equally, to him at least, heavyweight negative aspects of his life.

'What negative aspects?' his second or was it third
cousin Guy Cooke had asked him drily when they had
been discussing the subject of his impending return.

'How about an ill-judged early marriage followed predictably, I suppose, by a divorce.'

Guy's eyebrows had lifted as he shrugged dismissively, 'Divorce isn't exactly a social sin any longer Seb, and from what you've told us your ex-wife has remarried very happily and the two of you are on relatively comfortable terms.'

'Oh yes, from Sandra's and my own point of view the divorce was the best thing we could have done other than not to have married in the first place.

'No, it's not the fact that we married far too young and for all the wrong reasons that I feel bad. It's…' He had paused, grimacing before continuing, 'Sandy always used to complain that I was a selfish bastard not really fit to be either a husband or a father, too wrapped up in my career and my own professional goals. I thought at the time that she was being ridiculous. After all, I was working to provide a decent standard of living for her, or so I used to tell her and myself, but of course that was just the excuse I used to conceal the fact that she was right that I *was* being selfish, and that the rush I got from knowing I was right in there at the cutting edge of discovering new drugs that were going to provide the kind of breakthrough that would change the world was far more important to me, far more compelling and addictive than any pleasure I got from being with her.'

Guy and Chrissie, his wife, had exchanged ruefully happily married looks while Chrissie had lifted their son Anthony up off the floor to give him a hug, and although they had both made the right kind of protestingly reassuring noises Seb hadn't been deceived. Of course privately they must both have thought that he had been selfish. How could they think otherwise?

Seb had seen the loving commitment Guy was making to his own family, had witnessed at first hand during his stay with them when he had attended his initial interview the 'hands on' fathering that Guy was giving his son.

'But at least you and Charlotte have formed a proper father and daughter bond now,' Chrissie had reminded him gently.

'Yes, more thanks to Charlotte's maturity than any good parenting on my part,' Seb had returned, adding, 'After all she could very easily have refused to see me when I wrote and asked her if she would consider allowing me back into her life. George, Sandra's second husband has been far more of a proper father to her than I have.'

'Maybe so from a practical point of view,' Guy had agreed, 'But biologically *you* are her father and you only have to see the two of you together to see that.'

'Oh yes, she's got my genes when it comes to her physical looks,' he agreed.

'And she's got your brains by all accounts too,' Chrissie had laughed.

'Well, Sandra and I met originally at university so I suppose that aspect of her nature is down to both of us, but I admit that I was surprised when she told me that she intends to follow much the same career path as I've chosen.'

'And since she's going to be studying for her A levels at a private sixth-form college near Manchester, you're bound to be able to see a lot more of her.'

'I hope so,' Seb had agreed. 'Although at sixteen she's almost an adult now with her own life and her own friends. Sandra did say though that she was relieved to know that I would be on hand for her at the weekends especially now that Sandra and George are likely to be based abroad for the foreseeable future.'

'Well we certainly loved meeting Charlotte,' Chrissie had told him warmly. 'Although I suspect she felt a little bit overwhelmed by the massed ranks and fervent curiosity of the Cooke clan in force.'

The Cooke clan. How he had hated and chafed under the burdensome weight of his family's reputation when he had been growing up, Seb reflected now. Of course he hadn't known then that he wasn't on his own and that Guy, too, had suffered his own personal war between his inner needs and the town's expectations. But then Guy had met Chrissie and in helping her to make peace with her family history Guy had come to terms with his own unhappy childhood memories.

Seb knew that without the incentive of having Charlotte at college in nearby Manchester there was no way *he* would have come back to his birthplace in the small historical Cheshire town where, or so the story went, his family line had come into being following the seduction of a local girl by a member of a notorious band of Romany travellers who visited the town every year.

The children—the *clan*—that union had given birth to down through the centuries, whether rightly or wrongly, had garnered a notorious reputation in the town for not always walking on the right side of the law, and of course predictably it had often been a case of 'give a dog a bad name...' Certainly it seemed that historically, their family had been a convenient peg for the townspeople to hang all their local crimes of theft and unlawfulness on.

Now, of course, those days were gone and his relatives so far as Seb knew were, in the main, sturdy and worthy citizens, and so intermarried and interwoven with the families and fabric of the area that they could not in all fairness any longer be considered to be a separate and dangerously untrustworthy clan of outsiders.

Even so the lusty lifestyle of the original ancestors had left its mark on the collective conscience of the other families in the town. Cooke men had a reputation for fathering sturdy sons whose dark eyes tended to hold the kind of gleam that mothers and young impressionable girls quite rightly found dangerous.

Seb had known from an early age that he wanted to escape from the restrictions of living in a smalltown community where everyone knew everyone else. He had wanted to break through the glass ceiling imposed on him by the expectations and reservations of those around him simply because of the surname he carried. It had been his interest, cultivated and encouraged by his grandfather and a fascination with the problems that manifested themselves in the plants his grandfather grew because of their genetic make up which had initially led to his choice of career.

University might have freed him from the restrictions imposed on him by his small-town upbringing but in order to get there he had had to focus on the more self-absorbed, self-interested side of his personality and that ultimately had created a blinkered concentration on his career to the detriment of his personal relationships.

It had taken a comment he had overheard from a female colleague to make him realise the error of his ways. She had been talking with another co-worker unaware that he was in an adjacent room and could hear them.

'He actually hasn't seen his daughter in over ten years. Can you believe that?'

'It happens,' the other woman had pointed out. 'Divorced men *do* lose touch with their children.'

'Yes, I know, but he just doesn't seem to care. Doesn't he have any human feelings?'

That night at home alone in his empty executive apartment Seb had replayed the overheard conversation in his head and he had asked himself the same question.

The answer had shocked him.

Yes, he did care, more than he had known, and he had cared even more after that first fateful reunion with Charlotte when he had recognised not just in her face, her physical features, but in her personality as well, such a strong resemblance to him that he had felt as though someone, something, some emotion, was cracking his heart in a vise.

It had not been an easy task building bridges that would allow them, allow her, to lower the guard she had quite naturally put up against him. She'd been outwardly pleasant and friendly, but he had nevertheless known that inwardly she was extremely wary of him. And who could blame her? But that had been three years ago, and now he was very much a part of her life. But he was still aware that nothing, no amount of remorse, or regret could totally eradicate the past.

Sandra, his ex-wife, had gone on to have two more children, both boys, with her second husband George and Charlotte was very much a part of that happy close-knit family, but she *was* also his daughter and, like him, a Cooke.

'All these relatives,' she had marvelled laughingly when she had visited the town with him. 'I can't believe it. We seem to be related to half the population.'

'At least,' Seb had agreed drily, but unlike him Charlotte seemed to delight in her heritage.

'Things have changed,' Guy had told him. 'There's been a large influx of new people into the town, opening it up, broadening both its boundaries and its outlook.

'The women of the Cooke family have always had a special strong grittiness and that's really showing itself now. There are Cooke women on the town council, running their own businesses, teaching their children that their inheritance is one to be proud of. Yes, of course, a proportion of the babies at Ruth Crighton's mother and baby home *are* Cookes but on their *fathers'* side and not their mothers'. Cooke girls are hard-working and determined, university and self-fulfilment is *their* goal…'

Seb knew all about the Crightons. Who living in Haslewich *didn't*? Like the Cooke's, the Crighton name was synonymous with the town even though they were relative newcomers to it having only arrived there at the turn of the century.

Chrissie was in part a Crighton although that fact hadn't been realised even by Chrissie's own parents until she'd become involved with Guy.

Jon Crighton was the senior partner in the family's law firm. Olivia, his niece, the daughter of his twin brother David, was also a partner. David himself was someone who was surrounded by mystery, having left the town, some said under highly dubious circumstances. Jon and David's father lived in a large Elizabethan house outside the town along with Max Crighton, Jon and Jenny's eldest son, and his wife and children.

Max was the apple of his grandfather's eye and, to Ben Crighton's pride, was no mere solicitor but a barrister, working from chambers in Chester alongside Luke and James Crighton, sons of Ben's cousin Henry.

The Crighton family had originated from Chester, but a family quarrel had led Josiah Crighton, Ben's father, to move away from Chester and set up his own legal practice in Haslewich, and until relatively recently a certain degree of rivalry had existed between the two branches of the family.

Jenny Crighton, Jon's wife had once owned and run an antiques business in Haslewich in which Seb's cousin Guy had been a partner, but the pressure of her own family commitments had led to her giving up her share in the business, which Guy had kept on as a sideline.

Guy had, in fact, recommended Jon Crighton to Seb as someone to deal with the legal conveyancing side of his house purchase when he moved back into the area.

As yet Seb hadn't found a property he wanted to buy and so instead he was renting somewhere.

'Local property prices are high,' Guy had warned him, 'Thanks to Aarlston-Becker. Not that we can complain, they've brought prosperity to the area even though there are those who claim that their presence threatens the town.'

Seb changed gear as the traffic slowed to a crawl as he entered the town proper. He had thought that in rebuilding his relationship with Charlotte he had laid to rest the guilt he had felt at his shortcomings as a father, but returning to Haslewich had brought back some painful memories.

'What you need Dad, is to fall in love,' Charlotte had told him several months earlier, and even though she had laughed Seb had seen in her eyes that she had been semi-serious.

'Falling in love is for people of your age,' he had told her drily.

'Why have you never married again?' she had asked him quietly.

'Do you really need to ask?' Seb had returned sardonically. 'After all, you've had first-hand experience of the mess I made of it the first time. No Lottie,' he had shaken his head, 'I'm too selfish, too set in my ways. Falling in love isn't for me.'

'No you're not, you *just think* you are,' Charlotte had told him, adding with surprising maturity, 'You're just punishing yourself, Dad, because you feel guilty about me. Well, you needn't. I wasn't even two when you and Mum split up, and she and George were together by the time I was three. At least I never experienced the trauma of being torn between you and Mum, and she told me that that was thanks to you agreeing to let George bring me up.'

'So what are you saying…that I did you a favour by turning my back on my responsibility towards you,' Seb had asked her grimly. 'That my selfishness was almost praiseworthy…'

'No, of course not, but at least you did come to feel ultimately that as father and daughter we *should* be part of one another's lives. At least I do know that you love me,' she had added in a soft whisper.

Love her. Yes he did—now—but if he was honest with himself there had been years of her life when he had scarcely allowed himself to remember that she existed and he would carry the burden of that guilt for the rest of his life. Marry again? Fall in love? He cursed abruptly as just in front of him a young woman started across the road without looking causing him to stamp his foot down hard on the brakes. As his car screeched to a halt in front of her she froze in fear, her face turned towards him.

Seb had a momentary impression of her shocked expression, wide eyes set in a piquantly-shaped delicately feminine face, her hair tousled by the light breeze. Small and slender she was wearing a soft, brown linen wraparound skirt, the pale colour of the cream silk top tucked into it complementing both the warmth of the skirt and the even more alluring light tan of her bare arms—and legs. But as his brain mentally digested these peripheral visual facts, the feeling, the emotion uppermost in Seb's mind was one of anxiety fuelled by anger.

What on earth had possessed her to step right out in front of him like that? Didn't she realise how close she had come to causing an accident. The narrow town street was busy with shoppers and if his brakes had failed to work so swiftly or if he had skidded…or not been able to stop… And yet as the shock faded from her eyes, it wasn't guilt or gratitude he could see replacing it, but rather a sharply condemnatory anger, as though he were the one to blame for what was quite patently her foolishness. Indeed, for a second it almost seemed as though she was about to walk right up to his car instead of finishing her journey across the busy street, but then the car driver behind him, growing impatient with the delay, tooted his horn and she hesitated and then turned aside, shooting him a searing look before marching stiffly away from him.

Just as equally infuriated by her behaviour as she seemed to have been by his, Seb shot her departing back a fulminating look of male contempt for her female foolishness before slipping the car back into gear and continuing with his journey.

As Katie walked through Haslewich's busy main thoroughfare she was aware of a heavy weight of unhappiness dulling what, by rights, should have been a joyous and hopefully positive return to the bosom of her family.

She was twenty-four years of age, in excellent health, a fully qualified solicitor who had been not just asked, but beseeched by her father and her cousin to join them in the family partnership in their home town. Indeed she had even had the satisfaction of having her elder brother no less, add his persuasive arguments to those of the other members of the family.

'Dad needs you Katie,' Max had told her. 'They're absolutely inundated with work, and we all know how grandfather would react if Dad were to suggest taking on a non-Crighton partner, just as we all know that no solicitor worth his or her salt would join the partnership without the expectation of being offered their own partnership. For you to come home and join Dad and Olivia would be the ideal solution to the problem. You're young in terms of legal experience at the moment, but a partnership in the not too distant future is assured.'

'Yes, I daresay it is,' Katie had agreed quietly. 'But you seem to forget Max that I already have a job.'

'I know you do,' Max had agreed, 'but I'm not completely blind Katie, something's gone wrong in your life. Look, I'm not going to pry or ask questions, God knows I don't have the right to act the big brother with you now, after all I was hardly a caring one to you when you and Louise were growing up. What I will say to you, though, is that some people need to seek solitude, to lick their wounds and heal themselves, and others need the care and comfort of their close family, and we both know which camp you fall into.'

It was true, Louise, Katie's twin sister was more the type to seek the solitude Max had just described than her, but then Louise was hardly likely to need to do so. Louise after all was blissfully in love with and loved by Gareth.

Louise and Gareth.

Katie had closed her eyes thankful that no one had guessed her shameful poisonous secret. It made no difference that she had loved Gareth quietly and sedately and from a distance a long time before Louise had realised the exact nature of her feelings for him. And the reason it made no difference was not just because Louise was her other half, her dearly beloved if sometimes somewhat headstrong and exasperating twin, but because Gareth himself did not love her... Gareth loved Louise.

Stoically Katie had accepted the agonising searing burn of her own pain, claiming pressure of work for her increasingly infrequent visits home and her even more infrequent get-togethers with her twin, but then as though fate had not done enough she discovered that it had another blow in store for her.

Her boss, for whom she had worked ever since she

had joined the legal department of the charity to do her articles after leaving university, had resigned, and the man who had taken his place…

Katie closed her eyes in midstep. Jeremy Stafford had at first seemed so charming, so very much on her own wavelength that even now she couldn't properly come to terms with what had happened.

When he had started asking her to work late, she had done so willingly, enjoying not just the rapport between them but the knowledge that the work they were doing was ultimately benefiting people who were so very desperately in need of help.

The first time Jeremy had suggested dinner as a "reward" to them both for their hard work, she had felt nothing but pleasure, no sense of wariness or suspicion had clouded her happy acceptance of his suggestion. How naive she had been, but then from the way that Jeremy had always talked about his wife and small children she had assumed that he was so happily married that any kind of betrayal of his wife and their marriage vows—well, it had simply never crossed her mind that it might have crossed his… But she had been wrong…not only had it crossed his, it had lingered there and quite unequivocally taken up a very lustful and leering residence as she had so unpleasantly discovered.

At first when he had started to compliment her on her face and then her figure she had simply assumed that he was being pleasant, but then had come the night when he had put his arm around her when they were leaving the restaurant and then attempted to kiss her.

She had fobbed him off immediately, but to her consternation instead of apologising as she had expected him to do he had turned on her claiming that she had led him on; that she was a tease and worse, oh yes, much much worse. Of course after that there had been no more intimate dinners and no evenings working late, instead there had been hostility and even victimisation: accusations about missing reports which she knew she had filed, mistakes which she knew she had not made, errors which she knew were simply not hers.

Not that she had any intention of telling Max any of that. The change her elder brother had undergone following the attack he had suffered on a Jamaican beach while he was in that country trying to trace their father's missing twin brother, David Crighton, had not merely converted him into a passionately devoted husband and father, it had also turned him into a surprisingly caring and concerned brother and son. If Max guessed for one moment what was going on, Katie knew that he would lose no time in seeking out Jeremy Stafford and demanding retribution for his behaviour.

Had they been children still involved in playground jealousies and quarrels that might just have been acceptable, but they were adults. She was supposed to be in charge of her own life. As a modern independent woman she was expected to be able to deal with her own problems. The sadness was, she loved her work, loved knowing that what she was doing no matter how small, was a benefit to other people.

The Crighton women carried a strong gene of responsibility and duty towards their fellow men and women. In her great-aunt, Ruth Crighton, it had manifested itself in the establishment of an enclave of charitably run accommodation units for single parents and their children. In her mother, Jenny, it showed in the way she gave so much of her time and energy to others. Katie's sister had become involved in a programme to help young drug addicts in Brussels where she and Gareth lived and worked.

Katie froze as the sudden sharp screech of a car's brakes brought her back to reality.

Without realising what she was doing she had started across the road without looking properly, but that in no way excused the manic dangerousness of the speed at which the driver of the car, now stopped in front of her, had to have been driving to have been forced to halt with such a screech. Katie knew nothing about cars and the fact that the very powerful engine of the Mercedes the man was driving was responsible for the intensity of his braking rather than his speed was therefore completely lost on her. Instead what she was aware of was the look of totally unwarranted fury in his eyes as he glowered ferociously out of the car at her.

As her own shock held her motionless she was distantly aware of the fact that he was outrageously good-looking with thick, virtually jet-black, well-groomed hair, chillingly icy grey eyes and a mouth that even when clamped grimly closed still betrayed the fact that he had a disturbingly full and sexy bottom lip.

But none of that compensated for the fact that he had nearly run her over. Determinedly Katie took a step towards the car and then stopped as the driver behind him hooted impatiently. Much as she longed to give Mr Sexy Mouth a piece of her mind, she really didn't have time. She was due at the office ten minutes ago, hardly a good start to her first official working day with her father and Olivia.

It had been a wrench leaving her job, despite the problem she had suffered with Jeremy and she still wasn't sure she had made the right decision in agreeing to join the family practice. Both her father and Olivia had held out the inducement, as Max had already indicated, that in time she could expect to become a full partner, even if right now she was simply being retained by them as a salaried employee. Money had never motivated Katie, but then to be fair she knew that it didn't motivate either her father or Olivia either.

She was to start by taking over the conveyancing side of the business, the legal work attached to the buying and selling of properties. She had pulled a small face when her father had told her this.

'Well at least I should have some practice by the time it comes to my buying my own home,' she had told him ruefully.

Although her parents had offered her back her childhood room permanently, after several years of living independently at the University and then in London, she had felt that it would be more sensible to find her own separate accommodation. In London she had rented and while she waited for the right property to buy to present itself to her at home, she had, just temporarily she had told them, moved back in with her parents.

It had felt distinctly odd to be back in her old room—without her twin.

Louise had been more excited about Katie's decision to return to Haslewich than she had herself; trying to cajole her into a flying visit to Brussels to spend the week with them before Katie took up her new duties.

'Why don't you go?' her father had asked her when he had learned via Jenny of her decision to turn down Louise's invitation.

There wasn't any logical explanation she could give and she had been grateful to her younger brother Joss and her cousin Jack for creating a small diversion as they both pleaded with Jon to be allowed to take up Louise's offer in her stead.

Since it was Joss's all important GCSE year Katie had well been able to understand her father's refusal to agree until after his exams were over and loyally Jack, who was two years older than his cousin, had announced that he didn't want to go until they could both go together.

The pair of them were almost as close as the pairs of twins the Crighton family produced with such regularity, Jack having made his home with Katie's parents after the break-up of his own parents' marriage and the disappearance of his father David.

Ten minutes later, as Katie walked into her father's office after a brief knock on the door, she apologised.

'Sorry I'm late… I'd forgotten how busy the town is and I couldn't find a close by parking spot…'

'Mmm…if you think *this* morning is busy just wait until market day,' her father warned her good-humouredly.

'Olivia won't be here until ten,' he added. 'During term time she does the morning school and nursery run. Caspar picks the children up in the afternoon.'

Caspar, Olivia's American husband, held a Chair at a nearby university where he lectured in corporate law and it had been while she was on a course that Olivia had met and fallen in love with him.

'It can't be easy for her, working full-time with two young children,' Katie commented.

'No, it isn't,' her father agreed, adding briskly, 'We've cleared out a room for you to use and I've organised some preliminary file reading for you. We'll start you off on some straightforward conveyancing…'

'That's fine,' Katie responded absently.

'Is something wrong?' he asked, sensing her preoccupation.

'Not really…not unless you count nearly being run down by some speed-crazed driver,' Katie told him, briefly explaining what had happened.

'Mmm…it has been mooted that the town be made a no traffic area, but…'

'But…' Katie raised her eyebrows. The town had been there before the Romans, its surrounding salt making it a highly prized asset. The Normans had built a castle which the Roundheads virtually destroyed during the Civil War, and the town's streets dated in the main from the Middle Ages and were consequently narrow and tortuous and certainly not designed for the volume of modern-day traffic that used them.

'Well in order to make that a viable proposition, a new ring road would have to be built, and you can just imagine the cost of it…'

'Mmm…but if it keeps drivers like Mr Sexy Mouth off the road…'

'Like who?' her father questioned.

Katie flushed a little. Now what on earth had

prompted her to use that particular description of him out loud?

'Er… Nothing,' she denied hastily, quickly turning her attention to the files her father was showing her.

CHAPTER TWO

'JENNY Crighton is giving an informal supper party in a few weeks' time,' Guy gave his cousin the date, 'and she's invited you to go along with us, Seb. You'll enjoy it,' he encouraged when he saw the way Seb was frowning.

He had called round to see him expressly to deliver Jenny's invitation as well as to see how his cousin had settled in at Aarlston-Becker.

'Shall I?' Seb challenged him.

'Which reminds me,' Guy added before Seb could continue, 'Chrissie said to tell you that you're more than welcome to come round and dine with us any time you wish.'

'Thanks, I really do appreciate the offer, but right now I'm so involved at work...' Seb stopped and shook his head. Despite his misgivings about returning to the town of his birth, Seb had to admit that the sheer scope of the work he was involved with at Aarlston was proving enormously challenging and satisfying. The company was right at the forefront of research into and the creation of a new generation of drugs.

'I had planned to drive over to Manchester that weekend to see Charlotte, but it seems she's organised to go away with a group of friends, which means...'

'Which means that you'll be free to accept Jenny's invitation,' Guy told him firmly. 'You'll enjoy it. Saul is bound to be there. Have you met him yet? He's

head of a section of the Aarlston legal department
and…'

'Yes… I was introduced to him the other day. Nice
chap…'

'Have you found a house that appeals to you yet?'
Guy asked him.

'Not so far. Ideally I'd like somewhere large
enough for Charlotte to have her own space when she
comes to stay, which means somewhere with two bedrooms and two bathrooms, but I don't really want
something quite as large as a three- or four-bedroom
house, from a practical point of view if nothing else.'

'Mmm…well there's a large Edwardian house on
the outskirts of town which was recently converted
into a series of luxury apartments, although I think
most of them have already been sold. From the sound
of it one of them would suit you ideally.'

'Mmm…who are the agents? It's certainly worth
looking into,' Seb agreed.

The small terraced house he was currently renting
was only two streets away from the one he had lived
in as a child and Seb was finding staying in it faintly
claustrophobic. His mother had moved away to live
with her widowed sister following the death of Seb's
father and Seb had no immediate family left in the
town, but it seemed that everywhere he turned he was
confronted with the Cooke name and the Cooke features, battalion upon battalion of assorted aunts, un-
cles and cousins.

And as for the Jenny Crighton supper party, that
was something he would have preferred to have got
out of attending but he suspected that there was no
way that Guy was going to allow him to do so.

There was a certain something in Guy's voice when

he mentioned Jenny Crighton's name that made Seb wonder if those rumours about Guy's feelings for Jenny before Chrissie had come into his life had been just mere rumour. Whatever the case though there was no doubt about the fact that he loved Chrissie now.

'Mmm…that looks interesting,' Olivia commented as she walked past Katie's desk and saw the estate agent's details lying there.

'Who is the prospective purchaser?' she asked curiously as she studied photographs of the elegantly shaped Edwardian rooms and the sweeping views of the grounds that surrounded the newly converted apartments.

'Me, hopefully,' Katie told her, adding ruefully, 'although the price they are asking is rather high.'

'Can't you bargain them down?' Olivia suggested practically.

Katie shook her head. 'I doubt it, there are only two apartments left.'

'Mmm…well I can see why they've sold so well, two double bedrooms, each with its own bathroom and dressing-room, a large sitting-room, dining-room and good-sized kitchen, and those views…'

'Yes, and because this one is on the top floor it's got its own balcony,' Katie told her.

'I went to view it with Dad last night and I must say that I was really impressed even if it's still an awful lot of money, but with Mum and Dad so generously offering to help me out I can just about afford it.'

'Well, you certainly won't lose out by buying it,' Olivia told her, 'not with Aarlston-Becker expanding at the rate it is and the demand for housing expanding along with them.'

'True… I see we're getting an increasing number of farming clients applying for change of use in planning permission for some of their agricultural land.'

'Yes, and there's been a lot of controversy about it with a huge continuing debate in the local press. Those against any kind of new building on existing farmland are claiming that there are plenty of infill sites which should be used up first, while those who are in favour of granting planning permission insist the infill sites simply aren't adequate to cope with the growing demand for housing, stating that the town's prosperity is too closely linked with Aarlston to risk the threat of the company moving elsewhere because their employees can't find homes.'

'I should imagine that argument is something of a double-edged sword,' Katie murmured thoughtfully.

'Very much so,' Olivia agreed. 'The old die-hards are bitterly opposed to the Aarlston presence on the outskirts of the town claiming that it threatens its identity as a traditional market town in the centre of an agricultural area.'

'It's going to be a long-running battle, I suspect.'

After Olivia had left, Katie picked up the telephone receiver and punched in the number of the estate agents. There was no point in trying to persuade them to get the developers to drop the price of the apartment, she would just have to bite the bullet and offer the price they were asking. The apartment was, after all, perfect for her in every way, and if Olivia and her father were to be believed it would ultimately appreciate in value and prove to be a good financial investment.

While she was on the phone to the agents she decided that she would also arrange to look over the apartment again so that she could take proper measurements. Her mother had offered her some pieces of furniture she herself no longer needed including some very pretty antiques, but she would need to buy new carpets and curtains if the purchase went ahead.

Seb frowned as he studied the details of the apartment he had looked over the previous evening. On the top floor of the original Edwardian house it was one of a pair and ideally suited to his requirements. Guy had been right about that, it was exactly what he wanted even if the price was a little on the high side—not that that was a prime consideration for him—it was easily within his price range.

He had phoned Charlotte to tell her about it and she was going to travel to Haslewich from Manchester today after her classes had finished in order that she could see it. He had given her directions so that she could get a cab there and find it, and had arranged a time to meet. Afterwards he had promised to take her out for dinner.

One of the reasons Sandra had been so comfortable about accepting George's overseas posting had been because they had known that the live-in, sixth form private college where Charlotte was studying, which specialised in her chosen subjects—and where she had begged her parents to be allowed to go—placed a huge priority on its students' welfare and safety. It had been agreed that she could go, but only after a long, reassuring discussion with the school's principal about the precautions they took to supervise the students and ensure their safety. Charlotte would, also, have the benefit of members of her father's close-knit family on hand to turn to should she ever need to do so.

That of course had been before Seb himself had been headhunted by Aarlston-Becker and everything seemed to fall into place for him to be near his daughter.

Reaching for the telephone he punched in the numbers of the selling agents to confirm the appointment he had made to re-view the property this evening with Charlotte and to tell them that he was prepared to offer the full asking price.

The next stage of the purchase would involve him finding himself a solicitor and once again he suspected he would be wise to accept Guy's advice and instruct Jon Crighton to act for him.

Katie glanced at her watch. Time for her to leave if she was to meet the agent on time. Tidying up her desk she reached for her mobile phone, popping it into her bag. They were having a spell of good weather with long sunshiny days and high temperatures, which made the wearing of traditional formal office clothes too heavy and uncomfortable.

Instead, aided and abetted by her mother and her cousin, Katie had paid a visit to Chester, which she had combined with a brief but very enjoyable lunch with Luke Crighton's wife, Bobbie, and a whirlwind shopping trip that had resulted in the purchase of what she had complained to her mother was virtually a completely new wardrobe.

She had felt even more guilty about the extravagance of her purchases when her mother had insisted 'these are my treat, Katie.'

Now though, as the elegant cut of the smart black linen mix, button-back dress swirled softly round her legs, she had to admit that she was glad she had allowed herself to be persuaded. The dress was smart enough for the office without being too stuffy or formal. She had also bought a complementary jacket to go with it, and a couple of wrap skirts which could also be worn with the jacket in addition to one of several tops in matching tones.

It had been a long time since she had had any new clothes. Although her work for the charity had not involved working at the front line, she had nevertheless been conscious of the fact that a huge discrepancy existed between her comfortably affluent Western lifestyle and those of the people they were trying to help, and besides…

She could feel the back of her throat starting to tighten with emotion. What had been the point in making herself look attractive, and allowing herself to feel womanly and sensual when she already knew that the man she wanted to be those things for would not and could not ever be hers?

Perhaps it was one of those ironic twists of their twinship that her own unrequited love for Louise's husband Gareth should echo the love Louise had once had for a married man. But then Louise had found love with Gareth and although Katie doubted that she would ever find a man to match him, she knew, too, that for her own inner peace and happiness she had to find a way of moving her life forward and of leaving that love behind.

Katie walked towards the window of her small office and stared out into the busy town square. To one side of it stood the church and running parallel to it but outside her view was a prettily elegant close of Georgian houses where her father's aunt, Ruth, lived with her American husband, Grant, whenever they were over in England.

The other three sides of the square were filled with a jumble of mixed-era buildings, Tudor wattle-and-daub cheek by jowl with Georgian town houses. The square itself had, thanks to the determination of its townspeople, retained much of its original medieval aura even if the stocks were now purely decorative and the original well had been turned into an ornamental fountain.

As young girls she and Louise used to call to see their father on their way home from school, specifically on 'pocket-money' days, hoping that he might be persuaded to add a little extra to the permitted allowance. They had giggled over the boys as they sat side by side beneath the trees on the bench donated by past worthy citizens. Together they had visited Aunt Ruth and helped her with her innovative displays of church flowers. Together they had attended regulation church services. Together they had cycled through the square to the small antique shop their mother had once half owned with Guy Cooke. Together...

As twins they had always been close, even though temperamentally they were in many ways so very different. Together they had gone to university and it had been there that they had both met Gareth Simmonds who had been one of the course lecturers.

Gareth with whom she had fallen quietly and idealistically in love...

Gareth who epitomised everything she had ever wanted in a man... Gareth who was so kind, so calm, so gentle and perceptive… Gareth who loved her sister, her twin… Gareth who could never be hers…

The view below her wavered and swam as her eyes filled with tears. Quickly she blinked them away. She had promised herself when Louise and Gareth married that she would find a way to stop loving him, that she would make herself accept him simply as her brother-in-law, as her beloved twin's husband, but every time she saw him the ache of loneliness and pain she felt at seeing the two of them so happy together was still there. She knew that Louise was hurt by her rejection of her constant invitations to go and stay with them, and she knew, too, that the gulf that was developing between the two of them disturbed her parents, especially her mother, but what could she do? What could she say? There was no way she could admit what the real problem was. And now there was the additional pain of seeing Louise with her new baby—hers and Gareth's child.

A small bitter smile twisted the softness of her mouth. Was she destined always to be wanted by men who were already committed to someone else; to always be 'second best'? She knew that Gareth would never approach her with a view to an illicit affair the way her ex-boss had done. He loved Louise far too much for that. He was so totally unaware of Katie's own anguished feelings that it seemed to her, in her present state of low self-esteem and self-respect, that it was almost as though she didn't deserve to be loved or treated well, that something about her actively encouraged men to think they could treat her badly.

No man would ever have suggested to her twin that she should have a seedy, hole-in-the-corner sexual relationship with him. No man would dream of suggesting it to any of her female cousins either, she was sure of it. Even Maddy, her brother Max's wife, who had always been regarded as the most downtrodden and to-be-pitied member of the family because of Max's appalling uncaring behaviour towards her, had turned out far stronger and determined than any of them could ever have imagined. Look at the way she had taken control of their marriage and of Max following his return home after his attack.

At last year's wedding of Bobbie's twin sister, Samantha, all the family had remarked on how much of an adoring husband and father Max had become. He was even taking on his full share of parenting following the birth of their third child, another little boy, so that Maddy could continue with her work for the charity Aunt Ruth had originally set up. Once, the very idea of Max changing nappies and bathing babies would have been a total impossibility, but now...

So what was it about *her* that denied her the emotional happiness and support all the other Crighton women, both by birth and marriage, seemed to expect and get as their birthright? Sometimes she felt as though there was something about her that meant that she was forever condemned to live in other people's shadows...*other* people's or her twin's.

She could still remember the plans that Louise had made for them as they were growing up, plans which involved the two of them practically running the world, or at least Louise running the world; with Katie's devoted support. And Katie of course had willingly given her that support, that loyalty, that commitment, but now Louise had someone else in her life to give her those things...now Louise had the man that she, Katie, had loved and she, Katie...she, Katie had...nothing...

Outside in the square the church clock chimed the hour. Hastily Katie gathered her scattered thoughts. If she didn't leave now she was going to be late for her appointment with the selling agent.

Reaching for her jacket she headed for the door.

Half an hour later when Katie drove into the visitor's section of the apartment's car park the only other person there was a young girl who was obviously quite patiently waiting for someone. Tall and slim, wearing jeans and a cropped white top she gave Katie a warm smile as she climbed out of her car. Instinctively Katie smiled back. The girl had long dark hair and widely spaced apart warm grey eyes. For some reason Katie felt that there was something familiar about her although she had no idea what because she was certain she had never seen her before.

'Hi, I'm just waiting for my father,' the girl told Katie. 'I can see why he's decided to buy one of the apartments, Mum will love the location. I don't know where Dad is,' she added, glancing at her watch. 'He said to meet him at four-thirty. Has he telephoned you to say he's going to be late for his viewing appointment?'

As she listened to her Katie realised that the girl must have mistaken her for the viewing agent, but before she could correct her mistake the girl continued, 'I expect Dad's already told you that he works for Aarlston-Becker. He's head of their research department,' she confided with touching daughterly pride. 'I'm at a sixth form college in Manchester and we've got family in Haslewich so...

'Oh, here he is now,' she exclaimed as a large Mercedes swept round the curve of the gravel drive.

Behind it was the much smaller car driven by the estate agent which Katie recognised from her previous meeting with him, but she wasn't paying either the agent or his car any attention, instead she was concentrating on the Mercedes—and its driver. *Now* she knew why the dark hair and grey eyes the young girl had seemed so familiar. The man now stepping out of his stationary car was none other than the man who had virtually tried to run her down on her first day at work.

It was plain from his expression that he had recognised her, too, but before Katie could challenge him over his behaviour the estate agent was hurrying to join them, announcing, 'I do hope that neither of you mind but since you both want to view the properties at virtually the same time I thought we could combine the appointments.'

'*You're* buying one of the apartments?'

The words came out before Katie could silence them and she knew that her expression and tone of voice betrayed exactly what her feelings were.

The cold look she was thrown in disdainful response informed her that her dismay was more than matched by his reaction to the thought of having *her* as a neighbour, but since his daughter was flinging herself into his arms and hugging him lovingly and claiming his attention, Katie was relieved to recognise that he wasn't going to be able to respond verbally to her impetuous and betraying comment.

'Very well, if you'd like to come this way,' the estate agent suggested.

'You are interested in and are planning to purchase

flat nine, Miss Crighton,' he checked as he activated
the main alarm system and lock to the entrance lobby
to the apartments and waited to usher them inside before continuing, 'And you are purchasing flat number
ten, Mr Cooke, is that correct?'

Cooke…this man who looked nowhere near old
enough to be the father of a teenage daughter was a
Cooke, Katie reflected. Curiously she flicked a discreet look in his direction and then wished she hadn't
as she realised that he'd caught her studying him.

She looked away as quickly as she could, but not
before she had recognised that he did indeed bear the
very distinctive dark and sensual Cooke good looks—
the rakish and very disturbing aura of maleness and
danger they all seemed to have inherited in some measure or other from their long-ago gypsy ancestor.

'In fact,' the agent continued, as he led the way to
the discreetly concealed lifts that serviced the house's
upper floors, 'seeing as you are going to be close
neighbours—yours are the only two apartments on the
top floor—perhaps I should introduce you to one another.'

Turning to Katie and before either of them could
stop him he announced, 'Miss Katie Crighton… Mr
Seb Cooke…'

She was a *Crighton*, so where exactly did she fit
into the extensive family tree? Seb wondered curiously as he gave Katie a narrow-eyed contemplative
look. He could see at close quarters she was far pret-
tier than he had realised that day in the street.

Her eyes were veiled now as they mirrored her
body language's mute dislike of both the situation and
him. Her hair, smoothly brushed instead of tousled by
the breeze, hung in a thick soft wave down past her

shoulders. The black dress she was wearing hinted at rather than revealed the femininity of her body.

It might not be revealing the lushly full curves of her breasts but he had a vivid memory of just how she and they had looked with the wind pressing the fabric of the top she had been wearing against their softness. In fact, unless his memory was playing tricks on him, she possessed a surprisingly voluptuous body for someone so slim.

Without realising how stern or disapproving it made him look Seb frowned. What on earth was he doing even registering the voluptuousness of an unknown young woman's body, never mind remembering it? He may not have lived totally like a monk in the years since his divorce but the demands of his work coupled with his awareness of just what an appalling husband and father he had been ensured that he kept whatever relationships he had had to discreet liaisons with women who shared his beliefs that he was simply not good marriage material.

As she saw him frown, Katie immediately felt a return of her earlier dislike of him. Heightened by her lack of self-esteem, this fuelled her inner conviction that such a sensual, rawly male man, must surely find her lacking in the kind of feminine attributes that would appeal to him. Not that she would *want* to appeal to him. Not under any circumstances.

One look at him at close quarters had confirmed that he was most definitely not her type. Too aggressive, too arrogant and far, far too sexy. Oh yes, far, *far* too sexy, because, hidden away among all the other emotional burdens she was compelling herself to carry, Katie had what she considered to be a most uncool and unappealing secret and that was…

'If you're a Crighton, can I ask… Are you one of the twin Crightons?'

As Charlotte's semi-shy but wholly warm voice broke into her thoughts, Katie focused bemusedly on her. Charlotte too, like her father, had heard all about the Crightons from Guy and Chrissie, but unlike her father she felt no self-consciousness about wanting to satisfy her curiosity about just where Katie fitted into the family jigsaw. For Charlotte, the most fascinating and interesting part of the Crighton family saga was the fact that they so regularly produced sets of twins.

'Charlotte…' Seb began warningly, but Katie shook her head. Unlike her father Charlotte was someone she had immediately felt at home with. She knew instinctively that the younger girl's question was simply a natural expression of her justifiable curiosity and so it was easy for her to smile and nod her head, explaining easily, 'Well, yes, as a matter of fact I am.'

'Does your twin live in Haslewich too? Are you and she going to share the apartment?' Charlotte pressed her.

Katie shook her head. 'No.' A small shadow crossed her face dulling her expression, a fact which Seb noticed but which Charlotte, too engrossed in waiting for her to answer and too youthfully immature to be aware of, did not.

'No, Louise my twin is married and is presently living in Brussels with… Gareth, her husband…'

Now why had she hesitated and then stumbled so awkwardly over saying her brother-in-law's name? Seb wondered thoughtfully as he caught the note of desolation in Katie's voice. Had the two women fallen out perhaps…had a rift developed between them due to the fact that their closeness had been breeched because one of them had married?

Frowning, he stood back to allow Katie and Charlotte to step into the lift ahead of him. Why on earth was he wasting time wondering about a young woman whose acquaintance he had neither the time nor the desire to pursue? Without realising what he was doing Seb let his gaze drift down to Katie's mouth. It was soft and full and oh, so infinitely kissable. He could just imagine how it would feel under his…how *she* would feel…how she would *look,* her eyes blind with a vulnerable haunted look of longing and desire that would make him want…

'Here we are… This lift is, of course, exclusively for your use and both of you will have your own passkey.'

With a start Seb dragged his thoughts back to reality.

As Katie preceded Seb into the private hallway into which both their apartments opened she was aware of feeling distinctly wobbly. What on earth was happening to her? Why had she experienced that extraordinary sensation just now, as though…as though…

Instinctively she lifted her fingers to her lips. The only man she had ever fantasised about having kissed her, the only man she wanted to have kiss her with the kind of intimacy and passion she had just been imagining was Gareth. *Gareth* and not…as her thoughts skittered to a frantic halt, refusing to allow her to question just why she had experienced that extraordinary sensation of having her mouth so expertly and intimately kissed, and by a man she neither knew nor even wanted to know, she told herself that Gareth was just about as far removed from Seb Cooke as it was possible for two men to be. Gareth was gentle, kind, reassuringly safe in his manner, while Seb Cooke was aggressive and possessed the kind of sexual aura that… Katie shuddered. What on earth would she want with such a raw, dangerous outright hunk of male sexuality…?

'This is your apartment,' the agent was saying chirpily to her, unlocking the door for her. 'As you know, you have the benefit of your own private balcony while your flat…' he turned to Seb, 'has the addition of an extra room which could be used as a third bedroom or a study.' Still smiling he crossed the hallway and unlocked the other door.

Taking advantage of Seb's preoccupation with the agent, Katie slipped inside her own apartment.

Five minutes later, having completed a closer inspection of all the rooms, she was forced to admit that she was unlikely to find anything that would suit her better. All the rooms were a good size, all the period decorative details had been retained, giving the apartment a feeling of elegance and even grandeur, and the views from the windows, which she had not really taken full account of on her previous visit, extended not just over the grounds of the house itself, all of which were there for the residents to enjoy and which were tended by a firm of gardeners, but over the surrounding countryside.

Left alone in his own apartment with Charlotte while the estate agent went to check to see if Katie had any questions she wanted to ask him, Seb turned to his daughter lifting one querying eyebrow as he asked her, 'Well…'

'It's cool,' Charlotte responded with a wide grin.

'Love the bathrooms... Yours is even big enough to have a Jacuzzi fitted if you want one.'

'*If* I want one,' Seb agreed, adding firmly, 'which I don't...'

'Dad, why *haven't* you ever re-married?' Charlotte asked him seriously now.

While Seb was frowningly wondering how best to answer her, she continued a little uncertainly,

'It isn't because of me is it... I mean I know that...well Mum never really said much about...about things, but I did once overhear her talking to George about it and she said that having me had been the final straw for you...'

Seb studied her downcast head wondering what on earth he could say. As close as they had grown the subject of his marriage to her mother and their subsequent divorce was not one they had ever discussed, and man-like he had always been reluctant to raise a subject which, he was forced to admit, did not reflect well on himself.

'I rather think what your mother was trying to say was that my adolescent and totally selfish reaction to the demands a baby made on her time and our marriage were the last straw for *her*,' Seb corrected Charlotte gently.

'The reason our marriage didn't survive was wholly and totally down to me, Charlotte... I was a selfish wretch, and far too immature when we got married to think about anyone other than myself. Your mother and I met at university, fell into what we believed was love but what, with a bit of perspective, I think we both soon realised was really only lust, married...and...and then you came along and you have no idea how much I regret the years I've lost with you and my own unforgivable selfishness...'

'M-Mum did say once that had the pair of you been older or a bit more worldly-wise, you'd both have known that what you had together was wonderful for an intense and passionate affair, but not for marriage. She said, too, that while *she* was the one who initiated things between the two of you, you were the one with the old-fashioned moral principles who insisted that you should get married—if you were going to have sex.'

Seb grimaced. What Charlotte had just said was quite true. Eighteen months his senior, Sandra had had other boyfriends, other relationships, before she had met him—neither of them had come to their own affair as novice lovers. But with his own upbringing, his knowledge of what could happen in the aftermath of a passionate relationship for the woman who was left on her own, seen first-hand through the history of his own family—Cooke men had a certain notorious reputation for their alleged propensity to father children outside wedlock—he had felt it necessary to prove that he was different, above the kind of much criticised behaviour his name had branded him with. Perhaps his insistence on marrying Sandra had been a righteous and ridiculous piece of over-reaction, but if he was honest with himself Seb knew that, given the same situation again, he would probably have reacted in exactly the same way.

His father had always been a stern critic of the haphazard morals of some members of the Cooke clan. As a boy growing up, Seb could remember that there had been tight-lipped conversations between his parents about the sudden arrival of a new and unexpected member of the family who did not always carry his or her father's name. Both of his parents had been insistent that that was a family inheritance of which they most certainly did not approve. And nor, no more so, did Seb.

Seb was brought back to the present as Charlotte squeezed his arm lovingly and kissed his cheek.

'I'm glad we've had this little talk,' she told him almost maternally. 'And I wish that you could find someone nice to marry Dad... I liked Katie Crighton, didn't you?'

Seb frowned as she looked at him, but Charlotte only returned his look with one of filial innocence and before Seb could warn her that even if he had been looking for someone, Katie Crighton was most definitely not his type, the estate agent had returned.

Ten minutes later as Seb drove out of the house's grounds behind Katie and the estate agent, he made a mental note to get in touch with Jon Crighton and set the wheels in motion for the purchase of the apartment. Now that he had decided to buy and had had his offer accepted, he wanted to get the formalities over and done with as soon as possible so that he could move in.

As she drove out of the house's grounds ahead of Seb Cooke, Katie was wishing that she might have had someone else, anyone else, but him, for her new and nearest neighbour. Not that she was likely to see much of him she acknowledged, on two counts. According to what Charlotte had told her she could guess that his job would be very demanding and from the way he had looked at her she had seen that he was as pleased about having her for a neighbour as she was him. What was his wife like? she wondered. Very glamorous and sexy no doubt. He was that kind of man—you could see at a glance. He just exuded sexuality... Not like Gareth. Gareth was a man for snuggling up to in front of a lovely log fire... Gareth was a comfort and reassurance, safe and...

And there was no way that anyone, any woman, would ever describe Seb Cooke as any of those things, but most especially safe. Why, you only had to think about his family's reputation. There was a smouldering sexual energy about him that rubbed her up the wrong way and brought all of her own antagonism towards him out making her feel prickly and on her guard, wary and filled with unfamiliarly strong emotions.

Even the way he had looked at her. Katie tensed as she tried to banish the unwanted memory of that startling reaction she had experienced when she had almost felt as though she could sense the heat of his breath, his *mouth* on hers. It had been a mistake, an accident, a ridiculous fluke caused by heaven alone knew what mix up of signals inside her body. No doubt Seb himself would have an explanation for such awareness. He, after all, was the research scientist and no doubt fully *au fait* with the confusing mixture of chemicals and in-built programming which were responsible for what less rational people called 'emotions.'

To her relief as she looked in her driving mirror she saw that they were going in opposite directions to their different destinations as she indicated to turn left to drive home to her parents' house.

CHAPTER THREE

'Mmm... What a wonderful smell,' Katie enthused as she walked into the kitchen where her mother was busy cooking. Originally a farmer's daughter from Cheshire, Jenny Crighton had the kind of homemaking skills that at one stage of her young married life had made her feel very dull and old-fashioned. Who wanted a wife who could grow, preserve and cook her own fruit and vegetables in an era which had fallen in love with Twiggy look-alikes; fragile, big-eyed dolly birds? Who wanted a wife with a healthy build, thick curly hair and freckles when the fashion was for chalk-white pallor and long straight locks?

It had taken a long time for her to learn that Jon Crighton, her husband, loved her very deeply, but these last few years since the birthday party thrown to celebrate her husband's and his twin brother's half century, had seen a renaissance in their marriage and had brought her more joy and happiness than she had once believed she could ever have—and it showed. She still had the trim feminine figure of her youth, but as a young girl she had been self-effacing, a little awkward and shy, now she had a mature self-confidence that came not just from knowing how much her husband loved her nor even from being the pivot of her busy family household, but from feeling at ease with herself.

'It's for supper tonight. You haven't forgotten that we're having an informal party have you?'

425

Katie gave her an apologetic look.

'Oh heavens, yes I had,' she admitted, adding by way of explanation, 'It's been such a frantic week, what with my own conveyance and then Olivia having to take extra time off.'

'Mmm… Well at least the doctor has confirmed the fever and temperature is only a childhood upset and not meningitis as Olivia first feared. You will be joining us this evening though, won't you?'

'Mmm… What time are you expecting people?'

'In about an hour,' her mother told her.

'Right, I'll go up and have a shower and get changed and then I'll come down and give you a hand. Is Dad back?' she asked as she helped herself to one of the too-tempting and still-warm fruit buns her mother had just put onto a wire rack to cool.

'Yes…just… That will give you indigestion,' she warned Katie with a mock serious look as she tapped her hand.

'Oh, and by the way, I rang Louise this morning…'

Katie, who had been about to go upstairs, tensed, her heart starting to thud unevenly. Every mention of her twin reminded her of Gareth and brought home to her the emptiness of her own life in contrast to the love that filled Louise's.

'You know we're having a special party for your grandfather soon,' her mother was continuing. 'Well, both Maddy and I think that we ought to have as many from the family there as possible. Having the family around him means so much to Ben and he's getting so frail…'

Katie's eyebrows rose.

'The family means so much, does it? Well he certainly doesn't *show* it,' she told her mother dryly.

'With the exception of Max and of course uncle David, I get the impression that he doesn't care that much for anyone.'

'Oh, that's just his way,' Jenny assured her sunnily. 'You wouldn't believe how proud he is of all of you.'

'No, I wouldn't,' Katie agreed wryly. 'He told me when he learned that Lou and I were going to study law that women and the law simply didn't mix, and that women were far too emotional to make good lawyers…'

'He *is* a bit old-fashioned,' her mother acknowledged, 'and since David left…' She paused and sighed.

'Do you think Uncle David *will* ever come back?' Katie asked her mother curiously. 'I mean, to just disappear like that… I know that Olivia makes no real secret of the fact that she doesn't want him to come back, but Jack…'

She paused and frowned as both she and her mother remembered how, when Louise had first moved to Brussels to work, Jack and their brother Joss had illicitly taken time off school to go and search for Jack's missing father. And then later, undeterred by Louise's father's decision that his twin brother should be allowed to make his own decisions as to whether or not to be reunited with his family, Jack had secretly made arrangements to fly out to Jamaica on the same plane as Jon's eldest son, Max.

Max had callously played on his grandfather's love for him and for his son, David, on what was to have been, for Max, an all-expenses-paid luxury holiday and an escape from his wife and a difficult situation professionally, all cloaked in the disguise of wanting to look for David at Ben's behest.

The ensuing near tragedy had resulted, not just in Max's total transformation and metamorphosis, but also in a much deeper and adult understanding between Jack and his Uncle Jon, but all the family knew that a small part of Jack would also always be scarred by his father's disappearance and his apparent rejection of him, no matter how much love and reassurance he received from Jon and Jenny.

'I don't know if David will ever come back,' her mother admitted now. 'We don't even know where he is. For Ben's sake…' She paused and bit her lip but Katie knew what she was thinking.

'Grandfather *is* getting very frail,' she agreed quietly. 'If Uncle David is going to come back I hope he doesn't leave it too long…or until it's too late…'

'It wouldn't be easy for David to come back and I'm not sure he actually possesses the courage he would need to do so…' Jenny replied.

'Mmm… He and Max were very alike, weren't they?' Katie acknowledged. 'But Max has changed and so…'

'Max *has* changed,' her mother agreed. 'He and Maddy will be here this evening, by the way. Maddy did say she wanted to have a word with you. They're hoping to buy another house for the mums and babes and I suspect she's going to ask you if you'd do all the legal work for them.'

The family charity originally begun by Ben Crighton's sister, Ruth, had grown from a single house with individual rooms for young single mothers, into an organisation which now provided homes for single parents of both sexes as well as their young children, and which was constantly having to find more accommodation for its protégé's parents.

One of Maddy's contributions had been the development of a scheme which allowed the young parents to train for jobs and then to go out to work while their children were looked after safely at an in-house crèche.

And not all of their single parents were female. They now had a small group of young men who, for one reason or another, were the sole parents to their children.

It was a very worthwhile cause and one which all the Crighton women both supported and were involved in to some extent or another. Katie and Louise had both worked voluntarily with the scheme during their university breaks and Katie was not surprised to hear that Maddy, as the charity's main working executive, was in the process of obtaining further housing.

'Who else is coming?' she asked her mother as she scooped up the last few crumbs of her pilfered cake.

'Mmm… Olivia and Caspar, Tullah and Saul and a handful of other people. Oh, and Chrissie and Guy…'

'Guy Cooke?' Katie enquired so sharply that her mother frowned.

'Yes. Why?'

A long, long time ago, or so it seemed now to Jenny, Guy had made it plain to her that if she had a neglectful husband then she most certainly had a very appreciative business partner and one who, given the opportunity, would like to put their relationship on a much closer intimate footing.

But that had been before she and Jon had sorted out their problems and before Guy had met Chrissie, and so far as Jenny knew, there was now no reason whatsoever for Katie to have *that* particular note of reservation in her voice when she repeated Guy's name, and certainly none for her unexpected emphasis on the Cooke part of Guy's name.

Katie, of both her girls, was the one to whom Jenny felt the closest, the one who was most like her in temperament and yet, conversely, Katie was also the one who was the least forthcoming, the least given to confidence.

For a long time Jenny had been concerned about her daughter, knowing with maternal instinct that she wasn't happy, but Katie had never been the kind of person you could coax or persuade into discussing anything she did not want to discuss. Jenny had her own ideas and thoughts about what was making her so unhappy and if she was right…

Katie had always tended to idealise people, to put them on a small pedestal, to invest them with virtues of her own making. She had a far gentler and more romantic nature than Louise, her twin, a far less robust attitude towards life—and men.

And now as she looked at her withdrawn expression, Jenny decided that it might not be a good moment to tell her that she had invited Guy to bring another Cooke along to her supper party with him.

Jenny had not yet met Seb Cooke, but she had heard all about him from both Guy and Chrissie. Naturally maternal and warm-hearted as well as being a generous hostess, Jenny had immediately suggested to them both that they should bring Seb with them when they came over to supper. From what Guy had told her about him it sounded as though, despite all his family connections in the town, he might be feeling a little isolated.

'He isn't the easiest of people to get to know,' Guy had warned her. 'In fact, some folk find him a little bit off-putting and intimidating. He's a scientist, of course, and very analytical, and like me he's known the burden of being a Cooke who doesn't fit into the normal and expected male Cooke mould.'

As Katie went upstairs to change and prepare for the evening she was frowning. Her father had asked her if she would take over one of his few remaining conveyancing cases, explaining that what was to have been a simple court case had developed into something much more complicated, meaning that he couldn't do the work as quickly as their new client wished.

'Nice chap. You'll like him,' he had told Katie with a smile. 'Seb Cooke... He...'

'Seb Cooke! You want me to act for *him*?'

Her father had raised an eyebrow when he had heard the antagonism in her voice.

'What's wrong? I thought...'

'Nothing's wrong...' Katie had fibbed. The situation and her own feelings were far too complicated and personal to be explained to her father. How could she tell him that the main reason she disliked Seb so much was because of his intense sexuality...that something about him, about his power as a man, made her all the more aware of her own incompleteness as a woman.

'He's buying the apartment adjacent to mine,' was all she could allow herself to say.

'Yes, I know,' her father agreed, and then wisely decided not to pursue the subject.

Katie had changed since she had reached maturity. Something had happened to her, hurt her, and much as he longed to help, he felt that it was impossible for him to pry. She was an adult now and if she wouldn't even confide in her mother then who was he, a mere man—a mere *father*—to push for confidences she quite plainly did not want to share.

Her father had an appointment with Seb on Monday, an appointment *she* would now have to keep in his place. Fortunately most of the work had already been done and it was simply a matter of Seb signing some forms and then, hopefully, at the end of the week when completion for the sale would take place, that would be an end of the matter. He would still be her neighbour of course, but there she would be able to keep her distance.

What kind of man was he anyway? she fumed a few minutes later as she stood under the warm lash of the shower. He was buying the apartment in his own name and not putting it into the joint names of himself and his wife. That old-fashioned kind of chauvinism was something she detested and fortunately was rare now. The majority of men accepted that their wives, their partners, *were* equal to them in every way and behaved financially accordingly.

She might, Katie conceded, be a little old-fashioned when it came to matters of personal intimacy, but she was thoroughly modern in outlook when it came to matters of equality between the two sexes, whether that equality related to financial aspects of a relationship or the emotional and physical ones, and so far as she was concerned, a man who was selfish towards his partner financially, who refused to accept that she had absolute parity with him, was just as likely to be selfish both emotionally and physically.

Max, her elder brother, had once been that type of

man and she had seen at uncomfortably close quarters just how destructive an effect that had had on his marriage. What was Seb Cooke's wife like? Katie wondered curiously. Attractive? Very, she suspected. Seb had struck her as the type of man who would, as an arrogant right, demand perfection in every aspect of his life, and then there was the stunningly attractive daughter as living proof of her parents' good looks.

Was this wife clever, witty…fun to be with? Did those steel-grey eyes glow with warmth and passion when their glance rested on her?

Katie gave herself a small mental warning shake. If she wasn't careful she was going to turn into the kind of sad person who, without an emotional focus of her own in her life, worried incessantly and even perhaps a little obsessively, about the flaws of people who were at best mere acquaintances. And that was behaviour that was…what? Typical of what, one hundred and fifty years ago, might have been the ways of the unmarried, and therefore supposedly the unwanted daughter of the family who remained at home to look after her ageing parents.

Well, her own parents were far from ageing and she was living in a time when it was publicly documented that the women who enjoyed the best health and the least stress both physically and mentally, were those who had elected to remain independent—who had *chosen* to remain independent, Katie reminded herself inwardly, not those who were forced to confront the unhappy knowledge that they loved a man who did not return that love, and had no option other than to remain alone.

Perhaps it was inevitable in a way that both she and Louise *should* love the same man since they were twins…but Bobbie and Sam were twins and Bobbie loved Luke and Sam loved Liam.

But then there were certain personal similarities between those two men, both in looks and in character, and there was only one Gareth, could only ever be one Gareth.

Outside the sun was still shining. It was a lovely warm evening and Katie knew from past experience that her parents' guests would spill out of the house to explore and enjoy the gardens, so she opened her wardrobe door and looked for something appropriate to wear.

The soft chambray skirt she decided upon was both practical and pretty and with it she put on a white cap-sleeve T-shirt which had been a present from Louise.

'It's too tight and too…'

'…sexy,' Louise had teased her, her eyes sparkling with amusement. 'It's meant to be. It suits you, Katie. Since you've been working for that charity you've started wearing things that are far too dowdy and matronly for you. You've got a gorgeous body…much better than mine… Oh, yes you have,' she had insisted before Katie had been able to protest that the last thing she wanted to look was 'sexy,' but then Louise had unwittingly touched a nerve when she had added teasingly,

'Gareth commented the last time he saw you that Ma dresses more stylishly than you do. I know how you feel about ostentatious consumerism when other people are having to do without, but there's no reason why you shouldn't wear inexpensive clothes that flatter you instead of opting for ones that don't. And don't forget,' she had added winningly, 'every time you buy something you're helping *other* people to earn…'

Remembering the seriousness of her twin's voice as she delivered this piece of wisdom made Katie smile as she slipped on the pretty delicate gold earrings which had been Louise and Gareth's Christmas present to her. They matched the gold bangle they had given her when she had been their bridesmaid.

Arriving downstairs five minutes later, Katie shooed her mother out of the kitchen so that she too could shower and get ready for her guests, reminding her, 'Ma…don't worry, I'll finish off everything down here…'

'Would you? Oh, and Katie, could you do something with the flowers I've put in the laundry room. You really have inherited Aunt Ruth's talent with them.'

'Mmm…and I wonder which ancestor *you* inherited your silver tongue from,' Katie teased her mother as she obligingly headed for the laundry room and the flowers.

CHAPTER FOUR

'YOU'LL like Jenny and Jon,' Chrissie told Seb warmly after they had picked him up from the house he was renting, adding ruefully, 'Oh, but I'd forgotten you'll have met Jon already, won't you, since he's handling the legal side of your property purchase.'

'As a matter-of-fact I haven't,' Seb informed her. 'I've got an appointment on Monday to sign my contract, but it seems that he's going to be tied up in court so his daughter will be dealing with it.'

'His daughter…' Guy frowned and then smiled. 'Of course I'd forgotten that Katie was working with Jon and Olivia now.'

'Katie… Katie Crighton?' Seb questioned him sharply so that both Chrissie and Guy exchanged automatic close-couple looks before Guy turned to Seb and asked him,

'Yes, do you know her?'

'We've met,' Seb told him brusquely. Then, sensing their mutual curiosity, informed them drily, 'As it happens she's buying the apartment next to mine.'

'Oh really,' Chrissie looked interested. 'Jenny did say when I last spoke to her that Katie was looking for somewhere local. It's such a shame about her having to leave the charity. She was really enjoying working for them.'

'Of the two of them, she always was more intensely caring in that sort of way,' Guy informed Seb. 'I can remember how when they were children, both of them

436

were involved in sponsoring African orphans, but it was Katie who not only gave her spending money but came down to the shop and insisted on spending all her spare time polishing the furniture to earn extra money for them.'

'Well I suppose there is bound to be an element of competition between them,' Seb commented briefly and with what Guy felt was an unfamiliar and an uncharacteristic note of censure in his voice. Then, before he could correct Seb's misapprehension and inform him that in fact Katie had insisted on quietly and discreetly sharing the earnings with her twin so that their shared contributions were ultimately 'equal,' Chrissie was asking Seb if he remembered the family from his own childhood in the town.

'Obviously I know the name,' Seb confirmed, adding cynically, 'After all, it's almost as synonymous with Haslewich as the name Cooke, although for a very different reason. From what I can remember, old man Crighton was considered to be very much among the great and good of the area, a very traditional *pater familiae*... I do once remember going to a children's party up at Queensmead but it was quite definitely an "us and them" affair, the rich distributing alms to the poor sort of thing...'

'Mmm... I remember those days,' Guy confirmed. 'But things are completely different now. Jon is as different from his father as chalk is from cheese and the current young adult generation of Crightons are a lively multi-talented bunch whose company I'm sure you'll enjoy.'

Seb forbore to inform his cousin that his two previous encounters with Katie Crighton did not incline him to share his optimism.

He had not exactly been enthusiastic about the evening to start with and had he known just who Katie Crighton was he would've made every effort to exclude himself from the event. Now, of course, it was too late.

He started to frown as he had a sharp mental picture of Katie the first time he had seen her. Seb felt his stomach muscles tighten in protest at the feelings *that* memory evoked. At thirty-eight he considered himself, if not exactly past being sexually aware of and aroused by the sight and thought of a pretty woman, then certainly well able to control the physical effects of such thoughts. But now, as then, his body was proving him wrong.

Irritably he tried to deny the impact of his visual memory of her as Guy drove in through the gates to Jon and Jenny's comfortable home.

The heady summer warmth of the evening had prompted Jenny to organise a buffet table under the trees in their pretty orchard and as Seb followed Guy and Chrissie in under the rose and honeysuckle hedge which separated the orchard from the rest of the garden, the first person he saw was Katie.

She had her back to him and was standing beside Saul Crighton, who Seb recognised from work, pouring him a glass of what Seb later discovered was her mother's special and highly potent strawberry wine cooler. The scene in front of him couldn't have been more idyllic, Seb recognised. The meadow grass was sprinkled with wild flowers, the breeze was scented with roses and the still warm air hummed with harmonious happy voices. Even a half-dozen or so young children who were playing together in one corner of the orchard seemed to be sharing one another's company rather than squabbling noisily or quarrelling.

As Seb watched, one of the slightly older girls detached herself from the group and walked over to Saul Crighton leaning against him whilst he wrapped his arm tenderly around her.

As Seb looked on Katie reached out and brushed a stray lock of hair out of the girl's eyes. Quickly Seb turned away. The small scene being enacted in front of him reminded him of his own loss as a father. When he looked back now it appalled him that he could ever have behaved so selfishly and how it hurt to recognise how much he had missed.

'Come on, let me introduce you to Jenny and Jon,' Guy was saying, touching him on his arm and directing him towards the older couple standing a few feet away.

Five minutes later he was forced to admit that Guy had been right when he had told him he would like Jenny and Jon Crighton as Jenny in particular possessed a warmth which was extremely attractive and welcoming. And before he knew what he was doing Seb found that he was confiding to Jenny that one of the main reasons he had moved back to the area was so that he could be close to Charlotte.

'During the early years of Charlotte's life I was guilty of being an absent father,' he heard himself telling Jenny ruefully. 'I've been very fortunate in that Charlotte has forgiven me, and *she* has been very fortunate in that my ex-wife's second husband and her stepfather has given her the love and security I failed to provide.'

'We all mature at different stages,' Jenny responded

gently. 'You must have been very young yourself when your daughter was born.'

Several yards away on the other side of the orchard Katie was just about to pour a glass of cooler for Saul's wife Tullah when Tullah enquired in an admiring whisper,

'Who on earth is that with your mother?'

As Katie turned round to look, her eyes widened in disbelief and dismay.

'He's...it's Seb Cooke,' she told Tullah curtly.

'You've met him?' Tullah questioned, her eyebrows lifting a little as she readily interpreted the dismay in Katie's voice and expression.

'Briefly,' Katie admitted reluctantly, and then knowing that it was bound to become common family knowledge, she added even more reluctantly, 'He's buying the apartment next to mine...'

'He is? *Wow*! Lucky *you*...' Tullah sighed mock-enviously while Saul raised his own eyebrows and questioned teasingly, 'What's this?'

'No one for you to worry about,' Tullah quickly reassured him, linking her arm with his and snuggling up to his side. 'But he is gorgeous and now that you've told me who he is I can see his likeness to Guy.'

'Mmm...he's already caused quite a flutter in the research labs,' Saul admitted. 'I think some of the girls are running a book on who will be the first to have a date with him.'

'He's a married man,' Katie protested stiffly, looking disapproving.

'You mean he was a married man,' Saul corrected her. 'According to the Aarlston-Becker grape-vine he is very much divorced and has been for a considerable length of time.'

Seb Cooke was *divorced*. For some inexplicable reason Katie discovered that her legs had gone oddly weak and that she wanted to sit down. Quite why the discovery that the elegant wife she had visualised for Seb did not actually exist should have such a dramatic physical effect on her she had no idea and nor did she wish to have, she warned herself hastily as her thoughts threatened to go into overdrive.

'Why don't you go and offer him a drink?' Tullah suggested giving Katie a sparkling-eyed look.

'I'm sure if he wants one he'll come over and ask…besides I've just remembered, there's something I've left in the oven,' Katie fibbed, pink-cheeked, as she hastily thrust the jug into Tullah's hand and started to hurry back to the house making sure as she did so that she took a circuitous route through the orchard that would keep her as far away from Seb as possible.

Unfortunately though, her father had seen her and remembering that he had asked her to handle Seb's conveyancing, he called her over.

Reluctantly Katie abandoned her flight and walked warily towards the small group which included her parents and Guy and Chrissie as well as Seb.

'Katie, I was just explaining to Seb here that you are going to be handling his conveyance,' her father told her calmly as she reached them.

'Your daughter and I have already met,' Seb informed Jon formally as her father prepared to make the introductions.

As she responded to Seb's unsmiling greeting, Katie wondered if anyone else other than herself had noticed his distancing reference to her as 'your daughter'.

'It's quite a coincidence the two of you buying adjoining apartments,' Chrissie Cooke commented lightly.

Seb gave a small shrug before responding,

'They're ideal for anyone living alone who wants the space and privacy they afford. The size of their rooms is an asset together with no maintenance of the beautiful gardens.'

'Mmm… I believe the builders have even renovated the tennis courts so that the residents will be able to use them,' Chrissie enthused.

'Do you play tennis, Seb,' Jenny asked conversationally.

'I used to,' Seb acknowledged. 'Although…'

'Katie plays,' Chrissie chimed in.

Hot-cheeked, Katie denied quickly, 'Not any more… I don't really have time, and since Louise got married…'

'Louise is Katie's twin,' Chrissie explained to Seb. 'She and her husband are living in Brussels at the moment.

'When are they next coming over, Jenny?' she asked Katie's mother.

'We're hoping to arrange a family party for Ben soon,' Jenny responded, turning to Seb to tell him, 'Ben, my father-in-law, hasn't been in very good health for quite some time. This celebration isn't for a particular reason other than the fact he likes to get to see all the children. As much as he pretends his grandchildren and family irritate him, privately he would be dreadfully hurt if they didn't all come to see him every once in a while.'

'I suppose he *does* love us in his way,' Katie agreed, momentarily forgetting her discomfort at seeing Seb. 'But it's Uncle David he really wants…'

'David is my husband's brother,' Jenny explained quietly to Seb.

'Did I hear you mention my father's name?' Olivia Crighton suddenly chimed in on the point of walking past with her husband Caspar, but instead coming over to join them as she heard them discussing David.

'The family's black sheep.'

Seb frowned a little as he heard the challenging bitterness and dislike in her voice and noticed that it was Jon who moved over to her taking hold of her hand and patting it almost paternally as he soothed her, 'We were just saying how close he and Dad always were Livvy…'

'Don't remind me,' Olivia responded, refusing to be mollified. 'If Gramps hadn't spoiled him so much…' She stopped and shook her head, apologising to Jenny, 'I'm sorry, but gramps was criticising me the other day for continuing to work even though I've got the children…'

'He can be very difficult, I know,' Jenny agreed, turning to Katie and suggesting, 'Katie, why don't you take Guy, Chrissie and Seb up to the house so they can get themselves something to eat. I like to make sure my victims are well fed and slothful before I go on the attack,' Jenny told Seb beguilingly with a warm smile.

'Go on the attack?' Seb couldn't resist questioning as Katie started to lead the way back to the house.

'Mmm…' Guy began to explain, but Katie beat him to it telling Seb protectively,

'My mother is a very caring person. She works very

hard to raise funds to help support and maintain a local charity which was originally founded by my father's Aunt Ruth.'

'Mother and Baby homes,' Chrissie told Seb enthusiastically. 'We all do what we can to help but Jenny and Maddy between them carry the heaviest responsibility for everything.'

'Thanks in the main to Saul, Aarlston-Becker already underwrites a special fun day for the children, which is held annually. That's due to come up quite soon, isn't it, Katie?' Chrissie asked her.

'Mmm... Aarlston combined it with a group day off which means that nearly all the staff are also involved in the event.'

'Yes, it's held in the grounds of Fitzburgh Place and I warn you now, Seb,' Guy teased, 'you can fully expect to be roped in.'

'Guy organises the marquees and the entertainers as his contribution,' Chrissie informed Seb.

Guy gave a modest shrug.

'It's nothing really. What we normally do is arrange the event to tie in with one that we're giving commercially up at the Hall so that we can give the kids their day out either for free or at a minimum cost. Lord Astlegh allows us to use the parkland for free and you'd be amazed at the amount of talent there is among Aarlston employees.'

'...and among your family,' Chrissie reminded him. 'Last year's fortune-teller was a really big hit. Who was she? You never would tell me...'

'No, and I'm not going to now,' Guy informed her. 'Her identity is a professional secret.'

'Mmm...well, she was definitely a Cooke,' Chrissie murmured.

'Well, of course. What else would you expect with our gypsy genes?' Guy countered teasingly.

They had reached the house and as Katie led the way into the large conservatory off the kitchen where the main buffet table had been laid out she decided that now that her duty was done she could safely escape. Seb's brooding presence was having a decidedly disturbing effect on her senses. Was that really his aftershave she could smell and was so acutely aware of, that potently musky odour?

As they started to help themselves to the buffet another group came in including Saul and Tullah and their children. Almost immediately Saul and Seb began to discuss some mutually interesting aspect of their work at Aarlston-Becker but for some reason, instead of retreating back into the garden, Katie discovered that she was simply staying where she was listening and observing.

Saul said something which made Seb laugh. It was the first time Katie had seen him properly relaxed and a warning feathering of an emotion she didn't want to name curled dangerously down her spine. She wasn't attracted to him she told herself fiercely, she couldn't possibly be, she loved Gareth.

Saul's daughter Meg tugged on her father's sleeve and Katie saw quite plainly the look of sombre reflection that darkened Seb's eyes as he watched Saul turn to respond to his daughter.

He envied Saul. But why? Katie had recognised immediately when she had seen him with Charlotte just how close and loving a bond there was between the two of them.

As though she had guessed what was going through Katie's mind, Chrissie who had been standing beside her and who had also observed the small bit of byplay, explained in a quiet voice, 'Seb feels very guilty about the fact that he was an absent father for much of the time when Charlotte was young.'

'He *abandoned* his wife and child?' Katie demanded sharply.

She had turned her back towards Seb to speak with Chrissie and was therefore unaware of the fact that he had both disengaged himself from his conversation with Saul and overheard her own sharp question until he spoke from immediately behind her, his voice bitingly harsh as he told her quietly,

'No, I did not *abandon* them…'

Katie felt her face start to burn as Chrissie discreetly melted away leaving her to confront Seb on her own.

Katie knew that by rights she ought to apologise, if only because Seb was a guest in her parents' home, but for some extraordinary reason, a streak of wilful stubbornness normally more likely to manifest itself in her twin than in her, suddenly propelled her into defensive action, causing her to walk angrily towards the door at the same time throwing acidly over her shoulder,

'But you did *leave* them, *desert* them…'

As she walked into the narrow passage which linked the conservatory to the laundry room through which she had intended to make her escape, to her consternation Seb followed her, pulling the door to behind him, his height and breadth of shoulder taking up so much of the narrow space that as she turned to face him, Katie felt almost as though she was actually being deprived of air to breathe.

'Why you…!'

Katie's eyes widened as she saw how very angry Seb was, a dark flush burning along his cheek bones, his eyes the colour of molten metal. A sharp frisson of fear ran through her body, but she refused to give in to it or to be intimidated by it, or by him. Stubbornly she stood her ground.

His close proximity to her in the passage though was making her feel acutely claustrophobic. She had always had a fear of small enclosed spaces, something to do perhaps with the fact that once as a young child she had become trapped in a cupboard, but as she turned intending to walk away, she froze with shock as Seb suddenly reached for her, taking hold of her upper arm to restrain her as he told her furiously, 'Oh no you don't.... *What* gives you the right to sit in judgement of me?' he demanded curtly. 'Have you ever been married? Have you ever had a child? No, of course you haven't, you're…'

You're one of fortune's favourites he had been about to tell her. You're cushioned and protected from the realities of life by your parents and your background, but when he saw the white, tight look that drove the colour from her face and felt the way she froze, tensing her body almost as though he had physically hurt her, he stopped while his scientist's analytical brain tried to process all the conflicting information he was receiving.

Katie stared at him. *How* had he guessed her increasingly humiliating secret? She could feel her heart racing, her body taut with anxiety. He couldn't possibly have actually guessed how she really felt, could he?

From the moment Gareth and Louise had announced their love for one another Katie had made a fierce promise to herself that she would somehow find a way of making a fulfilling life for herself without Gareth in it. And she had worked hard and determinedly towards this goal.

She had a career that she found very challenging and fulfilling, a family and friends who she truly loved and who she knew truly loved her in return. And she was determined that she would never ever allow her love for Gareth to turn to bitterness or envy over her twin's happiness. But at the same time, deep down inside, she knew there was a part of her that suffered, not just a sense of loss but a sense of insecurity as well over the fact that she had not experienced the kind of sexual fulfilment she had often heard her peers discussing.

She had tried to reassure herself that there was nothing to be ashamed of in feeling not just a little enviously curious about how it must feel to share true sexual intimacy with a lover, but also a little anxious about the fact that because of her love for Gareth she had allowed herself to become isolated on her own small personal island of inexperience and inhibition.

Of course, the thought of sex for sex's sake was naturally totally repugnant to her, but she couldn't help wishing sometimes that way back before she had met and fallen for Gareth she could have known the rite of passage that would have meant that she did not now have that irritating gap in her life's experience, that worrying chink of insecurity in her female armour.

And certainly the last thing she wanted now was to have Seb Cooke finding that chink and taunting her for it.

Pulling away from him she demanded sharply,

'Let go of me…'

Let go of her… Seb hadn't even realised he was still holding her arm, but once he did…once she had drawn his attention to the fact that she was virtually his prisoner, she who had dared to accuse him…to criticise and condemn him…

The passageway wasn't very well lit by its single solitary small window, but there was more than enough light coming in through it for Seb to see the shocked disbelieving expression widen Katie's eyes as he closed the distance between them and tightened his grip on her arm.

'Stop it…*what* are you doing?' Katie protested frantically as she felt the hard heat of his body pressing hers against the passage wall, one hand on her shoulder, the other on her waist as he held her pinned there.

There wasn't time for her to feel frightened or to do anything more to try to express her outrage as he bent his head and covered her half-open mouth with his own.

Thanks to the unwanted attentions of her ex-boss Katie knew exactly how it felt to have a man kiss her against her will, but the sensations, the emotions, that coursed through her body as *Seb* kissed her bore no resemblance whatsoever to those she had experienced then.

Dizzily she wondered where they were and why in their place she was experiencing this odd feeling of lightheadedness; why she was hearing this deafening, thudding rushing sound that reminded her of breaking surf, pounding on a beach. She recognised it was, in actual fact, the roar of her pulse combined with the frantic surge of her heartbeat and she wondered, too, why her mouth seemed to be actually enjoying the sensation of the hard warmth of Seb's expertly caressing it, but before she could answer any of these questions, her brain went into overload, short circuiting its own ability to reason or analyse *any* of what was happening.... Her eyelashes fluttered, her body softened, her hand lifted to touch Seb's face as a small sound of sensual pleasure purred in her throat.

Seb lifted his hand from Katie's waist to the temptingly soft curve of her breast. Through her top and her bra he could feel the delicate pout of her nipple. Desire kicked through him in a shocking breath-stopping surge. Against his hand Katie's nipple hardened provocatively.

As Seb's body read her responsiveness to him it reacted instinctively and Katie's sensually soft purr gave way to a shocked strangled gasp as she felt the betraying hardness of Seb's body.

Outside, behind the closed door, one of the children called Katie's name. As Seb heard it, it brought him back to reality. Immediately he lifted his body away from Katie's releasing her and just as immediately Katie pushed herself away from him and darted down the passage.

The hallway was empty—thankfully—and Katie headed instinctively for the stairs and the sanctuary of her bedroom.

From outside in the garden she could hear the laughter and chatter of her parents' guests but *she* felt as remote from them as though she were on another planet, their voices nothing more than a backdrop to the appalled anguish of her own thoughts. Her whole body was trembling, shuddering from head to foot, galvanised by what she told herself was her total revulsion for what had happened.

The way Seb Cooke had treated her, *touched* her, was unforgivable...*unforgettable*...an insult...an *assault* against both her emotions and her most dearly held moral beliefs. She hadn't *encouraged* him, she hadn't *wanted* him.

Hot-faced she closed her eyes, choking back the devastatingly honest inner voice that told her that she wasn't being truthful with herself.

Squeezing her eyes tightly closed Katie whispered under her breath, 'All right, so I did...react to him, but that was just *physical...any* man could have...' Biting her lip she opened her eyes. Any man could have *what*? Exacted the same response from her. If *that* was true...

Frenziedly she whirled round and paced the floor. It was because she had been thinking about Gareth... It was *Gareth* who she really wanted...who she loved, and it had been a combination of that love for him and her anger at Seb's obviously intended, if not actually uttered, jibe that she was sexually untouched and frustrated...that she was—oh the shame of it— still a virgin.

How had he guessed...known...? Katie closed her eyes as a fresh wave of anguish-fuelled despair drenched her.

At her age she was past the stage where her virginity could be considered a praiseworthy indication of her respect for herself and her determination not to rush into sexual experimentation simply for its own sake.

Her discovery while at university that she loved Gareth had prevented her from following the path taken by most of her peers and forming an intimate loving relationship with a fellow student. The result was that now she was almost something of an oddity, an adult who was not really properly a woman at all. Only she knew how left out, how uncomfortable, how ashamed she felt on those occasions when her female family peers and most especially, her twin sister, appeared with that bemused, slightly dazed and wholly femalely smug look in their eyes which said that they had recently enjoyed good sex. But even worse than that were those times when her twin Louise tried to coax her to confide in her.

'Who are you dreaming about?' she had teased Katie the last time they had seen one another. 'Do I *know* him...?'

Katie had shaken her head of course, retreating immediately behind a protective wall of cool hauteur which had left Louise looking both bewildered and hurt. But how *could* she tell her that the man she had been daydreaming over was Louise's own husband?

Determinedly Katie gritted her teeth. What had happened with Seb Cooke had simply been an expression of her very natural longing to be able to offer someone her own sensuality, she was sure of it. A very dangerous expression of course, but the relief of knowing there was a plausible, *acceptable* reason for the way she had let herself go in his arms, the way she had not just responded to him but allowed him to *see* how much he was arousing her, was such that she immediately began to feel more like her normal self.

It would have been unbearable to have had to face him knowing that she had actually wanted Seb. But *he* still thought that, she reminded herself.

Downstairs, Seb was saying his 'goodbyes' to his

hostess. Fortunately their stay had only been a brief one as Chrissie was expecting her parents down to visit the following day and she and Guy still had to pick up Anthony from Guy's sister.

He still had no idea what on earth had come over him for those few minutes he had held Katie Crighton in his arms, or rather he was perfectly well aware *what* had, but what he did *not* know was *why* it had. He had known far more forthright women, women who had made it *more* than plain that they would love him to take them to bed, and had been able to turn away from them without even the merest twinge of the savage flood of desire that *Katie* had aroused in him.

Anger and desire. As a scientist he ought to know that there was no more potentially dangerous sexual combination and as a scientist, too, he ought also to know that as a *man* his desire and his arousal were simply physical reactions… Maybe. But as a *man* he *also* knew that what he had felt when he touched Katie had had the same raw, powerful energy that nature herself possessed and as yet man had found no satisfactory way of controlling. Ask any scientist who had tried to find a way of combatting a hurricane, a tidal flood, a volcano or an earthquake… Damn the woman, she was the *last* kind of complication he needed in his life, now or at any time. Even so, just for a moment he allowed himself the luxury of closing his eyes and briefly reliving that moment out of time when she had opened hers and looked at him, her eyes full of shocked liquid pleasure. Had she looked into his and seen there just what he was thinking? Feeling…wanting…? Just how *much* he had yearned to have her then lying naked on a bed beneath him while he licked the damp salt taste of her pleasure from her body and felt her quiver in the aftermath of her orgasm while he did so.

A bad father and a bad husband he might have been, but as Sandra had once openly and frankly told him, as a lover his sensuality had totally overwhelmed her.

A sensual scientist. It was a contradiction in terms, two imperfect halves that when put together rubbed and jarred against one another causing friction and pain.

In the front seat of the car Chrissie commented quietly to Guy, 'Katie still doesn't look very well. I don't think she's been as happy as she used to be since Louise got married... I suppose it must be hard for her, them being twins...'

'Mmm....' Guy agreed. 'She did seem rather subdued, but then she always has been the quieter of the two of them. Well, at least she's got Louise's visit home for Ben's party to look forward to.'

'What did *you* think of her, Seb?' Guy asked and then laughed, 'Or shouldn't we ask? There were certainly some sparks flying between the two or you.'

'I found her rather too idealistic and over-emotional,' Seb responded curtly. 'Not my type at all.'

In their front seats Guy and Chrissie heard Seb's response. It had been unexpectedly curt and did not exactly bode well for Katie and Seb's future as close neighbours.

CHAPTER FIVE

FOR the umpteenth time since she had arrived at work, Katie smoothed down the skirt of her impressively formal black suit. She couldn't remember ever having dressed for work with such anxiety and awareness. This suit was one she had bought in London at Louise's urging and was much more her sort of thing than Katie's own.

The jacket was immaculately tailored, the skirt short and straight. It was an outfit that breathed professionalism and power. In it, with her hair smoothed back she looked, Katie had decided, impressively formidable and there was no way that *anyone*, but most especially Seb Cooke with whom she had an appointment in fifteen minutes' time, was going to get the wrong impression about her attitude towards him. He was a *client* and, of course, that was *all* and she intended to treat him as such.

'Goodness. *You* look smart,' Olivia commented as she walked into the room and did a small double take as she studied Katie's suit. 'Very elegant.'

'It's Armani,' Katie felt impelled to tell her, admitting wryly, 'Louise chose it…'

'Mmm… It's the kind of suit that men visualise a woman wearing with absolutely nothing on underneath,' Olivia murmured teasingly. 'Or so Caspar would have had me believe when I bought one.'

Normally Katie would have taken her comment with a good humoured pinch of salt but the way Seb had behaved towards her, her own reaction to him, their aggression and the passion which had burst into life between them, had put her so much on edge that instead she demanded flatly,

'I hope you aren't serious.'

'Men are *never more* serious than when they're talking about sex,' Olivia responded dryly. 'I promise you that when Caspar saw me wearing what I had innocently imagined was a perfectly respectable and business-like suit to go to court in, he told me that the only "briefs" that would be on everyone's mind in the courtroom would be mine and that in those *male* minds they would most definitely be black and silky. Absurd, I know.' She gave a rueful grimace. 'I had a hard time getting my *own* head round it, but apparently there's a deep in-built male psychological reason for it, something to do with their need to compete with and diminish a woman's worldly power, a throw-back to their childhood when they had to learn to detach themselves from their mothers and learn how to become men... They're quite sad sometimes really, aren't they, poor things,' Olivia continued cheerfully, pausing as their receptionist came in to tell Katie, 'Seb Cooke is here to see you.'

'Mmm... Seb Cooke.' Olivia rolled her eyes naughtily and told Katie robustly,

'Now, in *your* shoes, were *I* single and fancy free, I rather suspect that if I had a Seb Cooke seated across my desk from me, *I'd* be the one doing the mental undressing and the sexy intimate visualisation...'

'Olivia!' Katie protested. 'I'm *not*... He *doesn't*...'

But Olivia was already on her way to her own office, leaving Katie to ask the receptionist to show Seb into her own small cupboard-like room.

She hadn't seen him since the incident at her parents' home and as he walked in and she indicated to him that he was to sit down, Katie was sharply aware of how relaxed and in control *he* appeared in contrast to her own nervous discomfort.

'This shouldn't take very long,' she told him as crisply and professionally as she could as she, too, sat down. 'The contracts are pretty straightforward and it's only a matter of reading and signing them and then completion can take place virtually immediately.'

'Good. I've got a business conference to attend soon and if possible I want to move in to the apartment beforehand.'

Katie didn't say anything. She, too, ought to have been looking forward to her own occupation of *her* apartment—she *would* have been doing so had it not been for the fact that *he* was going to be her closest neighbour.

Had what happened over the weekend occurred before she had made her decision to buy the apartment, *would* she have changed her mind?

Like her, Seb was wearing a formal business suit, its jacket unfastened over an immaculately laundered crisp, white shirt and a subtly patterned tie. Who *ironed* his shirts? she wondered absently. Surely not Seb himself. Her father had occasionally ironed his own when they were all growing up and he had needed one of his 'court' shirts in a rush. He had even ironed their school shirts once when her mother hadn't been well. Katie could still remember how oddly creased they had remained despite his best efforts, the mystery not being explained until her mother had discovered he had had the iron on the wrong setting.

Seb watched her furrowed forehead as he recognised both the deliberate distance she was putting between them and her not quite totally hidden anxiety.

What did she think he was? Some kind of potential sexual bully who might pounce on her given the least excuse? There was no point in him saying anything. How *could* he when he couldn't even furnish himself with a rational explanation for what had happened…for what was *still* happening he recognised as she leaned across the desk pushing the contract towards him and he caught the clean, freshly washed scent of her hair and his stomach muscles contracted sharply in reaction to the savage surge of desire that kicked through him.

As she watched Seb virtually openly recoil back from her as she pushed the contract towards him, Katie could feel her body and then her face start to burn with chagrin. What did he think she was going to *do*…flirt with him; come on to him? The urge to tell him that he was wrong, that she loved someone else, was almost overwhelming.

Deliberately keeping her eyes down so that she didn't have to look into his face, she watched him sign the contract. He had very long, strong looking fingers with well-kept clean nails. His hands, while large, possessed a flexibility that for some reason made her heart start to beat far too heavily.

Briefly she closed her eyes and then wished that she had not done so as she had a momentary vision of those hands, *his* hands resting against her own skin, her *naked* skin, stroking and caressing it, cupping the soft flesh of her breasts whilst his fingers…

In her mind's eye she could see the hard darkness of his hand contrasting with the softer paleness of her own flesh. She could *feel* the hot, dizzying ripples of sensation spreading through her body from that point of contact like liquid fire. She could actually see, as though somehow she were standing outside herself as another observer, the way she was lifting her own head and looking at him, focusing on his face…his eyes, his mouth, but what shocked and appalled her most of all was not what she was mentally visualising but the *sensations she was experiencing*—the hot, sharp female pleasure she was feeling…the longing.

Her office was suddenly as claustrophobic as the passageway of her parents' home had been and she could feel the same sense of panic and anxiety beginning to rush through her. She felt hot…faint… weak…and she wanted…

Seb had finished reading the contract, which he had signed and was now passing it back to her. With a tremendous effort of will Katie forced herself to focus on the reality of why he was here in her office.

Seb, meanwhile, was already standing up, patently anxious to leave, but surely not so anxious as she was for him to go.

So why then, as she witnessed his signature, did she have this absurd desire to cry?

Shakily she pushed her own chair back and stood up.

'We'll inform you just as soon as contracts have been exchanged and completion takes place so that you can pick up the keys to your apartment,' she told him quietly.

'I take it you're still going ahead with your own purchase?' Seb asked.

Katie tensed. What was he trying to say? That he had expected her to pull out of her purchase? That he didn't *want* her as his closest neighbour?

Lifting her head she looked him fully in the face for the first time since he had walked into her office.

'Is there any reason why I shouldn't?' she asked him shortly.

To her relief he didn't take up her challenge, instead merely shaking his head and walking away from her towards the door pausing once he got there to tell her, 'I shall be getting in touch with the agents to make arrangements to have the key made available so that measurements can be taken for carpets and curtains.'

'That's a matter for you to sort out with the agents,' Katie told him briefly. 'As your solicitor I have, of course, to tell you that they are under no legal obligation to allow you to have access to the property until completion actually takes place.'

'Indeed,' Seb drawled, equally briefly, opening the door as he informed her dryly, 'However, I wasn't actually *seeking* your *professional* advice, I was simply taking the precaution of warning you as my closest neighbour that should you happen to see anyone coming to or going from my apartment it will merely be the interior designers I'm commissioning to furnish the place for me in case their presence alarmed you.'

Interior designers. Katie digested this information in silence. *She* was planning to call on the combined expertise and advice of her mother and female relatives for help to decorate and furnish her own apartment.

Neither did she have any intention of telling him that the only person whose presence was likely to alarm her was his.

After he had gone she opened the office window and breathed in deep lungfuls of air. But even after she had closed the window she could still smell the subtle scent that was purely *him* and in the end she had to resort to taking her work out into the general office to escape from the effect it was having on her.

'Oh Dad, *please*, I'd *love* to go.'

Seb grimaced a little at being confronted by his daughter's enthusiasm for something he himself had hoped to avoid becoming involved in.

'It is a very special day,' Chrissie told him winningly adding her own form of gentle persuasion to Charlotte's enthusiasm.

'Mmm…and as a member of Aarlston hierarchy here in Haslewich I suspect that you will be expected to put in an appearance,' Guy chimed in.

They were discussing the weekend's forthcoming 'Fun Day' that Aarlston were sponsoring at Fitzburgh Place for the single parents and their families who lived in Ruth Crighton's sheltered accommodation and to which Aarlston employees were also permitted to take their own families.

'Have you met Lord Astlegh yet?' Guy was continuing, and when Seb shook his head Chrissie informed him with a smile,

'You'll like him. He's charming. Very much a gentleman of the old school.'

'Mmm… I can remember scrumping apples from the estate when I was a boy. His gamekeeper certainly wasn't very gentlemanly when he evicted us and threatened us with horrible reprisals if we ever set foot there again,' Seb remembered, looking rueful.

'*You*, scrumping apples? Dad… I *can't* believe it,' Charlotte laughed, shaking her head teasingly.

'Oh, he was quite a young tearaway as a boy,' Guy

told Charlotte straight-faced. 'You ask my sister Laura…'

'No such thing,' Seb denied.

'But we are going to the Fun Day, aren't we?' Charlotte coaxed. 'It will be fun.'

As he looked into his daughter's hopeful face, Seb knew that he had no real option.

Although he hadn't shown it he had been thrilled when Charlotte had telephoned earlier in the week to ask if she could spend the weekend with him.

He had finished work a little earlier in order to spend as much time as he could with her and it had been Chrissie's suggestion that they all have dinner together at the restaurant owned and run by Guy's sister Frances and her family.

Charlotte had fast become a favourite with those members of the Cooke family she had met, and if anything she fitted in far better and enjoyed their company much more than he could remember doing as a child, Seb acknowledged.

'So, it's decided then. What time are we going to go?' Charlotte demanded excitedly.

'Well, I'd recommend a reasonably early start,' Guy suggested, but then he paused and frowned and turned to Seb asking him, 'Didn't you say you had someone to see at the apartment in the morning?'

'The interior designer you recommended,' Seb told him. 'I've got this conference coming up and…'

'Oh yes, of course. Well Jamie is very professional. Once you've given her an idea of what you want you'll be able to leave everything safely in her hands.'

'Has Katie Crighton moved into *her* apartment yet?' Charlotte asked Seb interestedly. 'She's nice. I…'

'She'll be moving in next week,' Chrissie told her, adding with a smile, 'She was complaining the other day that Maddy had walked her feet off when she took her on a tour of some fabric warehouses. Maddy is married to Katie's elder brother Max,' Chrissie explained for Charlotte's sake.

'She and Max and their children live at Queensmead which is Ben Crighton's home and I still can't believe how Maddy has managed to turn it from the rather drab and almost unwelcoming house it was into the lovely, warm *home* it is now.'

'I think it's called love,' Guy told her softly.

'Mmm… Well, she's certainly transformed the place. She's marvellously multi-talented and seems to have a gift for finding a good bargain.'

'Katie was telling me that thanks to Maddy, she's found the most wonderful fabric for her curtains at a fraction of the original price.'

The arrival of Frances to chat with them and take their order put a stop to Chrissie's conversation for which Seb was profoundly thankful. He had not seen anything of Katie since he had visited her office to sign his contract and he suspected that she was deliberately avoiding him. He had told himself that he was glad, that the last thing he wanted was the kind of complications in his life that getting involved in any kind of relationship with her would bring him.

He was bound to see her tomorrow though, of course. From what he had heard, the Crighton family would be out in full force at the Fun Day. Ruth Crighton herself was apparently flying over from America with Grant, specially to be there.

'Come on everyone, it's time we were leaving.'

As Katie took a last gulp of her coffee early

Saturday morning, she reflected that the annual Fun Day, with the constant stream of arrivals milling about in her parents' comfortable kitchen, was becoming almost as much of an institution as the charity itself.

Up at Queensmead, Maddy would have a full house, too, and down in the town square the coaches hired to take everyone to Fitzburgh Place would already be filling up with excited children and their families.

One innovative practice that Ruth and Maddy had brought into existence had been the creation of special family rooms within the houses occupied by single mothers and their children so that the men, or more often boys, who had fathered them but who, for one reason or another, had not previously been a part of those children's lives, could be encouraged to visit and establish contact with their children.

Another innovative scheme, recently been put into practice, taught the young parents parenting skills, and Maddy was currently trying to persuade the local secondary school to allow her to establish a scheme that would mean teenage girls and boys became responsible for a computer programmed 'baby doll' which would mimic the responses of a real baby and give them a taste of just what parenthood was *really* all about.

'It's not about frightening them into *not* having sex, but rather of showing them, warning them, just how much an unplanned pregnancy will change their lives,' Maddy had told Katie earnestly when she had been explaining what they hoped to do.

'I'm so pleased that Louise and Gareth were able to make it,' Katie heard her mother enthusing as she expertly loaded empty breakfast dishes into the dishwasher. 'I can't believe how much little Nick has grown.'

Nick was Louise and Gareth's young son and Katie forced herself to smile as her mother started to extol the virtues of her small grandson.

'Goodness, just look at the time,' Jenny Crighton exclaimed. 'Katie, will you run upstairs and warn Louise that we've got to leave in ten minutes.'

By the time Seb and Charlotte reached Fitzburgh Place the Fun Day was in full swing. They had stopped off on the way at the apartment where Seb had arranged to meet the interior designer who, as Guy had promised him, proved to be extremely professional and knowledgeable.

'You want something comfortable and homey,' Charlotte had informed him when Jamie had been asking him about his own preferences for the decor of the apartment. 'Not something high-tech and modern...'

'I want something that's in keeping with the period of the building and the features of the rooms,' Seb told the designer calmly. 'The office you can leave to me... I intend to commission a desk specifically to house my computer and files. Oh, and I shall need a proper bed in the master bedroom, so please make sure it's both large and comfortable.'

'What are you planning to do in there?' Charlotte had teased him. 'Hold orgies?'

'Believe it or not...*sleep*,' Seb had corrected her dryly.

Predictably Charlotte had had her own opinions about how she thought *her* room should be furnished, explaining to the designer just what she wanted and then pausing breathlessly to ask Seb if he approved of her choice.

'I don't mind, just so long as you don't have it Barbie-doll pink…' Seb told her truthfully.

Charlotte had flashed him an indignant look.

'I grew out of *that* years ago, Dad.'

Now, as they left his parked car, Seb surveyed the excited throng of people milling around and reflected that it was just as well that it had turned out to be a warm sunny day.

'Oh look Dad, over there, that must be Katie's twin sister and her husband,' Charlotte told him tugging on his arm and directing his attention to where a girl who was quite definitely Katie's twin was standing, or rather leaning against the impressively tall man standing with her.

Yes, she was quite definitely Katie's twin, Seb recognised, and yet at the same time he knew that he would have known instantly that she *wasn't* Katie, even without the difference in their hairstyles.

'I wonder where Katie is?' Charlotte mused. 'Perhaps we could go over and ask her sister.'

Seb raised his eyebrows. 'I don't think that's a good idea. Katie will probably be very busy,' he warned her.

Ten minutes later as they walked past the informal crèche, which had been organised for the children, Seb realised that he had been right.

Katie was in the middle of a large circle of children reading them a story oblivious to their presence until Charlotte waved to her.

Although her voice faltered and her face changed colour slightly, she continued with what she was doing causing Seb to suggest to Charlotte that they should move on and leave her in peace.

'No, she's almost finished, but *you* don't have to stay if you want to walk round. I'll catch up with you at the tea stall in half an hour or so,' Charlotte told him.

Shrugging his shoulders Seb left her where she was and walked away to talk with Saul who he had spotted standing several yards away with his family.

'Charlotte,' Katie smiled, as her story finished. Charlotte came hurrying towards her.

'I've just seen your twin sister,' Charlotte told her warmly. 'She was over past the bouncy castle with her husband and the most gorgeous little boy.'

'Their son, Nick,' Katie agreed.

'I think what you're all doing here is wonderful,' Charlotte told her. 'My mother always says how lucky she was that after she and Dad decided their marriage wasn't working out, Dad always made sure that he provided for me financially and then, of course, Mum met George and they fell in love.' She gave Katie a rueful grin.

'Dad tends to beat himself about the chest with guilt a bit because he wasn't there for me when I was growing up, but to tell the truth, George was such a wonderful loving step-father that I didn't even realise for ages that he *wasn't* my birth father, and then once I did... I was curious about Dad of course, but once Ma had explained that she had felt that it would only confuse me and make me feel torn between them both if she encouraged Dad to be there more for me, I felt she'd made the right decision.'

'It was actually *George* who encouraged me to go for it when Dad did contact me. I was apprehensive about how he would react but when Dad explained to me how much he regretted the break-up of his and Mum's marriage and how bad he felt about it and me, how much he'd wanted to make contact with me but hadn't felt that he had the right to do so...

'He and Mum have both said separately to me that they never should have married... They confused lust with love. Have you ever been in love?' she asked Katie curiously.

Too taken aback to feel offended by the intimacy of her curiosity Katie didn't know what to say, but fortunately Charlotte didn't seem to notice her hesitancy, continuing instead,

'I wish that Dad could find someone to love... I think part of the reason he buried himself in his work when I was a baby was because it was so hard for him to face up to the fact that he and Ma had married for the wrong reasons and that they didn't really love one another,' she told Katie wisely. 'I'd hate to get to Dad's age without ever having loved anyone properly and being loved back by them,' she added abruptly.

She giggled, confiding, 'Dad thinks that every boy I date is going to seduce me, but I'm not ready for that kind of relationship yet. I've got too much to do, but one day soon I *shall* be. Dad has this bit of a thing about the reputation of the Cooke men as wicked seducers. Although he never really talks about it, I think that's why he insisted on marrying Mum instead of just going to bed with her. Of course, I know things were different when they were young but I don't think there's anything wrong in someone wanting to explore their sexuality. It's part of growing up, isn't it?

'When I *do* commit myself to a man, a relationship, I want it to be because I know beyond any kind of doubt that I love him, so I want to make sure that I've got the sex thing sorted out first. I mean for both sexes, losing one's virginity is kind of a very major rite of passage, isn't it, and of course I want it to be with the right person.

'I expect you felt the same when you lost yours,' she added questioningly.

Katie could feel herself floundering, lost in a sticky morass of conflicting emotions and thoughts. Was Charlotte trying to seek her advice or was she simply using her as a sounding board? The age gap between them wasn't huge, but it was enough for Katie to know that in Charlotte's eyes they stood on opposite sides of the chasm that was experience. If only Charlotte knew the truth. From what she had just said Katie felt that Charlotte's outlook and attitude towards sex was far more mature than her own, but then Charlotte wasn't in love with a man she could never have.

Charlotte's comments about her father had been equally enlightening, although after the way he had behaved towards her, Katie was finding it extremely hard to reconcile the man who was so moralistic that he had married a woman he didn't love with the one who had behaved so sexually demandingly towards her.

'Hi… I've come to relieve you.'

Katie looked up and smiled as Tullah, Saul's wife, came up to join them.

'Oh good, that means you can come with me and help me find Dad,' Charlotte informed Katie as she slipped her arm through hers.

Find *Seb*! That was the *last* thing Katie wanted to

do, but Charlotte obviously wasn't going to take 'no' for an answer and so reluctantly Katie found herself walking beside her as Charlotte led the way to the spot where she had arranged to meet Seb.

CHAPTER SIX

'LOOK who I've brought with me,' Charlotte told Seb as she gaily wriggled her way through the crowds to his side, tugging Katie after her.

'I'll bet you're dying for something to drink after all that story-telling,' she teased Katie as she slipped her free arm through her father's so that she was standing between them.

'Dad…' she began, but Katie, guessing what was coming and knowing that Seb would have as little appetite for her company as she did for his forestalled Charlotte, telling her quickly, 'No Charlotte, it's alright. My mother has brought a family picnic and she'll be expecting me to join them.'

Oddly as she looked at him, instead of seeming relieved at the prospect of being freed from her company Seb was actually frowning. She was just on the point of disengaging herself from Charlotte when a small boy suddenly dashed towards her carrying a sharp pointed stick which must at one stage have had a balloon attached to it from the strips of brightly coloured plastic dangling from it. It wasn't the burst balloon that caused Katie to dart forward anxiously snatching him up as he started to fall, however, but the knowledge that the sharp end of the stick was potentially dangerous to him.

As she grabbed him he gave a loud wail of protest that quickly turned to a broad beaming smile as Katie

471

deftly distracted his attention by cuddling him and asking him who he was.

'Me Joey,' he told her flashing her an impishly devilish Cooke smile so like Seb's that her heart suddenly lurched against her ribs causing her to miss a breath.

'Joey…there you are…'

Katie turned round as a plump dark-headed woman came hurrying towards them. Immediately Joey stretched out his arms wriggling to be handed over as he cried eagerly,

'Mum…'

'He was going to fall,' Katie told the young woman as she handed him over, not wanting her to think that she had had any ulterior motive in picking him up.

'Yes, I know… I saw you,' the other woman told her. As she cuddled her son her eyes studied Katie; their velvety dark gaze so intense and hypnotic that Katie couldn't drag her own gaze away.

'Here,' the woman added meaningfully as she touched her forehead. 'I sensed he was in danger and then I saw you reaching for him…' Her eyes flashed with pride and hauteur as she saw Katie's expression.

'If you don't believe me ask him,' she told Katie with a small toss of her head looking at Seb. '*He's* one of us and he knows that some of us have the sight…the gift…'

Katie knew it too. The ability for certain female members of the Cooke clan to foretell future events was a well documented local fact, but this was the first time *she* personally had been the focus of witnessing it in action.

'I wasn't doubting you,' Katie reassured her, gently reaching out her hand to smooth the little boy's tangled curls. His hair was dark like his mother's—like his

Seb's—and wonderfully soft to touch. Seb's child…
Seb's son would have just such hair. For a moment
she thought she must be falling under some extra-
dinary spell the gypsy woman had cast, for unbeliev-
ably she suddenly had a mental image of Seb's child,
as potent and lifelike as though he actually already
existed. But almost immediately her common sense
reasserted itself and she told herself that she was simply being over-imaginative.

But then, just as they were about to walk away, the
gypsy woman reached for Katie's arm and told her
softly, nodding in Charlotte's direction,

'She is not a child you have made together but there
will be one and very soon.'

Releasing Katie she turned to Seb who had listened
to the entire exchange in silence.

'*You* do not believe me, but it is true,' she told him
fiercely. 'Give me your hand,' she instructed Katie,
reaching for it and taking hold of it before she could
draw back from her.

It was ridiculous of her to feel that she was in the
presence of a mystical power as awesome and ancient
as life itself Katie acknowledged, and yet that *was*
how she felt as the girl pored over her hand and then
pronounced firmly, 'It is written quite clearly here.
You are one another's fates, although neither of you
has recognised it yet, but before you can do so, you,'
she told Seb, turning to him and addressing him almost sharply, 'must close the door on what you are
using to deny yourself your future. There is no need
for it, no place for it. And you,' she told Katie a little
more gently, 'must close the door on that which you
know can never rightfully belong to you…'

For a moment none of them spoke. A stillness—a

silence—seemed to envelop them like an invisible cloak and then excitedly Charlotte was holding out her hand to the girl pleading, 'What about me? What can you see in *my* hand?'

The woman's expression lightened as she released Katie's hand and took hold of Charlotte's.

'I see that you still have a long journey to complete along the path of knowledge before you begin your life's work. And I see, too…' Very gently she closed Charlotte's fingers over her palm and then told her slowly, 'I see that you will be among those who will give to the world a very great deal of good.'

And then abruptly she released Charlotte's hand and was gone, disappearing into the swirling crowd leaving the three of them to stand in silence while they digested her predictions.

'Well…' Charlotte gasped. 'Wasn't that *extraordinary*… Did you notice her eyes? I felt almost as though she was hypnotising me.'

'She probably was, or at least attempting to do so,' her father told her curtly, adding grimly, 'It's all rubbish, of course.'

'I really must go,' Katie told them both. There was absolutely no way she could bring herself to look at Seb, not after what the girl had said. Seb was right, it *had* all been rubbish, a piece of ineffective guesswork on the other woman's part based on the fact that they were together. She had probably assumed that they were already a couple and that Katie, who quite obviously couldn't be Charlotte's mother, *must* want to have Seb's child herself. It was silly for her to feel so hyper-sensitively aware of that mental image she had had of that small dark-haired boy so very, very like Seb. That had simply been a coincidence that was all.

'She obviously thought that the two of you were a couple,' Charlotte commented with a wide smile.

'No.'

'No way…'

Charlotte looked from her father to Katie and then back again as they both uttered their denials at the same time.

'Oh, but you heard what she said,' she teased. 'It's inevitable…*fate*…'

'I'd say the explanation is much closer to hand and owes far more to a vivid imagination than any supernatural influence,' Seb announced dryly.

'Katie—there you are. Ma has sent us to look for you so that we can eat lunch.'

With the sudden appearance of Louise, with Gareth at her side and their son in his arms, it was tempting to tell Seb that he was wrong and that a certain mischievous and even malign unseen force appeared to enjoy wreaking havoc with her composure, but of course Katie knew she would do—could do—no such thing, not without revealing just *why* the arrival of her twin sister with her husband and baby should be so uncomfortable for her.

It was normal custom in the Crighton family and most especially her own generation of it for both its female and male members to embrace, hug and kiss one another in greeting, but after the first time she had frozen back in anguish when Gareth had attempted to hug her when he and Louise had become a couple. Gareth had always kept his distance from her and Katie had been profoundly grateful to him for doing so. But contradictorily on this occasion, all too aware of Seb's keen eyes and Charlotte's curious ones on them, she almost wished that he would step forward and give her a brotherly hug.

Of course introductions had to be made and while Charlotte cooed enthusiastically over Nick, Gareth and Seb exchanged male pleasantries, each patently calmly assessing the other.

'You'll never *guess* what's just happened,' Charlotte started to tell Louise excitedly, while Katie's heart sank. Only let her twin get wind of what the girl had predicted... But to her relief instead of immediately teasing them both over the girl's prediction, Louise was uncharacteristically tactful and silent on the subject, simply reiterating their parents were waiting to begin lunch.

'Mmm...lunch, that sounds like a good idea, Dad,' Charlotte told her father enthusiastically. 'I'm starving...'

As she saw the rather rueful look Seb was giving the fast food outlets close by, Louise suggested promptly,

'Look, why don't you join us. Knowing Ma there'll be more than enough...'

'Oh, no...'

'Thank you, but no...'

As both Seb and Katie spoke together, Louise raised her eyebrows a little, her attention focusing rather too keenly for Katie's liking on what she knew to be her give-away flushed face.

But before she or Seb could reiterate their rejections of Louise's suggestion, Guy and Chrissie were coming towards them.

'I was just inviting Sebastian and Charlotte to join

us for lunch,' Louise explained immediately to her mother's ex-business partner.

'You were...that's good because I've just seen Jenny myself and accepted her invitation that the five of us should join you...'

Her heart sinking Katie automatically turned to go to her sister's side but as she did so, Guy asked her apologetically, 'Katie, would you mind taking your father's keys and going to the car to get the cutlery your mother asked me to collect. Anthony needs changing before lunch and our car is parked on the other side of the field, so...'

Only too glad to have an opportunity to get away from Sebastian Cooke, Katie immediately nodded her head and took her father's car keys from Guy.

'We're in our usual picnic spot,' Louise told her sister cheerfully as she fell into step beside Chrissie to exchange mother and baby stories.

Katie had gone less than a few dozen yards when she suddenly heard Seb calling her name.

Turning round she watched warily as he hurried to catch up with her.

'I just wanted to have a few words with you before we join the rest of your family for lunch,' he told her curtly. 'All that rubbish that fake ''fortune teller'' was spouting had absolutely nothing to do with me,' he informed her unnecessarily.

Immediately Katie could feel her temper starting to burn.

'Well, I certainly didn't have anything to do with her predictions,' she snapped back immediately. 'The very idea is ridiculous. For a start we'd have to...'

She stopped, her face going scarlet at the unexpectedly explicit mental images of just what they would have to do to make the woman's predictions come true filled her mind.

'We'd have to what?' Seb picked up softly for her. 'Go to bed together. Is that what you were going to say?'

Primly Katie looked away from him before answering in a very stifled voice, 'Actually no. What I was going to say is that we would have to...to have a very different relationship from the one we do have...'

'Like I said, we'd have to go to bed together,' Seb told her succinctly. 'And there's no way that's going to happen.'

Katie couldn't help it, she gave a small gasp of chagrined pride as he delivered his immediate and unequivocal rejection of her.

'You're right,' she agreed quickly and decisively. 'It isn't. The kind of man I would want...the kind of man I find attractive,' she hastily amended, 'Is... would be...'

'Would be what?' Seb challenged her sharply.

Katie was too caught up in her feelings to be either cautious or tactful.

'He wouldn't be anything like you,' she told him pointedly. 'He'd be kind...gentle...caring...' Her voice softened betrayingly, her eyes suddenly remote and dreamy as she continued a little huskily, 'He'd be wise and...and understanding and he'd...he'd never...' She stopped and then told him fiercely, 'he would never, ever, be anything, anyone...like you...'

'No, he wouldn't,' Seb agreed grittily. 'Not me, nor any other red-blooded male. He sounds more like some mythical sexless cardboard cut-out of a man than the real thing,' he told her scathingly. 'A fictional hero who bears as much resemblance to a real man as...'

'You're just saying that because you're not like that,' Katie interrupted him defiantly. 'There are men like that...men who...'

'Men who what?' Seb immediately challenged her, falling into step beside her as Katie, fearing that she was losing ground in their argument turned on her heel and started to hurry towards the field in which her parents' car was parked.

'Let go of me,' she protested as Seb reached for her arm when she continued to ignore him.

'Not until you've answered my question,' he told her grimly. 'Men who what? Tell me exactly what it is about this mythical mate you deem so desirable— because it certainly can't be his sexuality.'

'Seb!' Katie flashed back at him immediately. 'There's more to a relationship...to love...than that...'

'Indeed there is, but I think you'll find most men— and women—want the pleasure of enjoying and arousing their chosen partner's sexual desires. You must have experienced that for yourself,' he continued curtly when Katie made no response other than tensing in his grasp as they both came to a halt opposite one another. His expression changed subtly as he looked down into her wary eyes.

'You have experienced it, haven't you, Katie?' he asked her softly.

'What I have or have not experienced is no concern of yours.' Katie defended herself valiantly.

'Perhaps not,' Seb agreed, but instead of releasing her and turning away as she had expected, he suddenly moved closer to her causing her stomach to turn in anxious protest. 'Or perhaps our fortune-teller does know something that you and I do not... Shall we find out...?'

'No...' Katie started to protest, but it was too late. Cloaked as they were by the shadows cast by the trees at the edge of the field it was dangerously easy for Seb to draw her fully into his arms, imprisoning her there as he bent his head and his mouth came down expertly and inescapably over hers.

It was a kiss more of anger and retribution than anything else, Katie was not so naive that she didn't recognise that fact.

He had resented the fortune-teller's prediction and he was angry with her because he didn't like her and this was his way of punishing her.

'No...' she managed to protest sharply against his mouth as she struggled to break free of him, her teeth accidentally grazing his bottom lip as she did so.

'What the...'

As she heard him curse Katie froze. She could taste the slight saltiness of his blood on her own tongue and was horrified by what she had done, even if he had provoked it.

'...and what you want is a gentle passive lover,' she heard him demanding savagely. 'You're a liar, Katie. You want a man whose passion matches your own, a man who...'

'What I don't want is you,' Katie told him frantically.

'And I don't want you,' Seb assured her sharply, his expression changing and holding her in paralysing thrall he added rawly, 'but I want this...'

Katie whimpered in protest as his mouth possessed hers, possessed it, seduced it...ravished it...the pres-

sure of his mouth on hers making her own lips feel
so sensitive that her whole body shook with the tiny
quivers of sensation she was feeling.

Through the dapple of the leaves on the trees she
could feel the warmth of the sun on her face but its
heat was nothing to the heat Seb was generating inside
her.

She tried to break free of him. She knew she had
to. Why were her arms entwined around him, why
was her body pressed so close to him, why was her
mouth parting beneath the pressure of his...why...?

'See, I told you you were passionate,' she could
hear Seb telling her huskily. 'The only reason you'd
ever want a meek and mild apology for a mate is so
that you could destroy and devour him like a praying
mantis...'

'Oh...'

As the cruelty of his words jerked her back to reality, Katie pulled away from him.

'You were the one who... I did nothing,' she
amended quickly, unable to look at him.

'Nothing...'

As she attempted to move away from him Seb
reached out, cupping her jaw in his hand and turning
her face up so that he could look down at her.

'Then, what's this,' he demanded, lifting her hand
to his mouth and pressing her fingers against the
bruised rawness of his bottom lip.

Giving a small, choked protest Katie pulled away.
Her eyes were beginning to fill with tears. She was
dizzy and lightheaded and somewhere deep inside her
there was a small insidious ache that frightened and
shocked her.

But before she could say or do anything she heard Guy's familiar voice calling out semi-scoldingly,

'There you are you two, Jenny thought you must have got lost...'

Later Katie assumed that she must have said and done everything that was expected and required of her during lunch. Certainly no one seemed to find her behaviour odd or out of character, but she herself was intensely, uncomfortably aware of Sebastian Cooke's presence all through the light-hearted alfresco family meal. While the others were chatting and exchanging pleasantries and banter, she was finding it hard to force down so much as a mouthful of her mother's delicious cold spread.

In fact, she noticed a little bitterly at one point, Seb seemed more at ease and relaxed than she did and as for Charlotte...it was plain that she was enjoying herself hugely. Katie could hear her telling Jenny enthusiastically how much she was enjoying life at her sixth form college.

'Being a boarder there makes it even better,' she gushed. 'The other girls are great and I've made so many new friends.'

'It must have been quite a difficult decision for you to make,' Jenny remarked to Seb.

'It was,' he agreed. 'Sandra, George and I all sat down with Charlotte to discuss it. I know she believes at sixteen that she's an adult, but while we accept that she is mature enough to make most of her own decisions about her education, it is an unfortunate fact that this modern world we live in is not always a very safe place for a young woman.

'However, the school has an excellent policy which

allows the girls some freedom while at the same time ensuring their safety.'

'Yes, we're allowed evening exeats and we can even go clubbing, just so long as there's a group of eight or more of us and we all come back together in the school minibus.

'Mum and George and Dad did take a bit of persuading to allow me to go, but it's the best "A" level college in the country for my subjects and since I'm hoping to get a place at Manchester University it made sense to move here.'

With her own cousin and younger brother at a very similar stage in their education Katie was not surprised that her mother should be so interested in Charlotte's 'A' level studies, but she wished her mother would not be quite so warm and welcoming towards Sebastian Cooke.

She was uncomfortably aware that by some fluke of circumstance, the group of adults around the picnic had separated themselves out so that she was actually now sitting closer to Seb than she was to anyone else. Unfortunately, the nearest other person to her was Gareth and she had determined to remove any remaining longings for him from her life by keeping as much distance—in every sense of the word—between herself and her brother-in-law as she could.

Still, at least she could comfort herself that Louise had not told the rest of the family about the fortuneteller's prediction and Louise, Katie fervently hoped, would never refer to it again.

However later in the day Katie discovered that her relief had been premature.

At Louise's insistence she had driven her over to

see her new apartment while Gareth had been left behind to bathe and feed Nick.

'It's *fabulous*,' Louise pronounced once the short tour was over and they were standing in the apartment's living room. 'When do you expect to move in?'

'Well, hopefully by the end of the week. The carpets should be down by then, although I'm not sure whether or not all the curtains will be finished, but Mum has offered to lend me some in the interim if they aren't.'

'Mmm… It's a *very* sophisticated bachelor-girl place,' Louise approved. 'Although…' with a twinkle in her eye she told Katie, 'Although, if what your *gypsy* friend predicted is true…'

'Seb and I…' Katie interrupted her quickly. 'We…'

But before she could finish her denial Louise was reaching out to touch her, asking her seriously and quietly, 'Can we talk? Properly, I mean…'

Katie's heart sank. This was the moment she had been dreading ever since Gareth and Louise had announced their love for one another.

'Of course…' she responded with what she knew was a forced note of jollity in her voice. 'What do you want to talk about? We…'

'Katie, come on…this is *us*…you and me… Look, I know…'

Katie froze. Louise knew *what*? That she, Katie, loved *her* husband…?

But, instead of continuing Louise shook her head and said huskily, 'We used to be so *close*, you and I. We told one another *everything*…but since Gareth and I married… You're my *twin*… I still *need* you… I always will and I *hate* feeling that there's this distance, this *barrier* between us. If I've said or done something to hurt you…'

'No. No, of course you haven't,' Katie denied quickly, terrified in case Louise continued to question her and somehow discovered the truth. It wasn't *her* fault that she, Katie, loved Gareth. It wasn't *anyone's* fault, except her own and the last thing she wanted to do was to widen the rift which Louise had so correctly pinpointed by admitting how she really felt. All that admitting her feelings could do would be to embarrass Louise and Gareth and to humiliate herself.

'It's just…' She stopped, frantically hunting for a satisfactory explanation to silence her sister's questions. 'Well, obviously things are different now that you and Gareth are married and that you have Nick.'

'Well, yes, of course,' Louise agreed, her mouth curling into a wide smile as she laughed. 'Still, by the sound of it, it won't be long before you and Seb have a child of your own… He's gorgeously sexy, Katie. *Seriously* sexy,' she underlined, rolling her eyes appreciatively. 'And if I weren't so very much in love with Gareth…'

'Louise, Seb and I…' Katie began frantically, appalled by the direction the conversation was taking and the assumptions Louise had so mistakenly leapt to.

'It's a pity the two of you didn't discover you were in love before you bought this place though. Still it's obvious that you'll make a good profit on it when you sell it. Have you made any plans yet, or…'

'Louise, we barely *know* one another,' Katie protested. 'I don't even…' Like him, never mind love him, she had been about to say but typically Louise wasn't giving her time to finish her conversation before continuing enthusiastically, 'I could see how much Charlotte has taken to you as well. That's wonderful. Mind you, you're so gentle and loving that you'd be able to cope with even the most difficult of step-children and anyone can see that Charlotte is not that. And, of course, it couldn't be better, you and Seb living so close to one another.'

'Louise...' Katie began desperately and then stopped as Louise glanced out of the window and exclaimed,

'Oh, here's Gareth. He must have wondered why we've been gone for so long. Oh Katie, I'm just *so* happy for you,' Louise told her excitedly and she turned to embrace her twin in a loving hug. 'I can tell you now that there was a time when I wondered...well, you were always so determined to defend Gareth in the early days when I was so antagonistic towards him, and I suppose because we *are* twins and because *I* love him so much, I worried that you might...'

With every word Louise spoke Katie could feel her anxiety and anguish growing. It lay like a block of ice against her heart; weighed like the heaviest of lead weights on her conscience. It was all her worst fears come to life. Louise had intuitively sensed her own feelings despite *everything* she had done to try to prevent her from doing so. Louise was her twin, her other half, and there existed between them a bond which called forth from Katie, not just her fiercest loyalty, but also a need to put Louise's needs above her own, to protect her from the hurt and pain that knowing that she, Katie, loved Gareth would cause her. She struggled with her conscience not wanting to deceive her twin but as she already knew, it was almost impossible to stop Louise once she took hold of an idea and started to run with it. And, after all, the truth would very quickly become apparent—it was so obvious that she and Seb loathed one another.

'And you won't forget about your grandfather's party, will you?' Jenny Crighton reminded Louise as she kissed her goodbye.

They had brought the car across from Belgium and were driving on to see Gareth's family in Scotland before returning to Brussels. As she hugged her mother, Louise promised her, 'We'll be there. How could we possibly miss it when it will be Katie's first formal opportunity to show Seb off to the family?'

'Seb?' Jenny questioned in surprise, 'But...'

'I could see that there was something between them straightaway,' Louise continued happily, 'and I'm just so glad for Katie, Mum. She's been so unlike her normal self just lately. That's worried me. It's funny the way things work out, isn't it?' she continued conversationally. 'If she hadn't had to give up her old job because of that awful boss who was making life so miserable for her, she would never have come home and then she wouldn't have met Seb.

'You should have seen her face when Charlotte told us what the girl at the fair had predicted for her and Seb,' Louise had chuckled. 'A baby boy no less,' she enlightened her bemused parent. 'Charlotte was thrilled to bits. No potential problems there, that's *very* clear, but then Charlotte's almost a young woman herself and since, from what Guy told me, Seb and his ex-wife's divorce was mutually agreed and they get on tolerably well together, at least Katie won't be walking into an unpleasant situation.

'She's so sensitive, *too* sensitive for her own good I sometimes think. She always puts other people's feelings and other people's needs above her own.'

'Yes, she does,' Jenny agreed soberly.

It was news to her that Katie was romantically involved with Seb Cooke, but Louise was quite correct when she stated that Katie had been unlike her normal self over the last year or so. Always quiet she had become to a mother's anxious eye worryingly withdrawn, and it had been at least in part because of her concern that Jenny had suggested to Jon that they persuade Katie to come home and join the family business when she admitted that she was thinking of changing her job.

Not that Jenny had any objections to Seb Cooke as a prospective son-in-law, far from it. She had taken to him virtually immediately and she thought that Charlotte was a honey. No. What *did* surprise her was that her normally hesitant and even reticent daughter should have committed herself so immediately.

'Oh, yes, Guy, I'm sure that Katie would be thrilled with it,' Jenny enthused as she studied the pretty little desk which Guy had invited her to come and see. The antiques shop they had originally begun as a joint venture was now managed by one of Guy's many relatives, Didi Fowler, while Guy concentrated on the other aspects of his small financial empire.

'I remember how much she loved the one I found for my sister Laura,' Guy agreed, 'and when Didi said that this one had come in I thought of Katie and her new apartment straight away. When does she actually move in, by the way? I know that Seb has terminated the lease on his rented property and that he intends to start living in his apartment on his return from this conference he's gone to.'

'Katie said that she'd like to move in as soon as she can and, of course, now that she and Seb are seeing one another I imagine she'll want to move in when he does.'

'Katie and Seb?' Guy whistled soundlessly. 'I hadn't *realised*…' he began and then shook his head.

'Neither had I,' Jenny admitted. 'But Katie confided in Louise and Louise mentioned it to me without realising that Katie hadn't said anything yet herself.'

'A Cooke and a Crighton…that will cause something of a stir. Ben isn't going to like it. How is he by the way…?'

'Not too good, I'm afraid,' Jenny told him worriedly. 'Maddy says he's becoming increasingly distressed about David's absence—we don't use the word "disappearance" around Ben, we never have done, it upsets him so much. You know how much he's always thought of David. He was always the favoured son.'

'Mmm… If you ask me, that was probably the root of David's problem. It wasn't just that Ben had such high expectations of him, it was that he gave David the belief that he had the right to expect the world to place him on the same pedestal his father had done. Well, personally, I can't see how he could ever come back.'

'It wouldn't be easy,' Jenny admitted, 'for any of us. But I can't help wishing for Ben's sake if nothing else that he would at least get in touch with us… In truth, Guy, I'm afraid that if David leaves it too much longer it could well be too late,' she told him sombrely. 'The doctors say there's no valid reason why

Ben shouldn't have made a much better recovery from his last operation than he has. In theory he's got every reason to have done so. Just on the basis of the dedicated nursing Maddy's given him, and we had all hoped that having Max based in Chester and living permanently at Queensmead would help—you know that after David, Max has always been his favourite.'

'But Max isn't the person he originally was any longer, is he? Max is much more Jon's son now than he's David's nephew.'

'Yes. As Max himself would be the first to say, what he went through in Jamaica was very much a "Saul on the road to Damascus" conversion for him.' The seriousness left Jenny's eyes and she laughed, explaining to Guy, 'Little Leo must have heard his father using that particular phrase himself because he asked Max what his Uncle Saul was doing on the road to Damascus.'

When they had both finished laughing, Guy went over and patted the desk they had been admiring and told Jenny in amusement, 'Perhaps I should keep this and present it to Katie as a wedding present.

'Seb's a good man,' he told her reassuringly. 'Very highly principled which will suit Katie.'

Having confirmed to Jenny that he would keep the desk for her daughter, Guy went home to tell his wife that they might shortly expect to be celebrating another wedding in the family.

'Seb and Katie. Oh, that's wonderful,' Chrissie enthused. 'Charlotte will be thrilled. She's really taken to Katie,' she added, reiterating Louise's comment to her mother earlier.

Meanwhile, totally unaware of the future being

mapped out for them, the two supposed lovers were both independently going about their daily business.

Katie had a busy day filled with appointments all morning and an appearance at court in the afternoon, while Seb was on his way to attend a large conference on the moral implications resulting from the giant strides forward the scientific world was currently making in the field of genetics.

Seb's last telephone call before he had left had been to the interior designer giving her the go-ahead on the designs she had submitted to him. He would be gone less than a week but she had assured him that, given her contacts, enough of the work would be completed to enable him to move into the apartment on his return.

The conference was being held in Florida. Not an ideal venue so far as Seb was concerned, not with the long flight involved. Closing his eyes he settled back in his seat preparing to go to sleep using a relaxation technique he had perfected over the years, but for once neither his mind nor his body were prepared to respond to the commands he was giving them. Instead, behind his closed eyelids, an image formed of the last person he wanted to think about.

Infuriatingly, instead of achieving his normal Zen-like state of pre-sleep calm, Katie Crighton's features kept forming themselves in a series of intimate pictures, the most disconcerting of which set Katie's eyes and hair and mouth in the tousled-haired solemn-expressioned face of a small boy child.

'Oh, no. Oh, no way, no way at all.'

Seb wasn't aware that he had muttered his denial out loud until he saw the curious look the man in the adjacent seat was giving him.

Scientifically he knew it was totally impossible for anyone to 'see' into the future—true, they *could* make accurate assumptions based on the hard evidence of given facts—and it was perhaps predictable that the gypsy woman should have assumed that he and Katie were a couple and therefore, that she should at some stage bear his child, but there had been something not so much about her predictions, but about the woman herself that had touched an almost primeval chord inside him.

He shifted uncomfortably in his seat. All right, why not acknowledge it—*admit* it to himself, he *did* want Katie. Sexually she pressed buttons he had forgotten he had long ago, if in fact he had ever known.

Sex for him, while a pleasurable experience, had never driven him, never obsessed him, never *possessed* him as it did some men. Because his awareness of how people viewed Cooke men and their supposedly uncontrollable sexuality had subconsciously made him determined that he would not just rise above the low expectations people had of his family academically, but also determined to rise above the taint of their notorious sexual profligacy.

It was because of that that he had insisted on corralling his youthfully sexual desire for Sandra within the acceptable, *respectable* confines of marriage. Time and experience might have shown him the foolishness of that, but he had never again allowed his sexual desire to get out of control or indeed to have any real input into his life.

Since he had passed thirty he had come to consider himself as a man who had the maturity and the ability to treat the sexual side of his nature as less important to him and with less value to his life than the cerebral atisfaction it gave him to distance himself from any ower it might have threatened to have over him.

Now, irritatingly, ridiculously, here he was at nirty-eight discovering that, far from being a thoroughly tamed and unimportant facet of his nature, it ad become an out of control hydra-headed monster nat sprouted ten new heads for every one he destroyed. Right now, for instance, he had gone from visualising Katie to remembering how it had felt to iss her; how soft and warm her skin had felt, her breast…how betrayingly her nipple had pulsed and er breathing quickened…how betrayingly, too, she ad flushed and looked away, unable to meet his eyes when the gypsy had spouted all that rubbish about nem being a couple. Oh yes, she was as physically nd intimately aware of *him* as *he* was of her, although he doubted that she had gone as far as entertaining, *envisaging*, the kind of sexual fantasies about im that were plaguing him about her.

Charlotte had been conceived by accident, the result of a missed birth control pill, her conception omething neither he nor Sandra had recognised until everal weeks later. But if he was to father a child *ow*, he would want to *know* it, *sense* it, *feel* it, share with Katie the knowledge that the heat of their passion ad ignited the spark that was life.

What the *hell* was he doing…thinking? Catching he passing stewardess's eye Seb ordered the drink he ad refused earlier. He must be suffering from some ind of altitude sickness. Either that or that damned ypsy had put some kind of spell on him. Disbelievingly he closed his eyes. Now he knew he was *really* losing it. Spells, predictions…these were things that belonged to the superstitious, the Middle Ages, to a time when people had still believed that the world was flat. He was a scientist, for heaven's sake.

CHAPTER SEVEN

IT'S beginning to look like home already.'

Whirling round Katie hugged her mother gratefully.

Jenny had just spent the best part of the afternoon hanging the curtains she and Maddy had made for Katie's sitting room.

'This damask really looks wonderful,' Jenny murmured, adding feelingly, 'Mind you, it was murder to sew... I've been trying to persuade your father that we ought to give the drawing room a face-lift and this fabric would be perfect.'

'Mmm...it even looks as though it could be antique,' Katie enthused. 'And I love this soft gold colour.'

'Mmm... Maddy has a very good eye. It goes perfectly with your carpet.'

The carpet which had been fitted throughout the apartment was like the curtain fabric, a bargain tracked down by Maddy. Originally ordered by another customer and dyed to her specification, the order had been cancelled when the customer had decided at the last minute that she wanted a different colour.

Her expensive mistake had been Katie's lucky bargain. The soft, pale gold plain wool might not have been to everyone's taste, nor particularly practical, but as both Maddy and Jenny had reassured her she was hardly likely to have much dirt trodden into it living in a top floor apartment.

It had been at Maddy's suggestion that Katie had

been persuaded to spend what she had considered to be a very large sum of money on a wallpaper border to go beneath the room's elegant coving. The border formal swags of gold on a cream background was Katie had to admit, perfect with the carpet and curtains and she had liked Maddy's suggestion, too, that she might stencil rope tassels on either side of the chimney.

However, rather than employ a decorator she had decided to paste them up herself. An old sofa, again unearthed by Maddy from the attics at Queensmead was currently being re-upholstered and the bits of furniture which her parents had donated were already in place, along with the double bed she had bought.

'I've hung the old curtains from the guest bedroom at home in your bedroom for now. They'll do until you find a fabric you like. Come and have a look at them.'

As Katie followed her mother into her bedroom Jenny looked at the bed and remarked dryly,

'Wouldn't a king-sized one have been better? I know your father always complained that our old double was too small and Seb's a good inch or so taller than him.'

Speechlessly Katie stared at her mother, the colour draining from her face.

'Louise told me,' Jenny said gently.

'Louise *told* you,' Katie croaked in shock. 'Louise told you about…'

'…about you and Seb. Yes,' her mother confirmed.

Walking over to Katie she put her arms around her and hugged her tenderly.

'I'm so pleased for you, darling. I didn't want to say anything but…well, I know these last couple of

…ears haven't been very happy ones for you. Of
…ourse, your grandfather isn't exactly thrilled, not
…ith Seb being a Cooke, but then I'm sure that Seb
…ill be more than a match for Ben. You've both been
…ummoned to present yourselves to him at his party,
…eedless to say.'

Katie had to sit down. Why? *Why* hadn't she cau-
…oned Louise not to say anything? *Why* hadn't she
…ealised what would happen if she didn't? This was
…readful. Awful. Worse than the very worst possible
…ightmare she could ever have conjured up. Worse
…han Louise discovering that you love Gareth? an in-
…er voice demanded grittily. No, not worse than that.
With this, the only person who would be hurt would
…e her. What on earth was she *going* to do? Thank
…oodness Seb was safely out of the way, out of the
…ountry. Somehow she was going to have to find the
…ourage to tell her mother that Louise had got it
…rong—and before Seb came back.

Taking a deep breath she closed her eyes and then
…aid shakily,

'Mum…'

But it was too late, her mother was already speak-
…ng. 'When I told Guy he wasn't sure whether or not
…e ought to keep the desk for a wedding present,
…ut…'

'Guy knows…' Katie interrupted her hollowly.

Her mother nodded her head.

'Mmm… Apparently Chrissie wasn't all that sur-
…rised…'

Silently Katie looked at her mother, totally unable
…o find the words to express the enormity of the sit-
…ation she was in.

Guy knew!

Chrissie knew!

Everyone, it seemed, knew that she had told he twin that she and Seb were in love. Lovers, in fact to judge from her mother's unexpectedly frank com ment about her double bed earlier…

Everyone… Everyone *except* Seb. A feeling of sick panic filled her. What was she going to do? Even i she told her mother the truth now, it was far too late to stop what was going on getting to Seb's ears. Ever if she admitted, retracted, everything, he was bound to hear something. Heaven alone knew how many people were already involved.

She could plead with her own family for silence and, yes, even with Guy and Chrissie, but they were in almost daily contact with Guy's family. Guy's fam ily, like Seb's were Cookes.

Katie could almost see news of their supposed re lationship spreading and gathering momentum as i did so, so that she could easily envisage some distan Cooke connection working at the airport who migh greet Seb with the news of his impending marriage to her on his arrival back in the country.

She was beginning, Katie decided, to feel extremely ill and she could well understand what had prompted Victorian women to go into a decline. If only there had been some convenient convent, preferably one be longing to a silent order, for her to disappear into.

'Heavens, is that the time? I *must* go,' her mother was saying. 'Your father will be wondering where on earth I am.'

Weakly Katie got up and accompanied her mother to the door. Once she had gone, Katie walked into her immaculate, hand-painted, newly finished kitchen. She had never been much of a drinker but right now he was badly in need of something restorative and ourage-boosting. The only alcohol she had though vas the moving-in gift of half a dozen bottles of good vine from her father.

This was all the fault of that woman. If *she* hadn't made that prediction… Reluctantly Katie forced herself to acknowledge that she was being unfair. The blame lay fairly and squarely on her own shoulders, firstly for having involved Seb and secondly for not correcting Louise. Now her own weaknesses were being held over her head like a veritable sword of Damocles, waiting, not so much to fall but to be brought down on her unprotected neck by the full weight of Seb's fury.

In the meantime she might as well occupy herself unpacking and putting away her possessions.

Several hours later she was just closing the last of the drawers in her bedroom, the scent of the lavender bags she had placed among her things making her smile ruefully.

The lavender was from her mother's garden and just to smell it evoked memories of hers and Louise's childhood.

If there could be a silver lining to the leaden weight of the cloud threatening her then it had to be the closing of the rift which had sprung up between her and Louise.

Seeing Gareth had hurt as it always did, but oddly this time, the hurt had been less intense, more a soft ache rather than a sharp agony, her daydreams of him as her lover somehow dulled and put out of focus by the far stronger acid-sharp bite of the sensual passion she had felt for Seb.

But that had just been sex and she loved Gareth.. Loved...past tense... Katie started to frown.

The conference had been very demanding, they always were, but normally Seb found such concentration challenging and adrenalin-releasing, a recharge. This time, concentrating on the speeches had been hard work and yet, conversely, he somehow hadn't been able to give them his full attention, his thought. constantly performing clever tricks to take him where he didn't want to go.

Katie Crighton!

By now she would no doubt have moved into her apartment where she would be his closet neighbour, where they would be living as intimately as though..

Abruptly Seb put a clamp on his thoughts. His mood, already affected detrimentally by what he considered to be his own weakness, hadn't been improved by the long flight nor the delay waiting for his luggage at Manchester.

Guy, who had offered to pick him up from the airport, saw him coming out of the Arrivals hall. He went to meet him exclaiming, 'Cheer up. Mind you, I suppose you'd much rather have had Katie picking you up than me.'

Stopping abruptly—so abruptly that the man behind him almost walked into him—Seb demanded sharply.

'Katie! What?'

'Mmm... The pair of you have created *quite* a stir. *I* can tell you. A Cooke marrying a Crighton... Chrissie's got Crighton blood too, of course, but she isn't a "Crighton Crighton". I'd have loved to have seen old Ben's face when they gave him the news.

enny says he's demanding that the pair of you put in in appearance at his party.'

Quickly Seb assimilated what Guy was saying and hen demanded ominously,

'Are you telling me that the whole town…?'

'..knows that you and Katie are an item? Yes, I'm ifraid so,' Guy agreed ruefully. 'That's what comes of being a member of such a large extended family. I wouldn't even think of trying to deny it if I were you,' Guy counselled him with a grin. 'The females of the family are already planning a mass exodus to Chester to hunt for wedding outfits.

'Pity the pair of you had agreed to buy your apartments before you declared your feelings for one another. It could be hard work for Katie with a baby carriage up and down those stairs, especially if our gypsy relative has got it wrong and her "one" turns out to be "two",' Guy told him with a wicked grin, adding mock-sagely, 'After all *someone* has to be the first to provide the Crightons with the next generation's pair of twins.'

'Twins.' Seb frowned.

'Yes, twins, you know, two babies who are identical to one another,' Guy told him helpfully, tongue in cheek. 'Twins like your Katie and Louise. According to Jenny it was Louise who wheedled it out of Katie about the two of you.

'Mind you, *I* can't say too much,' Guy confessed. 'Chrissie and I fell in love virtually at first glance. Have you told Charlotte yet?'

'Er…no…she's away on a field trip at the moment,' Seb told him. Just what was going on…what the *hell* was Katie playing at? Was this some sort of crazy scheme she had dreamed up to punish him for kissing her, touching her…making it public that they were supposed to be a couple and then equally publicly dropping him? She was a Crighton after all, a member of a family who, historically, considered themselves to be a cut above everyone else, and he was a Cooke, a member of a family who equally historically had been considered to be the lowest of the low.

An hour later, when Guy dropped him off outside the house he was renting it was late evening. Unlocking the door Seb picked up the pile of mail off the mat.

He felt tired and irritated and in need of a shower, but more than any of that…

Taking the stairs two at a time he opened his bedroom door and quickly stripped off his clothes.

Florida had been hot and humid and he'd remained pretty much in the air-conditioned hotels, but the colour of his skin had still darkened slightly. He was naturally olive-skinned like Guy, and as he stood under the shower and soaped his body, the muscles in his arms and back stood out beneath his flesh.

While he towelled himself dry he replayed the messages on his answer machine. There was one from the interior designer telling him that the apartment was finished and ready for him to move into, as they had agreed.

Seb frowned as he reached out and switched off the machine. By rights what he ought to do if he had any sense was make himself a light supper and then go straight to bed. He was jet-lagged and in no mood to behave calmly or logically, so why, he asked himself sardonically half an hour later, if he knew that why was he right now in his car heading for the apartment, knowing that Katie had moved into hers?

He had every right to demand an explanation he justified to himself and he fully intended to do so.

Katie had had a very difficult day. One of her clients had been so late for his appointment with her she had had to go without any lunch break or even a cup of coffee in order to catch up, and then in the afternoon when she arrived in court, she had discovered that some of the papers she needed were missing and consequently she had been faced with the embarrassment of asking the judge for a postponement and that had not gone down well.

Add to that the fact that her car exhaust had disintegrated on the drive home from Chester and Katie felt it was no wonder that all she wanted was some peace and quiet and an early night.

She was soaking in the bath trying to relax the tension out of her shoulders when she heard the faint shrill of her intercom.

Cursing under her breath she climbed out of the bath, grabbing a towel on her way as she padded damply towards the intercom, flicking the switch and saying tiredly,

'Yes. Who is it?'

'Seb Cooke.'

Seb! Seb was *back*. Panic squeezed the breath out of her lungs, rendering her incapable of making any kind of verbal response.

'Katie.' Seb's voice was ominously charged with quiet fury.

'I was just on my way to bed,' she told him, not untruthfully, even while her conscience warned her that she was being a coward and that by far the most sensible and responsible thing to do was to see him and explain what had happened... Explain...! If only it was *that* easy.

She closed her eyes and then opened them again as she heard Seb saying softly,

'On your way to bed. Well, how very appropriate...in view of our...relationship...'

So he *had* heard. Not that she had doubted it, the very tone of his voice had told her that he knew.

Katie took a deep breath. There was nothing else for it. She was going to *have* to face him.

'I... I can explain,' she whispered into the intercom. 'But not now...tomorrow...'

'Now!' Seb returned implacably. 'Unless of course you want me to telephone your parents and inform them that their daughter is a...'

'No... No...now, then...' Katie agreed, momentarily forgetting that all she was wearing was a damp towel as she hurriedly activated the button to unlock the front door.

She froze as Seb walked in. There was a faint dark shadow along his jaw and he looked every bit as angry as he had sounded, but when he saw her, instead of unleashing the torrent of angry questions she had expected, he checked and looked at her very deliberately and lengthily.

Her face burned as Katie suddenly realised how he must be seeing her, her hair bunched up on top of her head, her body still damp from her bath, her only covering her soft cream towel.

'I... I'll just go and get dressed,' she heard herself stammering as her body reacted instantly and uncontrollably to the way he was looking at her, as instantly and uncontrollably as it had done when he had kissed her, touched her. Not that the heat burning her skin now had anything to do with her earlier apprehension or self-consciousness.

Mesmerised Katie stared right back into his eyes, her breathing suddenly laboured and shallow. A shocking surge of sexual heat shot through her veins. It must be the anxiety of the last few days that was having such a dangerous effect on her she told herself weakly. It must be because of that that she was experiencing this extraordinary reaction to Seb... that she was...

Dizzily she blinked but without being able to break the intensity of his burning stare. What was happening to her? Why was she feeling her whole body trembling, aching with a need that seemed to have been conjured up out of nowhere, like a whirlwind, a tornado, ready to wreak total destruction on her?

'I... I can explain,' she told him huskily, and she didn't know herself whether she meant she could explain why everyone thought they were a couple or that she could explain why she was feeling the way she was, but instead of agreeing Seb simply walked towards her, telling her softly,

'Don't bother. I've changed my mind. It isn't an *explanation* I want...'

'It...it isn't...?'

Wide-eyed, Katie watched him, knowing instinctively what was going to happen but totally unable to respond in the way she knew she ought to be doing to her own danger. Instead of shock or fear or anger, what she was actually feeling was a roller-coaster surge of frantic excitement, of having stepped outside her normal cautious carefulness.

'No, it isn't…' Seb confirmed.

He was a hand span away from her now and as she walked back from him, her eyes never leaving his face, he followed her until she was backed up against the wall.

'Seb,' she protested shakily.

He had placed his palms flat against the wall either side of her, effectively imprisoning her.

'Apparently, it's common knowledge in Haslewich that you and I are…together,' he told her softly and quietly, spacing out every word so that she could feel the warmth of his breath against her skin. '…that we are…lovers…'

'No!' Katie protested. 'No…!'

'Yes,' Seb insisted. 'And since that's what supposedly we are—'

And then he lowered his head and kissed her with a mixture of passion and desire and infused anger that left her mute and helpless, his mouth burning hers as he refused to end the kiss, punishing her, savaging her with its angry heat.

And yet, beneath that anger, some age-old female wisdom told Katie that there was something else, relaying the information to her along all the most sensitive pathways of her body, tiny trickles of knowledge, awareness and emotion that together became a swift unstoppable flood of powerfully female response, as though independently of her brain, her senses knew *exactly* what to do, how to use Seb's passion to burn away his anger, leaving in its place a pure and almost unbearably intense fiery passion.

She had, Katie recognised dizzily, as her lips parted beneath the thrust of Seb's tongue, aroused him to the point where his need was a white-hot driven urgency blinding him to reality and tempting her, tormenting her, to give in to her own body's wild inner clamouring to respond to him with an equal lack of inhibition. After all, she was as human as any other woman, wasn't she? She was just as capable of experiencing sensual desire and longing, just as capable of needing to satisfy the ache deep down inside her own body, which was rapidly becoming an overriding, overwhelming, out of control force; a tumultuous flood of fiery, bitter-sweet urgency sweeping aside all obstacles in its path, all logic and reason, all thoughts that warned her that what was happening, that what she was contemplating, must not be allowed to happen.

What, after all, was she holding back for? Why was she denying herself the sexual fulfilment that other women of her age took for granted. Why was she marooning herself on an isolated island of inexperience and self-conscious ignorance. Because she loved Gareth? Was she then to remain as she was all her life? Was she to remain untouched, unfulfilled... unknown by any man and unknowing of her own sexuality? Tonight, with Seb, she could experience all that she had previously denied herself. Tonight, with Seb, she could become fully a woman and fulfil her destiny. With Seb she could...

As her mind registered the dangers of her thoughts it rejected them instantly and totally, but her body seemed to have divorced itself completely from her brain, following a path of its own choosing, recklessly taking control. Her tongue touched Seb's, delicately sparring with it, a sharp shudder of reaction galvanising her body as Seb instantly responded to her silent encouragement. His hands left the wall and cupped her shoulders, his body hard against the softness of her own and so intimately close to it that she could feel, not just the fierce pounding of his heart but the far more intimate beat of his body pulse as well.

As though someone else had directed their movements, her arms reached out towards him, wrapping themselves around him while his hands moved urgently down over her body coming to rest against the round curves of her buttocks as he pulled her off the wall and even tighter into his intimate embrace.

Neither of them spoke. There was no need. Both of them knew what was happening, what was going to happen, and where the passage of arms between them to which Seb's passionate kiss was merely a prelude was leading.

When Seb shifted her body slightly in his arms, dragging his mouth from hers so that he could caress the soft flesh of her throat and then the curve of her naked shoulder, Katie made no move to stop him, and no move either to do anything to conceal from him the openly visible shudders of reaction coursing through her body. Her eyes open, silently she witnessed every touch of his hands, his mouth on her body, her expression registering every nuance of reaction and response she was feeling.

The heat of what was happening made her feel as though it was burning her up; as though she was being consumed, broken down, into the basic components of her essential self. And while a part of her was shocked by what was happening and by what she was doing, another recklessly urged her on.

There was a moment when, looking deep into her eyes, Seb slowly stood back from her, before reaching out to remove the towel from her body. She knew she should stop him, when she was helplessly and painfully aware of how very different this, her own first experience of male desire, would be from the tenderness and gentle joy her twin must have known with Gareth, a moment when she shivered and hesitated, but then some deep fierce inner force urged her on, drove her past that barrier. She was *not* Louise, and Gareth would *never* love her. She would *never* experience the gentle, tender warmth of his possession and so, instead, she must take this darker, deeper and far more dangerous pathway to sexual fulfilment.

Seb was still watching her as though waiting for her to do or say something. Katie looked at him. She had crossed her Rubicon and made up her mind. Very calmly she unfastened the towel herself and let it drop to the floor, her gaze on Seb's.

For a second she thought he wasn't going to move. His eyes met and held hers without the involuntary betraying drop to her naked body she had expected, and then she saw the muscle twitch spasmodically in his jaw and that gave her the courage to let her gaze move very deliberately from his face to his body and to the tell-tale straining of the fabric of his trousers across his groin.

As though that one tiny glance had electrified him, Seb moved, closing the distance between them and sweeping her up in his arms.

The light from the two bedside lamps Katie had switched on before having her bath bathed the bedroom in a soft warm glow. The antique quilt Olivia had given her as a moving-in present lay across the foot of the bed, the heavy ivory damask curtains which had come from home covered the windows, enclosing the room and making it feel almost cocoon-like.

Katie had expected Seb to carry her over to the bed and immediately place her on it but instead, just short of it, he lowered her to her feet, gathering her up against the hard heat of his own body and then, bending his head to kiss her slowly at first and then, as his passion ignited, with a white-hot heat that made Katie feel as though the air surrounding them could self-combust. But even more shocking than Seb's fierce passion was her own response to it.

A long time ago in another life, another Katie would have been totally shocked at the wantonness—the *eagerness* with which *this* Katie pressed her naked body against Seb's fully clothed one, opening her mouth to his kiss just as fiercely and passionately eager for Seb to take the moistness, sweetness of her mouth, as Seb was to devour it. Their tongues met, meshed, stroked, caressed, tangling and entwining as erotically as they both knew their bodies would soon be doing, gliding against one another. Flesh to flesh, soft and smooth, hard and hot, each seeking out and fitting every curve and plane of the other.

In the distance Katie could hear a soft keening sound rising and falling as rhythmically as each thrust of Seb's tongue against her own, but she had no idea that she was the one making that sound. All she did know was that this was what she had been born for, this was something so fierce, so elemental, so necessary to her that she had no idea how she had ever lived without knowing it.

Seb had lifted one hand to cup her head while the other…

She shuddered deeply as it swept, stroked over her

naked skin leaving in its wake a trail, a starburst of tiny fiery darts of aching pleasure, imposing on her body's memory a yearning, a hunger, to be touched that way again, and again…and again…

She wasn't even aware of speaking her need out loud until she felt Seb's hands sweep her body a second and a third time, both hands this time caressing her from the rounded ball of her shoulders right the way down to the equally rounded curve of her bottom and then back up again, the pads of his thumbs exquisitely abrasive against the sensitivity of her nipples.

This was what she had been made for, her whole body seemed to be singing with wild wanton pleasure as though somehow he had unearthed from deep within her a hitherto unknown chord of such strong sensuality and passion that the beat, the throb of it, was so powerful that it made her feel dizzy and faint.

Just to have Seb's thumbs brush lightly against her tight hard nipples exploded a sensation inside her like a flash fire, shocking, elemental, hot, out of control, an aching quivering life-force over which she had absolutely no control, a need, an urge, that made her want to reach for his hands and hold them against her breasts to reach for his mouth and…

Sensations exploded deep in the pit of her belly and Katie was lost. She no longer recognised the woman she had become or the emotions and desires she was experiencing. What had happened to her longing for a quiet, gentle, tender lover, a man who would treat her as though she was as fragile as delicate porcelain, who would woo her with gentle words and the lightest of careful touches? What had happened to that inner fear which had always made her recoil, even from the thought of a sexual role for herself that wasn't completely passive and restrained? Never had she imagined herself being capable of such sexual hunger, such sensual womanly aggression.

She closed her eyes on a deep shudder of intense reaction as Seb, without needing her to say what she wanted, cupped her breasts and then lowered his head towards them.

Even the warmth of his breath against her skin was enough to make her tremble wildly in response and when he opened his mouth and started to circle the hard point of her nipple with the tip of his tongue Katie thought she was going to faint with the violence of her own reactions. Frantically she wound her fingers through Seb's hair, urging him closer and closer to her breast moaning out loud, begging for him to end her torment and take the whole of her erect pulsating nipple into his mouth and slowly suck the tormenting ache of desire from it.

And yet, when he did so, instead of satisfying her and stilling that hunger, it only seemed to increase it, feed it, stoke it so that her hands were tugging at the fastenings on his shirt, almost tearing the buttons from their button holes in her need to experience the reality of his flesh beneath her own fingertips.

Distantly she was aware of Seb helping her, of him removing his clothes at the same time as he continued to caress her, but the mechanics of what he was doing were lost on her as she whimpered in pleasure at the discovery of his naked flesh against the hands touching it, touching him with the blind hunger, the need of a starving person facing the most sumptuous banquet imaginable.

Seb's body was, she recognised dizzily, a feast for

each and every one of her previously starved senses. Sight, sound, scent, touch…taste… She wanted to satisfy them all, to positively gorge herself on what she was being offered.

Vaguely Katie was aware that she ought to be shocked by what she was feeling, by how she was acting. Her whole behaviour was so totally unlike her, her needs were so unfamiliar to her, but there was no space, no time, no will within her to listen to any unwanted warning voices. This was the real her. She felt as though she was a chrysalis shedding its restrictive coat to emerge for the first time with the freedom to be as she really was.

As Seb placed her on the bed she reached up and kissed his shoulder, closing her eyes in open appreciation as she breathed in the heated aroused scent of his body, tasted it on her tongue.

'You feel so good,' she whispered huskily to him, the words tumbling from her lips in the brief spaces of time she could allow in her eager oral exploration of his body. 'You smell so good… You taste so good…'

Her words seemed to snap the final cords binding Seb's self-control. Katie heard him groan, a low exciting growl of sound that sent actual physical shock waves of sensation racing over her own skin and then he was holding her, lifting her, positioning her so that every part of her body was open to the intimate caress of his hands and mouth. The sensation of him touching her, caressing her, leaving her with the moist heat of his tongue, sending wave after wave of arousal crashing down over her until she was drowning in her own longing and need for his full possession.

There was no time for her to feel apprehension or

even hesitation, only a growing vortex of need that drew her into the maelstrom of its tumultuous heart, the only sound she could hear the thud of Seb's heartbeat and the sobbing cry of her own piercing longing.

There was no sense of shock or pain, only the intensity of her own longing, her own urgency. That, and her awed comprehension of how perfectly they fit together, of how dizzyingly strong her own sensual reaction to him was. He moved and she moved with him, their bodies in perfect harmony, creating between them a rhythm that echoed the life force of the universe itself, so completely at one with one another, so perfectly complementing one another that Katie felt as though she was being buoyed up, swept along, carried by a force as pure and spiritual as it was sensual and earthly.

What was happening for her was so sublimely perfect that she felt as though not just her body, but her mind, her heart, her whole being had entered another dimension. Awash with the waves of sensation that had crashed through her, carrying her over that final barrier and safely into the calm place that was the other side of the chasm she had crossed, she reached out to Seb, touching his throat with questing fingers, the smile she gave him beneath her suddenly too heavy eyelids, soft and womanly, full of knowledge and fulfilment.

Seb though wasn't returning her smile. His eyes were dark and unreadable, his face set and something close to anger breaking through the quietly controlled pitch of his voice as he demanded,

'Why didn't you tell me…*warn* me?'

Self-consciously, Katie looked away from him, her

euphoria disappearing at the cold disapproval of his voice.

'It was your first time, wasn't it?' Seb was demanding sharply as she looked away from him unable to hold or endure the searching look he was focusing on her.

There wasn't any point in denying the truth, not when he had so obviously realised.

'Yes. It was,' Katie agreed calmly.

She heard Seb curse under his breath and winced at the anger she could hear.

'You should have *told* me, and…'

'…and what?' Katie found the courage to question, her own lips only trembling very slightly as she twisted them into a wry smile. 'You'd have stopped?'

She saw from the dark surge of colour burning up under his skin that Seb knew what she meant. *He* had been as incapable of stopping as *she* had been of drawing his attention to her virginity.

'*Why* should I have told you?' she asked him and then looking at him she said simply, 'It…it couldn't have been any…any better and I…'

Seb cursed again.

'You were a *virgin*,' he reminded her furiously, 'and I…'

'You made love to me as though I were a woman and not a girl,' Katie suggested. Pride darkened her eyes, her head lifting as she spoke to him.

'Perhaps I *didn't* tell you because I *wanted* to be treated as a woman…an equal…'

'No…you're lying,' Seb denied sharply. 'No woman of your intelligence and your age waits so long without having a purpose, a reason for doing so, and certainly a woman like you would *never* allow such an important rite of passage to be... No...you must have been waiting for something or someone...

He was so close to the truth that Katie held her breath praying inwardly that Seb wouldn't inadvertently stumble on it and realise...

Realise what? That she had dreamed up for herself a totally false image of her own sexuality? That she had spent years fantasising about a sexual experience and a man so far removed from the reality of what her body had told her tonight it really wanted, that the enormity of the gulf between what *she* had believed she *had* wanted and what in fact she really *had* wanted was so huge that even now she could barely grasp how wrong she had been?

The person she had believed she was before tonight could never have felt, wanted, needed, *enjoyed* what she had just experienced with Seb. By rights she knew she ought to feel, at best self-conscious and at worst downright ashamed of what she had done and why she had done it, and certainly it was something she couldn't envisage ever discussing even with someone so close to her as her twin.

How on earth would Louise react if she were to tell her that she had been so overwhelmed by her own sexual longings that she had practically begged Seb, a man she knew she didn't love, but who in that mad moment of intensity she had wanted with an urgency and desperation far stronger than anything she had ever previously experienced, to take her, possess her, fill and complete her?

She had, she recognised on a shocking surge of self-realisation, wanted exactly what had happened and worse, she had wanted it to be with Seb who she knew didn't love her and who she knew was just

bout as different from Gareth as it was possible for
man to be.

'Why?' Seb was asking her tersely. 'Why now?
Why me?'

He reached out, taking hold of her by her shoulders,
dragging her upright to face him before she could stop
him.

'What's going on, Katie? I arrive home to discover
that you and I are supposedly having a relationship,
that we are effectively *already* a couple, although you
and I both know that that just isn't so…or rather it
wasn't,' he corrected himself grimly.

'*That* was an accident,' Katie told him immediately.
'I never…' She stopped, biting her lip and then winc-
ing as the touch of her teeth against its tenderness
reminded her of the intimacy of the kisses they had
shared. Her face flushed a soft rosy pink as she tried
to wriggle free of him and another part of her body
reminded her even more insistently of just how intimate that intimacy had been.

'An accident?'

'Yes,' she insisted. 'Louise jumped to the wrong
conclusions about… about us…I…'

She stopped. How could she explain just why she
hadn't totally and immediately corrected her twin. 'I
tried to tell her, but it…it wasn't easy…' She hung
her head. 'She feels uncomfortable with me sometimes, guilty almost because she's…because she has
Gareth and their life together and it's hard to make
her understand that I'm happy as I am.'

'She wants you to be like her, part of a couple—
settled…' Seb interrupted her, adding intuitively,
'And so it was easier to allow her to think that her
assumptions were correct.'

'Yes. Yes, it was,' Katie agreed. 'I never dreamed that she would tell anyone else or that...'

She stopped and shook her head. 'I couldn't believe it when my mother started talking to me about you...about us, as though... I should have admitted the truth then, I wanted to... I knew how angry you'd be once you got to hear about it.'

'I *was* angry,' Seb admitted brusquely. 'But that's no excuse for what I did... Why didn't you stop me...tell me?'

'Perhaps I didn't want to,' Katie told him honestly, her eyes clouding a little with the pain of her private thoughts.

She wasn't being totally honest with him. Katie knew that. She hadn't told him the truth about why she had allowed Louise to believe they were involved with one another. But how could she tell him without exposing herself to even more humiliation and, anyway, how could she tell anyone else about her feelings for Gareth when she hadn't told her twin? And now if she told him about Gareth, could she then go on to admit that, despite the longevity of her love, despite what she had believed to be the strength and permanence of it, the moment Seb had touched her she had been overwhelmed by such a compulsive urgency, such a white-hot burn of desire that it simply hadn't been possible for her to think of anything or anyone else?

She gave him a direct look and said quietly and ruefully, her mouth curving in a semi-self-mocking smile,

'Perhaps I was beginning to feel that my virginity was getting dangerously close to the end of its shelf-life. But I wanted you Seb... I can't explain why or now and I wasn't even thinking about my virginity, I wasn't capable of that kind of logic, of any kind of reasonable thinking... I can't explain why or what... I just...'

She stopped, her eyes momentarily shining with emotional tears as she admitted with painful honesty,

'Yes, perhaps I *should* have warned you...told you...or stopped you...but...'

'But...' Seb prompted her when she fell silent and bowed her head so that all he could see was the top of it.

'...but I didn't want to,' Katie repeated huskily as she lifted her head to meet his gaze. 'I had no idea that sex could be so...so...'

'...so dangerous,' Seb offered sardonically.

'So *total*,' Katie amended as she added bravely, 'I'm not going to allow myself to feel guilty or ashamed about what happened or about the way I felt, Seb. I...it was...it was wonderful,' she told him recklessly, the words little more than a shy whisper of sound as her face grew pink and she looked away from him.

'*Wonderful*!' Seb repeated explosively. 'Have you *any* idea! None of this should have happened. None of it. You and I...'

'...don't even like one another. I know...' Katie agreed sadly. 'Maybe that's the way passion is, I don't know. Perhaps you would be able to say better than me.'

'You think so?' Seb shook his head. 'What just happened between us was as much of a "first time" for me as it was for you. I don't make a habit of allowing myself to lose control like that and I certainly don't enjoy knowing that...'

He stopped, shaking his head while Katie suggested practically, 'Well, at least no one other than ourselves need ever know about it. Tomorrow I'll explain to my mother that Louise got it wrong and…'

She tensed as Seb suddenly moved abruptly away from her pulling the disarranged bedclothes over his lower body.

His rejection of her and his patent lack of interest in what she was saying hurt her more than she liked having to recognise and the warmth and happiness that had followed their lovemaking was quickly being replaced by a sense of loss and loneliness.

'If you want…' she began stiffly and then she saw the way he was looking at her body and she knew immediately and exactly just what it was he did want and her face burned bright scarlet with a heart-stopping mixture of shock and excitement.

Excitement because Seb still wanted her, because the reason he had reached for those concealing covers was because his body was reacting to the proximity of hers, because…

Before she could stop herself or even think critically or sensibly about what she was doing she heard herself whispering softly, 'Seb, please stay with me tonight…*all* night…'

'Stay with you…'

His voice was slurred and gruff as though his throat was hurting him somehow. Fascinated Katie watched as he closed his eyes and swallowed, her whole body shivering in mute reactive awareness of the strong tide of need which was already building to threaten their defences.

'Yes. I want you to,' she told him. 'I want you…'

She gave him a brief look full of female knowledge

s she reminded him, 'After all, I'm not a virgin any-more now.'

She could see the heat leaping in his eyes as im-mediately and dangerously as though she had thrown a lighted match onto petrol. When he reached for her his skin felt like hot satin and when she touched him he cried out, suffering the eager exploration of her hands and then her mouth until his whole body was racked by seismic shudders of uncontrollable reaction.

'Stay with me' she had begged him and he did, through the tumult of her own hungry desire and be-yond it, holding her through the night as she slept.

What the hell was happening to him? Seb asked him-self defeatedly. He had come to see her tonight intent only on demanding an explanation from her, furiously angry with her and now… He looked down at where she slept in his arms. Now he knew that ridiculously, illogically, he never ever wanted to let her go.

'Stay with me' she had asked and in doing so he had somehow rewritten all the rules he had laid down for the way he intended to live his life.

CHAPTER EIGHT

'COFFEE…'

Sleepily Katie opened her eyes and then sat bolt upright in her bed as she saw Seb standing in the door-way to her bedroom, fully dressed and holding a mug of fragrantly scented coffee.

Wide-eyed, she watched him as he walked towards her without waiting for her response. Less than a handful of hours ago, as the dawn had started to lighten the sky, she had woken him from his sleep, whispering to him that she wanted him. She blushed now to recall just how wantonly insistent she had been, and just how femininely persuasive as she had eagerly caressed his body. Not that he had needed very much persuasion. She winced as she moved and felt her own body's sharp response to the intensity of the long hours of lovemaking they had shared.

'You don't have to stay now,' she told him huskily as she took the mug of coffee from him and avoided looking into his eyes. 'You must want to get back to your own place…you must have things to do…'

'Well yes,' he agreed, informing her laconically, 'I do have some telephone calls to make and I shall certainly need a change of clothes before we meet your parents for lunch. Your mother called.'

'*What*?' Katie sat bolt upright in bed.

'She rang earlier while you were still asleep. I answered the phone,' Seb told her matter-of-factly.

Katie stared at him as though she couldn't believe what she was hearing.

'My mother rang and *you* answered the phone?'

'Mmm…' Seb agreed.

'What did she say? What did you say?' Katie began wildly. 'Oh, but this is awful. Now she's never going to believe that you and I aren't…'

'That you and I aren't what?' Seb asked her ironically. 'That you and I aren't lovers…but we are!'

Nonplussed Katie looked at him.

'But that was private,' she told him huskily when she eventually found her voice. 'It was…' She stopped.

'It was what?' Seb probed, but Katie shook her head. How could she tell him that what they had shared, what she had experienced was for her, even in the sharp clear light of morning—even knowing logically what she did know—something so special…so mystical, that she knew that even if she could she would not have changed a single heartbeat of it?

Every thought, every image she had ever had with Gareth as her lover had been completely extinguished by the heat of Seb's passion, extinguished and obliterated.

'None of this should be happening,' Katie told him helplessly. 'You shouldn't… You don't… My parents think we're a couple, but we're not…'

'No,' Seb agreed, 'but then I could hardly tell your mother that when she telephoned and learned that I was here, could I? What would I have said? Yes, I've spent the night in bed with Katie but that was all it was…just a night in bed…'

Katie's face drained of colour as she listened to

him. If they knew the truth her parents would be so shocked, so shamed by her behaviour.

As he watched the emotions chase one another across her mobile face, Seb reflected inwardly that he was going to be in big trouble if she found out that *he* was the one who had suggested to her mother that they should all meet for lunch and that *he* was the one who, by the tone of his voice and the careful words he had used, had made it clear to Jenny Crighton that he and Katie had spent the night together, rather than her assuming it.

Tradition might have it that it was the woman who trapped the man into a relationship with sex and not the other way around, but last night had proved to him, if he had needed any proof, just how unreliable tradition actually was. Katie might have been a virgin but there had been no shrinking hesitancy, no fear or apprehension, no holding back or coyness in the way she had responded to him, the way she had *given* to him.

Early that morning, while she had slept, he had gone for a solitary walk along the river needing the time alone to make sense out of the jumble of thoughts and emotions jostling for supremacy inside him.

As he had walked he had admitted that he would be a fool to pretend that he had not known even before last night, just how strong and dangerous his feelings for her actually were. You simply didn't get so hyped up and angry about a person who didn't matter, and *he* certainly wouldn't have had the kind of physical reactions he had had last night without... As he paused to watch a pair of swans with their offspring he had been forced to recognise a truth he had been hiding from himself all along.

Right from the very start, the very first time he had seen her, Katie had had a profound effect on him. The anger, the intensity he had experienced that very first time he had seen her had been too strong, too alien to his normal behaviour pattern. It was as though at some deep-seated buried level his senses had locked on to her, reacted to her, and he had suppressed that reaction. What was he trying to say to himself, that he had fallen in love with her and then gone into denial?

Well, he certainly hadn't been in any kind of denial last night, had he? he had mocked himself.

As he had watched the swans he had acknowledged that while he might love Katie, she most certainly did *not* love him.

No, but she *wanted* him. His body had quickened fiercely and hungrily in response to this thought and his need to turn round and go straight back to rouse her from her sleep and take her in his arms had been so strong that the effort of controlling it had made him grunt out loud in protest at his own pain.

As he walked back towards the house, he was ironically aware of how the whole of his life had come full circle. He and Sandra had married, confusing their physical desire for one another with love, but now that he had actually come face to face with the real thing, now that he actually *knew* love, he could see so plainly the world of difference that separated what he had felt then with what he felt now. But if he had made the mistake of committing himself to a relationship based on physical desire once he wasn't about to do so again. Katie deserved better. She deserved not just to be loved, and he most certainly *did* love her but to know love, to feel it, experience it, share it for herself.

He had walked back into her apartment fully intending to make it plain to her that he had no expectations, that what had happened was an isolated incident, over and done with, when the phone had rung and he had answered it and without even knowing himself what he was going to do he had subtly confirmed to her mother that they were lovers, trapping Katie in her family's expectations and his own love. He was old enough to have known better, old enough to have *done* better by his love and by Katie herself.

'This can't be happening,' Katie was whispering plaintively as she nursed the now cold mug of coffee he had brought her. Perhaps it shouldn't be happening, but it quite definitely was and contrary to her expectations, instead of accusing her of messing up both their lives, Seb seemed to be totally relaxed about the whole situation.

'*I* wasn't the one who started it,' Seb reminded her wryly.

Katie frowned. No he wasn't and she had only herself to blame for the situation she now found herself in—and in more ways than one.

'I'll ring my mother and cancel lunch,' she told Seb quickly but, instead of greeting her suggestion with approval, an expression she found hard to define crossed his face then he shrugged and told her curtly,

'If you wish.'

Ten minutes later when he had left to return home Katie decided that she couldn't fathom him out at all. But was she any more capable of understanding *herself* than she was him? Last night her behaviour had

een completely out of character. So much so, that
ven though she was now on her own she still blushed
ɔ recall some of the things she had said—and done!

he telephoned her mother as soon as she had show-
red, explaining with her fingers crossed behind her
ack that Seb wasn't going to be able to make it for
ınch as he had realised he had some work he had to
ttend to urgently.

'In fact,' she began, taking a deep breath, suddenly
etermined not to end the telephone call until she had
ɔld her mother the truth, but before she could do so
er mother was saying quickly, 'Darling, I have to go,
ıere's someone at the door. Never mind about lunch,
ɩe'll fix something for another day, and besides,' she
ıughed gently, 'I'm sure that you and Seb would
ıuch prefer to be on your own…'

She would certainly like to be on her own Katie
dmitted, completely and *totally* on her own. Dressing
ıuickly she picked up her bag and her car keys. She
eeded time to think, time to let the reality of what
ad happened sink in fully.

While Katie was hurrying down to her car, Seb was
etting out of the shower. As he padded naked across
is bedroom he caught sight of Charlotte's photo-
raph. She had been telling him with increasing in-
ıstence that it was time he fell in love and remarried.
he had taken an immediate liking to Katie. Look at
ıe way she had reacted to that gypsy girl's ridiculous
rediction. Seb froze and closed his eyes, muttering a
ious prayer-cum-plea beneath his breath as he sud-
enly remembered what, in the heat of last night's
assion, he had so recklessly forgotten.

He knew he had a clean bill of health so what they

had done, while irresponsible, was not hazardous, bu
from the point of view of potential conception.
There were modern methods, though. Safeguards.
As he hurried towards the door the telephone rang
He hesitated and paused and then quickly reached fo
the receiver, his heart starting to thud with anxiety a
the leader of the field trip Charlotte had been attend
ing the past week explained that there had been
small mishap and that she had suffered a fall.

'They're keeping her in hospital to check that sh
isn't suffering from concussion,' he explained to Set
'but I can assure you that there's nothing for you t
worry about.'

'Where is she? Which hospital?' was Seb's uncom
promising response.

Before he left he telephoned Katie's flat, waiting
for her to answer for several minutes before hangin
up. He couldn't delay any more, not with Charlotte i
hospital. He would have to ring Katie later on hi
mobile and warn her of the danger he had left he
exposed to.

Later, Katie couldn't explain, even to herself, wha
had prompted her to do what she did or quite how c
why she was on her way, virtually at a moment's no
tice, to Brussels. She'd made a brief telephone call t
her twin to warn her that she was coming, and anothe
and even more muddled one to her mother, disjoint
edly explaining that she was at the airport and on he
way to her sister and that she didn't know how lon
she would be gone. 'It will only be for a couple o
days,' she reassured Jenny. 'Tell Dad and Livvy tha
I'm sorry to spring this on them, but…'

On the other end of the line Jenny simply listened

It was totally unlike Katie to behave so impulsively, but she couldn't help but be glad that the rift she had seen slowly growing between the two girls was now being mended. If Katie needed her twin enough to drop everything to fly over to her then Jenny knew that Louise would be there for her.

'She's gone where?' Jon demanded in astonishment when Jenny broke the news to him of Katie's unplanned visit to her twin sister.

'It will only be for a few days. It's just a short break,' Jenny soothed him while he sighed in exasperation and then smiled ruefully at her.

'I certainly hope so. We're hellishly busy at the moment. What on earth brought this on?'

When Jenny simply looked at him he gave another rueful paternal sigh and guessed.

'Love trouble!'

'A small crisis of confidence I suspect,' Jenny told him.

'In *Seb*?' Jon frowned. He might not be either a possessive father nor the type who became vehemently verbally proactive on behalf of his children—right or wrong—but he was nevertheless *very* protective of them.

'If that's the case then I should have thought she'd be better off without him.'

'No, not in Seb,' Jenny told him gently. 'I suspect that the confidence she lacks is in herself... I noticed particularly how when she was at university she developed the habit of standing in the shadows as it were, of accepting second place...second best...'

'Like father—like daughter,' Jon offered ruefully as he and Jenny exchanged mutually understanding and loving looks. For many years Jon himself had stood in the shadow of his twin, so much so that his resultant lack of self-esteem had affected every aspect of his life and he and Jenny had been determined that their twin girls would not suffer similarly; encouraging them both to develop and be proud of their differences as well as their similarities.

'Seb will be good for her. He won't allow her to take a back seat in life. As a Cooke he'll know just what it means to sometimes have to fight to win other people's respect and, even more importantly, to maintain one's own. He will understand Katie's vulnerabilities and she'll see through his outer image of toughness to the sensitivity that lies beneath it.'

'Mmm…well, it all sounds very positive and hopeful.'

'I can see a very happy future ahead for the two of them.'

'And I can see a very expensive one ahead for us,' Jon riposted. 'Why couldn't fate have arranged for them to meet a little earlier? That way she and Louise could have had a double wedding, two for the cost of one, so to speak.'

The airport was exceptionally busy. After she had gone through to the departure lounge Katie checked the board for her flight and then made her way through the crowd to the coffee shop. As she did so, out of the corner of her eye she glimpsed a tall dark-haired man crossing the concourse in front of her.

Immediately a fierce surge of joy and excitement raced through her.

'Seb.'

His name was on her lips, her heart pounding. He was here. He had come to look for her. He *wanted* her. He *loved* her just as she loved him. She loved him! She loved Seb. For a few seconds Katie stood perfectly still as the world kaleidoscoped around her and the revelation of her own emotions hit her with all the devastating effect of a strong drug taking over her senses, entering her bloodstream. Her thoughts, her emotions were so searingly intense that she was oblivious to everything else going on around her. She might have been standing completely alone so little did the busy crowds around her impinge on her awareness.

She *loved* Seb.

She closed her eyes and said his name slowly, savouring it and then opened them again frantically searching for his familiar figure. But as she started to hurry towards him, he stopped and turned and with a sickening jolt Katie recognised that the man she had been following wasn't Seb at all and that now she had seen it she saw that his face bore no resemblance to Seb whatsoever. His features lacked the patrician nobility of Seb's. His bone structure was nowhere near as masculine, his eyes nothing like Seb's cool grey ones. He was quite simply not Seb and how on earth she had ever believed that he was, she couldn't imagine. Why, after all, would Seb be here? He didn't even *know* she was at the airport. He didn't know and would probably not have cared if he had. He certainly wouldn't have cared enough to come rushing here after her, to take her in his arms and declare undying love for her.

Seb love her?

This must be what the intense intimacy of the kind of sex they had shared did to a woman Katie decided, shivering almost feverishly. It made her vulnerable. It made her love the man who had shown her…given her such pleasure. Slowly Katie shook her head trying to clear the miasma of painful thoughts crowding into it.

Had she fallen in love with Seb when they had been making love or had she perhaps, unknown to herself, been attracted to him *before* that? She didn't know and had no way of ever knowing, but what she *did* know was that that moment, that split second of time when she had thought she had seen Seb, when she had believed he loved her, would be engraved on her heart and her memory for the rest of her life. There was no going back now from the discovery she had made or going back from the knowledge she had gained. No, there was no going back from *anything* now.

Absently Katie glanced at the departure board and then realised that they were boarding her flight. Like an automaton she made her way to the appropriate gate. *Now* she knew why she had felt so impelled to be with Louise, why she was being urged to seek out the one person who could help her to make sense out of what was happening to her. People didn't fall in love without knowing they had done so…did they? It just wasn't possible—was it? How *could* she have loved Seb without knowing that she did so?

Once on the plane Katie took her seat like a sleep-walker. Her mind, her heart, *all* of her was filled with images and thoughts of Seb. Seb striding angrily into her apartment. Seb kissing her with such furious passion. Seb touching her body; looking at her, his anger transmuted into pure molten desire. Seb…

Why hadn't she had some inkling, some suspicion, some built-in protective warning system to tell her

at this would happen; that she would feel like this—
ve like this?

'Katie…over here…'

Automatically Katie turned in the direction she
ould hear her twin's voice coming from. Louise was
aiting for her on the other side of the flight gate.
uickly Katie hurried towards her, all the things she
ad planned to say; the logical explanations she had
itended to make, forgotten as they rushed into one
iother's arms.

Tears filled her eyes, rolling down her face as she
old Louise chokily, 'Lou, I'm in love…with Seb…'

Releasing her Louise studied her and then asked
ently, 'Is that a problem? I thought the two of you
iade a good couple.'

'Us being a couple isn't the problem,' Katie ad-
iitted. 'Or rather… Where's Nick?' she asked,
hanging the subject and looking round for Louise's
ittle boy.

'With Gareth,' Louise told her promptly. 'Gareth
iad a few days' leave owing and so I told him it was
ime that he and Nick did a little bit of father and son
ionding. They've gone to stay with friends for a few
ays.'

There was no way that Louise was going to tell her
win that until she had received her phone call she *too*
ad been planning to take part in this short family
reak. Gareth had raised his eyebrows but made no
emure when she had told him that there had been a
hange of plan.

'Katie *never* asks for anything,' Louise had told
im soberly. 'Of the two of us *I'm* always the one
ho makes demands on her. She needs me Gareth. I

have to be here for her. I owe it to her,' she ha
finished softly.

Now, as she looked at her twin's pale face, Louis
knew that she had been right to listen to that sma
inner voice.

'Come on,' she announced, taking hold of Katie'
arm. 'You and I are going to go and have a prope
girlie lunch. There's this fabulous restaurant we'v
discovered not far away from the house.'

Katie started to protest and shake her head. The la
thing she felt like doing was eating, but typicall
Louise wasn't giving her the opportunity to objec
tucking her arm through Katie's and urging her to
wards the exit.

As Seb drove towards the Yorkshire Dales, the site o
Charlotte's field trip, a sudden bottle-neck in the tra
fic slowed him down enough that he had the oppor
tunity to reach for his mobile phone and punch i
Katie's number. He had made a mental note of it ea
lier in the morning while he had been on the phon
to her mother, never guessing how soon he was goin
to need to use it.

Impatiently he waited as the phone rang, willin
Katie to pick up the receiver, smothering the sense o
anguish and disappointment he felt when there wa
no reply. Charlotte had been taken to the hospita
nearest to the field trip site and although Seb had spo
ken to the staff nurse in charge of her ward and ha
been reassured that keeping her in was only a precau
tion and that she was fine, he knew his natural paren
tal fears would not be allayed until he had seen her

He just hoped that he would be able to reach Kati
by telephone before too long. If he couldn't… 'You'

have a boy child' the gypsy had said. A child…a boy…a son… Katie's son… There was no way he was going to abdicate his parental responsibilities a *second* time. No way he was going to be an absent father. No way he was not going to be fully and totally a part of his child's life…

Charlotte had been lucky… He had been lucky in that his absence had not damaged her, but he still had to carry the guilt of knowing he had not been there for her when he ought to have been, he still had to bear the guilt of knowing that his own selfish behaviour could have compromised her happiness and her life… Just as his own selfish behaviour could have resulted in the conception of another child.

Unplanned this baby may be, he acknowledged, but not unwanted. The sensation that had ripped through him at the thought of Katie carrying his child had shocked him. Charlotte was his daughter and he loved her, but he had never once felt anything for Sandra like he had just experienced now thinking about Katie conceiving and carrying his child.

He liked Sandra as a person, respected and admired her as a mother and as a wife—someone else's wife—but he didn't love her, had never loved her the way he did Katie. But Katie didn't love him and if she should have conceived because of his lack of self-control… God, what a mess he had made of everything.

Truthfully, Louise, I'm just not hungry,' Katie protested. 'All I want…' A single, solitary tear slid down her face causing Louise to change her plans and the direction in which she was driving.

'What are you doing?' Katie protested in alarm as

her twin did an illegal U-turn virtually in the middle of the busy city street.

'Don't worry,' Louise grinned. 'No one was watching... We're going home,' she added by way of explanation. 'We can talk properly there.'

The house Louise and Gareth were renting in Brussels was down a pretty, leafy road; a small town house with a good-sized, private rear garden.

'Come on,' Louise smiled reassuringly at her twin as she parked her car and then got out, walking round to the passenger door and waiting for Katie and then taking hold of her hand almost as though she thought she might run away, Katie acknowledged wearily.

But where, after all, was there for her to run to? Who was there for her to run to? Nowhere and no one. She just wished she hadn't made that ridiculously overemotional statement at the airport. No wonder Louise was treating her as though she had less common sense than her small son Nick.

'We'll sit out in the garden,' Louise announced as she led the way into the house and then through it out onto a pretty paved patio area, virtually pushing Katie into one of the comfortable garden chairs before telling her,

'Stay there. I'll go and get some wine...'

'I don't...' Katie began but Louise shook her head and told her ruefully,

'Well *I* certainly do. Just one glass,' she suggested in a more gentle voice. 'It will do you good.'

The wine Louise poured for them both was clear and crisp and deliciously cold. It tasted good, Katie admitted, shaking her head over the plate of sandwiches Louise was offering her.

'So...tell me *everything*,' Louise commanded her

You're in love with Seb. Well, I could see that. What's troubling you? Is it the thought of making such a big commitment...marriage can seem very scary. I know.'

'No. It's nothing like that,' Katie interrupted her, taking a deep breath before saying starkly,

'What I let you think before, what I told you, simply wasn't true. Not then... Seb and I weren't... hadn't... There was *nothing* between us and...'

'But there is now,' Louise cut across Katie's stumbling explanations. 'Now you're in love with him...'

'Yes...' Katie looked down at her almost empty wine glass feeling her face grow hot as certain memories flooded through her. Then she drained the last of her wine and turned to face Louise, telling her with a bluntness that ordinarily would have been totally out of character for her, 'It... I... I went to bed with him. We had sex...and it was...' She paused, her face growing even hotter, but when she searched Louise's face and could see no hint of shock or criticism there she took another deep breath and continued, 'It was wonderful. I hadn't... I never thought... He was angry at first. Angry with me because he'd discovered that people were talking about us as a couple. I tried to explain and apologise, but...he took hold of me and started to kiss me and then what had started out as... I couldn't help myself... I just wanted him so much,' Katie confessed in a low voice.

'I'd never imagined *I* could feel like that. Not me. My own feelings just overwhelmed me... I just wanted him so much. I know this must be hard for you to understand,' she told Louise, unable to fully look at her now. 'You and Gareth…you love one another and…'

'I didn't love him the first time I had sex with him, Louise interrupted her to tell her matter of factly. 'Actually…' She stopped. 'Perhaps we're even more alike than either of us has ever recognised. Gareth was very angry with *me* the first time *we* made love, Katie, and I felt just the same as you've said you felt. *I* was the one who drove things on, who insisted…who seduced…' she underlined ruefully.

Katie lifted her head and listened warily.

'The first time I went to bed with Gareth I was convinced it was Saul I loved, not him. I was furiously angry with Gareth and with myself and he was equally furiously angry with me, but somehow all that anger became transmuted, transformed into something else.'

Katie closed her eyes and then opened them again.

'When I went to bed with Seb,' she confessed gruffly, 'I thought…' She stopped and bit her lip and then, looking right at her twin, she confessed huskily 'I thought…felt…believed that it was really Gareth I loved.'

For a moment the silence between them was so intense, so profound, that Katie feared that she had gone too far, said too much, violated their twinship so severely that their lifelong bond had been severed but then Louise moved, pushing back her chair, coming towards her, taking hold of her and hugging her so hard that Katie had to gasp for breath.

'Oh Katie, Katie, it's so awesome that we should both have experienced the same thing, that we should both have shared almost exactly the same things. You *know* what this means, don't you?' Louise demanded in a portentous voice.

Katie looked at her, her heart starting to beat heavily and painfully. What was Louise going to say? That because Katie had admitted to having loved Gareth things could never now be the same between them, that Louise could never again trust her…?

'No…what does it mean?' Katie forced herself to ask.

'It means that you and Seb are quite definitely meant for one another,' Louise told her excitedly. 'Just like Gareth and I were…'

Katie hated to disillusion her but she had to. Sadly she shook her head.

'No. Seb doesn't love me,' she told her positively.

'He took you to bed, made love to you,' Louise reminded her.

'He *wanted* me,' Katie agreed. 'But he doesn't *love* me,' she said painfully. She hesitated and then looked uncertainly at Louise.

'You won't say anything to Gareth about…about me having thought I loved him, will you?' she begged Louise. 'I realise now that…' She stopped. Even if she hadn't already recognised how unreal and unsupportable her supposed love for Gareth had really been, she knew that hearing Louise describe his anger with her when they had made love, and recognising that Gareth was the tender almost detached gentle lover she had imagined was nothing more than an unreal fantasy would have destroyed the fragile romantic image she had built up around her brother-in-law.

She had believed she loved him because there had been no one else there in her life for her *to* love, she realised with sudden wisdom. Loving Gareth had been a subtle form of emotional protection, of safeguarding her emotions. Rather like that thicket of briars which

had grown up around Sleeping Beauty, and like th
prince who had hacked his way through that thicke
Seb had found a way through *her* emotional protec
tion and into her heart.

If she had gained nothing else from what had hap
pened, she had at least gained maturity and a muc
deeper knowledge of her real self. And of course, sh
had regained the special closeness with Louise he
twin.

An hour later as they strolled together throug
Brussels' shopping area, Katie paused to study th
display in a small boutique window.

The dress, a cobwebby knit creation that clung lov
ingly and seductively to every curve of the manne
quin's body was both impossibly expensive and eve
more impossibly provocative.

'He'll be furious with you for wearing it in publi
where other men's eyes could see what he wants t
keep only for himself,' Louise murmured to her be
fore adding temptingly, 'Why don't you buy it?'

'Certainly not,' Katie demurred. 'Have you seen th
price, and besides where would I wear it? Mind yo
I could do with something,' she admitted ruefully
'There's Gramps's "do" coming up...'

Louise rolled her eyes expressively and groaned
'Don't remind me,' and then, as her voice change
tone and became quieter, she asked gently,

'What will you do?'

'...about Seb?' Katie responded. 'I don't know
Perhaps I should look for another job...move away...

'Why not move here?' Louise suggested promptly
'You'd get a job easily enough and we've got plent
of spare bedrooms... Or,' she added, pausing and the
looking at Katie before saying firmly,

'You *could* always tell him how you feel, and then
e…'

'No! That's impossible,' Katie denied immediately.

Ten minutes later while they were sitting in a café
drinking coffee, Louise suddenly gave a small exclamation and got up. 'I've just remembered, I didn't put
nough money in the parking ticket machine. You
ait there while I go and get another ticket. I shan't
e long…'

'No,' she insisted when Katie started to get up.
There's no need for you to come. Finish your coffee
nd order us both a second cup… You don't know
hat a treat…a luxury…it is for me to simply be able
o sit and drink coffee. I love Nick to pieces but just
ccasionally it's absolute bliss to have some time to
myself. When you and Seb have that baby of yours
ou'll understand what I mean,' she added wickedly
efore hurrying down the street.

'Dad! What are *you* doing here?'

Seb grimaced as Charlotte came bounding into the
oyer to the ward stopping dead as she saw him. He
ad arrived at the hospital ten minutes earlier and had
ust reached the ward where Charlotte had been hos-
italised.

'What do you think?' he responded grimly.

'You came because of *me*?' Charlotte shook her
ead. 'But I'm fine, I promise. In fact I've just been
ischarged. Heaven knows why they insisted on keep-
ng me in here.'

'You had a bad fall,' Seb pointed out curtly.

Charlotte rolled her eyes protestingly.

'I had a bit of a tumble,' she corrected him. 'Hardly
fall at all and if I hadn't bumped my head I doubt

there would have been any of this silly panic. Heav
ens, if I'd been rushed off to hospital every time I fe
over when I was growing up I'd have spent half m
life there. Mum always used to complain that it mus
be the Cooke gene that made me so clumsy and s
addicted to danger. According to her, *she* never s
much as sustained the smallest scratch when she wa
growing up. I suppose I was a bit of a tomboy,
Charlotte allowed ruefully, a huge smile dimpling he
face as she slid her arm through Seb's and teased him
'You're going to have to get used to visits like this
you and Katie have that baby boy. No,' she correcte
herself firmly, '*When* you have him... How *is* Kati
by the way, is she here with you?'

Here with him?

'No, why should she be?' Seb demanded sharply

'No reason,' Charlotte pacified him. 'I was ju
hoping...thinking...that it would be nice to see her.

Normally her teasing and almost maternal probing
would have been something he could have side
stepped with ease but today, after last night, it wa
activating pain cells he hadn't known he was capabl
of possessing. Just the sound of Katie's name wa
enough to produce a series of flash cards inside hi
brain.

Katie wearing just that damned towel. Katie he
mouth swollen from his kiss. Katie reaching out t
touch him. Katie as *he* touched *her*... Katie...

'Dad...where *are* you?'

Collecting himself he frowned down at Charlotte.

'Are you sure you're well enough to be dis
charged?'

'Ask the doc if you don't believe me,' she retaliate
flippantly.

An hour later, having spoken with the duty doctor, the admissions staff and, in addition, having insisted on seeing the specialist in charge of the ward, Seb acknowledged that Charlotte had been right when she claimed that she was in perfect health.

'Dad, you're over-protective. You're practically Neanderthal,' she said as they finally left the ward.

'I'm your *father*,' Seb reminded her tersely looking at her in bafflement as she suddenly gave him a smile and hugged him.

'Yes, I know,' Charlotte conceded. 'But when the time comes when I finally meet a man…*the* man, Dad,' she emphasised with a sidelong look at him and a soft pink tinge to her skin, 'There's no way that I'm going to tell *you* about it. At least not until afterwards.' Her skin colour deepened a little more betrayingly as she added defensively, 'You'll terrify him.'

'Good,' Seb told her, but her semi-teasing words had set off a chain of thoughts of his own and there was no way he could share them with her.

The man she had said, meaning quite plainly the man who would be her first lover. Charlotte and her peers looked on sex as a responsibility that had to be treated with caution and respect and that, of course, was a legacy of the tainted inheritance other generations had left them.

He had been Katie's first lover. What would Jon Crighton think of him if he knew? Jon would not love his daughter any less than Seb loved Charlotte and Jon Crighton thought that he and Katie were a pair, a couple.

If he were to disappear out of Katie's life now, what would Jon Crighton think of him? Would he think that

he had used Katie, betrayed her, abandoned her.
Would he condemn him as being every bit as bad a
the worst of his Cooke ancestors? Would Seb b
tarred by the same brush as them, a man totally with
out morals, without any kind of finer feelings?

'Dad… Dad…' Abruptly he realised that Charlotte
was talking to him. 'Dad, are you okay?' Charlotte
asked him in concern. 'You were miles away again…

'I was thinking about…something…' Seb told he
quickly.

'Something or *someone*?' Charlotte suggested, he
face breaking into a wide smile when he wasn't quit
quick enough to hide his reaction.

'I *knew* it. It is Katie, isn't it? You do love her
don't you, Dad? Oh, I'm so pleased,' Charlotte sai
hugging him excitedly. 'But just don't expect me to
be a bridesmaid and dress in a pink tulle meringue.
Charlotte pulled a face. 'Okay, I know, Katie has fa
too much taste to want me to wear anything so un
cool.'

'You're running ahead of the game,' Seb admon
ished her gently, changing the subject determinedl
by telling her, 'Come on, let's get you back to
Manchester.'

'Manchester! No way!' Charlotte announced firmly
'I'm finishing my field trip first.'

They argued for several minutes but, in the end
Seb was forced to concede defeat and acknowledge
that Charlotte was right to insist on continuing with
her field trip.

'I'm an adult now, Dad,' she reminded him. 'And
even if *I* wasn't… I love it that you are so protective
of me, but sometimes I have to be allowed to feel the

ain you know. It's called living.'

'Tell me about it,' Seb advised her sardonically.

So what are you going to do when you get home?'
ouise asked Katie. They were at the airport waiting
or Katie's return flight.

'You mean *after* I've called a meeting in
aslewich's town square to explain why Seb and I
e *not* an item?' Katie replied ruefully.

'Sorry about that,' Louise apologised. 'If I hadn't
id anything…'

'It's not *your* fault,' Katie reassured her. '*I* should
ave had the courage to tell you the truth.'

'…and I should have realised that you were holding
ack. At least something good's come out of all this,'
ouise murmured.

Their shared confidences had brought them closer
an Katie could ever remember them being, closer
nd on a much more equal footing. With Gareth and
ick away, they had spent their first evening together
xchanging confidences and swapping memories of
eir shared growing-up years, talking long into the
ight but returning again and again to the extraordi-
ariness of the circumstances surrounding the way
ey had both come to realise where their true feelings
y.

On the final day of Katie's visit Gareth had returned
ome and it had been the most natural and the easiest
ing in the world for Katie to go up to him and give
im a sisterly hug and kiss.

She had known then when she did so, the fantasy,
e *fear* that had gripped her for so long had gone.
areth meant nothing to her apart from the fact that
e was Louise's husband.

'It isn't over with Seb yet,' Louise reminded her.

'Yes, it is,' Katie responded fiercely, adding gently
'I know that for my sake you'd love this to have
happy ending—for Seb to love *me*—but it isn't going
to happen Lou. You said yourself that Gareth told you
that he had loved you that first time you were lovers
even though *you* hadn't known it at the time. But Seb
doesn't love me…'

'How do *you* know that?'

'Because *if* he did, he could have told me so,' Katie
pointed out softly. 'Gareth *couldn't* tell you because
you'd told him you loved someone else.'

'I hear what you're saying, but I still think you're
wrong,' Louise insisted firmly.

'*Don't* Lou,' Katie begged her, her eyes suddenly
darkening with pain. 'Don't give me any hope, all it's
going to do is to make things worse.'

Louise saw the pain in her twin's eyes and hugged
her tightly before reminding her,

'It won't be long before we come over…'

'…for Gramps' party, the one *I'm* supposed to produce Seb at for his inspection,' Katie replied dryly.

As she gave her a final hug, Louise sent up a private
mental prayer for her sister's happiness, waiting until
the last minute to thrust a prettily wrapped package
into her sister's hand.

'What is it?' Katie asked her in surprise.

'It's the dress…the one we saw in the boutique
window—the "for Seb's eyes only" dress. Remember?' Louise told her. 'I went back to get it when I
told you I had to get a parking ticket for the car. I
knew you wouldn't buy it yourself…'

'You knew right,' Katie told her feelingly and then
remembering the cost of the silky sensual slip she

rotested, 'You shouldn't have, Lou… There's no
ay I can ever wear it.'

'Of course you will…. Wear it for the family gath-
ring,' Louise told her.

'What?'

'I dare you,' Louise challenged her wickedly, add-
g, 'You'd better go, otherwise you're going to miss
ur flight.'

Without giving Katie any chance to respond she
ave her a little push and then stood watching her
ntil she had disappeared.

CHAPTER NINE

'AND SO, if you would face the Court please and te
the jury exactly what you saw on the night of th
eighteenth of October last year...'

Katie closed her eyes and tried to concentrate o
what the witness who had just taken the stand wa
saying.

The delay in the jury reaching a verdict in a cas
in which Olivia had been acting had resulted in Kati
having to take over from her at the last minute o
another case being heard at Chester's Crown Cou
which had been brought forward. Although in man
ways she was grateful to have the excuse for havin
to spend several days in Chester while the case wa
being heard, and therefore not having to run the ris
of bumping into Seb, Katie was forced to admit tha
she was finding it hard to give her work her full a
tention; to blank Seb out of her mind completely.

'The Court will rise.'

Automatically Katie stood up. The judge had de
clared a recess. It was hot and stuffy in the courtroo
despite the whir of the fans, and she was glad to b
able to go outside and breathe in some fresher unre
cycled air.

Her head had started to ache, a tight band of pai
gripping her forehead. There was a chemist's sho
close to the court, so she crossed the road and mad
her way towards it.

There was a queue at the counter and as she waite

o be served she looked absently around. The array of rugs on sale was bewildering. Out of the corner of er eye Katie caught sight of a display of condoms nd contraceptive products alongside pregnancy testng kits.

'You never know,' Louise had told her during their ate night heart-to-heart. 'You may have already coneived Seb's child…'

'I haven't,' Katie had told her immediately and positively. 'Don't ask me how I know. I just *know*, but ven if I *had*…that would be something, wouldn't it?' he had added sardonically. 'Having to tell the family hat I'm pregnant and that Seb doesn't love me. Not hat they'll need much telling about that. After all it vill be pretty obvious I should imagine when I turn p at Gramps's "do" without him.'

She reached the till and paid for her headache tabets. Quite how she knew so positively that she wasn't arrying Seb's child she had no idea, she just knew hat the gypsy woman had got it wrong, there wasn't oing to be any baby… Any little boy so like his ather… At least not for her.

t was a perfect afternoon as Katie drove back to Iaslewich, the Welsh hills sharply clear against the kyline, the rich fields of the Cheshire plains laid out efore her. Roman soldiers and merchants had once rossed this plain on their way from their port at Chester to the salt mines of Northwich, Nantwich, Middlewich and Haslewich. Salt mining had been the rincipal industry of the area along with farming right own through the centuries. Until the introduction of rozen and refrigerated foods, salt had been the only vay that meat could be stored and safely preserved.

Now the old workings had been turned into a museum and a tourist attraction. There was a local story that during the Civil War, when the area had been heavily fought over by the rival Cavalier and Roundhead forces, a certain very famous royal fugitive, the Stuart prince who would ultimately be King Charles II, had taken refuge in Haslewich's mines, but it had never actually been proved.

At her own suggestion, instead of returning to her own apartment, Katie drove over to her parents where she had arranged to spend the night so that she would be on hand from early in the morning to help her mother and Maddy with their preparations for Ben's party.

As she walked in her mother's kitchen she was welcomed by the warm scent of baking and as Jenny enveloped her in a hug and asked her how her court case had gone, Katie thrust away the image that had been tormenting her all the way home of walking up to her apartment to find Seb waiting there for her with open arms.

But of course, that was never going to happen.

Over supper she chatted with her parents about her visit with Louise and the recent concluded court case.

She'd met with Max while she'd been in Chester and he'd confided to her, 'It looks very much as though I'm going to be elevated to the ranks of Queen's Counsel.'

'Oh Max,' Katie had beamed with sisterly pride. 'That's wonderful.'

'Well, it should help to cheer Gramps up a bit,' Max had agreed. 'I've talked it over with Maddy and we've both agreed that I should tell him during the party.'

'So that he can boast about it to everyone who's there,' Katie had teased, adding truthfully, 'Max, he will be so thrilled, this is what he's always wanted, to be able to claim a member of his own immediate family has those all important initials after his name—Max Crighton, QC. Oh Max…' She had hugged him excitedly and then shared the bottle of champagne that Luke had insisted on opening in their chambers when Max confessed to him that he hadn't been able to resist telling her his good news.

'You deserve it, Max,' Luke assured him and the two men had exchanged such a look of warmth and respect that Katie had felt her eyes start to fill with emotional tears.

'I've already told the folks,' Max had added to Katie just before she left.

'They will be thrilled,' Katie said.

'Yes,' Max agreed, and then giving her a wry look he had added, 'but like me, they feel that what I've got with Maddy and the children is of far more value.'

Katie had hugged him again knowing how much soul-searching and pain had been endured by both Max and Maddy before they had reached the loving intimacy of the marriage they now shared.

Now, seated at the table with her parents, Katie reflected that at least Max's news would take the pressure off her. With Max's elevation to boast about, her grandfather was hardly likely to concern himself with her relationship—or lack of it—with Seb. The female members of the family had never been accorded or merited as much importance in her grandfather's eyes as the males and for once Katie was happy to let that be so.

'Have you seen Seb since you got back?' her

mother was asking her in a little concern now. 'You must have missed one another this last week…'

'I…' Now was her chance—her golden opportunity—to tell her parents the truth, Katie recognised, but as she took a deep breath ready to do so the phone rang and her mother got up from the table and hurried out of the room to answer it.

Before she returned, Max's wife Maddy had arrived to drop off the fruit that Jenny needed to fill the tart cases she had been baking and then, within the hour, Maddy was on her way back to Queensmead where various members of the family were going to be staying for the weekend. Then Louise, Gareth and Nick had arrived and any chance Katie might have had to talk to her parents in private had gone.

'Well, that's the last batch of food delivered to Queensmead and it's time for us to get ourselves ready,' Louise announced, deftly removing the chocolaty crumbs her son was about to scrunch into her clean outfit.

'I can't wait to see you in that dress,' she enthused to Katie who immediately looked down at the floor, causing Louise to stop what she was doing and demand determinedly,

'You *are* going to wear it, aren't you, Katie?'

'I can't,' Katie protested. 'It's not…it's too… anyway, I don't have it here with me, it's at the apartment and there isn't time…'

'Lou,' Katie protested as her twin immediately reached for Katie's handbag and deftly extracted her keys, telling her in a voice that brooked no argument, 'There *is* time. I shall *make* time, and you my dear darling twin will wear it. Gareth,' she called over her shoulder to her husband who had just walked into the kitchen with Jon, 'You're going to have to wash and change Nick. His things are all laid out on the bed upstairs…'

'Louise,' Katie protested but it was too late, her sister was already out of the doorway and heading for hers and Gareth's rented car.

Seb frowned as he put down the telephone receiver. He had just rung Katie's flat for the fifth time without getting any reply that morning.

It had only been when he had telephoned the office and spoken with Olivia that he had discovered that Katie had returned from an unplanned visit to Brussels and then had virtually gone straight to court in Chester.

Was it a set of freak circumstances that was preventing him from being able to speak with her or was she *deliberately* avoiding him? Today was the date set for her grandfather's party—an event to which *he* was supposed to be escorting her—at least according to Guy.

Oh yes, he had enough, and to spare, practical reasons for needing to see Katie, but it wasn't those that were causing the aching longing which had taken over not just his emotions but his thoughts and time as well. Like a series of vivid flashbacks he kept getting mental images of the night they had made love, images which tormented every one of his five senses.

Broodingly he wondered what Katie herself was thinking and feeling. Did she regret what had happened? Did she blame him for it…hate him for it? Was she avoiding him out of embarrassment or anger? Did she… Did he really need to ask himself those questions he derided himself bitterly? He only had to remember what he had said to her before they had made love, the accusations he had made, the anger he had shown. But once they had touched, kissed, held one another... There was no point in him staying here, he decided, he might as well go out.

Louise was just crossing the hallway to Katie's flat when Seb opened his own front door.

'Katie...' he began and then stopped as he realised his mistake and Louise, who had seen the hope and longing flare quickly in his eyes only to die when he saw *her*, made a mental promise to herself that her twin would most definitely wear her new dress even if she herself had to dress her in it and drag her forcibly to the party.

'Katie's at home helping my mother get ready for Gramps's party,' Louise told him easily.

'Yes. Yes, of course. I...er...how is she?' Seb asked lamely.

Louise looked at him. Although they were identical twins, Seb knew that he could never mistake Louise for her twin. Katie was special, unique, she was...

'If you're *really* concerned, if you *really* care...' Louise emphasised, 'Then perhaps you should tell her so,' she suggested firmly.

Seb frowned.

Had Katie discussed what had happened between them with her twin? It seemed out of character for her. He knew instinctively that she was a very private and even reserved person, but twins shared a relationship and an intimacy that went far beyond that shared by non-twin siblings.

Louise brandished the elegant carrier bag she was holding.

'Katie's dress…for the party…' she told him conversationally, adding more pointedly and not entirely
ruthfully, 'She bought it in Brussels to wear today.
For you…'

She was taking a huge risk, Louise knew that, and
even worse she was not the one she was doing the
risk taking for. If she had got it wrong and Seb did
not care… If he was merely being polite…if what had
happened between the two of them *had* simply been
an impulsive act of the moment with no emotional
importance in it for him, but no…there had been no
mistaking that uncertain moment when he had asked
about Katie, the very way he had been there, wanting
to ask about her.

'The party starts at three,' she told him quietly, and
then before he could say anything she hurried towards
the lift.

Back at her parents' home Louise made no mention
of seeing Seb much less of having spoken with him.
Instead, she bundled Katie upstairs ignoring her protests that the dress was far too over the top for the
nature of the event, pausing only to kiss Gareth as he
emerged from their bedroom holding Nick.

'Mmm…you both smell wonderful,' she told him,
adding impishly, 'Baby powder is soooo sexy on a
man…'

'Lou, I can't *possibly* wear this,' Katie wailed. 'You
can see right through it.'

'No you can't, it's got a nude slip, you just think
you can…'

'That's what I mean,' Katie told her despairingly.
'It looks as though I haven't, as though I'm not…
it's…'

'It's provocative and sexy and you look stunning in it,' Louise told her firmly.

She *did* look stunning in it Katie acknowledged as Louise determinedly turned her round to the mirror and commanded,

'Look…yes, I *know* you can see through it, but like I said, all you can actually see through to is the lining Yes, I *know* it's flesh-coloured but look, it isn't as though you're showing masses of cleavage, not with that neat little round neck-hugging neckline, and, in fact, the only bits of you that are really bare are your arms and legs…'

'Maybe, but everyone will think that *all* of me…'

'Let them,' Louise interrupted her and then said with quiet sincerity, 'Katie, it looks wonderful on you You *must* wear it. It makes you look…it makes you look like you should look…'

As she gave Louise an old-fashioned glance Louise shook her head and said, 'No, not like that. Yes, all right, it *is* sexy, but it's also stylish, elegant and sensual, not sleazy as you seem to be trying to say There's nothing cheap or sleazy about it…or about you…

'Come on, it's time we went down, otherwise we're going to be late. Oh no,' she added when Katie told her that she needed to get her car keys, 'You don' think for one minute that I'm going to let you out of my sight, much less into your own car so that you can sneak back to your apartment and get changed behind my back. You're coming with us…come on…'

Queensmead was a big house with plenty of spare bedrooms which was just as well, Maddy had told

Jenny, because they were certainly going to need them to put up all those members of the family who wanted to stay overnight.

'And when you add in all the children…it's just as well that most of them are still small enough to share their parents' rooms.'

As Katie walked into Queensmead's drawing room she could see what Maddy had meant, large though the room was, it was packed, filled with people.

Saul and Tullah were standing with their children talking with Saul's parents. Luke and Bobbie were in another group which included James, Luke's brother, their two sisters and their families and their parents.

'Looks like there's a full turn-out from the Chester contingent of the Crightons,' Louise remarked to Katie as they stood together just inside the doorway.

'Mmm…that's definitely going to make Gramps's day,' she began, thinking of how pleased their grandfather would be at being able to boast to the two cousins he had always secretly felt he had had to compete with, of Max's good news, but Louise who didn't as yet know, gave her a puzzled look.

Bobbie, Luke's American wife who had just caught sight of the twins, was waving to them and, detaching herself from her own family group, came over, bringing her children with her.

'Wow…love the dress,' she approved as she studied Katie appraisingly. 'It is just soooo sexy…'

As Katie coloured up Louise groaned and then laughed, 'Don't tell her *that*. I've just spent the last hour convincing her that it isn't…'

'*I* never said you'd succeeded,' Katie pointed out dryly.

'So…' Bobbie teased her gently, 'Where is he?'

Katie knew perfectly well who the 'he' Bobbie meant was and she closed her eyes as a wave of sharp pain clawed her.

Louise was nudging her, warning, 'Katie... Katie...' causing her to open them again but the words of protest she had been about to deliver to her twin were lost when she saw Seb standing framed in the open doorway.

Even among the collective force of her male Crighton relatives, all of them tall, all of them dark and all of them extremely good looking, Seb stood out as she slowly scanned him. Katie avidly allowed her starved senses full rein to enjoy themselves and then Seb turned his head and saw her.

Katie sucked in her breath. The way he was looking at her made her feel—made her think...made her *believe*... Her heart was pounding heavily, the interested massed ranks of her family faded into total oblivion. Seb was still looking at her and in his eyes she could see... She saw his lips form her name and then he was moving towards her. At her side Louise gave her a firm push in Seb's direction and somehow she was taking one step forward and then another and all the time he was looking at her with 'that' look.

Seb was used to large families. His own was huge, but the Crightons were a family apart, or so Ben Crighton liked to think, and as he stood looking into the packed drawing room Seb could see why. But there was only one person there *he* really wanted to see. Quickly he searched the room and then he found her, standing next to her sister, wearing a dress that made her look as ethereal as a wood sprite, as delicate and fragile as a piece of thistledown, as... He caught his breath as he saw the way she was looking at him, her whole heart in her eyes.

'Katie...' he breathed her name and the crowd of people separating them seemed to part as though by magic.

'Katie...'

As he reached her and said her name Katie closed her eyes unable to stop the ecstatic shudder of happiness that shook her and then she was in his arms and he was holding her, kissing her.

Eagerly she returned his kiss, her lips parting hungrily as she clung to him.

'Seb.' She gasped his name.

'I've missed you,' she heard him groan. '*Why* didn't you ring...get in touch? Why am I wasting time talking? Why are *we* wasting time here?' he muttered thickly against her mouth, 'And why are you wearing that damned dress that makes me want to...'

'Seb,' Katie protested, pink cheeked, but smiling as she placed a cautionary finger against his lips. His hand curled around her wrist and he kissed her finger, nibbling tenderly on it while his thumb monitored the frantic thud of her pulse. With give-away bemusement in her love-dazed eyes, she reminded him shakily, 'There are children here and...'

Children...a sudden shockingly explicit look darkened his eyes so that they smouldered and burned.

Shielding her from everyone else with his body he told her quietly, 'You could be carrying my child...our child...'

Katie couldn't help it, she gasped out loud, her whole body reacting to the intimacy of what he was saying.

'No, I don't think so,' she told him. 'Not...'

'…not this time,' he suggested.

Not *this* time… Katie felt as though she might faint she was so incandescent with happiness and disbelief. How *could* this be happening? How could her emotional skies have gone from darkest grey to brightest blue and all within the space of a single breath, all because of one specific look?

'I never thought you'd be here,' she whispered. 'I was going to tell everyone that there's been a misunderstanding, apologise to them for not saying anything before. I never dreamed…'

'No,' Seb was giving her a very rueful look. 'Did you think then that what we shared together was so common-place and mundane…'

Katie shook her head immediately.

'Oh no…no…it was…' She paused and looked at him, her eyes, her gaze direct but a little shy. 'It was wonderful, Seb…magical…something I never imagined. It frightened me a little to go from not knowing, from not realising just what I felt to recognising that all that anger, all that aggression I'd been feeling towards you was really nothing more than a barrier I'd built up because I was afraid to acknowledge what I really felt.'

'And what do you really feel?' Seb asked her.

Katie looked at him. The look she could see in his eyes was telling her to trust in him, to believe in him, to have the courage to be honest with him.

She took a deep breath.

'I… I love you,' she told him huskily.

As she said the words she felt his fingers tighten around her wrist.

'Let's get out of here,' he told her thickly. 'What I want to say to you…what I want to *do* with you…'

Katie heard him groan. 'That damned dress,' he whispered vehemently. 'It's driving me crazy…*you're* driving me crazy, Katie Crighton, crazy with longing, crazy with need, crazy with love…'

'We can't go yet,' Katie protested unconvincingly. Her relatives had discreetly drifted away leaving the two of them surrounded by a protective moat of empty space and silence, but…

'If you don't stop looking at me like that I'm going to have to make love to you right here and now and be damned to the consequences,' Seb growled. '*That* will impress your grandfather, won't it? I must be more of a Cooke than I've ever realised and I'm certainly enough of one not to give a damn who knows or sees just how much I want you, Katie…and enough of one to carry you off, steal you away with me as my notorious ancestor was reputed to have done with *his* lady love.'

'Seb,' Katie protested breathlessly. 'Just let me go and say my farewells to Gramps and then we can go.'

'I think you're going to have to do a bit more than just wish him farewell,' Seb told her wryly, 'at least if the looks he's been throwing in our direction for the last few minutes are anything to go by.'

'Give me a few minutes to explain to him,' Katie suggested, 'and then I'll introduce you to him.'

Nodding his head, Seb slowly released her hand and then, just as she was about to slip away, reached for her possessively and kissed her briefly but very passionately. 'A few minutes,' he warned her. 'That's all. You and I have got a lot of lost time to make up.'

'Mmm…a whole week of it,' Katie teased him blissfully before wriggling out of his arms and heading towards her grandfather.

Tenderly Seb watched her. She was his joy, his future, his hope, his love and he didn't care who knew it. And he intended to prove it to her very, very thoroughly and protractedly indeed just as soon as he could get her to himself. That dress... He closed his eyes as he imagined touching her through it, kissing her and then opened them again as close at hand he heard a woman's voice saying quietly, 'My goodness me, what a change in Katie... I hardly recognised her.'

Alison Ford raised her eyebrows a little as she listened to her sister Rachel. Their father, Henry Crighton, was Ben's cousin and their brother Luke was married to Bobbie, Ruth Crighton's American granddaughter. Nearly two decades older than Louise and Katie, they were both married with growing families.

'Mmm...quite a change from the way she looked at Louise's wedding,' Alison agreed.

'Yes indeed. It's never been mentioned, but my private suspicion was that her feelings for Gareth weren't just those of a sister-in-law...'

'You mean she was in love with him?'

As the two women started to move away from Seb their voices faded but the damage was done. Fiercely he searched the room until he found who he was looking for. Gareth, Louise's husband, and there, right beside him was Katie, looking up at him, smiling at him, standing so close to him that she was within easy kissing distance of him... *His* Katie...

Seb was not by nature a jealous man but the sight of Katie standing so intimately close to Gareth after what he had just overheard and while his own love for her was so newly declared and his ego so fragile

nd vulnerable, overwhelmed all his logic and self-
ontrol.

How dare Gareth stand so close to his beloved?
low dare he talk so intimately to her? How could he
ossibly resist her especially when she was wearing
uch a dress, a dress that would make a saint want…?

Katie chuckled appreciatively as Gareth reached the
nd of the amusing anecdote he had been relating to
er. It amazed her how much she was enjoying this
ew relationship she had developed with him, the
ense of camaraderie, of sisterly closeness and warmth
vhich she could tell he happily reciprocated. She felt
o sense of discomfort or self-consciousness in his
resence now. The Gareth she had believed she loved
ad simply been a creation of her own imagination,
n impossibly one-dimensional and, yes, virtually sex-
ess figure who bore absolutely no resemblance to the
eal Gareth at all.

'I thought you said you wanted to say goodbye to
our grandfather.'

Katie jumped as out of nowhere, or so it seemed,
eb suddenly materialised at her side, somehow or
ther managing to stand in between her and Gareth,
is eyes hard and angry, his voice unmistakably harsh.

'Yes. I did… I do… but…'

'But you found someone more…interesting to talk
o…' Seb suggested grittily to her.

Katie stared at him.

'I…'

'Oh, you don't have to explain to me,' Seb told her
irmly. 'I've just heard a very enlightening conversa-
ion.'

Out of the corner of her eye Katie could see the
urious looks they were attracting. Gareth who was

standing the closest to them was starting to frown a little bit.

'Seb,' she protested, but he ignored her, propelling her towards the door.

'*Who* was it you were really saving your virginity for Katie?' he demanded. 'Not me, that's for sure.'

'Seb,' Katie protested again just as soon as they were on their own in the hallway.

'It was *Gareth,* wasn't it?' he demanded, ignoring her. 'Gareth, your brother-in-law!' he emphasised. 'You're in love with him. Don't bother denying it. Is *that* why you're wearing that dress? For *him*… Hoping that *he'd*…'

'You're jealous,' Katie gasped as she saw the emotions darkening his eyes. 'And…and you're wrong… I don't love Gareth…'

'Gareth—what?' Seb demanded savagely. 'Gareth doesn't *want* you because he's married to your twin… Well that certainly wasn't the impression I just got. He was looking at you as though…'

'Seb, you've got it all wrong,' Katie protested swiftly.

'No, *you're* the one who's got things wrong. If you think for one moment that I'm going to let another man—*any* other man come between us. I love you Katie and I'm pretty damn sure that you love me, no matter how much you might think that another man… Just give me a chance to prove how good it could be for us, Katie, that's all I ask, and I promise you…'

He stopped when he saw the searchingly solemn-eyed look she was giving him and then, taking a deep breath, he decided to use his trump card, the card he had promised himself he would never play; the one that came so loaded with emotional dynamite that

e'd have to be either a fool or desperate to use it—
r maybe even both.

'Remember what the gypsy said,' he told her
ruffly. 'It was *my* baby she saw you with, Katie.'

His baby… Katie stared at him, his jealousy, his
assion, his determination, all of them were so un-
xpected, so very much the opposite of what she had
ssumed to be his feelings towards her, his indiffer-
nce towards her that she still couldn't quite totally
bsorb them.

His baby… Her heart and with it her doubts melted
n the sweet hot-honeyed tide of love that spread
nrough her.

'No,' she corrected him softly. 'Not *your* baby,
eb…' The look in his eyes made her reach out im-
ulsively to touch him reassuringly, her fingertips
esting on his arm, hard and tensed beneath the cloth
f his jacket as though he was both fearing her rejec-
on and bracing himself for it.

'*Our* baby, Seb… *Our* baby. *Yours* and *mine*.'

As she looked at him she saw him swallow and
nen heard him say in a thick emotional voice,

'Come on, let's get out of here…'

In the drawing room Max had just given Ben
Crighton his news. Through the open doorway Katie
ould see her grandfather's face quite plainly. Max's
ews had totally eclipsed anything she might have
aid to Gramps or anything he might have wanted to
ay to her—thankfully.

Breathing a small sigh of thanks to her brother she
ooked up into Seb's face.

'Yes,' she agreed softly. 'Let's…'

Have I told you just how much I love you…just how
vonderful you are, how gorgeous, how adorable, how
exy and…'

'Mmm…but you can tell me all over again if yo
like,' Katie said happily as she snuggled deeper int
his side.

The late-afternoon sun shining in through the win
dow of his apartment brushed their naked bodies wit
a soft gold wash of colour. Seb's skin was muc
darker than hers, his body hair dark and silky.

Idly she stroked her fingers through it and the
leaned over teasingly, kissing one of his nipples an
then the other.

'Do you know what you're doing?' Seb growled
his growl turning to an urgent low groan of reactio
as she tugged sensually on the small hard nub of flesh
her palm spread flat on the concave plane of his belly

'I never really loved Gareth, you know,' she tol
him gently a few minutes later as she propped hersel
up on one elbow and looked lovingly down into hi
face. 'I just thought I did, but the Gareth I imagine
I loved never really existed, he was just someone I'
created in my own head, and as for you being jealou
of him…' She gave him a searching look and the
said quietly, '*You've* been married, Seb. You mus
have loved Sandra once…and…'

Quickly Seb shook his head.

'We thought we loved one another but it was jus
an infatuation, something which by rights we shoul
have got out of our systems with a few nights of ex
perimental sex, but I was too strait-laced, too awar
of my Cooke heritage to do that. Sandra and I shoul
never have married and we certainly should neve
have had a child. I *do* feel guilty about that, about no
being there for Charlotte when she was growing up

but when Sandra told me that she felt it was for the best that Charlotte didn't have any kind of contact with me rather than be torn between the two of us I felt that she was right and then she married George and to all intents and purposes he became Charlotte's father.'

'That must have been hard for you,' Katie said gently, 'knowing that another man was taking your place.'

'It wasn't always easy,' Seb agreed wryly, 'but for Charlotte's sake…' He stopped. 'When I first got in touch with her I was terrified that she might be disappointed in me, that I wouldn't live up to her expectations and that I might somehow have damaged her by not being there for her, but she's just about the most well-adjusted human being I know…'

'Mmm…' Katie agreed and then asked him a little hesitantly, 'How will she feel, do you suppose, about us?'

Seb looked at her and then shook his head gravely, 'That's going to be a problem, I'm afraid,' he told her solemnly.

Katie's heart lurched. 'It…it is?'

'Mmm… She's already told me that there's absolutely, totally no way she will ever…' He paused while Katie looked anxiously at him. 'Ever…' he continued dramatically, 'wear a bridesmaid's dress that makes her look like a pink meringue…'

'What?' Katie glared at him and then burst out laughing.

'She thinks you're wonderful,' Seb told her softly, 'and she can't *wait* for us to provide her with another clutch of half siblings…'

'Oh Seb,' Katie whispered, her eyes full of emotional tears.

'Oh Seb, what?' Seb repeated equally emotionally but Katie couldn't make any rational vocal response because he was kissing her, pressing her back against the pillows, pinioning her arms in a tender mock masterful lover's embrace as he kissed her, slowly and softly at first and then with increasing passion and urgency as his body hardened and Katie gave a low female moan of arousal deep in her throat. The soft rose-pink colour staining her breasts now didn't come from the dying sun but from the slow sensual suckle of Seb's mouth. As he kissed the soft curve of her belly Katie arched frantically beneath him. His hand caressed her thigh and then tenderly touched her sex Katie moaned out loud.

'We shouldn't be doing this,' Seb reminded her with a soft groan as she turned towards him, 'Not without...' But Katie was already touching him, stroking him and the urge to bury himself deep inside her was far too strong for him to resist.

Later, lying in Seb's arms, Katie gave a blissful sigh and told him softly,

'I saw him...just now, when...he was so beautiful Seb...'

'Yes, I know,' he agreed quietly, 'I saw him too.'

They looked at one another sharing the awe of what they had both experienced.

'He looked so like you,' Katie told him tremulously.

Seb frowned.

'No,' he corrected her, '*He* looked like *you*.'

Katie's eyes widened.

'Twins,' she whispered chokily, 'We're going to
ave twins. Oh Seb… Seb…'

'Mmm…' Seb breathed as she kissed him. 'Care-
ıl…it could be triplets…'

Katie laughed.

'There are no triplets in the Crighton family,' she
nock scolded him.

'We'll have to get married…and soon,' Seb warned
er.

Katie pursed her lips and pretended to frown.

'I mean it, Katie,' Seb told her fiercely. 'This isn't
"let's live together and see how it works out" thing
or me. You're the woman I love and it's a "forever
ove" for me…'

'…and for me,' Katie assured him happily.

'A quiet simple wedding,' Seb continued, stopping
vhen Katie started to laugh.

'No…no way can we do that,' she told him joy-
usly. 'You're a Cooke and I'm a Crighton, Seb, and
ne whole town is going to want to see us married.
t's just as well Haslewich has such a large church.'

'Mmm…but does it have a large *font*,' Seb mur-
nured before drawing her down against his body and
hen silencing whatever reply she might have made
vith a long sensual kiss.

EPILOGUE

'IT'S just as well that Haslewich has such a larg
church,' Jenny Crighton told her husband, uncon
sciously echoing Katie's own comment to Seb.

'Mmm... I know they're in love, but does every
thing have to happen in such a rush?' Jon proteste
ruefully, stopping when he saw the look Jenny wa
giving him.

'Oh,' he exclaimed, 'I see...'

'Katie hasn't *said* anything,' Jenny warned him
'but Louise is pretty sure, and you know how it i
with them, being twins...they seem to share a specia
bond and...' Jenny broke off as she saw her husband'
expression. Gently she touched his arm. Her Jon wa
a twin himself, even if he and his brother Davi
weren't in contact with one another anymore.

'Your father still believes that ultimately David wi
return home.'

'Yes, I know,' Jon agreed heavily. 'You know
had the oddest feeling when I went to Jamaica that...

'...that what?' Jenny pressed him, but he was al
ready shaking his head.

'Oh, nothing... So we've got another wedding t
look forward to. Which reminds me, we're coming u
to Olivia and Caspar's anniversary.'

Jenny started to frown.

'What is it?' Jon asked her.

'I don't know,' Jenny admitted. 'It's just that Olivi
seems to be rather on edge at the moment.'

'Mmm…well, we are under a lot of pressure at the
practice which, of course, is one of the reasons why
I was so pleased when Katie agreed to join us. Which
reminds me,' Jon joked, 'we're very definitely going
to have to think about buying that dining room table
you were telling me about!'

'The one that extends to seat twenty?' Jenny asked
him. 'You said it was too big.'

'Mmm…that was before I'd added up the number
of grandchildren our family is blessing us with.'

Jenny laughed and agreed. 'Yes, Katie was saying
only last night that it's just as well the church has
such a long aisle…for all the little bridesmaids she's
going to have,' she explained. 'Close on a dozen at
the last count.'

'A dozen!' Charlotte exclaimed, looking bemused
when Katie outlined her wedding plans to her that
same evening.

'Mmm…all of them dressed in little pink mini-
meringues,' Katie told her solemnly, tongue-in-cheek.

'Like *what*?' Suddenly realising she was being
teased, Charlotte burst out laughing.

'All right, I agree to take charge of them and to act
as yours and Dad's support, but no *way* am I wearing
pink or tulle.'

'No way,' Katie agreed, her eyes dancing with
laughter and love.

'Oh, I'm so glad you and Dad have found one another,' Charlotte told her happily.

As Katie smiled at her and then looked across the
room to where Seb was watching them, her eyes spar-
kled with happiness and love.

'So am I…' she told Charlotte tenderly.

* * * * * *

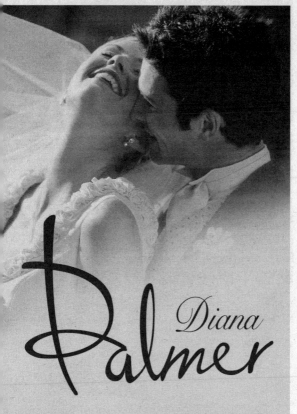

Diana Palmer

WEDDINGS IN WHITE

*A fabulous collection of three
irresistible wedding stories*

On sale 20th September 2002

*Available at most branches of WH Smith,
Tesco, Martins, Borders, Eason, Sainsbury's
and most good paperback bookshops.*

Coming home...to heal the past

THE
BEACH
HOUSE

MARY ALICE MONROE

Published 16th August 2002